WHEN THERE'S NO MORE ROOM IN HELL III

LUKE DUFFY

www.severedpress.com

ISBN: 978-1-925047-13-4

1

The city was dead.

It had been devoid of human life for twelve years. Its buildings slowly decayed and crumbled as the streets below were gradually reclaimed by Mother Nature. *She* stole back more and more each year and slowly but surely, the landscape began to transform.

Steve took another cigarette from the pack and lit it. He inhaled deeply and let the wisps of curling smoke drift up into the air. He checked his watch, and then looked out across the landscape to check on the position of the sun. It was still mid-afternoon; plenty of time yet.

Apart from the twitter of the birds in the trees and the occasional mournful wail lingering in the distance, the air was silent. The wind was down to nothing more than a gentle breeze that was barely enough to make the long grass sway.

Imagining that things had once been different to how they were now was hard. In the old days, the stillness and quiet that covered the land had once been completely alien to him. Even during the night, the streets and roads would have been lit with lights that came on automatically at pre-programmed times. Houses and places of work would have glowed with illumination from within.

Even the silence would not have been complete. There would have always been the steady drone of distant traffic. The hum of factories and power stations, as they continued to work throughout the night, would have added to the ambient light and noise of the dark hours.

As he looked out at the slowly crumbling metropolis, he sighed and raised the cigarette to his lips for another drag.

The city loomed on the skyline in the low sunlight, like the black silhouette of an old graveyard. Its dull buildings, towers, churches and monuments stood in solemn silence like monoliths. They clung on stubbornly, as testament to the old world and the once prosperous human civilisation that had built them, as though waiting for the return of the architects and engineers to repair and restore them to their former glory.

Most of the large panes of glass in the tall buildings were cracked or smashed as the elements had taken their toll on the manmade structures. The wind and rain poured into the office blocks and apartment buildings, laying waste to the interiors and creating high-rise eco systems that lived and thrived in the places where humanity had once dwelled.

Weeds and plants flourished, using every crevice and crack to take root and make a life in a place where they would have once been ripped up or poisoned the moment they began to grow. Creeping vines and ivy slowly scaled the buildings, climbing higher each year, and one day, they would cover the concrete and brick surfaces like a death shroud on the dominance of man.

The city was not completely dead. Birds and insects continually flocked and swarmed in the air, high above the buildings, looking like black, swirling clouds from a distance, as they fed on the remains of the lifeless world below and dominated the skies above. Their populations had exploded since the rising of the dead. With no one to control their growth and treat them as pests, they had multiplied at an expeditious rate.

No one collected the waste and rubbish that was left behind or carried out maintenance and cleaning of the city anymore. Stored and discarded food, animal carcasses and the dead bodies of the human populace provided meals for the smaller creatures that were stealthy enough to pick from them. The supermarkets, restaurants, and even the fridges and freezers in the homes had become easy pickings and great sustenance for the lesser inhabitants of the urban areas. Their numbers had soon increased and rose sharply as the once dominant species of the planet succumbed and began to fade into obscurity.

At ground level, the rats and other small vermin had the run of the city. They scurried through the gutters and sewers, through the empty buildings and between the cars, scavenging and feeding on whatever they could. Like the birds and insects, initially, the rodent population had expanded quickly with the abundance of food. However, after many years of prosperity, their numbers settled and the colonies shrank to a more sustainable number.

The abandoned cars, many parked neatly at the roadside, as though waiting on their owners to come and retrieve them, slowly rusted away. Their paintwork flaked and their tyres had become flat, leaving them as static, immovable homes to the plants and creatures that took up residence in them.

Shops, homes and businesses sat quietly, their dark doorways and windows gazing out onto the desolate streets like traumatised eyes that had witnessed such unimaginable terror. They looked on in silence, unwilling to speak of their horrors, staring out onto the roads and pavements that were scattered with the debris of civilisation.

Personal and beloved belongings of the thousands of people that had tried to flee now lay discarded and left to decay along with the rest of the city.

Bones, bleached white by the sun, lay unburied and unceremoniously strewn along the pavements and roads. The skulls and ribcages of men, women and children sat as if witnesses to the panic that had swept over the world in the beginning as old newspapers drifted and fluttered by them through the streets on the wind. Their headlines, *'The Dead Walk'*, speaking ominously of what was to come.

'Twelve years...,' Steve thought to himself, as he remained sitting on the grassy hillside overlooking the city. *'Jesus, it seems like so much longer. I can't even remember the old world.'*

The figure, struggling to negotiate the slippery hill below him, continued to fall and tumble back down the slope. It never gave up. Steve wondered to himself how many more times the thing could fall down the wet grass before its limbs were smashed to the point where it could no longer stand.

He looked back up and closed his eyes for a moment, trying hard to picture what the city was like in the old days. The roads would have been clogged with revving engines and tooting horns. People would have scurried along the streets as they went about their daily business. It would have been a hive of activity.

He opened his eyes again and looked down at the decaying buildings and silent cluttered roads. If he had not known better, he would have found it hard to believe that the world was once very different. It all seemed so long ago.

He glanced down at the rifle in his lap, then down at the walking corpse that stubbornly attempted to climb the hill below. He thought about all the people that he had known before and after the dead began to walk and wondered what had become of the ones he had lost touch with when the old world died.

His brother, Marcus, and the remains of his team had made it home after many months of struggle and fighting in Baghdad. They had slogged and battled their way across the Middle East and Europe, then finally, to the Safari Park where Steve and the other survivors waited.

However, that was not the end of their ordeal.

2

The machine seemed cumbersome and fought against her as she struggled to control it and keep them stable. The steady thump of the engine was muffled in her ears by the headset that she wore, but she could still hear and feel that something was wrong.

The cockpit shuddered and the seat beneath her vibrated as the machine buffeted and rattled around her, while the sound of her own heavy breathing and pounding heartbeat in her ears was enough to drown out the noise of the motors. She felt a stream of sweat begin to pour from beneath her helmet and down her forehead as she strained and battled to keep control. She blinked hard, attempting to clear her vision from the moisture that had begun to accumulate beneath her visor. Clenching her teeth, she growled under her breath, willing the machine to comply with her commands.

The anti-torque pedals pushed back against her feet and she had to tense the muscles in her thighs as she pressed down, controlling the angle of the rear rotor to stop them from going into a spin. The cyclic stick and collective trembled in her hands, as though fighting to break free of her influence.

She looked down at the panel in front of her. No warning lights flashed and no alarms sounded. The gauges and readouts all seemed to be in order. There was no sign of any pressure loss from oil or hydraulics and the fuel levels were still within the green. Their altitude was exactly where she wanted it to be; sitting level with the horizon and the cockpit gyroscope, while the readout indicated a forward ground speed of forty miles per hour. She glanced to her right and out of the window, looking down at the rooftops, roads and sprawling fields as they passed over them, confirming their speed and altitude with her own eyes and sense of judgement.

The cockpit instruments seemed to be correct.

'Ancient bag of bolts,' she thought to herself. *'This thing belongs in a museum. Please don't fail me now, old girl.'*

The engine sputtered and they began to oscillate; the horizon swinging before her like a pendulum as the machine lurched violently from side to side, threatening to turn them upside down, resulting in an inevitable crash.

Her stomach knotted and she tensed every muscle in her body as she wrestled with the pedals and levers. Dread was creeping in fast and a film of sweat began to coat her skin. Her ears subconsciously registered the whining sound of the struggling engines as they rose and fell in pitch. She automatically adjusted the pressure on the anti-torque pedals and the lift on the cyclic and collective to compensate.

In her left hand, she twisted the throttle attached to the head of the collective lever, hoping that an increase in revolutions to the engine would help to settle the old helicopter in its flight. She eased back slightly on the cyclic stick with her right hand, changing the down angle on the main rotor to prevent their speed from increasing due to the sudden rise in engine power output.

Lone dark figures, shambling through the fields and staggering along the roads below, stopped and looked up as the swerving and swaying aircraft passed over them. They remained motionless, watching the curious flying machine. Their longing moans were drowned out by the sounds of the engine and thumping rotors.

The helicopter began to stabilise.

She looked across to her left and blew out a sigh of relief at her co-pilot. He looked back at her, a grin spreading the entire width of his face.

"Fuck me, you're good, Kelly," he stated through the intercom.

Kelly shook her head. She had been a pilot for ten years and there was very little that she did not know about when it came to flying a rotary wing aircraft. Nevertheless, it did not stop her from experiencing the gut-twisting fear in her stomach during situations when she thought they were about to drop out of the sky.

"Tell me that on the day I end up crashing this thing into a mountainside, or have to touch down in the middle of a swarm of those infected down there, Joey."

"Nah, you're far too nice to do that to us," Joey replied.

She nodded and smiled, but she was under no illusion of what could happen should she lose control of the aircraft. At best, she would crash land and they would manage to climb from the wreckage unhurt, but then they would be exposed and vulnerable to the hordes of walking dead that roamed the land.

Since the collapse of civilisation, the logistics of the armed forces had also drastically declined. The helicopter was old and parts were hard to come by. Maintenance was performed to the best standard that the mechanics could manage with the tools and equipment that were available, but it was never at one hundred percent serviceability. It was only a matter of time before the machine would fail to start, or drop out of the air. Kelly just hoped it would not be the latter.

"Zero, this is hotel three zero, over." Kelly paused and waited for a reply from their base. "Zero, hotel three zero, over," she repeated.

A voice suddenly crackled in her ear. "Zero, send, over."

"That's our sweep complete. No survivors seen; looks like another dead city, over."

"Roger that, three zero, move to your next safe haven and shut down. Remain on alternate means until phase-two is complete."

"Will do, but be aware, we're experiencing some mechanical difficulties, possibly from the rear rotor, causing stability problems," Kelly replied.

"Roger, three zero, go static at the RV and assess. Report on your condition in your evening sit-rep."

The succinct and detached tone of the radio operator made her feel as though they were alone and insignificant. At times, whilst flying missions over a dead and perilous wasteland, she just wished that she could get a warmer, more human conversation with base. At least then, she would feel that there was a real person aware of their position and situation and not just some robot.

Kelly nodded to herself. She did not like the prospect of being stranded with a broken down helicopter, but she also remembered what happened to the last pilot who returned to base with mechanical problems without specific orders to do so. He had been court-martialled and found guilty of negligence, dereliction of duty, and failing to follow orders in a time of war. General Gibson had ordered him to be hanged as an example.

Kelly, shaking the memory from her mind, decided that she would rather take her chances with a downed helicopter and the swarms of infected, than face the gallows.

"Roughly fifty kilometres, on this bearing," Joey informed her.

He had a set of charts and surveys in his hand, and he studied the lay of the ground around them, relaying it to what he saw on the map, confirming their exact position.

"We should be pretty secure up there."

"You think so?" she replied.

Joey looked up, glanced out the window towards the city, and then back at Kelly.

"Well, yeah. Safer than being here when phase-two happens, anyway. Besides, there's a team of SAS guys, dug in up there. They've been on the ground since this whole thing began. We'll be safe enough, I think."

Kelly shook her head. "I still can't believe they're really going to do this. They've lost their minds."

Joey nodded, but said nothing. He did not want to get into a conversation about the rights and wrongs of the decisions of their commanders. Over the months, he had learned that it was better to play the grey man and keep his thoughts and views to himself.

"Well, anyway, we have two days to ourselves before phase-two goes ahead. I'm looking forward to a well earned rest," he said, changing the subject.

Kelly smiled. She knew him well and was aware of his discomfort when it came to conversations on political matters. Not that he was a coward, but because he chose self-preservation over upsetting a status-quo that he could do nothing about. Things were different now, and free speech and stating your opinion was something that could get you in serious trouble.

She pushed down slightly on the cyclic and twisted the throttle, increasing the revolutions. The thump of the rotors increased in frequency and the screech of the engine grew. The nose of the helicopter dipped and the aircraft picked up speed. They flew low over the city one final time as they headed to their next position.

The grey buildings and dark streets drifted by silently beneath them as the aircraft passed over, just above the highest rooftops. The chaos of the last days of civilisation was evident on the ground below them; collapsed barricades, overturned and burnt out vehicles littered the narrow streets. Charred and crumbling buildings stood testament to the anarchy.

Kelly and Joey could also see the dead below. In some streets, they were scattered, looking like small black insects slowly making their way through a model city. In other places, seething dark masses, packed in tightly to one another, filled the roads between the buildings as they swarmed together.

"Why do so many of them stay in the towns and cities?" Joey asked rhetorically.

Kelly felt the need to theorise.

"Maybe, it's instinct? Cities were once important places to us and those things just feel the need to be there."

Thousands of gaunt faces and dead eyes were turned upwards towards them, staring into the sky as the helicopter passed overhead. They swarmed out the doors and broken windows of office blocks and shops, spilling into the streets and adding to the seething mass. Kelly could see ripples, like waves, passing through the crowds as they heard the helicopter above and worked themselves into a state of frenzy, reaching and clawing at the air above them in a desperate attempt to bring down the flying machine and reach the living flesh inside.

Kelly shuddered and looked away, focusing her eyes on the horizon in front of them.

"Completely dead," she stated.

Joey nodded in agreement, unable to tear his eyes away from the spectacle below.

The helicopter picked up more speed and headed away from the city.

3

Stan sat hunched with his shoulders riding high, as though he was trying to force them into his ears. He clutched the hot steaming mug in both hands and watched the wisps of steam drifting up into the cold air as the liquid slowly cooled. He gingerly sipped at the coffee, pulling a face as the hot fluid assaulted his cold lips and struck his teeth.

"Jesus, it's cold this morning."

Kieran was pacing, stomping his feet in an effort to keep warm. The blanket draped over his shoulders added to his large bulky appearance. He clapped his gloved hands together, the noise muffled by the padding as he attempted to increase his circulation and warm his numb fingers.

They had drawn the short straw and had been on watch the whole night. Now, as the sky above them slowly changed from a deep purple to a myriad of pink, orange and dark blue, they eagerly awaited the sun to cast its warming rays over the distant horizon.

"Aye," Kieran replied, "winter is going to be a bitch this year."

He stopped at the edge of the rooftop and peered out into the distance. Raising the binoculars to his eyes, he scanned the far side of the Safari Park, trying desperately to make out the high wall that ran the length of the perimeter. He knew it was there, but every now and then, he wanted to see it physically, to reassure himself.

"I hate the dark," he whispered hoarsely. "I used to like it. It meant that we could do the things we liked, without anyone seeing us. Now, it means those sacks of pus can do what *they* like, while *we* hide like frightened rats."

Stan rose to his feet, groaning with the effort and the sudden movement causing the cold material of his clothing to brush against his bare skin beneath. He let out a shudder and grunted as he walked towards his friend.

"I don't know about the 'rats' part, but I *am* frightened, Kieran. Those things scare the shit out of me and I don't mind admitting it either."

Kieran continued looking through the binoculars, but let out a grunt in agreement.

"What can you see?" Stan asked.

Kieran shrugged. "Nothing really, well nothing new anyway."

Stan took the binoculars and began to look for himself. Even with the naked eye, he could make out the dark swarm that stretched out for what seemed like miles beyond the walls. Through the binoculars, he could see the crowds more clearly. Though they were still cast in gloom, he could see the bobbing and weaving mass that seemed to pitch and tumble as though it were a choppy black sea.

He did not really need to see them. Their stench was thick in the air around them. It drifted to them across the wide-open plains of the park and stalked towards the house, like a creeping mist, as though it were an entity within itself, seeking the living people inside.

The noise of the dead was a constant, even though they were far away, but without any other noise to drown them out, the low hum of thousands of dead voices as they let out their perpetual moans and wails was carried to the survivors on the cold wind. The air around them seemed electrified with the faint ghostly chorus of the damned as all their voices were merged into one long, continuous low murmur.

Kieran hated the sound. To him, it sounded like a distant beehive or an electrical power grid, but those things were gone now and replaced with the poignant music of the dead.

At first, the survivors within the park had attempted to stem the flow of the dead by burning them. Hundreds of bodies that swarmed the walls and gates were engulfed in the flames but it was no use; more came to replace them, flocking from the outlying towns and villages. They flung themselves at the walls and attacked the gates incessantly, trampling on the charred remains of their fallen comrades.

"Jesus," Stan snorted and spat in disgust, "that bitch, Stephanie, really did a number on this place, didn't she?"

Kieran huffed. "Yeah, but the fat tub of shit is suffering for her efforts now though. How long's it been, three, four months?"

"About that, yeah," Stan nodded. "What do you think they will do with her?"

Kieran shrugged indifferently. "They can let her rot for all I care. Marcus is pretty much running the show now and I don't think he's in too much of a hurry to put an end to her misery."

"That Lee is a crazy bastard. I've seen him go in there a few times and piss all over her, and then give her a kicking, just for the fun of it."

"Understandable really," Kieran said as he blew out a lungful of air and watched as it misted and drifted upwards towards the slowly changing sky.

"They lost friends because of her, and from what I've heard, she was making moves to try and take over this place when she lived here."

"Yeah," Stan nodded, "fuck her. She deserves whatever she gets."

A sudden noise from behind and the two of them spun on their heels. Their eyes struggled to focus in the gloom as they peered into the dark shadows where the door led from the interior of the mansion and onto the rooftop. Stan could feel the hairs on the back of his neck standing on end in the cold crisp air. They were not expecting to be relieved from guard duty for another two hours, but someone was now on the roof with them.

A silent black figure stepped forward from the shadows; the sound of the gravel crunching beneath its feet as it slowly approached them was the only noise that it made. The lack of features and detail in the figure heightened the sense of anxiety in Kieran and Stan.

Kieran's shoulders relaxed and his body straightened as he recognised the man. Stan was a little slower to identify the new arrival, but the voice was unmistakable.

"You two expecting monsters or something?" the voice asked in a mocking tone.

Stan huffed and shrugged his shoulders, trying desperately to look casual and unfazed. "No," he snapped. "Just wasn't expecting anyone else to be up here."

"Ah, well I couldn't sleep so I thought I would take a wander," Stu replied as he stepped up to the roof's edge beside them.

"I'll happily go and do your sleeping for you, Stu," Stan grinned.

"I bet you fucking would," Stu beamed back at him. "But sorry, mate, I've done more than my fair share on 'stag'."

"Why do you lot refer to it as 'stag'?" Kieran asked with a raised eyebrow.

Stu smiled to himself. "I haven't a clue to be honest. It's just army slang and it's stuck." He looked out into the distance, towards the perimeter of the park, and nodded.

"Is there anything new happening out there this morning?"

"Not a thing," Kieran grumbled.

Stu turned slowly in a three hundred and sixty degree arc, scanning the horizon and forming an appreciation of the situation in his head. He nodded and hummed to himself as he did his turn, before stopping and looking out to the south, towards the main gate and perimeter wall.

"What are you thinking, Stu?" Stan asked expectantly.

Stu shrugged and turned to the two youngsters. He fixed them with a cold stare. "We're fucked!"

Stan and Kieran suddenly looked alarmed. Swapping glances with one another, they stepped closer to Stu, their wide eyes revealing their apprehension at Stu's sudden and unexpected statement.

"What do you mean? What's happened?"

Stu grinned. "Calm down fellas, nothing has happened. Well, nothing new anyway, but look at it." He swept his hand in a wide arc over the horizon. "There's a million of those things surrounding us. They can't get in…for now, and we can't get out."

"What do you mean *'for now'*?" Stan was feeling unsettled and it was apparent in his shaking voice.

"He's right, Stan," Kieran admitted.

Stan was rattled. It felt as though the pair of them had suddenly gained some knowledge of an impending catastrophe and he was desperate to be let in on the secret. He glanced from Stu to Kieran and back again, waiting for an explanation. None came.

"Stu's right," Kieran repeated.

Stu nodded to him and turned to head back towards the door. "We can't stay here forever, boys," he called over his shoulder as he disappeared in to the stairway.

Kieran and Stan stood looking at each other for a moment.

Kieran broke the silence. "We will have to leave here at some point."

Stan looked frightened and confused. He always felt less than comfortable around any of the tough looking men that had arrived with Marcus, but Kieran suddenly announcing that he was in agreement with Stu's statement unsettled him.

"Why, what do you think is going to happen? We're safe here, aren't we?"

"Yeah, for now we're safe, but look." Kieran nodded out at the mass of bodies that was packed against the outer walls of the park. They were more visible now and Stan suddenly realised that it was fast becoming light.

"At some point, Stan, they will get in, or we will run out of food. Maybe run out of fuel. Then we will *have* to leave."

"How could they get in? The walls are too big and we put the fuel truck up against the gate to reinforce it. We have tons of food. Marcus and Steve saw to that when they took us back to the supermarket and we pretty much cleaned the place out." Stan was doing his best to convince his friend.

Kieran shook his head and sat down on a rickety camping chair. "You still don't get it, do you, mate? Those things out there, they'll never give up. If they don't break through the gate, then they will starve us out."

Stan was pacing, looking out to the south at the swarms of reanimated dead then back at Kieran. "Nah," he said shaking his head. "We're safe here. They won't get in."

Kieran looked up at Stan. "You remember the supermarket?"
"Yeah, I remember, why?"
"We were stuck there for days and more and more of them showed up by the hour. They didn't get bored and they didn't give up. Now look down there." He nodded towards the large walls that surrounded them. "There are thousands and thousands of them. Eventually, *we will have to leave this place, Stan.*"

4

Jake's skin had turned deathly pale. Beads of sweat formed on his forehead, despite the biting cold of the winter's day. His head was beginning to spin and the nausea increased by the second. He held his hand up to cover his nose and mouth, fighting hard to hold back the gag reflex that threatened to bring up the contents of his stomach.

"I think I'm going to be sick," he warned.

Helen looked at him. He was swaying. She took a step to the right, increasing the distance between her and Jake, just in case he was unable to keep his composure, to avoid being covered in his vomit.

Lee turned and grinned at him. "I thought you would've been used to it by now, Jake. Come on, it's not that bad." He breathed in deep through his nostrils and exhaled loudly through his mouth, all the time, watching Jake for his reaction.

Still holding his nose, Jake shook his head defiantly and mumbled, "Never. I could never get used to it."

The large tanker that they had liberated from the supermarket blocked much of their view beyond the gate, but a metre wide gap on the left side revealed enough. In just that small space, where the railings met the high perimeter wall, hundreds of decaying faces forced themselves up against the steel bars, desperate to reach the five survivors on the other side. They thrust their arms through the gaps in the railings, their fingers clutching and their jaws snapping.

The stench was overpowering, at least for Jake. He could only describe it as a mixture of vomit and excrement. The sickly sweet smell seemed to penetrate through his pores and attack his senses. He wondered how the others had developed such a resistance to it. For Jake, the odour was just as horrific as the dead themselves were.

Steve and Stu stepped closer. They moved around to the front of the tanker, checking that it was still firmly wedged against the large stone pillars that held the gate hinges in place. The cab and trailer were sitting flush with the large heavy gate, reinforcing it against the increasing weight of the dead pushing against it. Steve remembered being impressed at how easily and precisely Jim had managed to manoeuvre the vehicle so close to the gate. The wheels were turned to the left at full lock, and then they had deliberately deflated the tyres to avoid any movement whatsoever. It was still secure and had not budged an inch.

They moved to the rear, towards the gap. They rounded the rear of the truck; immediately, the dead that pushed themselves up close to the gate saw the living humans at such close proximity and erupted with excitement. They increased their efforts to gain entry to the park, pulling and pushing at the steel rails of the gate, smashing their faces into the gaps. They moaned and wailed longingly as they heaved at the gate. Some even managed to obliterate their own skulls with the violence of their assaults, as their heads smashed against the steel barrier and their bodies crumpled to the floor, never to rise again.

The crowd surged as more saw the two living men just beyond their reach, no more than a metre beyond their grasping hands. The bodies at the front were being slowly crushed from the weight of the mob behind them. Stu and Steve watched as they were battered up against the steel bars. The dead did not complain or try to protect themselves from being squashed against the barrier, and continued to snap their teeth together, their eyes locked on Steve and Stu as they were trampled and obliterated by the mass to their rear.

A sea of pale grey and blackened faces; their moans long and in unison, continued to assault the gate. Steve stepped closer, not to agitate the crowd, but so that he could get a better look at the stone pillar and the condition of the brackets that held them in place.

"Careful, Steve," Helen called from behind.

He glanced back and saw her staring at him. At that moment, she reminded him of his mother, scolding him for climbing the garden shed as a child.

Jake had lost his composure and Steve saw that he was a few metres back from Lee and Helen, bent double, and vomiting violently into the bushes.

Steve gingerly moved closer still, one eye looking up at the gate housing and the other watching the bony claw-like hands that were shoved through the bars, reaching out for him. Their fingertips were just centimetres away from his clothing.

Stu stepped up with him, his pistol raised into the aim and ready to drop any of the dead, should they manage to get a grip on Steve.

The steel gate rattled and clanged as the mass of bodies continued to launch their attacks at it; Steve could see the cement around the heavy hinges flaking. With all the weight pressing against them over the months, it had slowly been crumbling away and now, the brackets had movement within the stone.

"Shit, it's..."

A loud bang to his rear forced Steve to raise his hands up to protect his head. He ducked and pivoted to his left as the noise echoed through his ears and sent his vision blurry. He spun and saw the barrel of Stu's pistol pointed in the area where he had been standing. A body, tall and thin, was sliding down the other side of the railings, its long reaching arm dropping to the floor and coming to rest on the exact spot where Steve had been.

"They nearly had you then, Steve." Stu continued to stare at the corpse that he had just shot through the head. "Jesus, he was a big lanky fucker too."

Steve stepped back towards Helen, Lee and Jake. His ears were ringing and a shiver coursed along his spine at the thought of the creature's long arms managing to get a grip on him and pulling him towards the gate, into hundreds of grasping hands.

"Why are so many coming here?" Helen asked as she stared out at the gate, rubbing her hand between Steve's shoulder blades.

"Because we're here, and they won't stop coming here until they get in," Stu replied.

Lee nodded. "And there's too many to burn now." He looked over at Steve and spat in anger. "Let me kill that fat bitch that brought them all here. I'll feed her to those things."

Steve shook his head, a finger pressed into his ear as he tried to stem the ringing from the gunshot.

"We'll decide what to do with her some other time. We have a bigger problem at the moment." Steve was speaking louder than usual due to his temporary impaired hearing.

"What problem?" Lee asked, glancing at Steve and then back at the gate.

"The hinges," Stu cut in, "they're starting to come loose."

Sitting in the foyer, as Stu and Steve informed him of the situation, Marcus felt like kicking himself. He wanted to beat himself up over it. Since arriving at the park, he had tried desperately to throw off the cloak of responsibility and settle down into a routine resembling some form of normality with his wife and children. Slowly, but surely, he had begun to relax.

It had been hard at first. In the beginning, he would wake up with a start during the night, confused and unsure of where he was. It would take a while before his brain fought its way through the fog and reminded him that they were safe at the park, and no longer on the long arduous trek across Europe where he needed to be alert and on his guard twenty-four hours a day.

During the first two months, he had constantly patrolled the park, looking for weak spots in its perimeter walls and gates, always asking himself, *'What if?'* It was an old habit and one that was hard to beat. He had spent his entire life forming tactical appreciations and risk assessments in his head. For every scenario or perceived threat, he would automatically begin planning a solution and a number of alternatives.

Now, with Stu pointing out what he already knew, but had refused to acknowledge, he felt as though he had let everybody down.

"Don't be fucking stupid, Marcus," Stu said, sitting on the one of the foyer's large leather sofas next to him. "It's not your job to sort out *every* problem here you know. Steve has done a good job of it while we were slogging our way home and *I'm* no retard either. I've done my own appreciations of the situation."

Marcus bit his lip. "So, what's the deal?"

Stu shrugged. "The way I see it, we need to have an evacuation plan."

"We do have an evacuation plan; down the cliff face at the north end of the park and across the fields."

Stu shook his head. "No, mate, that's an escape plan. We need to look at where we go from there. What are we going to do, wander around in the wilderness like a bunch of gypsies? We have kids, families and older folk here to think of. Not all of them are in the same shape as us, with tactical thinking and experience. So, we need a plan for what we do once we bug-out of this place."

"True," Marcus nodded. "I think it's time we started sending out a few recce missions, to find an alternate safe-haven."

"We'll do it," an eager voice suddenly volunteered from in front of them.

Marcus and Stu looked up to see Stan and Kieran standing ready, as though reporting for duty and with enthusiasm in their eyes.

"I'm sick of sitting on that roof and watching those things, so a day or two out of here would be a nice break," Kieran stated.

Stu smiled. "It wouldn't be a jolly, you know. I think I would rather have the likes of Jim and Hussein with me on this. They know more about what they're doing and what needs to be done."

"We know what we're doing. Look," Kieran sighed as he stepped forward and squatted down in front of them. "You need our help. We know this area and we need to learn how to do these *patrol* things and what to look for."

Stu remained silent and glanced at Marcus.

Kieran felt the need to state his argument a little clearer. "You've taught us how to use the weapons, and you've taught us how to drive."

During the first months after Marcus and his team's arrival, they had instructed everyone in the house on how to use the weapon systems that they had brought with them. Marcus had felt like he was an instructor again at the recruit depot, constantly drilling the trainees, including his wife and children, with the rifles and pistols.

They advanced quickly and Marcus and Stu believed that they learned fast from necessity, understanding that the world had changed, and regardless of their views on guns, they were vital to their survival.

Kieran looked to his left at Stan for support before he continued. Stan nodded, encouraging his friend to go on.

"I'm not stupid and the way I see it, we're pretty much under siege here. The cars we have here are useless. They're no use to us for escape because of the amount of dead surrounding us. If we need to run from this place, it will be on foot and over the cliff to the north. From there, we will need vehicles and supplies, and we think we know where best to get them."

"Agreed," Stu nodded. "Go on."

"Well, I think the main aim of this 'scouting mission', or whatever you call it…"

"A recce; as in reconnaissance," Stu corrected him.

"Yeah, that's it. Well the main aim, should be to get some cars, say a couple of four-by-fours and people carriers, stock them and leave them on the main road to the north of the park, beyond the open fields. That way, if we have to run, it's a short hard slog for a mile or so, then into the cars and away we go."

Marcus grunted and nodded. "You're not just an ugly face are you?"

Kieran nodded in reply, his eyes locked on Stu.

"Okay, you've convinced me, but like I said, this is not a jolly that we're going on. It seems to me that you were wasted as just a hoodie scrote-bag. You should've joined the army, could've made something of yourself, brains as well as brawn."

"Not my thing, Stu. I don't handle discipline very well."

"And what the fuck do you think this is?" Stu growled and leaned forward, glaring at the younger man. "You will be doing *exactly* as I say on this, Kieran, or I will drop you like a bad habit. Do you understand me?"

Kieran grinned back at him. "This is different, mate. This is survival!"

Jim stood in the gravelled parking area in front of the house, a cigarette hanging from his lips and talking loudly to Hussein in his Texan drawl as he checked his equipment.

"I tell you what; buddy, I'm actually happy to be going out there. I've been going stir-crazy, cooped up in this place."

Hussein nodded. "Yes, Jim, it's been a while since we went beyond the walls." He turned to the tall thin American, to whom he had become a close friend. "What do you think it will be like out there now?"

Jim puffed on the cigarette, keeping it clutched between tightly closed lips. A mist of blue grey smoke plumed out from his nostrils, reminding Hussein of a dragon that he had once seen in a children's book, many years ago.

"I don't know, more of the same shit, I guess. Dead people walking, dusty buildings, abandoned cars…you know; the usual stuff. I don't think we'll see many bars or clubs open that's for sure." Jim grinned at Hussein. "We are outnumbered by about twenty million to one I think, and it has been a long time since we heard or saw any news broadcasts. Maybe we're all that's left?"

"Yeah," Hussein replied, deep in thought.

Stu pulled back the cocking lever on his rifle, just a centimetre or two, enough to see inside and confirm that there was a round in the chamber and the weapon was ready to fire. He knew there was, but he always liked to be double sure.

"You all set?" Marcus asked as he stood beside him.

"Yeah, pretty much." Stu began checking that all his ammunition pouches were secure and that his radio was switched on. "Just waiting on those two lunatics, Ant and Dec, they know what time we're leaving."

Marcus smiled at the nickname for Kieran and Stan. The comparison to the Saturday night entertainers never failed to amuse him.

"Listen, Stu, don't take any chances out there. Get what we need and get back. We can start planning the rest once we have the vehicles in place."

Stu looked up from adjusting his pistol belt. "You worry too much, old man. We'll be fine."

Marcus was about to speak again when the doors to the house suddenly crashed open. His mouth involuntarily fell open as he gazed upon the spectacle that greeted them. More people began silently filing out from the house, glancing from one another and scratching their heads in disbelief.

Steve slowly walked down the steps towards Marcus and Stu, glancing back over his shoulder every now and then, checking that what he saw was real. He approached his brother, shaking his head.

"What the fuck is that?" Marcus asked with his eyes locked on the two figures at the top of the steps that led into the mansion.

"Uh, I think it is Kieran and Stan," Stu replied with an air of doubt.

The two figures standing before them looked around at the silent crowd and then back at each other.

"What, what's up with you lot?" Although he was unrecognisable, everyone identified the voice as belonging to Stan.

Marcus shook his head. "We're fine, Stan. We thought maybe there was something up with you actually. What the fuck are you wearing?"

Stan was clad from head to foot in a black leather biker's suit, including a helmet; the same one that Tony had brought with him when he arrived at the park.

Kieran was not as fortunate to find such equipment. Instead, he had kitted himself out in a mixture of sports padding along with the shoulders and breastplate from a rusted and discoloured suit of armour.

"We found this stuff in one of the store rooms. We thought it would stop those things from being able to eat us," Kieran replied in an unsure voice, now doubting his mastermind idea.

Jim grinned up at them. "Yeah, good idea if you're planning on walking into a crowd of them. Let me know how you make out. Me, I'd just prefer to avoid the pus-bags in the first place if it's all the same to you."

The ludicrousness of the sight finally broke through the initial shock and bewilderment. Stu burst into hysterics, unable to contain himself or his composure. He bent double with tears rolling down his cheeks as he fought for breath.

The rest of the assembled onlookers began to smile and look about at one another.

Marcus' chest heaved and bounced as he laughed quietly to himself, shaking his head. "You know," he folded his arms and nodded towards the two bewildered young men standing on the steps, "you look like a really shit *Darth Vader* and you remind me of the *Tin-Man*, from *'The Wizard of Oz'*, only more camp than the original."

Those assembled that had not already done so, erupted into laughter.

5

After scaling down the cliff face, Stu and his team had to trample their way across the open fields to the north. It was a hard slog. Over eight months' worth of un-harvested crops, tangles of weeds and the undulating ground that was hidden from view by the long grass, threatened to snare and trip them. On more than one occasion, a member of the patrol got his foot snagged and tumbled to the floor, huffing and cursing.

Stu imagined that it would be much more difficult in the dark, under pressure, possibly being pursued, and with less able-bodied people in tow. He stopped roughly half way across the field and dropped to one knee, allowing the others to close up around him.

Jim was the first to arrive. He squatted down in the dirt beside Stu and groaned with the weight of his weapons and ammunition.

"Is everything okay, Stu?" he grumbled.

Hussein, Kieran and Stan soon joined them. Stu looked up at the two young men who were sweating and panting as they crouched down.

"I told you it wouldn't be a jolly, didn't I? I bet you're glad you dumped that armour crap now."

Kieran shrugged. "Was just an idea, was all."

"What we stopping for, Stu?" Jim asked again.

"This field," Stu replied looking at the chest high strands of dried corn that swayed back and forth in the cold wind. "It could be a death trap for us."

Jim nodded. "Yeah, I nearly broke my fucking neck a hundred metres back when I fell."

Hussein nodded. "It's not just that, Jim. If we have to leave the house in the dark, we could get split up and lost here, especially if there is a panic."

Stu nodded at Hussein, a faint glimmer flashed in his eyes as the former Iraqi insurgent read his thoughts. "Exactly; we need to make this field more traversable. When we get back, we'll have to organize clean up teams to flatten the grass and weeds and create a channel leading up to the road; maybe even guide ropes and markers, and a way to make that cliff easier to climb down."

At the road, they paused. It had taken them the best part of an hour since leaving the mansion and according to Stu's pacing; they had travelled roughly fifteen hundred metres, just short of a mile. He shook his head. In an emergency, they would need to cover the distance much faster.

It was a single lane country road with high hedgerows on either side. Stu looked to his left, then to his right. There were no sign of any vehicles abandoned on the road and nothing stirred. A hundred metres further up, they identified an area to cache the vehicles once they had found some suitable to their needs.

"This will be the ERV," Stu said to his team, indicating the lay-by on the side of the road.

He pulled out the Global Positioning System from his assault vest and recorded the grid reference that would be the Emergency Rendezvous.

"Once we get what we need, we bring them here, equip and then secure them."

It was five kilometres to the area where Kieran and Stan said that they knew of a showroom that would have the sort of vehicles they needed. Stu adjusted his equipment, shrugging his shoulders and letting the straps of his harness settle on his body, distributing the weight evenly. He moved off, taking the lead in the patrol with the others following on behind him in single file.

It was not long before they came to a blockage in the road. A car, its doors hanging open, had been abandoned in the centre of the narrow lane. Stu approached with caution. His weapon was pulled tightly in to his shoulder and the safety catch was off, with his finger lightly pressing against the trigger. Each step that he took was short and deliberate, avoiding any possibility of trips or stumbles as he moved forward and scanned the area around the car for possible threats.

A figure sat motionless, hunched over the steering wheel. Its badly decomposed corpse was barely recognisable as human and dark stains surrounded it in the seat. The clothing had become a mix of mottled greys and browns as they had faded from the effects of the elements and bodily fluids had seeped into the fibres from the rotting cadaver. The head had been cracked open and Stu guessed that the windscreen had been responsible judging from the web of fractured glass.

Keeping his weapon in the aim, Stu crouched and looked beneath the vehicle, scanning for anything that may be waiting for them behind the car. Ten metres away on the other side of the smashed car, another vehicle lay on its side, half buried in the unkempt hedgerow. Its front was crumpled inwards and Stu surmised that the two vehicles had been involved in a head on collision.

Jim stepped forward from behind Stu and pushed around to the left of the vehicle. He moved in a semi-crouch, bending at the knees while his body remained rigid and upright, his weapon forced into his shoulder as he peered over the sights.

Quickly and silently, he checked around the other side of the crashed car.

"Clear," he hissed back to Stu.

Hussein then pushed forward and together, he and Jim moved towards the vehicle that was entangled in the hedgerow. A few moments later, Jim signalled back to Stu that the area was free of any threat.

"We got to move them," Jim noted when he returned.

"Move what, the bodies?" Stan asked, alarmed.

He did not relish the idea of mauling with a rotted corpse. The memory of the festering bodies in the builders supply shop when he and Kieran made their escape from the gym rooftop all those months ago was still fresh in his mind.

"No, you dumbass, the cars," Jim replied. "We need to move the cars. This is probably going to be our escape route if we have to bug out from the park."

"Ah," Stan heard the penny drop.

Kieran leaned over, close to Stan's ear. "Think before you blurt things, dick head. You're making us look like a pair of retards," he whispered.

Stan shot him a look. "Oh, and your fucking suit of armour idea helped with our image?" He spat back in response.

"At least I was thinking. Unlike you…"

Stu turned at the sound of the raised voices between Kieran and Stan. "Hey, Ant and Dec," he whispered loudly. "There's probably a hundred of those things in the area, so shut the fuck up and give us a hand pushing this thing off the road."

Jim reached in to the car through the passenger door. The smell of the decayed body at such close proximity was enough to make his eyes begin to water. He reached across and made sure that the car was in neutral and the handbrake was off.

"Just hope the wheels haven't seized up," he groaned as he and Stu leant all their weight against the rear of the vehicle.

Kieran and Stan joined them and together, began to heave the heavy car to the side of the road while Hussein stood watch just a few metres away.

After a long minute of shoving and straining, the four of them managed to get the road clear. The car rolled in to the hedge, a loud clunk resounding as the undercarriage scraped against the tip of the small ditch at the side of the narrow country lane. The nose of the car crunched its way through the underbrush and came to a halt, entangled in the thorns and branches of the hedgerow.

Nothing could be done with the other car, but Stu judged that the vehicles they had in mind, would easily pass through the gap between the crashed cars and the edge of the road.

They continued with the patrol.

A few hours later, after skirting around the outer edges of an infested village, they reached the showroom. The five of them crouched, hidden amongst stalled traffic and the debris left over from the chaos and mass exodus that had clogged the roads in the early days, turning them into death traps and easy prey for the hordes of dead that increased in number by the hour.

Their objective was just a hundred metres away, a once shiny and glittering showroom that had flaunted and showed off its expensive and pristine cars out front, almost gloating at the ordinary people that passed by, eyeing the vehicles with admiration and envy. Only a select few, with wealth and luxury at their fingertips, had had the means to own such machines.

Now, it sat in ruin. Its faded and torn banners fluttered pathetically in the wind. Tantalising billboards, introducing their latest deals, went unnoticed by the wandering corpses that stumbled by, oblivious to the reduced offers and extended warranties. The cracked and broken bay windows of the shop floor stood in testament to the anarchy that had reigned during the time when the dead began to rise, and no one cared anymore about what kind of vehicle a person owned.

Scattered between the five living men and the car showroom was the wreckage of burnt out vehicles and overturned trucks. Dismembered bodies, their bones and skulls bleached white by the sun and the torn and bloodied rags of clothing, littered the 'no-man's land' that Stu and his team had to cross.

Stu raised his head just high enough to see over the hood of the car that hid them from view. He could see a few meandering bodies, shuffling between the cars and other detritus that was spread over the roads. Their sorrowful moans and low grunts strummed on his nerves like guitar strings being plucked too harshly. He felt icy cold sweat run down between his shoulder blades as he watched and waited, looking for a route through that would prevent detection.

"Right," he said in a whisper as he dropped back down beside the others, leaning his back against the driver's door of the car. "We'll move that way," he nodded to their right. "We can use the line of traffic for cover. Once we get to the lights, we hang a left and cross the junction on the other side of that wrecked truck. From there, it's just twenty metres to the showroom."

Everyone nodded, understanding where he was going and how he would get there. Jim already had his toolkit stuffed in to the zip of his assault vest, ready to go straight to work on the vehicles as soon as they got there.

Stu took in a deep breath and began slowly raising himself into a half standing position. He raised his head to look through the driver's side window of the car, just high enough to give him one final look at their objective before they moved into action.

A grey face stared back at him through the opposite passenger window. Its lifeless dead eyes locked on his and opened wide with sudden realisation and excitement as it recognised a living human being within reach.

Stu felt his throat seize up and his heart skip a beat at the shock of the sudden comprehension that they had been detected.

"Shit, they know we're here," he hissed.

The face staring back at him from the other side of the vehicle opened its mouth wide, a long lingering moan erupting from its mangled throat. It launched itself at him, its head rebounding from the glass of the passenger window with a loud resounding thump. Its decaying brain was unable to understand that there was glass and steel between it and the human on the other side as it attacked again.

More figures heard the noise of the growling, agitated reanimated corpse, and began to emerge from between the vehicles to investigate. All around, Stu and his men heard the questioning moans of the dead as they shambled towards the commotion.

"Move, move that way," Stu ordered, heading in the direction of their original plan.

The others sprang to their feet and began to follow as the howls and wails of the dead broke out all around them.

Stu sprinted, his eyes locked to his front and his weapon tucked in against his hip, the muzzle pointing directly ahead of him, ready to open up on anything that appeared in his path. His footsteps seemed loud in his ears, even against the backdrop of the moans that appeared to be rising in volume and tempo on all sides.

"Don't shoot," Jim called over his shoulder to Kieran and Stan. "You'll just bring out more of them. Keep up, and don't shoot."

More and more shadowy figures emerged from the crashed cars and ruined buildings to join in the pursuit. They staggered, hobbled, and crawled in all states of decomposition, some with such damage that all they could do was drag themselves along at an extremely slow pace. Others were more mobile and moved at a much quicker pace as they closed in on the five living men sprinting towards the partially destroyed showroom.

Stu had reached the junction where the traffic lights had once controlled the thousands of vehicles that passed through them on a daily basis. Now, they stood in silence, watching over the dead roads and ruined cars.

He quickly turned to his left as he reached the battered frame of the large truck and headed directly towards the visitor's parking area at the side of the showroom. The area was fast becoming filled with the lurching dead, reaching out to them, moaning and growling as they advanced.

Jim could see the swarms of dead that appeared all around them as he sprinted after Stu. They appeared so quickly and almost out of nowhere.

"Where the fuck they all coming from…?" he growled between gulps of air. "It's as if someone's rung the goddamn dinner bell."

The side entrance to the building was just metres away. The door was closed and Stu began to time his run and adjust his stride. He launched himself off his left foot, throwing the weight of his body forward towards his target with his right leg raised and locked at the knee. The flat of his boot crashed against the hard wooden door, just centimetres to the right of the lock. His knee jarred and the shockwave from the impact juddered up his leg and into his hips. The door splintered at the lock and it smashed inwards from the frame with a loud crash while the momentum of the run and kick carried him forwards into the gloomy interior, where he landed on his feet in a semi-crouch.

He raised his weapon immediately, quickly scanning the area to ensure they were not running into a mob of flesh hungry ghouls that were waiting for them inside the showroom.

"In, get in here," he cried out to Hussein, who was close on his heels.

Jim piled in through the doorway next, quickly followed by Kieran and Stan.

They were in a small reception room where Stu imagined the potential customers would sit and be dazzled by all the jargon and statistics that the salesmen would bombard them with. Two interior doorways led away from the room; Stu guessed that one would be to the shop floor and the other to the garage at the rear of the building. There was a desk in one corner, still displaying a number of colourful and eye-catching brochures and a couple of large sofas placed up against the walls. In the far corner stood two vending machines, one for drinks and the other for snacks.

"Block the door," Stu ordered Kieran and Stan. "Jim, go to the back with Hussein and see if you can get any of the vehicles started."

Kieran and Stan began piling the office furniture against the exterior door. Stu helped drag the vending machines into place before barricading the door that he suspected led out to the shop front. He remembered the broken windows and did not like the idea of the dead realising they could just waltz in on them from the other direction.

The pursuing corpses had already reached the building and began to hammer and pound at the door as Stu, Kieran and Stan hauled the furniture against it. Stu stepped back, eyeing the barricade as the frame quivered and shook while the creatures smashed their bodies against it, their cries and wails muffled by the thick wooden door.

The defences would not hold for long; Stu knew that, but it was the best they could do and he hoped that the addition of the two heavy vending machines would give them enough time to get a couple of vehicles and get out.

"You two," he said, turning to Kieran and Stan. "Watch the doors. Don't go noisy unless you have to, and by that, I mean those fuckers are coming through the barricade."

Kieran nodded. "Just don't forget about us," he said, as Stu turned and headed for the workshop.

In the garage, Jim and Hussein conducted a sweep of the large workshop, ensuring that there were no surprises waiting for them. A thin layer of dust coated every surface and beams of sunlight drifting in through the frosted glass panes above illuminated the spacious room just enough for them to navigate their way around.

Tools, spare wheels and mechanic's diagnostic equipment lay scattered all about. There were a number of vehicles sitting silently in the open area by the mechanics stations. Jim nodded silently to himself, realising that Stu had already anticipated their situation.

The vehicles in the garage were more likely to be easier to start. Stu knew that when a customer had made a purchase, the mechanics would go to work on the car, carrying out final inspections and servicing before they were released to the buyer. There would also be battery packs, hopefully, still containing enough charge and power to get the engines started.

Jim and Hussein got to work and began collecting the keys from the board hanging above a workstation. Stu joined them, and after singling out two brand new Range Rovers, he hauled over the large battery pack and jump leads that he found in the corner. He touched the two points together and felt his heart soar as they crackled and sparked.

Jim was quickly flicking the bonnet catches on the vehicles and checking over the wheels. He climbed into one and pushed his foot down on the clutch, knowing that it would have the new style keyless ignition system. He pushed in the start button and the dashboard display lit up, revealing a full tank of fuel. He pushed the ignition again and the engine whined, but failed to turn over.

"I got it," Stu shouted without waiting for Jim to try again. He quickly attached the jump leads while Jim moved on to the next Range Rover.

Stu looked up as the engine in the second vehicle sputtered then turned over; clouds of dust and exhaust plumed from the rear before the engine settled into a low grumbling hum. Jim threw him the thumbs up and grinned as he jumped from the driver's seat and back into the first Range Rover. He nodded and hit the ignition. The starter motor clicked and whirred but still failed to start the engine.

"Shit," Stu hissed.

"Give it another minute of charge," Jim shouted from behind the wheel.

"We don’t have another minute," Hussein called back to them.

He was standing close to the large steel sliding doors of the garage. They rocked and vibrated as more of the dead attacked it from outside.

"Fuck it," Stu shouted, ripping the jump leads from the large battery pack.

He ran across to the vehicle that was running and connected the leads to the terminals. Jumping into the driver's seat, he pressed his foot down hard on the accelerator pedal. The revolutions of the engine soared and Stu watched as the needle on the dashboard shot over to the right and into the red. He released his foot, waited a couple of seconds, and then repeated the action three more times.

"Try it now," Stu shouted across to Jim with an encouraging nod of his head.

Jim's vehicle coughed and groaned but feeling a spark of life in the engine, he wasted no time and pushed his foot down on the accelerator. The motor caught and the engine snarled as it was brought back from the dead. Jim continued pumping his foot, watching the revolutions rise and fall for a few more seconds.

"That’s it, we got it, Stu," he shouted excitedly over the din of the two engines.

Hussein ran to the front, started securing the hoods to the cars while Jim and Stu threw them into gear, then began manoeuvring them inside the large garage so that they were facing the shutters. They could drive straight out when the time came to make their escape.

A series of loud cracks rang out, their report echoing around the large garage. A moment later, Kieran and Stan appeared at the door, their eyes like saucers. They were screaming something that Stu could not make out.

He did not need to hear what they were saying; their actions spoke volumes.

The dead were inside.

"Get the door open, Hussein," Stu shouted.

The young Iraqi sprinted to the far side and released the heavy lock. He would need to be fast on his feet to get to one of the Range Rovers once he opened the large sliding door. He gripped the steel handle and took in a deep breath. He was sweating profusely and his heart pounded in his chest.

He pulled with all his strength as more gunfire broke out in the confines of the workshop. Stan and Kieran were firing into the doorway leading from the reception room and into the garage, pumping countless rounds at the horde of reanimated corpses flooding in through the destroyed barricade.

The heavy steel door slid open a metre then jammed as Hussein continued to heave. A figure fell through the gap, quickly followed by another, then another. They turned and saw Hussein standing just a few feet from them.

He felt his stomach churn with terror but he could not run to safety. If he did not get the door open, they would all be trapped. Again, he pulled with all the force he could muster, growling and hollering with the strain.

The steel door moved again. It screeched and squealed in protest as it was dragged along its rusted runners, but it was moving.

More of the dead fell through the doorway and into the garage, and began to stagger towards Hussein. Stu leaned out from his driver's seat and began firing at the crowd with his pistol, taking out the closest with precision headshots.

Just one more heave and the gap was large enough. Hussein turned on his heel, and sprinted back to the passenger side of the Range Rover just as the first of the dead reached him. He lunged for the vehicle while the creatures began to stagger into the garage from the room that Kieran and Stan had been defending. He sidestepped the first of them as it reached out to him. He brought his rifle up and shot another at point blank range, its brains flying from the back of its head in a grey and black mist.

He turned and threw himself into the passenger seat, slamming the door hard behind him, trapping the hand of one of the dead and severing it at the wrist. Through the window, he watched as the deceased man pulled his handless stump away from the vehicle and studied it for a moment in confusion. He looked back up at Hussein, his eyes growing wide. Then he hurled himself at the passenger window, leaving dark smears of coagulated blood as he bit and gnarled at the glass.

"Go, Stu, let's go," Hussein screamed as fear gripped him.

Stu slammed his foot down and released the clutch. The gears caught and the heavy vehicle thrust forward towards the bright sunlight outside. More bodies were entering the workshop and hammering against the vehicle but the engines of the Range Rovers were strong and ploughed through the crowd as they picked up speed.

The passengers inside were tossed and buffeted about as the wheels churned the bodies into the floor of the garage; the four-wheel drive did its job well and easily cut a path through and over the dozens of dead that fell beneath the vehicle.

"Go, go, Stu," Jim screamed from behind the wheel of the rear Range Rover. He was terrified of a stall and being overwhelmed by the mass of bodies pressing against them.

Stu's vehicle thrust its way out of the showroom workshop and into the open. Keeping his foot on the accelerator, he quickly changed gear and spun the heavy car to the right, heading for the junction and the main road that led away from the swarms of voracious walking dead.

6

It was late morning and the old Land Rover rocked from side to side as it traversed the rough ground at the northern end of the Safari Park. Gary and Sophie were being tossed around inside like a pair of rag dolls as the wheels slid in and out of the deep, muddy troughs of the dirt track. They were on their daily rounds of the animal pens, checking on their wellbeing and conditions.

Gary forced the wheel over to the right as they reached the northeast corner and dropped the vehicle down into second gear in order to climb the steep rise in the ground. The engine raced as the wheels dug into the gravel and forced them up the bank.

To the left, Sophie watched intently at the area where the trees covered the track leading down to the rear gate. The dirt road disappeared into the gloom, swallowed up by the black cavernous mouth created by the shadows of the overhanging foliage. She shivered, knowing that just a short way along the track, thousands of rotting and ravenous walking corpses beat themselves at the barrier, trying to get into the park. She pictured the barricade becoming loose and the chains that secured the fence falling free during the night, the hordes of dead spilling into the interior of the park. The thought frightened her and she tried desperately to force it from her mind.

"I'm not sure how much longer this old thing is going to be able to carry on doing this sort of stuff, Sophie," Gary announced, breaking her train of thought.

"Yeah, well, according to what I've heard, we may not be here for too much longer. Once Stu and the others are back, Marcus says they will begin looking at other places, more secure than this," she replied.

Although the conversation was not a million miles away from what she had just been thinking, it was a welcome deviation.

Gary snorted. "How could we be any safer? We have big walls and heavy steel gates protecting us. We've been here since the beginning and we're *still* here."

"We haven't always been safe though, Gary," she reminded him.

The vehicle suddenly dipped again as it hit another rut in the road. She reached out and pushed back against the dashboard, stopping herself from colliding with the hard moulded plastic.

"Remember a few months back when they got in? John and Carl were almost eaten by them and got stranded in a bloody tree."

"Ah, but you're forgetting, Sophie," he said without taking his eyes off the track ahead of them, "it was Stephanie that let them in. They didn't get in by themselves."

Sophie was starting to get annoyed at his overconfidence in the ability of the park and walls to continue protecting them. She had listened as Stu and Steve told them about things that could eventually happen.

She knew about the weakening hinges and brackets of the main gate and she understood that there could be more unforeseen incidents of people letting the creatures in. They were surrounded and under siege by thousands of the dead and their supplies were far from endless.

She also remembered what Stu had said:

"Murphy's Law of Combat; 'what can go wrong...will go wrong."

Gary's refusal to acknowledge the possibility of having to move frustrated her; she struggled to understand why he was so determined not to accept the possibility that the park defences could eventually collapse.

"Look, I know you love this place..." she began, but Gary raised his hand.

"It's not that," he cut in, shaking his head. He sighed and glanced across at her. "It's Karen, she's sick."

He turned back to the road, biting his lip and waiting for the inevitable question.

Sophie frowned, but she knew what he meant. She just did not want to say the words.

"Maybe Stu and Helen could help her," she suggested, knowing there was nothing they could do.

Gary shook his head. "You know they can't, Sophie. Years ago, we went through this once before. She had the surgery that removed the lump, and the radiotherapy afterwards almost killed her on its own."

He brought the vehicle to a sudden halt and climbed out from behind the wheel, stepping into the cold air and breathing deeply, fighting against the emotions that bubbled up inside of him.

Sophie followed him and moved around to the front where he was leaning against the wheel arch, his hands folded across his chest and his eyes cast downward to the ground. She did not know what to say.

"There's nothing that anyone can do, Sophie. I cannot watch her suffer with this again. When the time comes," he looked up at her, his eyes wet with tears, "I will do what needs to be done to ease her suffering."

Sophie felt Gary's words wash over her like a tsunami of ice. "Surely you don't mean that?"

Gary nodded. "I do mean it." He looked up at her and smiled. "And please, don't call me 'Shirley'."

For a second, her brow furrowed in confusion, and then she got the joke. She smiled politely and shrugged.

"You need to think about this, Gary."

"I have done," he replied with an air of resignation. "I've thought long and hard about it and dragging her away from here, where she has made a home, would be more suffering for her. I feel that she wouldn't be able to stand it."

Sophie could see that his mind was made up. She looked down at the ground and scuffed at the gravel with the sole of her walking boot. She was about to speak again when they were suddenly bathed in a bright light. The whole area was immersed in a brilliance of white, more dazzling than the sun.

"What the hell is that…?" Sophie exclaimed as she squinted and pivoted on her heel.

The two of them turned, looking for the source. The light seemed to emit from a point on the distant horizon to the south. It was brighter than the sun, so strong that Gary and Sophie had to shield their eyes.

Above them, the thin wisps of cloud hanging lazily in the pale blue sky were suddenly swept away by an invisible and silent force that seemed to race through the atmosphere in all directions.

The light, after a few seconds of intensity, began to fade. Sophie and Gary remained standing still, watching the horizon and hoping that the cause would be revealed. As the light faded, the ground beneath their feet vibrated and a low concussion, followed by a continuous rumbling, reached their ears.

Gary's eyes grew wide as he watched the distant skyline reveal its secret. His head began to spin and he had to bend himself double, bracing his hands against his thighs as the realisation dawned on him and his eyes saw, what his mind struggled to comprehend.

"Oh shit," he grumbled.

Sophie was still watching the light, trying to make sense of the vision that was still not fully clear to her. She turned at the sound of Gary's voice.

"What? What is it, Gary?" she asked, desperate to know what it was that had clearly unsettled him from his usually rock solid foundations.

"No, no, it can't be," he said, speaking to the ground, shaking his head as his stomach flipped and churned. "Please, don’t let it be this."

Sophie turned back to look at the horizon. By now, the blinding white light had faded and in its place, stood a glowing billowing cloud, reaching up from the ground and high into the air.

Sophie now comprehended what she was looking at and suddenly felt an overwhelming urge to vomit.

7

"Stand with your body square to the front, legs slightly bent at the knee, Sarah," Marcus commanded. He was using his 'instructor voice', a tone that had no familiarity in it regardless of the pupil's relationship to him. Even his wife, Jennifer, did not recognise him when he was teaching her how to use the weapons.

Steve's daughter complied with her uncle's commands. She gripped the pistol with both her hands, her elbows loose and her shoulders braced, with the weapon pointing at the small white square acting as their aiming mark on the wall in front of them. She focussed, awaiting his next instruction.

The foyer was silent except for the voice of Marcus as he called out commands, criticisms and praise. They listened and concentrated intently to his advice. They knew what would happen if they did not.

Marcus was not shy of having them do push-ups as punishment for failing to get a certain drill correct, or order them to begin a routine of star-jumps while they repeated the drill over again verbally, making sure that it was firmly lodged in their minds.

For Sarah and the other younger members of the house, it was fun, even the punishment, but a few of the adults found it insulting and degrading. Marcus decided that the best way around dealing with some of the more difficult grown-ups was to join them in their punishment. Sarah had watched in amusement on many occasions as Marcus dropped to the floor, joining the others, raising and lowering his body to the ground and reeling off, at the top of his voice, the actions that had been expected of the trainees.

"I would not ask anything of you that I would not be willing to do myself," was one of his many encouraging words of wisdom.

The children had come on quickly in the weapons training. Marcus was particularly impressed with how adept his own son, Liam, was with the rifle and the pistol, despite his young age. They had been taught the basics to begin with, weapon safety, and stripping and assembling for daily cleaning.

Safety was his biggest concern. It was fine having a weapon, but being able to handle it without accidentally killing themselves, or someone else, was of utmost importance and it was something on which Marcus and Stu refused to take prisoners. On a few occasions, people had been reduced to tears after being bawled out by them over unsafe handling of a firearm. A fight between Lee and Stu had once almost broken out when Lee had taken exception to Stu's reprimanding.

"You too, David, don't lock your elbows. You will need them to give a little to counter the weapon's recoil when it fires," Marcus' voice echoed.

For months, Marcus, Stu and Jim had drilled the people of the house on how to care for and fire the weapons. From cleaning and loading, to unloading and dealing with stoppages. Some had quickly picked it up and after a month of daily instruction, demonstration, and practice, they were ready to be trusted to handle their own personally issued weapon. Lee was especially proud of the fact that he now sauntered about the park carrying his very own SA80 rifle.

Marcus was about to give the words of command for the next drill when the house began to shake all around them. The windows rattled and the floor vibrated beneath their feet. The children looked to him, fear in their eyes, searching for an explanation.

A commotion from the area of the stairs caught his attention. Carl was sprinting down the steps, screaming for Marcus to come and see something.

"What is it?" he asked in alarm as he grabbed his own weapons from the table. "What's happened, Carl?"

Carl was gasping for air. His eyes were like saucers and he had already turned and was running back up the stairs.

"You need to see this, Marcus. Come on," he called over his shoulder as he reached the top step and bounded down the corridor towards the door that led up to the roof.

Marcus took off after him. He could feel his throat seizing up as he dreaded the worst. *'They must have got in,'* he thought to himself. *'They must be inside the walls.'*

He had visions of reaching the sentry position on top of the house and seeing hundreds of wretched and horrifying figures staggering towards the house from all directions.

Others followed too, not wanting to be kept in the dark. Helen, Jake and Jennifer raced up the steps, close on Marcus' heels and out onto the roof.

Lee was standing close to the edge, his knees resting against the small wall running around the roof of the house, his binoculars glued to his face.

As the door crashed open, he turned to see Carl returning with Marcus in tow.

Marcus moved towards him. He could see the look of alarm etched across Lee's features as he turned and faced Marcus, holding out the binoculars for him and pointing to the horizon.

"They've done it, Marcus," he murmured, still pointing into the distance with a look of disbelief. "They've gone and fucking done it."

Marcus took the binoculars and followed the direction of Lee's finger with his naked eye. He could see it, clear as day without any viewing aids. His blood froze in his veins and his guts twisted and knotted. In all his years in the army he had trained for it, but never thought he would actually see it, especially now. With all the governments gone and armies destroyed, it was the last thing he expected to see.

"Fuck," he whispered.

The mushroom cloud was still growing, reaching high into the atmosphere. It glowed from within as the massive ball of fire, dust and debris rose up like a terrifying monster over the distant landscape.

Jennifer was sobbing, holding her face in her hands, unable to look at the horrifying sight that stood before them.

"No, it can't be. No," she whimpered continuously into her hands, the tears streaming from between her fingers.

"Where do you think that thing is?" asked Carl.

"It's south, I know that much, maybe thirty miles or so?" Marcus shrugged, staring at the tall fiery cloud. "Could be Chester or somewhere in that area," he said passing the binoculars back to Lee.

Jake and Helen were in shock. They stood silent, watching in a mixture of astonishment, fear and awe.

Jake was old enough to remember the threat of a nuclear war from when he was a child. He vaguely remembered the leaflets that were posted through their door by the local council, instructing them on how to build a shelter and what to do should the bombs fall. He also remembered the short government information broadcasts, explaining the effects of *'fall-out'* and what to do if someone in the shelter succumbed to radiation poisoning. He recalled his mother and father, sitting for hours, discussing what they would have to do, and hearing his mother crying and sobbing through the night.

It was only in later years, as a young man and with the threat of nuclear war dying along with the Soviet Union, that his father told him about the difficult decision his parents had come to on the matter. If the country were to be swept by a nuclear holocaust, to prevent them from suffering and dying a slow and agonising death, they would die as a family, at the hands of his father.

Now, staring out at the monstrous glowing mushroom cloud, the words of his father rang in his ears.

"You should get inside and shelter in the basement," a gravelly voice said from behind them.

Marcus turned and saw Johnny Boots standing there, eating a bar of chocolate and watching the expanding cloud from the nuclear explosion. No one knew how long he had been there for; he could have been there from the beginning. No one ever knew where Johnny was or what he was doing. He drifted about the park as his own entity and now and then, he would make an appearance.

Marcus suddenly felt a sense of urgency coursing through him.

"He's right," he announced as he turned to the others. "Everyone, get inside. Grab as much food as you can and get the children in to the basement. Move," he ordered.

The sound of an engine and a beeping horn caught his attention. Racing across the fields from the north, the old zebra coloured battered Land Rover raced towards them.

Gary and Sophie crashed through the large wooden doors to the house in a panic. More panic greeted them as they entered the foyer. People rushed about, carrying food, clothing and blankets while others herded the children towards the cellar door.

"Marcus," Gary called as he saw his friend carrying a large box of tinned food. "We need to secure this place."

"We're heading to the basement, Gary. We need…" Marcus began.

Gary was shaking his head. "No, I mean, yes, we need to do that, but we also need to make sure the house is sealed."

Marcus stopped, realising what Gary meant. He turned to Lisa as she passed him and gave her the box of food.

"Get to the cellar and keep everyone there," he ordered. "Lee, Steve, Jake and Carl, you're with me."

Gary had already run to the kitchen and was filling buckets of water and gathering as many towels and blankets as he could find. He threw them to Marcus and the others.

"Here, soak them and block any gaps you find; doors, windows, vents…everything."

Marcus was impressed that the old man remembered some of the advice from the old Cold War information pamphlets.

"My boy," Gary began as he worked furiously to seal the main door, "I was in my prime back in those days and I remember it all." His voice was strained as he slapped down another wet towel to cover the gap at the bottom of the door.

"It was all we could think about because it was rammed down our throats twenty-four seven. We came so close to nuclear war," he said, turning to Marcus, holding up his thumb and forefinger, just millimetres apart, as an indication. "Now we're fighting flesh-eating dead people *and* nuclear fucking bombs."

8

He watched how they moved, their grace and beauty as they effortlessly crossed the ground and handled the objects that they carried. A certain delight in observing them seemed to rise within him as he compared them to the masses of lumbering, clumsy husks that swarmed the cities and towns.

He remained unseen, watching them from the shadows. The mouldy and threadbare curtains ensured that he would not be detected as he peered out through the filth-encrusted window of the third floor apartment.

All around him, the once stylish and comfortable interior that had been home to a young family, slowly decayed and withered with time. A layer of dust had settled over every surface, leaving everything looking opaque and dreamlike. The personal effects of the previous occupants lay scattered all around him; children's toys and books littered the floor while upturned furniture, and discarded clothing bore witness to the panic that had ensued and prompted the people to flee.

The pictures on the walls and bookshelves showed a happier time that no longer existed. The smiling children and parents now either hiding, or dead, after falling victim to the ever growing population of staggering ravenous creatures now inhabiting and roaming the world they had once known.

At first, he had felt urged to get away from the people he watched, to put as much distance between them and him as possible, but something tugged at him from deep within and he felt an overwhelming need to observe them and stay close by.

He remembered their leader; a man that could have easily put a gun to his head and ended his existence, but instead, had set him free, ignoring the objections of the others around him. The man had shown him compassion and understanding and did not view him as a threat. As a result, he had been led down to the gates and released, while the others like him had perished at the hands of their captors.

Andy remembered the events well. He recalled his feelings of utter contempt and disgust for the others he had been locked inside the cage with. They were as vile and wretched as any that he had come across. They saw and felt nothing of their surroundings or of each other. They shuffled from one side of the enclosure to the other in their revolting state as Andy stood back and watched.

Only when they saw the vibrant and animated figures on the outside, speaking and moving with a pace that they were unable to match themselves, did their drab and dull existence change. They would scream and assault the cage, shaking at the bars as they tried desperately to reach the men on the other side.

They attacked the barrier relentlessly and with complete disregard to the damage that they were causing to themselves. They were intoxicated with their desire to feed on the flesh of the living, regardless of the cost.

Andy did not know which he despised more, their shambling, incoherent and oblivious meanderings; completely unaware of what was happening or what was likely to happen to them, or their loathsome and terrifying reaction to the presence of their captors whenever they were in view.

He remembered the feelings that had surged through him during his captivity, as his thought process and emotions had developed far beyond that of most others like him. Terror had gripped him, as he had seen all too often, what the fast moving figures did to his kind. Usually, they would not hesitate to shoot or smash the heads in of the others that were like Andy. Being held in the cage, with the possibility of the others turning on him, or being shot by the ones on the outside, had filled him with an overwhelming dread, an uncertainty of his fate.

He watched as the others around him fell, one after the other, as bullets smashed through their heads. He felt certain that his turn was next. He had nowhere to hide and no way of defending himself. Instead, he had accepted his fate and a great sense of defiance had urged him to remain standing, watching his would-be executioners. That same reaction had earned him his freedom; the leader of his captors had seen something different in him.

Andy leaned forward and peered down onto the road below. Dozens of twisted staggering figures aimlessly roamed the littered and decaying streets. A collection of grey shadow like mangled shapes wandered and stumbled along with no clear intention of where they wanted to go. They would continue that way until something blocked their path and forced them to change direction, or something caught their attention. They were mindless and of no interest to him.

They were capable of nothing other than death and destruction.

He looked down at his body. He was in much better condition than most like him, he was aware of that. For a long time, he had been conscious of how delicate he had become and how easily he could be damaged. To that end, he had done what he could to protect himself. He avoided anything that could harm him, especially the others like the ones in the street below. He was careful of where he placed his feet, avoiding falling or damaging his brittle bones. He took extra care to protect the soft tissue of his hands and fingers.

After being set free, he had taken to carrying a means of defending himself. A tyre iron that he found in the garage of a house was his only companion, and he felt the need to use it on a few occasions, despatching the confused and dumbstruck creatures that came too close to him.

Andy grunted.

He looked back up and focussed on the living people that he saw beyond the protective walls. The shambling things below had no inclination that warm living flesh was close by, just beyond their reach.

For a long time he watched them. He witnessed the days shorten and the clouds form overhead, and the rustling leaves of the trees turn from vibrant green to bright oranges and yellows before falling to the ground.

All the time he remained at the window.

Andy also observed the people as they silently crept in and out from the walls, clearing the area of the lurching and revolting figures that encroached upon their home. He looked on indifferently as the things like him were silently beaten and killed with clubs and knives, then dragged to the side and discarded like the unwanted and dangerous garbage that they were.

He watched with curiosity as the skies became filled with birds flying south before the cold weather arrived. He stood witness as the rains came, heavier and longer than they had in previous months. Now, as the first light flakes of dazzling white snow slowly drifted down from the dark clouds, he continued to observe the beings beyond the walls of the army barracks.

The fast moving figures were busying themselves, loading trucks with equipment and people. They seemed to be hurrying, a sense of panic spread amongst them as they intensified their efforts.

The next morning, as the first rays of sunlight touched the rooftops of the city, Andy watched as the living people drove out from the barracks, heading away from the infested metropolis. Their engines roared as they raced for the outskirts; their guns chattered as they mowed down any of the swaying figures in the street that stood in their way.

As quickly as he could, Andy chased after them. At best, he could only manage a speedy hobble as he urged his decaying legs to carry him along the street. He did not understand why he needed to follow, but he was compelled to. They had spared him and he felt drawn to them, as though, in some way, they would be able to help him or give him something back that resembled his former life.

He staggered through the suburbs, barging the other figures out of his way as they lurched into his path. Before long, and inevitably, a crowd began to follow him. They saw his haste, and in their typical herd mentality, they latched onto him, wailing and moaning as they stumbled along behind him.

He was starting to feel panic rising inside him. He had been caught up in a similar incident before, becoming the attention of a whole city as they swarmed around him, almost tearing him to pieces. The memory of that day burned through his mind, filling him with fear for his own safety and continued existence. He knew that if they caught him, they would destroy him, rip him apart and leave him scattered across the surface of the street.

A dark shadow stumbled into his path. It turned and moved towards him, reaching for him and letting out a low questioning moan as it approached. Its face was swollen to twice its normal size. The green flesh of its cheeks looked ready to burst and its swollen black tongue flopped from its mouth. It continued forward, shuffling on unsteady bloated legs with its sunken and clouded eyes locked onto Andy.

As the gap closed, the body became more excited; its moans changed in pitch and tempo as it reached out. It was completely oblivious to the raised shaft of steel that Andy held in his hands. It was still unaware of it when the weapon crashed down into its head and smashed a hole through its skull.

Andy searched desperately for somewhere to hide, to evade his followers. They moaned loudly behind him as they attempted to catch up with him, but he was determined not to allow them to get close. He gripped the tyre iron in his hand, ready to use it against any that approached him. He searched frantically for a place to conceal him and evade his pursuers. He turned in circles, eyeing and studying the dark buildings lining the road on either side of him, his panic growing to the point where it was almost blinding.

There was a sudden flash from behind and the street became filled with a bright and intensifying light. It swathed everything around with a radiance that was so dazzling, nothing other than a blanketing whiteness could be seen, not even his hands, as he raised them up to his face to protect it from the unknown attacker.

The air seemed to push against him, squeezing in a vice-like grip, and an immense booming sound, louder than anything he ever heard, echoed in his ears, threatening to cave his skull inwards upon itself.

Andy felt the enormous pressure, and he clasped his hands to the side of his head, expecting to feel something physically enveloping him. His body shook as the vibrations from the detonation raced across the land, threatening to knock him from his feet, as the ground below trembled violently.

He turned as the blinding light began to fade. Over the rooftops and in the distance, towards the dense city centre, he saw a cloud of fire reaching high into the sky, bubbling and pluming with flame and dust.

For a moment, he stood in silence, watching in wonder and awe. The crowd that had been following him also stood motionless, staring up at the burning cloud as they began to smoulder from the immense heat given off by the light. They stood with their rotting faces turned up to the sky, mesmerised by the sight, completely unaware of what the vision before them was.

Then, something inside Andy screamed. A flash of a memory, of a horror that he had once known and remembered from his past life, tore its way through his mind. The image of a similar event thrust itself before his eyes. In that instant, he saw death and destruction on a scale that his misfiring brain could not comprehend. An instinct of approaching danger coursed through his tangled thoughts and withering body. The only thing he could really grasp, was that he needed to find somewhere to hide, quickly.

While the crowd of grotesque and abominable monsters stood rooted to the ground all around him, Andy staggered towards a building close by. The door that once was barricaded now lay askew with the wreckage of its defences scattered across the ground. He smashed his way in through the entrance and into the darkness, searching for a place to hide and protect himself from the approaching doom.

The earth shook below his feet and the building began to quiver, as the initial blast wave arrived. An intense, thundering, bang rocked the very foundations beneath him. The windows exploded, shattering into a million pieces and sending their fragments in all directions like glass missiles. Plaster and large pieces of loose masonry fell from the walls and ceiling as the vibrations threatened to bring the building down around him.

Andy was out of time. He moaned loudly against the crescendo that filled his ears, as he realised he was about to be destroyed in the explosion that would arrive at any moment. He felt a sorrow rise up within him as he considered that he would never look upon the birds fluttering cheerfully in the sky again. He would never watch the sway of green and radiant trees as the wind gently blew against their branches, and the long blades of grass that danced in the fields.

He looked down at the floor, resigned, and waiting for the end.

In front of him was a set of concrete stairs built into the frame of the building. Below that, a door led into a cupboard on the underside of the staircase. Andy reached for the handle and pulled it open. The darkness of the interior loomed out at him, making him hesitate, but then he remembered the urgency of what he needed to do. He climbed inside, slamming the door shut behind him. He crawled into the corner, knocking over glass bottles and plastic containers that were scattered about the floor of the enclosure.

Through the cracks in the door, Andy could see an intense glow as the heat wave arrived and incinerated everything in its path. The others like him, which were still on the street, were engulfed by flames and turned to charred lifeless statues and ash in an instant.

The door to his sanctuary began to glow as the heat penetrated it and began to reduce it to nothing, leaving him unprotected against the fire. He looked down and saw that his fingertips were beginning to glow red, as the heat fought its way into the shelter, subjecting his body to the high temperatures.

In a moment of clarity, he reached for one of the closest bottles, which he knocked over as he crashed into the dark closet. Without further hesitation, he raised the bottle and emptied the contents onto his hands, extinguishing the flames that threatened to erupt from his dried leathery skin. He grabbed more containers and quickly poured them over the entire surface of his body, drenching himself in the fluid and staving off the effects of the heat wave that threatened to engulf him.

He watched, terror filling his every sense along with a feeling of complete helplessness. He knew that he could do nothing; there was nowhere left for him to hide. He was going to be destroyed in this place, cowering in the corner below the stairs as the world quaked around him in the roaring heat and howling winds.

The glowing door of Andy's hiding place was abruptly ripped away. The concrete stairs above him trembled violently as large clumps of stone fell from the structure. Outside, he saw the remainder of the building disappear into a whirling cloud of grey dust that enveloped him, as he remained protected beneath the stairs.

The ground shook and heaved beneath him as the screaming shockwave rocked the earth. Buildings exploded and crumbled beneath the onslaught, reducing the streets of the city to nothing more than piles of smouldering brick and twisted metal.

The steel frames of the building around him groaned as they were warped, and then ripped from their foundations. They carried tons of debris, exploding into deadly whirls of flying dust and metal, and smashing their way through anything in their path, as they were carried along in the blast wave.

Andy curled into a ball and raised his hands above his head in an attempt to protect himself from the collapsing building. The noise of the shockwave and erupting buildings drowned out the howls and moans that he involuntarily emitted, as everything around him seemed to be obliterated.

Gradually, the roaring winds and heat of the blast died down, leaving a trail of destruction behind as the dust slowly settled over him. He was afraid, there was no mistaking that, and he remained curled up in his hideout for some time afterwards, staring out through the gaping hole where the door used to be, and at the total devastation around him.

After a long time of sitting in silence in his protective shelter, Andy finally rose to his feet and climbed out through the warped and battered doorframe.

He paused, standing in the ashes and rubble, observing his new surroundings. The building looked distinctly different now.

All around him, walls burst and collapsed in on themselves, leaving large gaping holes peering out into the streets. Steel support beams tumbled from their housings, bringing down much of the upper floors as the building imploded. The floor was strewn with large lumps of concrete and wood, charred and discoloured from the immense heat.

Andy looked up and saw that the upper floors, including the roof, had completely disappeared. Even the top part of the staircase under which he sheltered was gone, torn away by the explosion.

The only thing that remained intact was the cupboard beneath the stairs where Andy had sought refuge. The thick and heavily built concrete steps, along with the enclosed space beneath was charred, but other than that, barely scratched.

Unbeknown to Andy, the building was old and had not been used or renovated for many years. The asbestos lining the walls of his hiding place absorbed most of the intense heat, and saved him from perishing like the others.

He looked down at himself to check on his condition. His skin was dry, blistering in parts and scorched in others, but overall, the damage was minimal. His fingers suffered the worst, singeing the tips to the point where the flesh crumbled, exposing the white bone beneath.

He grunted as he studied his damaged hands, but he remembered that he was fortunate to have survived at all. He turned to the area where the door once stood and carefully began to make his way across, conscious of where he placed each step.

Out in the street, the landscape of the city was transformed into a desolate wasteland of rubble and twisted metal. Fires raged all around and dense plumes of smoke rose into the sky. Very few buildings remained standing, and those that did, only their frames survived.

The destruction was complete.

Charred and misshapen bodies lay amongst the wreckage, burned and crushed as the buildings collapsed on them. All around, smashed skulls and dismembered limbs lay strewn over a vast area, all mixed in with the debris that were the remains of the city.

Nothing moved. There were no sounds; not even the moans of the despicable beings that just a short while ago, wailed incessantly as they staggered through the streets, *en masse*. Andy looked back towards where the centre of the city once stood. Still rising high into the sky, the remains of the dark cloud that created such devastation, slowly dispersed out into the atmosphere.

It was time for him to leave.

He suddenly remembered the people he had been trying to follow, and then a sense of urgency filled him, making him feel afraid. It was not fear for himself, but for the living people who had been human enough to spare him all those months ago.

He staggered forward, picking his way through the rubble, smouldering cars, and collapsed buildings as he headed for the country.

As he walked, he heard a thundering in the distance and the ground beneath him began to shudder. He turned in panic, thinking that it was all about to happen over again. This time, there was no giant cloud of fire or blinding flash. What he saw was a tall building close to the city centre that had stubbornly stood up to the blast, and now began to tumble to the ground. The upper floors collapsed in on themselves on one side, creating a chain reaction that brought the whole structure crashing to the street in a cloud of dust and flying rubble.

Andy let out a long mournful moan as he witnessed the final death throes of the city.

Despite its grotesque and horrific residents, the destruction created a great sadness inside of him, as he remembered how it would have once been in a time when the living people ruled the world.

A few days later, as he shuffled along a wide road that twisted its way through the countryside, Andy stopped. Up ahead, he saw columns of smoke drifting into the air and a mass of dark figures crowding the road.

He advanced carefully, keeping his distance from the roaming creatures that filled the area. Through the acrid smoke that hung low, shrouding the ground, he saw numerous shadows drifting in and out of the dense, black, swirling clouds.

On closer inspection, he saw that it was the remains of burning trucks; the same trucks he saw his captors leaving in as they escaped from the city.

They were riddled with holes and charred down to their frames. Glass and debris littered the road and amongst them, the stripped and dismembered bones of dozens of people.

The mass of feeding figures clambering around the vehicles fought and tore at one another over the scraps, gnawing at body parts, and growling at any that approached them while they ravaged the remains.

Andy kept his distance. He felt no desire to join in on the feeding frenzy, or to scavenge the scraps of flesh that still littered the road. Instead, he remained separated from the others like him, watching with a great sadness tearing at him from inside.

9

Stu saw the flash of light from the bomb and so did the others. Even the immense crowd of dead that swarmed and surrounded their vehicles stopped to gaze up at the dazzling white light and the fiery ball that rose up on the horizon. They were mesmerised by it, and every one of them seemed to forget about the five living people inside the two Range Rovers that they were so desperate to get at just moments before.

Stu reached for his radio. "Jim, you seeing what I'm seeing?"

Jim's voice came through in his earpiece, gravelly and little more than a whisper. "Yeah, someone dropped a goddamn atom bomb," he said slowly, stating the obvious.

"No, Jim," Stu replied, "apart from the bomb, look around you."

Stu nodded to Hussein at his side and gestured to the sea of bodies that now stood motionless around them.

"They're too busy watching the pretty lights, Jim. If we try to move the vehicles, we might grab their attention again, so we need to debus and make a run for it."

Jim's voice was more animated now. "Fuck, you serious, man?"

"Just a few seconds ago, we couldn't move because there were so many of them. We still won't be able to move now unless we go on foot. It's either that, or we die here once they've had enough of watching the giant pretty mushroom."

They were trapped in a street with the dead converging on all sides. Despite the power of the engines, the two off-road vehicles were bogged down due to the sheer number of bodies pressing against them. Their wheels lost traction in the organic swamp below, as putrefied flesh and bone churned up under the tyres. They became stuck in an ocean of gaunt dead faces with no possibility of escape.

The two Range Rovers had taken a beating for twenty minutes as the horde pressed in and assaulted the vehicles. Their endless attacks rocked the machines from side to side, tossing the occupants around like survivors of a shipwreck, clinging to a raft on a rough sea. Skeletal faces and emaciated, withered hands pounded at the windows, their howls and moans rising to a crescendo, attracting more dead to the scene by the minute.

Stu and the others believed that they were finished and would not be able to hold out for much longer. The vehicles were going nowhere and they did not have the ammunition to fight their way out of their predicament. They watched in horror as the windows were cracked and the doors slowly buckled and splintered. It was only a matter of moments before they would shatter the glass, leaving them defenceless against the thousands of flesh-hungry creatures.

Then, the bright white light appeared, bathing the whole area and making everything look as though they were in an old sepia photograph. As Stu and the others shielded their eyes from the intense glow, the mass of reanimated bodies around them stopped. They turned and stared up into the sky, completely forgetting their lust for living flesh.

The area had fallen into stillness and silence.

"It's now or never, Jim," Stu informed him. "We need to move before they get bored of looking at the bomb and realise we're still sitting here like a pair of giant lunch boxes."

"Roger that." Jim's voice sounded less than sure of the decision, but he obviously realised that Stu was right. "Where do we go?"

Stu looked around him. Thousands of grey, black, and brown, grotesque statues surrounded them, their faces turned up to the sky. He had no idea of where to go. He searched desperately, looking for even the slightest glimmer of hope to head for.

The street was lined with buildings, shops, businesses, and even bars. He looked past Hussein then back to his right. He saw an area where the dead were less densely packed. Beyond them, he saw the large leaded and colourful windows of a pub. Above the door, he read the name, *'The Nelson',* a building named in honour of the 'Hero of Trafalgar', Admiral Lord Nelson.

"Get out on the right, slowly and quietly, and head for the 'Nelson' pub," he instructed calmly over the radio.

Cringing to himself and praying that the doors would not creak and groan as they opened, Stu grasped the handle. He turned to Hussein and nodded, placing his forefinger against his lips, instructing his friend to remain silent. The locking mechanism clicked quietly and he began to push the door outwards.

An emaciated and misshapen figure was standing close by, only allowing him to open the door a foot or so. With his assault vest and weapons, he would not be able to squeeze through without becoming snagged or making a noise. He winced and began gently, and very slowly, pushing the door a little further.

The steel delicately made contact with the figure's back. Stu held his breath and gingerly began to press the door further still. He could feel the weight of the creature against it as he increased the gap between the door and the frame. The figure on the other side of the glass did not turn at the sudden pressure from behind. It merely shuffled its feet forward a little, its eyes glued to the heavens.

Stu breathed a silent sigh of relief.

He clutched his pistol in one hand, letting his rifle hang by his side, attached to the sling. At such close quarters, with so many of the dead surrounding them, the pistol would be much easier to wield. With the other hand, he gripped the doorframe as he carefully stepped out into the street, his toes touching the floor first, and then rolling on to the ball of his foot, and then his heel to avoid making any noise.

He stood still for a moment and looked around him. The natural light of the day was fading fast, but it was replaced by the artificial glow of the nuclear bomb that exploded in the far distance.

He could see Jim and the others doing the same, slowly emerging from the death traps that the two vehicles had become. Surrounding him, the dead stood motionless. He had never been so close to them without being attacked, and now a morbid curiosity caused him to hesitate as he studied the hundreds of rotting corpses that refused to remain dead.

Their stench was enough to make him want to hold his breath until he was far away from them. The air was thick with insects of all kinds, as they buzzed and crawled from one body to the next, nesting and feeding in the rotting flesh. Their clothing hung from their bodies, filthy, torn, and shredded. Trousers were frayed and shirts ripped to shreds and hanging open as they slowly dissolved into nothing. Some had lost their shoes, exposing their rotting feet, and the flesh slowly eroding from their bones as they continued to shuffle and scrape along the hard roads and pavements. A number of the dead were even naked, either having reanimated that way, or the clothing had been torn from them over the months.

There were all manner of injuries amongst them, but it was hard to guess what caused many of their deaths. Most of the bodies were missing a limb, or eye, even jawbones. Many looked to have exploded from within due to the build-up of gasses as the internal organs decayed. Cavernous holes where the abdomen used to be, were framed by grey white ribs jutting outwards. Some still had the remains of their innards hanging from their stomach; green and blue, fetid intestines that swayed like pendulums between their legs as they walked.

The one thing that most of them had in common, Stu noticed, was that they were all drying out. They had gone through the stages where the body breaks down and the fluids and bacteria eat and putrefy the flesh. Now many of them were turning to parched husks, their extremities were brittle and easily damaged. Many had missing fingers and hands.

All of them stood, transfixed on the horizon and the glowing sky in the distance. The street was on a hill, and standing close to the top of the rise, it was easy to see over the hundreds of rooftops of the town and view the giant geyser of smoke, ash, and fire that stood proudly on the distant skyline.

Stu turned to Hussein and motioned for him to follow. Treading carefully, he and the others navigated their way through the decaying statues that stood motionless all around them.

Stan had his eyes almost shut. His face was screwed into a grimace; terror gripped him like a mechanical claw that refused to let go. He was scared of looking at the figures around him for fear of making eye contact and alerting them to their escape. He hunched his shoulders high in an attempt to make himself as narrow as possible, so as not to brush against any of the dead as he passed.

He regretted volunteering for the mission. He knew that he was not cut out for it and that Kieran, his much tougher and stronger friend, could handle it emotionally and physically. Just inches ahead of him, Stan stared at the broad shoulders of Kieran as he slowly made his way through. He wished he could be more like him, smart and cool under pressure. *'Fearless,'* Stan thought.

They were almost there. Just a few more metres and they would be in the doorway of the pub. Stan fought against the urge to sprint the last few paces. His legs threatened to take on a mind of their own and began driving forward as fast as they could. He battled with his nerves and instincts, forcing his feet to continue moving at their slow and deliberate pace.

Jim reached the doorway first, closely followed by Stu. Without making any sudden movements, they pressed themselves up close to the building. Jim slowly reached to his left and grabbed hold of the handle to the door. Stu watched Jim's hand, sweat pouring down his forehead as the suspense and anticipation clawed at him.

'Will the door open? If it doesn't, we're well and truly in the shit,' Stu thought to himself.

He turned and looked back at the progress of Hussein and Kieran. Both of them were now at the curb, and Stan was closely tucked in behind the bulk of his friend like a child seeking protection from the shadow of its father.

Behind him, Stu felt a warm draft and sensed a change in air pressure as Jim opened the door to the pub. An overwhelming sense of relief rose up inside him, as he knew that their escape was now possible.

Hussein was just a metre away from him now, and Kieran would reach safety immediately after him.

Stu quickly eyed the dark interior of the pub from the doorway. Nothing moved. He nodded to Jim and indicated that they were to move inside. Stu took one last glance, to check on the progress of the others.

They were so close now.

The blood suddenly froze in his veins. Just behind and to the left of Stan, no more than an arm's reach, a figure stared back at him. Stu blinked, clearing his vision to make sure that he had not been mistaken.

It stood there, glaring at him with dead and unblinking eyes. In another time and place, Stu could be forgiven for thinking that maybe it was a grotesque sculpture, or a street artist pretending to be a statue, but it was not. It was a reanimated corpse that watched him, unlike the others still staring up to the sky, completely mesmerised by the sudden appearance of the atomic cloud and oblivious to the five living men in close proximity.

Panic flashed through his mind. In a split second, he considered numerous options. *Should he shoot it, call to the others to run? Maybe he should attempt to kill it quietly before it alerted the crowd to their presence. Should they continue silently in the hope that they did not register in the creature's mind?*

Before he could complete his appreciation of the situation, the body made the decision for him. It took a staggering step forward, reaching its hand out and barely missing Stan's back as it lunged. It let out a long and frustrated sounding moan as it clutched its fingers on thin air and stumbled after them.

Heads, hundreds of them, turned silently and stared in the direction of the noise. Their eyes fell on the creeping men that were attempting to escape their trap.

Stu raised his pistol, screaming to Hussein, Kieran, and Stan at the same time to alert them that they had been detected.

"Run, fucking run, they know we're here," he howled at them.

The barrel of his pistol erupted with a flash of light and a deafening bang in the otherwise still air, rang out, and echoed through the street. More heads turned. He fired two more shots in quick succession. The first, hit the creature in the shoulder as it staggered after Stan and the others, reaching out for him with its bony fingers. The round hit its rotting flesh, punching through and blasting out through its back, but did nothing to deter it or slow it down. The second shot smashed a hole through its cheek, drilling clear to the other side; the vacuum caused by the bullet dragged its brains through the hole in its wake.

The body crumpled to the floor, as Stu began firing into other faces that lurched towards them.

Hussein bounded up the small steps into the doorway, turned, and raising his rifle, began to pour fire in to the crowd, as they all seemed to come back to life. The whole area erupted into a crescendo as the weapons fired, men screamed, and the dead wailed.

Kieran jumped into the doorway and passed Stu and Hussein. He came to a stop, almost colliding with Jim; having returned from the darkness inside the building and checking that the area was clear.

"This way, son," Jim said, waving Kieran forward, "keep quiet and move to the rear door."

Kieran did as he was told. He began to stalk through the gloom, his shoulders hunched and his trembling hands gripping his rifle tight. He could vaguely make out a lighter area in the darkness directly ahead of him. He presumed it to be the rear of the pub and headed towards it. He could see nothing in his immediate vicinity. His legs bumped into chairs and tables, and his feet crunched on broken glass on numerous occasions as he made his way forward.

At the doorway behind him, the firing continued. Stan was now inside and all four of them were trying desperately to barricade the door. Jim was shouting orders to grab tables and gambling machines, and anything else that could help stem the tide of rotting flesh that now began to hammer at the outside.

Kieran heard the sound of the heavy furniture being dragged and the voices of men shouting out as they bashed themselves in the darkness.

He reached another doorway. It was open and led into the lounge area to the rear of the pub. He peered in, afraid to expose himself before he knew that it was safe. Nothing stirred in the shadowy room. He stepped forward, hoping to find the rear doors that would probably lead out onto a patio area.

Dozens of cold dead faces stared back at him from beyond the glass, and there were hundreds more behind them. Shoulder to shoulder, they stood there, packed in tightly to one another. When they saw Kieran move, they exploded with excitement. In unison, they began pounding away at the large panes of glass standing between them and the flesh that they so longingly desired.

Kieran froze on the spot. He stared back at them, vaguely registering the noise that they made, only seeing their grotesque faces, and dead, staring eyes. He did not even hear the sounds of the pounding feet approaching from behind him.

"Kieran," Stu called into the darkness, his voice full of panic. "Where the fuck are you, Kieran?"

Kieran snapped out of his shock when he heard his name being screamed. "Here, in the back room," he replied. "Here, follow my voice."

Stu appeared out of the gloom, crashing into the doorframe as he bounded into the lounge area. Jim, Hussein, and Stan were close behind, all of them sweating and panting.

Kieran turned to them, the wide windows and countless bodies pressing up against them, framing his silhouette as he stood with his back to the glass and the faint light that managed to shine through.

"We're surrounded, Stu," he said, "we aren't getting out this way."

A loud crash from the front of the building heralded the arrival of the dead and the collapse of the hasty barricade. The sound of splintering wood and the screech of moving furniture as it was pushed aside, assaulted Stu's nerves. His brain raced, trying to think of a solution.

"Here," Jim shouted as he pulled open a door that they had not noticed, and disappeared inside.

The rest of them followed. A set of stairs led upwards to the first floor of the building and to the rooms where the landlord and their family would have lived. Stu pulled the door closed behind him, hoping that none of the dead had noticed them as they fled.

At the top of the stairs, they were met by a long landing with doors leading off into numerous rooms. It was dark and the five of them struggled to see along the corridor to the far end.

"Where do we go now?" Jim whispered, close to Stu's ear.

Stu did not answer. Instead, he began to creep along the passageway, his rifle in one hand, braced against his shoulder, while his other hand fumbled in one of the pouches of his assault vest, searching for his small torch.

A narrow beam of light penetrated the gloom from behind him, Jim obviously having realised what Stu needed. The shaft of light illuminated the far end of the long hallway and the door that stood there, spattered with bloodied handprints.

"Well, we're not going in that room," Stu whispered back over his shoulder.

Together they tiptoed along to the first door. A sudden crash from below echoed up the narrow staircase. It was followed by the sounds of fists beating against the door leading to the narrow stairway.

"That door won't hold for long," Stan whispered, to no one in particular.

Stu and Jim positioned themselves on either side of the entrance to the closest room. Jim could see Stu silently counting backwards from three, using the fingers of his left hand to count down before they charged in through the door.

Jim nodded, bracing himself with his rifle locked into his shoulder and his eyes fixed on the entrance.

"Now," Stu hissed as he raised his boot and thrust a heavy kick at the wood around the locking mechanism.

The door swung open, crashing against the interior wall. Without waiting, he bounded into the room, his torchlight sweeping the floor and the corners, searching for any hidden threat.

"Clear," Jim whispered loudly.

"Everyone, get in here," Stu said urgently in a low voice.

Hussein, Kieran and Stan entered the room, quietly closing the door behind them. They were in a large open space that Stu took to be the master bedroom. At both ends, tall heavy wardrobes stood against the walls, with a sprawling king size bed in the centre directly under the window.

Jim moved forward and peered down at the rear garden of the pub. It was packed, wall to wall, with shuffling corpses as they all made their way into the building. More were coming in from the street behind them.

"Well, we aren't getting out this way, either," Jim grumbled.

They stood, side by side, at the foot of the bed, staring at the door. Stu could feel his heart hammering against his ribcage. His palms sweated profusely as he gripped the rifle tighter in his hands.

Quickly and quietly, he slipped off the magazine, checked the top rounds and pushed down on the spring. The spring depressed only slightly, confirming that the magazine was full, and then he pushed it back into his rifle. His right index finger pushed against the safety catch, switching it from 'safe' to 'fire.'

In his mind, Stu kept on reminding himself, *'Save the last round, save the last round.'*

He glanced across at Jim. They shared a moment of eye contact; a faint, almost undetectable smile creased Jim's face. They both knew that they were about to die.

The echoing footsteps and long drawn out moans of the creatures as they made their way up the stairs were like a brass band in Hussein's ears. They were getting closer. He pictured them stupidly trampling up the steps, many of them just mindlessly following the body in front. Nevertheless, as soon as the door was forced open, exposing the living men, every one of them would suddenly realise why they were there.

Hussein was unsure of his emotions. Of course, he was scared, but also disappointed. After everything they had been through; the battles, the losses, and the miles upon miles of struggle, they were to die in the bedroom of a pub. He had always felt, deep down, that he would not live long in the new world, but he had hoped that his end would have held more meaning.

In his previous life, he had been willing to die a glorious death, not in the name of Allah, but as a soldier of fortune, fighting in the name of Allah. He had never wanted to be a suicide bomber, or die a martyr like so many of the other young men that had fought alongside him. To him, the idea of suffering in this world in the hope of being rewarded in the next was ludicrous, and he had no desire to rush to paradise, but he had been willing to die, not as a soldier of God, but just as a soldier.

Silently, he said a prayer to himself. He finished by whispering, *'Praise be to Allah.'* He looked up as he quietly spoke the words, offering his prayer up to God. For a moment, he stared blankly, and then his brain registered what he had seen.

"Stu," he hissed, "look, a door."

Stu looked across at Hussein and followed his finger to where he was pointing. Above them, built into the ceiling, was a trapdoor. It was not the usual size expected of a loft entrance, but much larger.

A surge of hope coursed through Stu's body. In their final moments, a glimmer of salvation had presented itself. He glanced about them, searching for something they could use to climb. Dragging a chair from the dressing table, he placed it beneath the entrance to the sanctuary above them.

The door that led out onto the hallway suddenly banged as a body crashed against it. Stu froze with one leg on the chair and the other on the floor. A moment later, with no more thuds against the entrance to the room, Stu continued his ascent. He reached up to the ceiling and pushed against the hatch. It lifted free and he cast it into the darkness of the loft.

"Jim, push me up," he whispered loudly.

With just his fingertips able to reach the lip of the hatchway and the weight of his equipment, Stu needed help to gain a firm grip to pull him upwards.

Jim, wasting no time, stepped across, placing his hands into the seat of Stu's trousers and, with an almighty shove, launched him upwards.

Stu scrambled, kicking his legs and heaving with all the strength he could muster in his arms. He forced himself into the hole in the roof and rolled into position to help with the next person.

Hussein jumped, grasping Stu's hand and feeling the strength of the other man as he wrenched him up to safety. Inside the loft, he leaned through the hatch across from Stu to help with the next.

Jim was up and into safety quickly, leaving Stan and Kieran below.

Another thud hit the entrance to the bedroom, this time, much heavier and more deliberate. The dead had filled the landing and now discovered that there were doors blocking their path. More bangs rattled the door in its frame as numerous bodies joined in the assault. The door was juddering under each impact and the old wooden frame was already beginning to splinter.

"Go, Stan," Kieran ordered, staring at the faltering barrier. "Get up there, you're next."

Stan hesitated as he stepped on to the chair. "No, you go next," he said as he stepped down. "You're heavier than me and they will need your help to get me up after you."

Without wanting to get into a debate and wasting time, Kieran nodded and vaulted onto the chair and up to the grasping hands of Stu, Hussein and Jim. They groaned and winced as they struggled to lift his heavy bulk up into the loft.

The door continued to rattle and splinter under the assault.

Stan ran to the window and pulled at the large bed. It skidded with a loud crunching sound as he dragged it across the room. The noise made the dead outside attack the door more vigorously, alerting them to the presence of people inside. Stan could see that the lock was starting to give as he forced the bed against the entrance, hoping that it would buy him just a minute longer.

He ran to the chair and began pushing Kieran from below as he hung in mid-air. With bulging biceps and aching shoulders, he frantically thrust at Kieran's legs, allowing Kieran to gain a better grip on the frame of the attic door and haul himself upward.

Another crash from behind signalled the failure of the lock. Stan glanced over his shoulder, panic tearing at his composure as he saw the door open just a few centimetres as it collided with the foot of the bed. He pulled the rifle from his shoulder and squeezed the trigger, aiming at the small gap between the door and the frame.

Nothing happened.

"The safety, get the safety off!" Stu screamed from above him as they heaved Kieran up the final few feet.

Stan fumbled with the weapon, trying desperately to remember what he had been taught. He pressed the safety catch inwards, feeling it click as it was pushed to 'fire.' Without taking aim again, he loosed off a volley of shots, the rounds smashing through the plaster over a wide arc in the area of the door.

The blast of the rifle echoed around in the room, causing his ears to pop and ring. He squeezed the trigger again as he took a step backwards towards the chair. More plaster exploded in a cloud of white chalky mist and the wood splintered as the rounds punched through the door.

He turned and jumped to the chair as the door shifted again, this time moving the bed from behind it a few more centimetres. Cold hands forced their way through the ever-increasing gap and clutched at the air between them and their prey. The rotten faces and eyes squeezing through the doorway caught sight of Stan's warm living flesh.

Stan was wild with fear. He bounded and jumped for the stool. His foot landed flat on the chair and his body sprang upwards, his fingers reaching out for the hands of Stu and Kieran. His palm made contact with the forearm of Stu and he felt himself being lifted upwards, but the momentum of his vault from the chair was too strong. The kinetic energy of his leap was still carrying him forward, and before Kieran could get a grip on him, he slipped from Stu's grasp and crashed into the wardrobe that was placed against the wall.

The first bodies smashed through the door, forcing the bed away to the side. Stu began to fire into them, dropping them with precision shooting, as his bullets ploughed through their decaying brains.

More forced their way into the room, stumbling and falling over the bodies on the floor, their eyes fixed on Stan as he scrambled to his feet.

They were too close; Stan could see that. He would never make it for a second try at the loft. He looked up at Kieran, who was still reaching for him and screaming his name, and then he looked back at the creatures stalking towards him.

He fired again, spraying the advancing ghouls with a swarm of deadly metal projectiles. More of them fell before him as he backed away from them and into the corner.

His weapon stopped.

He looked down, terrified that his only defence had turned against him. The cocking handle was to the rear, showing an empty chamber and magazine. In his panic, his brain failed to fight through the fog of fear and remind him that he needed to eject the empty magazine and replace it with a full one.

"Shit," he screamed as tears ran down his cheeks.

Jim and Stu poured fire down from above him and Kieran was still calling his name and reaching out to him, but Stan could not move. He was frozen to the spot with terror as he watched the grotesque faces of the creatures as they crawled, staggered and slithered towards him.

Heads, limbs, and abdomens exploded as they were hit with bullets, but they refused to fall back under the torrent of fire.

Stan screamed over again, shaking his head and crying with fear, clutching his empty rifle in his hands as he slid down the wall, curling himself into a ball. He sobbed and wailed as he watched the feet of the corpses close in around him.

"No, please no," he pleaded, "please, no."

Stu could no longer see Stan. There were too many bodies in the room.

Kieran fired frantically with his pistol through the hatch and into the backs of the dead converging on the corner where his friend lay huddled.

"Stan!" he screamed, tears filling his eyes and blurring his vision. "Stan, I'm coming for you, Stan!"

Jim jumped across the hatch and smashed his shoulder into the chest of Kieran to stop him from throwing himself down from the loft. The impact sent them both sprawling across the floor, knocking the wind from Kieran and incapacitating him for a few moments as his eyes rolled and his senses jarred.

The screams began.

Blood curdling and ear splitting as the dead tore into Stan in the room below. They howled and wailed in reply, the excitement of the feast rippling through the crowd and sending the room into an eruption of flailing arms and thrashing heads, as their teeth snapped together in anticipation of gaining some flesh for their selves.

The shrieks of agony from his friend registered in Kieran's ears as his senses returned to him. He rolled and scrambled to the hatch, ignoring the pain in his chest.

"Stan," he cried.

His voice was weak and full of emotion. He called over again, each time his words becoming fainter and less audible as the tears coursed down his face, as his friend's howls and shrieks became fainter.

A short while later, the screaming stopped, but the dead continued their feast.

10

The basement echoed with the constant drip of water from the old pipes; the tightly packed enclosure reeked with the dank, mouldy smell from decades of slow rot seeping in through the brickwork from the ground outside. Sixteen men, women, and children were squeezed into the small, gloomy cellar, and already they were beginning to suffer.

The small confines of the subterranean room reverberated with the raspy coughs of people who had already spent too long in the damp conditions. No one washed for two days and the distinct scent of numerous body odours were becoming more prominent than the damp hanging in the air.

The far corner of the basement was cordoned off as the communal toilet, consisting only of a large bucket that had not been emptied since they moved down into their shelter. Beside it, a few bottles of bleach were placed as a means of keeping the odours and bacteria to a minimum. Despite their efforts to control the smell, the stink of sixteen people's waste was hard to suppress.

Water was already in short supply and the food they managed to grab from their stores before Marcus deemed that they had run out of time would not last them long. The people of the house felt prepared for most things, but the prospect of nuclear fall-out had occurred to no one.

Most spent their time in a slumber, sitting huddled together on what dry patches of ground they could find, staring into space and lost in thought. Others sat together, whispering and discussing what would likely happen. Their eyes always turned to Marcus and Steve in the end, hoping that they had some kind of solution to their predicament.

The children first saw it as an adventure, camping in the basement, but after the first day of being cooped up and watching their parents' despair, the novelty wore off, and now they looked on with scared eyes and a feeling of uncertainty. Their giggles and excited voices slowly turned to sighs and whimpers, as they huddled close to their parents for comfort and reassurance.

"When do you reckon we can go up top?" Gary asked.

He sat on the floor with his head resting against the mouldy wall of the basement. He looked tired. Dark circles had formed under his eyes and his usually immaculately combed white beard and grey hair, looked dishevelled and unkempt.

No one answered his question. They all remained silent, staring or drifting in and out of a bored and uncomfortable sleep.

Gary leaned forward, thrusting his head into the small group of men he was sitting with.

"Marcus, how long do you think we need to stay down here? We've been here two days, when do you think the fall-out will happen?"

Marcus looked up when he heard his name being spoken. His eyes were bloodshot and the lids seemed to glow red. He looked just as exhausted as Gary did. His skin was pale and pasty, and the lines in his face seemed deeper than normal.

"I don't know," he shrugged, blinking his stinging eyes.

"I thought you soldiers were all trained in this?" Jake said, as he took an interest in the conversation that consisted of the possibility of returning to the surface.

Marcus looked at him and chuckled. "You're fucking joking, aren't you? I was a Para and we spent all our time avoiding N.B.C training. We hated it and preferred to run about like lunatics with heavy kit, rather than sitting in a hole wearing gasmasks and carrying out contamination tests. The pissing and shitting drills alone were enough to make you want to rip the suit off and take your chances with whatever was floating in the air."

"What's, *'N.B.C'*?" Jake asked.

Marcus sighed, remembering the discomfort of the training exercises they had endured as recruits.

"Nuclear, Biological and Chemical warfare; a complete pain in the arse, so, sorry, I haven't a clue about any of it."

Carl huffed and shook his head. "So, what do we do? Just sit here for a year?"

Marcus looked at him with a grin. "You could always go up there, sit around for an hour, taking deep breaths and drinking the tap water, and if you come down shaking like a shitting dog with your skin falling off, then we will happily stay here."

Carl had a sudden idea. He sat upright, his eyes flashing with eagerness.

"What about Stephanie?"

"What about her?" Marcus shrugged. "Let her rot up there."

"Exactly," Carl added, "she can be our, uh...what's those things you use to detect radiation? You know, they make that crackling noise."

"You mean a Geiger counter?" Gary offered.

"Yeah, that's it. She could be our Geiger counter. If she is getting sick, then we know the place is contaminated."

Gary looked across at Marcus and raised an eyebrow. Although the idea sounded a little on the barbaric side to him, it was nevertheless a good idea. Stephanie was already on the surface and had been for a number of days, breathing the air. By default, she was their lab-rat.

"Okay, who is going to go up there to see how she is?" Gary asked.

Carl suddenly looked like a rabbit caught in the headlights of a car racing towards it. He sat back, attempting to make himself as small as possible, shrugging his shoulders.

"Uh, I don't know. It was just an idea."

"A pretty good one too," Marcus nodded. "We just need someone to go up there." He glanced about at the small group, then over to the other side of the basement where the others slept. "Alright, I suppose I'll have to do it," he sighed.

"I'll go up there," a voice suddenly volunteered from the gloom. "I'll do it."

Lee stepped forward from the shadows, running a grubby hand through his hair and stretching with an air of indifference to the potential risks of radiation poisoning if he was to go up to the surface.

Marcus shook his head. "Not you, Lee. Even if Stephanie were up there, a picture of health and in high spirits, you'd peel her skin off just for the fun of it. I'll do it."

"Suit yourself, then," Lee shrugged and turned back to his makeshift bed where Sophie lay asleep. "I was only offering to help."

"What about Johnny? No one has seen him since we all came down here," Jake said, with genuine concern.

Over the months, since the incident at the supermarket when they first met, he had grown a great fondness for the scruffy little vagrant.

"I'll keep an eye out for him, but I'm not going on a wild goose chase. If the place is contaminated, then he's as good as dead."

"And so are we," Gary added.

Everyone turned to look at him, startled by his sudden revelation. Gary looked back at each of them and let out a low, almost inaudible laugh.

"You all don't really believe that hiding in this cellar will save us, do you?" He looked down into his lap, shaking his head at their ignorance. "If the place really is flooded with radiation, this *'bunker'* buys us days, maybe less. I do remember that much from the days of the Cold War. Building a shelter under the stairs from doors and old lumps of wood was an exercise in futility."

Marcus nodded and the others remained silent, thinking on Gary's words. Marcus knew that Gary was right, but he focussed his attention on seeing for himself what the situation was first.

Within an hour, Marcus stood ready, covered from head to toe in black plastic bags that had been swathed around his body and head, leaving him looking like something from a cheap horror movie.

He argued for twenty minutes with Jennifer over being the one to go up top. In the end, he convinced her that he was the only one remotely qualified to do the job, even though he had no idea what he was doing, but as he was a former soldier, it sounded more tangible to the truth.

"I still don't want you to go," she said in a final protest. "You've done enough around here. Anyone could go up there and check on that fat bitch. It doesn't have to be you, Marcus."

"I'd rather do it myself, Jen. I need to see how we stand, with my own eyes."

Jennifer stormed off back to the corner, to where their sons lay sleeping, curled up together on a dirty mattress.

"Go on then, you be a hero," she grumbled.

Marcus stared after her, a slight smile creasing his face as he watched his wife stomp away from him. Her strong will and stubbornness were positive features in his eyes.

"That's got to be the shittiest gimp-suit I've ever seen, Marcus," Steve joked as he continued to wrap the sticky tape tightly around his brother, sealing the joins of the plastic.

Gary had constructed a crude respirator from a dust mask and a set of safety goggles that he found in a tool cupboard. Marcus doused a length of towel with water and wrapped it around his face, covering the mask as another form of filtration.

He walked across to the foot of the steps that led up in to the house.

"I wish I had a canary or something," he joked as he turned to Steve.

Beneath the makeshift radiation suit and mask, he was sweating profusely. His body heat was trapped inside the airtight seals, but it was not just because of the temperature. He was scared, too. He remembered enough of his training to know how high doses of radiation affect the human body, and the terrible slow death that can be the result.

Already, he could feel that his body was saturated in sweat beneath the layers of plastic. It trickled from his head to his toes, coursing along the contours of his muscles in endless streams and gathering in his boots.

A cold shiver ran the length of his spine as he looked up at the door at the top of the steps.

"Get up there, check on Stephanie and don't hang around, bro," Steve said as he made his final checks of Marcus' suit. "Once you've confirmed whether she is sick or not, get back down here."

Marcus stared back at him through the misted lenses of the safety goggles and nodded. His eyes were wide and blinking rapidly. His breathing was heavy, partially from the restrictions of the mask and partially, through fear.

"Okay, we're good to go," Carl called down from the top of the stairs, as he stood ready by the door leading in to the house.

Marcus slowly made his way up towards him.

"Be careful, Marcus," Carl reminded him. "You ready?"

"Yeah, good to go, mate," Marcus replied, raising his thump. His voice sounded muffled and distant beneath the multiple layers.

"One…two…three," Carl pulled the door open and Marcus jumped forward and through the gap without any hesitation.

Carl quickly slammed the door behind him, the draft of it blowing millions of dust particles into the air all around him. His eyes flashed with fear and he forced his face into his hands, holding his breath, he sprinted back down the steps and into the basement.

"You think he'll be okay?" he asked as he stepped backwards, brushing himself down with his hands and staring back up at the basement door.

"I fucking hope so," Steve grumbled.

Marcus paused in the foyer of the house. He could feel the adrenalin coursing through his body, causing his hands and legs to shake slightly. Shafts of light beamed through the large windows of the mansion, capturing tiny specks of dust in their brilliance as they drifted through the air.

For some reason, he had been expecting the house to look different, in ruin and rotting away under a bombardment of radiation. Instead, it looked no different than it did when they abandoned the surface for the cellar.

He walked over to the nearest window and peered out into the brilliant sunlight. Even with the layers of plastic, and from behind the mask, the sun's rays had a rejuvenating effect on him. It seemed like years since he felt the glow of the sun on his body.

Outside, everything seemed normal. The trees, devoid of their leaves, swayed in the winter breeze. The grass was as green as ever, not the tinged yellow he expected to see as it died due to contamination. It danced lazily in the cold wind that swept across the open fields of the park.

A noise made him look upwards at the clear blue sky. Birds fluttered in the air, whistling and squawking as they continued with their daily concerns, oblivious to any radioactive fall-out. They were not dropping from the sky in mid-flight, and from what Marcus could see, the ground was not littered with the corpses of any wildlife.

He turned away and began to make his way across the large empty foyer, and headed for the storerooms at the back of the house. In the narrow hallway, he paused outside the door that led into the room where they locked Stephanie. He hesitated, leaning his head close to the thick wooden door and listening for any sounds from within.

For months, the room had acted as her cell with the windows blacked out and in total darkness. She had not stepped foot outside the room or been released from her restraints the whole time; she had been left to exist like an animal in her own filth and squalor. No one had shown any sign of sympathy for her or voiced concern over her treatment. No one objected to the meagre rations given to her, or the conditions that she was forced to live in.

Six months before, some may have protested against such measures, but the survivors in the mansion changed. They became hardened through struggle, loss, fear, and their survival instincts. Most of all, they became a family, and in their eyes, Stephanie tried to destroy all of that and came very close to succeeding.

John, the burly man with a gruff voice, a warm and welcoming personality, and amateur lumberjack, was killed during the supply mission to gain more fuel because of Stephanie's sabotage. He was loved by all, and his loss was a blow to the group.

Simon, a man who none of them knew but had sacrificed his own life to help save those that were trapped inside the supermarket, died from the bites he received and subsequent infection that raged through his body. Though he had not been part of the group, his actions nevertheless, allowed many of them to survive.

Marcus reached down to the handle. It twisted in his hand and he pushed it open. The hinges creaked, sounding like the stereotypical haunted mansion door as it opened to reveal an impending doom for an unsuspecting victim.

Marcus swallowed hard. He felt silly admitting it to himself, but the sound of the door in the otherwise still air unnerved him. His imagination was beginning to get the better of him.

'Get a grip,' he whispered to himself inside the mask.

The door fell open, revealing only blackness, like a wall before him. He felt his shoulders tense as he attempted to see into the darkness. He gripped his pistol in his right hand, held at waist height with the barrel pointed into the room. His left hand began fumbling for the torch attached to his waist.

"Stephanie…?" he hissed into the room.

There was no reply.

"Stephanie, answer me. Are you still alive in here?"

He pictured Stephanie lying on the floor, her skin bubbling from the blisters caused by exposure to the radiation, vomit and excrement surrounding her as she lay close to death.

Another vision soon haunted his racing imagination. A blackened bloated corpse, her flesh peeling away from her bones as she reached out for him in the darkness. He gripped his pistol tighter in his hand, his trigger finger ready.

He heard movement.

A sound, like feet scuffing against the bare concrete floor, reached his ears through the layers of clothing and plastic covering his head. Finally, he had the torch free from his belt. Without taking his eyes from the darkness before him, he thumbed the switch, illuminating the ground at his feet as the bulb burst with light. He raised the beam upwards, quickly sweeping the small room. The shaft of light revealed nothing but an empty space, a pile of sacking in the centre and a white bucket.

Marcus squinted, involuntarily moving his right index finger from the trigger guard of the pistol and onto the trigger itself, squeezing lightly and taking up the first pressure. He stooped slightly, allowing flexibility in his knees should he need to leap from the doorway or into the room.

He focussed the light on the pile of rags in the centre of the cell. It was too small and did not hold enough mass to be the body of Stephanie, even if the months of captivity and near starvation rations had caused her to lose a drastic amount of weight.

'*Where the fuck is she?*' he thought to himself.

He swept the room with his light once again and saw the glint of metal as the beam bounced off the chains that they used to restrain her. In the far corner, Marcus saw a patch of wall that was darker than the rest of the room. With a moment to focus his eyes through the restrictive lenses of the safety goggles, he realised that it was indeed the body of Stephanie standing there.

The once large and bulky frame of the intimidating woman was gone, replaced by the broken and slumping form of a human being brought to the edge of despair. Her head sagged forward with long strands of greasy matted hair covering and obscuring her features. At her side, her arms dangled limply from sloping and withered shoulders. Her skin had turned the same shade of pasty grey as the rags of clothing still clinging to her shrivelled body, and her chained bare feet, blackened with filth and infections, stood planted in pools of human waste.

For a fleeting moment, Marcus felt a pang of regret for having subjected her to such torture. He wondered if it would have been better just to shoot her in the head at the beginning.

"For fuck's sake," he mumbled to himself, "she's turned."

"Fuck you, limp dick," a defiant voice rasped from inside the room.

Marcus almost jumped with shock. He had already been reaching for the door handle to close it behind him and return to the basement.

"Jesus, you're alive."

"No thanks to you bastards." The voice had turned to more of a whimper. "Why have you done this to me? What is happening? Are you going to let me go?"

Marcus blinked, unsure of what to say in reply, but then decided to ignore her questions completely.

"How are you feeling, Stephanie?"

"Please," she continued, "I promise, I will go far away and you will never see or hear from me again. Please, just let me go. I'm sorry, Marcus."

He took a step backwards, unsettled at the fact that after all this time, and despite the layers of plastic he wore to protect him, she knew exactly who he was. Until that moment, he felt a degree of detachment, but now she unravelled his suit of indifference.

"How do you feel, Stephanie?" he repeated.

The room was silent for a moment.

"What do you fucking care?" she spat from the darkness.

Suddenly, she sprang forward. Marcus raised the pistol, ready to fire into her, but before he could take aim, she disappeared from sight with a screech and a flurry of arms. The chains snapped taut, causing her to slip in the urine and excrement coating the entire cell floor. Marcus shone the light down onto her as she flopped and squirmed in her own filth, trying desperately to climb back to her feet.

"You fucker," she growled. "You fucking cunt, I'll kill the fucking lot of you. You bunch of fucking cunts."

Marcus watched as she slowly made her way to her feet. She stood in the centre of the room, the chains extended fully from the bolts that held them in place. She stared at him with wild eyes that seemed to glow in the darkness of the room. Her chest heaved up and down as she breathed through clenched teeth with white foam spilling from the corners of her mouth.

"You see, Stephanie," Marcus began to point out in a calm voice, "it's those kinds of comments that are delaying your parole. Now, please tell me, how are you feeling, chuck?"

Stephanie erupted.

"I'll fucking kill you," she howled, waving and thrashing her arms and once again, losing her footing and colliding with the floor and filth.

Marcus stepped forward and brought his fist down into the side of her head. She let out a squeal and her knees gave way as she collapsed under the impact.

"You threaten me or my family, and I will take it very seriously, Stephanie. You have already proven that you are willing and capable of it. So I suggest that you refrain from making further threats, or I will put you down for good," Marcus growled at the semi-conscious bundle at his feet.

Stephanie rolled over onto her back. Her eyes rolled in her head as she slowly regained her composure.

She looked up at Marcus standing over her and spat. "Go ahead, fucking do it. I'd rather be dead than stuck in this room."

"Well," Marcus crouched down, his voice sounding more agreeable but his hand firmly clutching his pistol, pointed at Stephanie. "That's what I've come to talk to you about, Stephanie. I have some questions for you."

She shifted and attempted to sit up. Her expression changed to one of eagerness and her eyes lit up with hope.

"You, you mean…," she stammered, "you mean you will let me go?"

"Maybe," he replied with a nod, "it all depends on how much you cooperate."

She nodded back at him. She tried to smile to show her willingness, but in the gloom and her condition, it looked more like a grimace. Her teeth were black and the multitude of sores around her mouth and nose cracked from the stretching of the skin and oozed with blood and pus.

"I'll do anything you ask, I promise. You will never see me again, Marcus. You can be sure of that." Her voice had risen in pitch with the anticipation of being set free.

"Okay, firstly, how are you feeling?"

She looked at him, confusion showing in her eyes, but she felt urged to comply with him and avoid jeopardising the possibility of freedom.

"I feel like shit, if that's what you mean, Marcus." She looked around at the squalor of her cell and then raised her pleading eyes back to his. "I've been here for God knows how long. I'm sick and weak, and no threat to you anymore, I promise."

Marcus shuffled his feet, moving back from her slightly. "Sick, how do you mean sick?"

"How do you think I mean? I am covered in my own shit. I've been living on scraps of food from your kitchen and I haven't seen daylight in a long time."

"What about headaches, dizziness, or vomiting, any hair loss or skin irritation?"

She looked at him quizzically; she could not understand his sudden concern. There was something else about him; something that she could not quite make out. Then she realised. He was dressed strangely. Her failing eyesight and delirium stopped her from noticing his clothing until now.

"All the fucking time," she remarked. "Why are you dressed like that and where is everyone else? What's happened?" She was hungry for information, something she had been deprived of for so long.

Marcus did not know exactly how to explain the situation to her.

"Uh, a bomb was dropped some distance to the south of us, a few days ago."

"A bomb, what do you mean a bomb?" She was not sure if her hearing was also deteriorating.

"The 'nuclear bomb' kind," he replied. "It looks as though someone has come up with the great idea of dropping bombs on the cities. We moved everyone to the cellar to avoid fall-out radiation."

Stephanie nodded and looked down at her hands as she realised what was going on.

"And you've come up here to see if it is safe?"

"Something like that, yeah."

"Well, I don't feel any worse than I did a week ago, if that helps," she said in a resigned voice.

"That helps a lot actually, Stephanie," Marcus said as he shone the torch beam over her body, studying her for any signs of radiation sickness.

She was a mess, but he did not believe it to be related to any fall-out. He stood up and began to edge his way back towards the doorway.

"I'll discuss your release with the others and arrange some food for you."

Stephanie turned to look up at him. She was about to say something when he held out his hand.

"Quiet," he ordered. "Do you hear that?"

She shook her head and was about to ask about her freedom when Marcus suddenly bolted through the door. She was left in the darkness and stinking filth, listening to the sound of his footsteps as his boots pounded down the narrow corridor, away from her and towards the door that led in to the cellar.

Gary and Steve remained stood at the foot of the stairs for the entire time that Marcus had been up on the surface. They watched the door at the top of the steps expectantly, hardly speaking a word and lost in their own thoughts. Neither of them said it, but they both feared the worst. They expected Marcus to return, describing the effects of the radiation on Stephanie and confirming their fears.

Gary's words regarding the fact that the cellar would only buy them a matter of days, seemed to endlessly rattle around in Steve's mind, and with each passing moment, their impact increased. He shuddered at the thought of Sarah suffering from the effects of radiation sickness. He had seen enough movies and documentaries to know how terrible a death like that could be.

The door at the top of the stairs flew open with a bang, causing Gary and Steve to jump backwards with the sudden shock. The black silhouette of Marcus paused for a moment in the doorway, the light behind him obscuring all but the strange looking dark insect-like outline created by the layers of black plastic.

They could hear him shouting but were unable to make any sense of his muffled words as he began to race down the stairs.

Gary saw that the door behind Marcus remained open.

"Marcus, the door, close the door," he began to holler, but Marcus ignored him and continued down into the basement.

He bounded past Steve and Gary and over to the corner where he had stored his weapons and equipment. He began frantically rummaging and fumbling with his assault vest and trying desperately to free something from one of the pouches.

Steve and Gary looked at one another in alarm. More people were beginning to take notice, including Jennifer.

"Marcus," she said in an unnerved and anxious voice, "what is it? Is she dead? What are you doing, Marcus?"

Her questions went unanswered as Marcus continued to struggle with his kit. Finally, he stepped back. He held a green case in his hand, no larger than a bar of chocolate, and began to remove items from it as he made his way back to the stairs, slinging his rifle over his shoulder.

"Marcus," Jennifer screamed loudly, bringing her husband to a dead stop.

She was terrified and had no idea what was going on. None of them knew what was happening and the lack of information was bringing them all to the verge of panic.

Marcus turned to her, resting one foot on the bottom step of the basement and looking as though he was about to bolt for the door. He glanced at the others as they stood watching him in fear and anticipation.

"Marcus, what the hell is happening? Are we contaminated, is Stephanie alive?" Jennifer asked the questions demandingly.

She had had years of practice with it. She knew all too well that when Marcus had something urgent to do, it took a lot to gain his attention, and her screaming voice had snapped him out of his zone.

He said something that was almost inaudible and pointed up the stairs, holding out the green packet in his hand. He realised that no one could understand what he was saying and began to tear at the makeshift respirator from around his face. He ripped the dust mask and goggles off, feeling the cool air of the cellar on his skin. The fresh air assaulted his lungs and almost sent him dizzy but he fought hard to remain coherent, knowing he had little time to waste.

"A helicopter, I heard it," he gasped and began to run back up the stairs.

Immediately, hushed voices began repeating the word *'helicopter',* and asking one another questions as they attempted to confirm for themselves that they had heard Marcus correctly.

"Marcus, wait," Steve shouted from below, "what about radiation? Is Stephanie alive?"

Marcus did not stop.

"She's fine. I think you'll be okay to come up," he called over his shoulder as he bounded through the door and into the main building.

On the roof, Marcus began loading the mini-flares from the green case and into the firing mechanism. At the same time, he fought desperately to focus his hearing and identify where the helicopter was.

He could hear nothing. The aircraft had passed them by without him having the chance to signal them.

"Fuck," he snarled.

He then remembered that Jennifer had delayed him in the basement, demanding to know what was happening. If she had not held him back, he may have been able to attract the helicopter pilot's attention.

"Stupid bitch," he growled, then immediately he regretted even thinking it. Jennifer was not to blame.

Steve and Jake appeared on the rooftop, closely followed by Helen and Gary. Soon, more were spilling out through the doorway, eager to investigate the phantom helicopter that Marcus had reported hearing.

"Where is it, then?" Lee asked as he shielded his eyes and began scanning the sky.

"Did you see it, Marcus?" Helen asked.

She watched him as he stood looking out over the park, still holding the mini-flare in his hand.

Marcus shook his head. "It's gone. It must've just flown straight over us."

He sighed and turned to head back inside.

He paused and turned to Steve. "Good news is though: I don't think we need to worry about radiation. I don't think it…"

"Wait," Jake called, "everyone, be quiet." He cocked his head and squinted.

Marcus heard it too. The steady thump of helicopter rotors, but it was hard for them to tell which direction the noise was coming from.

The sound was getting louder.

Marcus ran to the lip of the roof on the north side of the building.

"Lee, Jake, keep your eyes on the south. Gary, Helen, watch the east, it's coming closer."

He checked that the flare was securely screwed into the firing mechanism and the spring was pulled back; ready to release the firing pin. Soon, the swish and thump of the rotor blades was joined by the high-pitched whine of the jet engines of the helicopter. It was growing louder by the second.

Marcus felt a sense of urgency surge through him. He did not know why, but he *had* to find the helicopter and attempt to signal it. The fact that they could give them some information and maybe some news on the counter offensive was how he justified it to himself, but deep down he reasoned that it was because he spent too long being static at the park and maybe he became bored through the inaction. He wanted to go with Stu and Jim with the others, but convincing Jennifer of the importance of him being on the patrol was a battle he did not want to face at the time.

"Does anyone see anything?" he called back to the others.

The roof was now packed with the other members of the house. Carl and his family were there and so were Jennifer and the boys. Everyone was watching the sky.

"No, nothing," Helen replied.

"Can't see anything, but it's definitely getting closer, Marcus," Lee hollered from the south end of the roof.

"There," a small voice suddenly cried out.

Marcus spun to see Sarah, standing in the middle of the roof and pointing into the distance. She turned to Marcus and beamed.

"There it is, coming this way, I think."

Marcus followed her finger and saw the small faint shape of a helicopter just above the horizon. It flew low over the southeast area, beyond the park walls. The area that contained the junction that Marcus and his men had fought their way through and met Steve and Helen; the same junction that had guided them to safety when they had finally arrived from their long haul across the Middle East and Europe.

He raised his binoculars to his eyes and focused on the small silhouette as it travelled from the south, following the road that ran parallel to the Safari Park. The aircraft was flying slowly and no higher than twenty metres above the ground, as though studying something below.

"Well spotted, Sarah," Marcus smiled. "We should put you on lookout duty more often."

"Really, can I?" she asked excitedly.

Her mother, Claire, placed her hands on her shoulders and looked down at her. "There are two chances of that happening, Pumpkin; slim and none."

The others surrounded Marcus as he continued to eye the aircraft.

"What kind is it?" Lee asked.

Jake turned to him with a sour look on his face. "Does it frigging matter what kind it is? It's a fucking helicopter, Lee."

"Yeah, well, I'd just like to know if it is going to be able to shoot at us, *bender*."

Jake was about to retort but Marcus cut them off. "You two, shut up. Lee has a point. You never know in this day and age, and people may not be as friendly as we would like."

He turned to the others and handed the binoculars to Steve.

"It's okay though, it isn't a gun-ship. It's a Puma. French built and used by the British army. Time to get their attention, I think."

He moved away from the others and held up the mini-flare. He released the spring and, with a pop, a glowing red light shot up into the air. Immediately, he began to reload and sent another three lights into the sky in quick succession.

The helicopter seemed to slow down then, banked to its left, headed straight for the house.

"Clear the roof, go," Marcus ordered.

Gary began to usher everyone from the rooftop. Rounding up the children was the hardest part but a few stern words, barked at them from their parents, made them fall into line and comply.

"Gary," Marcus shouted to him as the older man attempted to dislodge Liam from his firm hold on one of the water pipes.

"You, Carl, Sophie and Lisa, get whatever you can use as a weapon and stay in the foyer."

"Will do," Gary nodded in return as he finally pulled the protesting Liam loose, dragging him into the doorway.

Marcus turned and quickly checked on the progress of the helicopter.

"Lee and Jake, you stay on the roof and cover us."

He passed his rifle across to Jake and pulled out his pistol. He pulled the top slide back slightly, checking that there was a round in the chamber, and then turned to his brother, Steve.

"You're with me, bro. Helen, you too, if you don't mind. Let's go welcome our new guests."

They both drew their pistols and followed him into the stairway.

11

Kelly and Joey were on their way to carry out visual confirmation of the effects of the bomb that was dropped on the city of Stoke-on-Trent. They did not expect to find much, except for a wasteland of destroyed buildings and rubble, and the scattered and twisted remains of the hundreds of thousands of walking dead that infested the city. Still, orders were orders and they were expected to follow them to the letter. Kelly was not prepared to question or disregard anything that came from the top.

They spent two days sitting on the cold and empty moors, waiting for phase-two. They expected to be able to rest and catch up on some sleep with hot meals to help them to recharge, but things did not turn out as they hoped.

After arriving at the rendezvous, where they were to lay up for a couple of days before phase-two began and the bomb was dropped, they soon discovered that the SAS team they were supposed to meet were nowhere to be found. There was no evidence of a fight or the position being overrun; they just vanished without any word or trace.

To be safe, Kelly decided that they should push further north, opting to touch down and rest on the secluded and windswept moorlands where they were unlikely to encounter many of the dead.

Joey was less than pleased. Exposed to the freezing rain and howling winds, they sat and waited it out, eating cold rations and taking turns to stand watch until it was time to move again.

Kelly endured forty-eight hours of Joey's endless grumblings.

"This is bollocks, Kelly," he shouted from outside the cockpit as he stood his shift on guard duty. "I'm fucking freezing."

She rolled her eyes and smiled at him through the windshield, rubbing her hands together and waving.

"Fuck off, Kelly," he snapped, "I mean, where were the SAS blokes? We could've been sat with them, eating hot food and..."

Kelly had heard enough. She opened the window and leaned out. The force of the wind, swept her hair in all directions, leaving it looking like a lion's mane as it framed her face.

"What would you like, Joey? The Hilton hotel?" She had to scream to be heard over the slashing rain and gale force wind. "There's one in Manchester, just ten minutes flying time from here. We could go there if you like?"

"Shit and fall in it," he retorted, raising his middle finger and slamming it against the windshield of the cockpit.

Two days up on the bleak moors seemed like two weeks. Neither of them was rested, but they could not wait to be moving again. When the order came that phase-two had begun, they gladly started up the engines and wasted no time in getting airborne.

Flying over a large town on a bearing that would lead them directly to Stoke, they saw an exodus of the dead, headed away from the built up area. Thousands of corpses roamed the streets below them, all headed towards the suburbs and beyond. Kelly was used to seeing the reanimated bodies headed towards the cities and towns, not away from them.

They followed the trail of shambling cadavers for a number of miles and reached a junction where they all seemed to congregate, clambering against a high wall that ran parallel with the roads leading off from the crossroads, towards the west and north.

Their numbers swelled until the crowds were so dense, it was virtually impossible to distinguish individuals. From a higher altitude, the multitude of blackened and swollen corpses made the ground look like it was covered with a seething and bubbling oil slick. On closer inspection, the sea of blacks and greys was revealed as the twisted and grotesque bodies of once living people.

"Jesus, there's so many of them," Kelly gasped as she looked down from the cockpit.

She eased back on the cyclic stick, slowing their forward movement, and adjusted the collective and throttle to settle the helicopter into a hover, positioned over the road junction below them.

"They must be in the hundreds of thousands, Kelly," Joey noted. "What do you think is attracting them?"

Kelly shook her head, unable to tear her eyes away from the scene below. "I don't know, but there must be something around here that is grabbing their attention."

Just fifty feet below the aircraft, a sea of rotting, maggot infested bodies stood staring up at them. The downwash from the rotor blades blew their matted hair from their features, exposing the thousands of skeletal rotting faces and dead eyes that were locked on the helicopter. They reached out into the air, grasping futilely and jostling one another for pole position directly below the hovering aircraft.

They pushed and pulled at the other bodies around them, snapping their jaws aggressively, like hungry predators around a fresh kill. Arms were ripped from their torsos and some of the bodies were even decapitated as the swarm grew with excitement, grabbing and clawing at one another.

Even over the loud thump of the blades and the screech of the engine, Kelly and Joey could clearly hear their wails. It was a constant barrage of monotone moans; all mixed together and creating a ceaseless hum that seemed to penetrate the souls of the living. It was enough to send cold shivers running the length of Kelly's spine.

She pushed down on the pedals beneath her feet, slowly turning the helicopter in a three hundred and sixty degree arc. Everywhere they looked, a mass of walking corpses covered every patch of road. They staggered, hobbled, swayed and crawled from all directions, bumping into each other and trampling on the fallen.

Despite the downwash of the whirling helicopter blades, the stench of thousands of rotting bodies managed to make its way into the cockpit of the aircraft. Joey gagged and looked across at Kelly pleadingly, grimacing and wafting his hand in front of his face.

"Come on, Kel, it's nothing we haven't seen before. Take us up to where the air is fresh and clean," he grinned.

Kelly nodded and obliged. She increased the throttle and pulled back on the collective. The machine gained altitude and again, when they were roughly fifty metres from the ground, she settled into a hover. From that height, they were able to see the extent of the crowd more clearly.

They were everywhere. Along the entire length of the wall, from the junction and into the far distance in both directions, a swarm of dead pressed themselves against the tall stone barricade.

Lofty fir trees grew on the opposite side of the wall, their branches overhanging the brick structure. Beyond them, sprawling fields and woods, devoid of any sign of the dead, stretched for as far as the eye could see towards the north and west.

"What do you think of that?" Kelly asked, nodding to an area on the western part of the main junction. "Looks like a link road running towards the west and someone's..."

Before she could finish, Joey butted in. "Set up a barricade to block it off..."

"Exactly," she replied.

Her voice betrayed a hint of enthusiasm, excitement at the prospect of finding other survivors. It had been a long time since they last came across people that had managed to stay alive on the mainland.

She did not doubt for a minute that there were probably thousands, hiding and living through the dead plague. However, given the extent of ground to cover and the fact that they were ordered not to waste fuel looking for survivors, they were unlikely to cross paths with any.

Kelly steered the helicopter over towards the junction, settling above it while they studied the barricade. A number of large trees had been felled. They spanned the entire width of the carriageway, blocking the link road beyond from view.

"Looks like someone did a little lumberjack work," Kelly remarked. "Look over there." She pointed to an area on the northern side of the road.

Between the mass of bodies she was able to make out a number of tree stumps, their pulp still much brighter in colour than the rest of their bark.

"Must've been a risky job to come out here and go to work with an axe."

"Not a bad job, though," Joey added. "They've pretty much cut off access to the road in this area."

"A lot of good it's done them."

Beyond the barricade and along the whole stretch of link road, a dense horde of ghouls was packed shoulder to shoulder, covering the entire road like a carpet of putrid flesh and bone.

Kelly pushed down on the cyclic and sent the aircraft moving forward. They followed the road down for another three hundred metres and came to rest, lingering over a turn off in the road that led up to a large iron gate, built into the high wall.

"There must be people in there," Joey stated, more to himself than trying to inform his pilot of the obvious.

Kelly nodded as she eyed the thick iron railings and the large fuel tanker that was parked on the opposite side, flush with the wall and entrance to stop the gate from collapsing under the weight of the horde pressing against it.

She kept the helicopter hovering for a few moments longer, studying the area beyond the truck. It was hard to make anything out. A road led away from the entrance and disappeared into a thick tangle of trees, cast in shadow and giving no inclination of what lay beyond.

"Why don't we just fly in there, Kelly?"

Kelly bit her lip. She considered the possibility of going straight in and having a look around for herself from within the safety of the cockpit, but she hesitated. If there were people beyond the wall, Kelly and Joey knew nothing about them. They could be well armed and very protective over their sanctuary, especially against a helicopter. The last thing she wanted was to be shot down or killed by a mob of fiercely territorial survivors.

"Let's have a look to the north," she said finally, and turned the aircraft back towards the junction.

At the crossroads, she pushed down on the anti-torque pedals and, with a gentle push on the cyclic stick, they swung around to the left, headed north along the outer perimeter of the wall and soaring over the thousands of staggering creatures below. It was the same story as the road and wall that led westwards, beyond the barrier of fallen trees. An ever-swelling river of rotting bodies flooded the ground below, coursing along the road like a repulsive alternative illustration of bubbling water rapids.

"Yup," Joey nodded to himself, "there's definitely someone in there, Kel."

A flash from the left caught his attention. In his peripheral vision, he saw something red in the sky. He studied the area while Kelly concentrated on watching the ground below.

Another red light, glowing brightly and soaring into the sky, erupted to the west from deep within the grounds beyond the wall.

Joey's eyes lit up but he struggled to find his voice. Instead, he opted to wave his hands around in front of the cockpit instruments, trying desperately to attract the attention of his pilot.

Finally, he was able to form one word.

"Flare," he squealed.

12

"How do we get out of this shit-trap, then?" Jim groaned.

Hussein and Stu looked at one another. Neither of them had any real solution to their immediate problem. They had been trapped in the loft of the public house for over two days, and they still had no idea of how to make their breakout.

Stu, Jim, Hussein and Kieran were tired and hungry but most importantly, thirsty. Sleep was a welcome distraction, but it never lasted long enough. A noise below, as one of the shambling corpses clumsily bumped about or tripped, would wake them with a start, or the thirst that they all suffered from would drag them from their slumber, tearing at their throats and their desiccated mouths.

Stu wondered how long they would need to be there for before someone began drinking their own urine. The thought of it did not particularly bother him, but he would have insisted that he drink only his own and no one else's.

Jim came up with the innovative idea of removing the bullet head from four rounds, one for each of them, and sucking on them to help encourage saliva to build up in the mouth.

"Like they did in the desert during the Second World War," he reminded them.

It seemed to work initially, but soon their whole body and not just their parched lips and throats screamed out for fluid to replenish them.

It was no use; their body was becoming more dehydrated by the minute. The headaches had already begun, along with moments of blurry vision and dizzy spells. Gradually, their bodies would begin to shut down on them. As every drop of moisture was slowly used up from within their organs, muscle, and skin tissue, they would eventually lose control of their limbs, ability to think clearly, speech, and finally slip into unconsciousness and die.

Stu detested the idea of dying from dehydration, especially when there were much greater dangers to fear. He especially loathed the idea of dying from thirst while he was in the United Kingdom.

'One of the wettest countries on the planet, and here I am, about to die from lack of water. The fucking irony of it,' he thought to himself.

"I'm not sure we *should* be in a hurry to leave just yet," Stu pointed out in reply to Jim's question.

"Why's that, Stu?" Jim huffed in an aggressive and questioning tone.

He was growing impatient. The four men had been trapped in the relatively small and cramped space in the roof of the building for what seemed like a lifetime, and his temper was beginning to flare.

"Well," Stu began in a tone that was just as hostile, "in case you've forgot, and as much as I would like to get away from this stinking, shit infested tomb." He nodded in the direction of the far corner, the area they were using as a toilet.

"A big nuclear bomb went off and I'm not sure if it will be safe to leave yet. Do you understand what I mean, or should I draw you a fucking picture?"

"Fuck you," Jim snapped, sitting up and thrusting out his chest towards Stu. "Don't patronise me, you Limey motherfucker."

Stu felt the hairs on his neck stand on end; his jaw clenched and his fingers rolled themselves inwards to form a fist.

"Who you calling a *'Limey'* you, hillbilly inbred twat?" Stu launched himself towards his friend, roaring with rage and grasping Jim by the straps of his assault vest.

Jim was caught off balance and with the weight and momentum of Stu's body, they both crumpled into a heap, pulling and pushing at one another as they rolled across the floorboards. Jim managed to thrust his hand under Stu's chin and forced his head backwards, while Stu folded his fingers around the American's neck. Both men snarled and grunted as they struggled, each trying to gain a better position to land a blow to the head and face of the other.

Stu let out a howl as Jim forced his knee up in to his groin, but the impact failed to dislodge Stu's clutching hands from around his throat.

The scuffle went on…

Kieran, sitting by the trapdoor that led down in to the main bedroom of the pub, stared at the grotesque scene below.

After Stan was pulled down and set upon by the mass of hungry ghouls, Jim, Stu, and Hussein managed to restrain Kieran from launching himself through the hatch to try to help his friend. They slammed the door shut and sat in silence, listening to the noises of the feeding frenzy below as the dead gorged themselves on Stan's flesh.

A day later, with complete silence from underneath them, the four survivors risked opening the hatch and peering into the room below. Bright morning light poured into the room through the windows, revealing an almost empty space, with none of the festering creatures in sight.

The room was not completely empty though. There were still a number of motionless bodies, sprawled across the floor, buzzing with flies as what remained of their brains seeped from their broken skulls, but the dead that were still mobile had left, leaving their fallen comrades behind.

They could still be heard throughout the building as they crashed and bumped about from room to room, rummaging through drawers, and turning over furniture, always searching for living flesh. The four surviving men chose not to risk leaving the sanctuary that was built in to the roof of the pub.

Kieran sat watching, unable to take his eyes from the squirming, limbless torso of the body in the corner. It was devoid of all of its flesh. Its arms and legs were torn from their sockets and carted away to be devoured. The stomach was ripped open and the contents dragged from the body and scattered in a wide area over the floor of the spacious room.

Blood spatters streaked the walls and below the body, a dark red patch seeped into the carpet, spreading out like a silent, creeping menace. Bloodied hand and footprints covered every surface of the room, standing testament to the horrific feast that had taken place the day before.

Kieran could hear the brawl going on in the darkness behind him but he remained at the hatchway, staring at the body of his friend, Stan. The pain in his chest was becoming hard to bear. His whole being was wracked with grief, an emotion he had never really experienced in its fullness.

In the past, sorrow and sadness had only been felt when his favourite football team was knocked out of the league, or when one of his endless strings of girlfriends rejected him. Now he felt the true impact of loss. It made him feel weak, both emotionally and physically. A feeling of helplessness and vulnerability infected his soul. For the first time in what seemed like a lifetime, he found himself thinking of and wanting his mother.

Stan's body lay there, grunting and gurgling as its shredded and destroyed throat failed to make any other noise. His lower jaw and tongue were missing, as was most of the flesh from his face, exposing the blood stained features of his cheekbones and eye sockets. His one remaining eye stayed locked on the hole in the ceiling and on Kieran, who sat in the hatchway staring back at him.

Kieran witnessed the reanimated body of his best friend as it tried repeatedly, but in vain, to move itself towards the patch of floor below the trapdoor. Stan's head continually slapped and bumped against the carpet and his chest heaved, exposing his bloodied and empty ribcage as his back arched in an attempt to shift his position.

Kieran reached up to his face and with his index finger, wiped the tears that had begun to run down his cheeks. He rubbed his nose, sniffing back the emotion that threatened to burst through his poise.

He gritted his teeth and snarled.

The growls and grunts of the two ex-soldiers fighting behind him continued. Finally, his patience wearing thin, Kieran jumped to his feet and stomped over to the bundle of men on the floor of the loft.

Hussein was trying desperately to break them up, tugging frantically at the back of Stu, but unable to pull him loose. Both men continued to grunt and curse at one another as they rolled around on the floor in a tangle.

Kieran reached down and in one swift movement, Hussein was tossed into the air and away from Stu and Jim, like a discarded child's toy. He landed in a heap, his head bouncing from the wooden floorboards with a loud thump.

Kieran stooped, placing his hands in between the two brawling men and heaved with all his strength, opening his arms wide and creating a void between Stu and Jim. Kieran's big hands clutched around Stu's harness and with a shove, he was also sent sprawling into the darkness, hitting the floor with a thud and a gasp.

"You two," he growled at them, glaring at each in turn, "get a grip of yourself. You're both making enough noise to bring all those pus-bags back up here to us. You're supposed to be professional soldiers, for fuck's sake!"

Kieran, his silhouette sinister and foreboding in the murky light of the loft, remained standing in the space between the two combatants for a few moments. He loomed over them, looking from one to the other.

Stu sat up, one hand rubbing his head and the other nursing his sore testicles. He looked up at Kieran and then glanced across at Jim. He shrugged his shoulders and shook his head.

"He started it," Stu grinned.

Jim's body went limp as he fell back, stretching himself out on the floor, shaking his head and smiling to himself as he caught his breath. Although just moments before, he and Stu had been trying to beat each other to a pulp, it was a relief to him that the matter was already forgotten, and swallowed up in the abyss of thousands of other cross words and insults that had happened between them since they first met.

Kieran turned on his heel and stomped back over to the hatch. As he crouched down, he looked back over his shoulder at the other three.

"We need to go back down there," he said calmly.

Jim sat up and looked across at him with concern. "Look, big guy, I know he was your best buddy and all, and I am truly sorry for your loss. I know it hurts, but there is nothing you can do for him, he's gone, Kieran."

Kieran shook his head without taking his eyes off Stan's body.

"I know he's dead and nothing can be done, but that's not what I mean." He paused for a moment. "We need the rifle. Stan's rifle is still there, just a few feet away from his body." He turned to look at the others again. "We need all the weapons we can get."

Jim crawled over to the hatch and looked down at the blood-splattered room, an unlit cigarette hanging from between his lips. He grunted as he eyed the door leading out into the hallway. It remained open with smears of blood trailing out along the floor and into the dark stairway over a pile of permanently dead and trampled bodies.

"Shit, he's right," he sighed. "One of us is going to have to go down there, Stu."

Stu made his way over to the trapdoor and squatted down beside the others. "You think it's worth the risk? I mean, those things could come through the door at any moment. The slightest sound could have them on top of us."

"You mean like the sound of you and Jim scrapping like a couple of school kid's on the playground?" Kieran asked sarcastically.

Stu looked sheepish and glanced at Jim.

Jim grinned back at him foolishly.

"I'll do it," Kieran volunteered. He was already shifting his position and readying himself to drop through the hatch.

"Forget it, big guy," Jim retorted, "you're too big and heavy. We'd never get you back up here quick enough if those fuckers turned up at the door."

"But, we need the rifle," Kieran protested.

"He's right," Stu cut in, still eyeing the room below them, "you're too big. I agree that *someone* has to go, but it can't be you."

In unison, all three of them turned their heads to look at Hussein. He sat just back of them, his face shrouded by the shadowy gloom of the loft. He began slowly edging his way forward, walking in a squat. As he moved closer to the hatchway, the light from the bedroom exposed his features, revealing the trepidation etched on his face.

"I knew this was coming," he mumbled to Stu as he took up position at the hatch.

"Sorry, my little Al-Qaeda buddy, but you're the smallest of the group and skinny Jim over there, he's an old man. You lucked out, I'm afraid."

"Strip down, Hussein. Make yourself as light as possible," Jim added.

"Not down to your under crackers though, I don't want you getting your little cock bit off," Stu joked.

"Yes, yes, let's just get this done, Stu." Hussein was in no mood for light-heartedness. He removed all of his equipment and ammunition and piled them into a heap, then turned to Jim. "Give me your knife," he demanded, holding out his hand.

Jim obliged, wondering what he would want the knife for as he unsheathed it and handed it over.

"You're not planning on getting into a knife fight with any of those pus-bags are you, Hussein?" he asked.

The young and lightweight Iraqi sat at the trapdoor, his legs dangling into the room below as he breathed deeply, preparing himself for the exertion and dangerous task ahead. Without taking his eyes away from the rifle and the squirming body of Stan, he shook his head.

"No, it's for Stan. We cannot leave him like that," he replied calmly.

Without another word, he leapt forward, his hands grasping the frame of the opening as his whole body swung into the air below the hatch. For a second, he remained hanging, tightly gripping the wooden ledge of the loft opening as his body came to rest with the floor just a metre below him.

He dropped down, his toes making contact first and his knees absorbing the shock. He landed with the grace of a ballerina, making virtually no sound as he touched down on the bedroom floor.

Above him, Kieran took up position, hanging his body out from the hatch with his arms reaching down, while Jim held him from behind, ready to help heave him up once he had a hold on Hussein.

Stu lay beside them, his rifle raised and aiming at the door to the hallway. His safety catch was off and at the first sign of any of the walking dead; he would drop them in an instant.

Hussein rose to his feet. He checked the door quickly, ensuring he was still alone in the room and remained undetected. He began to tiptoe, creeping his way towards the far side. He was sweating uncontrollably and his heart was beating like a bass drum inside his chest. He was sure that it could be heard outside of his body. His veins seemed to pulse with pure adrenalin, leaving no room for blood and forcing it all into his brain, making his ears throb to the beat of his heart.

He reached the area where Stan's blood stained weapon lay. The bag containing his magazines and ammunition was also close by. He avoided looking at the body in the corner, which by now had grown more excited as it watched the living flesh approaching. Stan's corpse made a sucking, gurgling sound, as it twitched and convulsed on the floor, never taking its one eye from its unreachable prey.

Hussein stole one final glance at the door as he crouched down and scooped up the weapon and ammunition. He lifted them gently, gritting his teeth and willing the floorboards beneath him to remain silent and not creek as his weight shifted on them.

With every passing moment, he expected to see a horde of flesh hungry rotting creatures to come crashing through the door. The silence of the immediate area unnerved him, even more so, because he could hear the distant echoing moans and grunts of the dead in the other rooms along the landing and stairway. They were close, just metres away from him, separated by a layer of plaster and wallpaper.

Carefully, he made his way back towards the waiting hands of Kieran, reaching down from the loft above. With one eye fixed on the door, he passed up the rifle and bag, and then turned to begin making his way over to Stan's reanimated body.

Hussein's mind raced and his nerves threatened to burst from his flesh. His heart pounded in his ears and he feared making even the slightest sound. Each step was carefully thought out and gingerly placed as he slowly inched his way back across the room.

Time seemed to slow down, but his heart and mind raced. The time that it took to make his way across the room felt like an eternity as his eyes darted from the door, to his feet, to the groaning flesh-stripped corpse of Stan in the corner.

He stopped and drew his knife, standing over their dead companion. He breathed deeply and silently spoke a prayer, apologising for what he was about to do, and asking *Allah* to look after their friend in Paradise.

He leant in close, the sound of Stan's gurgling becoming more vibrant as he sensed warm flesh.

"Forgive me, Stan," he whispered.

The knife thrust through the air as Hussein launched his hand forward, aiming directly at Stan's eye socket. The steel blade hit the soft flesh of the eyeball, then immediately, he felt the resistance as the shaft crunched through the bone directly behind the optic nerve. He pushed harder and felt the eye pop and the bone splinter, allowing the knife to sink further in, piercing the brain.

The body convulsed, letting out a gurgle as Stan's misfiring, partially reanimated brain was punctured. Hussein quickly twisted the blade, scrambling the frontal lobe and slicing deep into the central area.

Stan became limp and his head fell to the floor with a soft thud.

The knife was embedded to the hilt, deep in the skull. Hussein had to pull hard to try to remove it. He heard a squelching noise, created by suction, emitting from the eye socket as he attempted to dislodge the weapon. Placing a foot on the bloody pulp of Stan's chest, Hussein heaved. Finally, the knife came free.

He stepped back, staring down at the lifeless body. The job was done and Stan would rest in eternal peace.

The room suddenly exploded with a loud crack. Hussein spun to see a figure crumple at the doorway, dropping to its knees, and then onto its face as the round fired from Stu's rifle punched a hole through its skull.

"Run, run, Hussein, more are coming," Stu screamed from the hatch.

More shots rang out, deafening and disorientating Hussein in the relatively small confines of the room. The blast echoed around, rattling the panes of glass in the windows and causing his ears to ring and his vision to dance.

His central nervous system took control, urging his legs to take flight. He bounded across the room towards the clutching hands of Kieran, who was now screaming for him to move faster, as more shots erupted from the muzzle of Stu's rifle beside him.

Hussein focused on the hands of Kieran and began subconsciously timing his run before he made his leap. Just a few more steps and he would spring himself upwards to safety.

Another corpse fell at the doorway, sprawling face first into the room. Hussein was close and had to step to the side to avoid falling over it.

A shot snapped above his head with a deafening crack. The round smashed into the neck of an approaching figure as it crashed through the doorframe, but failed to slow it down. It lunged at Hussein with frightening speed as he passed. It caught him by the arm, knocking Hussein off balance and causing him to trip over the body of a motionless corpse on the floor, as he tugged himself away and to the side.

He tumbled and the growling body followed, regaining its grip on him as it gnashed its teeth.

Hussein was face down and defenceless against the attack. He screamed as he felt the creature's grip tighten and the weight of it press down upon him. He felt its cold rotting flesh against his back and the foul odour of decay assaulted his senses, causing the terror to rise within him.

Hussein squirmed and kicked, attempting to turn over onto his back in order to defend himself. He twisted just in time to see the creature's skeletal face cave inwards, congealed blood and grey matter spattering out from the exit wound in the rear of the skull as Stu's shot hit its target.

It fell limp, its whole weight pressing down upon him.

Hussein continued to kick and struggle, trying frantically to get the body from on top of him. He could hear Stu firing rapidly and screaming above him, but his words were muffled by Hussein's owns screams as panic threatened to overwhelm him.

Finally, he managed to slither free from the fallen body and wasted no time in regaining his feet. He glanced back at the door, seeing more figures falling as Stu tried desperately to stem the tide of putrid ravenous flesh.

Hussein took two quick steps and leapt upwards, reaching for Kieran's hands. Their palms made contact and he felt the strong man's fingers fold around his as his feet were lifted from the ground.

Kieran gripped as tightly as he could around Hussein's hands, forcing himself up onto his knees and backwards, as Jim heaved with all his strength at the belt around Kieran's waist.

Stu continued pouring rounds into the creatures forcing their way in to the room, dropping them one after the other, but more appeared to replenish their ranks.

With a final effort and his forearms threatening to burst from the strain, Kieran hauled Hussein to safety. They crumpled in a heap on the floor of the loft, gasping for breath and pouring with sweat.

Hussein turned onto his side and unable to contain himself any longer, began to wretch and vomit as spasms wracked his body.

Kieran leaned across and patted him hard on the back, partly to help him to clear his chest and throat, and partially to acknowledge his bravery and accomplishment.

"Thanks, Hussein," Kieran said between breaths, "I appreciate what you did for Stan."

Hussein said nothing but continued to dry wretch as he poured out more of the vital fluids from his already dehydrated body.

Stu rolled away from the hatch and exhaled loudly as he changed the magazine on his rifle.

"Fuck me, Hussein," he gasped, "you were almost a Jalfrezi there, mate."

Hussein, coughed and wiped his face as he propped himself up on to his elbows, turning to look across at Stu.

"What…," he sputtered with vomit and saliva dripping from his mouth, "what is a Jalfrezi?"

Stu chuckled, the relief of the incident washing over him like a cool breeze in the heat of the desert.

"It's an Indian dish, my friend."

Hussein coughed. "Well, I'm not Indian, I'm an Iraqi."

"Sorry, Hussein, you all look alike to me, mate. I get confused at times," Stu replied in mock apology.

"Yes, and you Englishmen all look alike to me."

Stu feigned annoyance and glared at him. "I'm not English. I was born in the Holy Land, God's Country."

Hussein looked at him quizzically, wiping the drool and bile from his lips. "You were born in Palestine?"

"No…Wales."

Kieran jumped to his feet. "Fuck this," he grunted as he stomped across the floor of the attic.

Stu and the others watched as he began tearing at the foil and fibreglass insulation that lined the underside of the roof.

Jim looked at Stu and shrugged. "What's he doing?"

Stu just looked at him in confusion and with no answer to give him. He turned back to Kieran who was still busy ripping off large sheets of insulation and tossing it on to a pile behind him.

"Kieran," he said, with concern that the man may have begun to lose his mind, "what are you doing, mate?"

"You want to get out of here, don't you?" The big young man growled with the effort without slowing down or taking his eyes away from the job in hand.

Stu glanced back at Jim and then to Kieran. "Uh…yeah," he replied.

"Well then, give me a hand here." Kieran stepped back for a moment, a film of sweat glistening on his heavy brow. "Unless you want to risk going out the way we came in?" He nodded to the trapdoor.

Stu leaned across and peered down into the room below. It was packed, wall to wall, with the dead. A sea of gaunt and grotesque faces loomed in the space directly below him, their dead, unblinking and lifeless eyes staring back up at him.

Stu gasped as the penny dropped. "Shit," he exclaimed, "why had we not thought of that sooner?" he asked rhetorically as he bounded across the loft.

Kieran was now kicking at the underside of the weatherproof layer of plastic, wooden lattice and slate, punching a hole to the outside.

Jim and Hussein joined them, watching as the shafts of light, created by the smashed tiles, poured into the attic, illuminating the darkness with their bright rays. Stu was throwing a barrage of kicks at the side of Kieran, creating his own hole that would eventually join with Kieran's escape route.

They both grunted and gasped with the effort, but with each blow, more daylight spilled into the gloomy interior. Stu began to laugh. The relief of finally having a solution to their problem was overpowering. Just five minutes before, their choices were limited to either dying from dehydration or risk being eaten alive, as they attempted to escape the way they had come.

Kieran also began to chuckle as he launched a new and increasingly vicious assault against the roof.

"You jokers hadn't even thought of this?" he shouted over his shoulder between kicks.

Jim shook his head. "Jesus, man…it hadn't even occurred to me."

"Me neither," grunted Stu.

Kieran shook his head and laughed. "Super troopers, I fucking shit 'em."

With a final bombardment of stomps and kicks, the last of the slate tiles were smashed through, leaving a large hole in the roof, big enough for the four men to squeeze through. Kieran pushed his head out into the open and immediately felt the effects of the cold winter air against his skin. He breathed deeply, smiling as he savoured the moment. What he could smell was freedom and salvation.

"Oh, the air has never smelt so good," he called back to the others.

Without warning, he was suddenly dragged back in by the other three. He turned quickly, glaring at them with anger.

"What's up?" he demanded.

"The bomb," Hussein replied, "we forgot about the bomb. The whole place could be contaminated."

Kieran looked back out through the hole and then up at the sky. "Smells fine to me," he remarked.

"Well it would," Stu pointed out, " you can't see or smell radiation."

He walked over to the hole and looked out at the landscape around them. Nothing looked any different to how things had been three days earlier. The sky was clear of any clouds and as blue as he had ever seen. Even the birds still fluttered around in the air, hopping from building to building as though nothing had occurred. Stu leant out as far as he could. He craned his neck in an attempt to gain a view of the street below to the rear of the building.

The alleyway and parking area at the back were empty. There were no sign of the hordes of dead that had surrounded them when they had arrived.

"Strange," he said as he pulled himself back in to the interior of the loft.

"What," Kieran asked, "what's strange?"

"There's no sign of any pus-bags down there."

Kieran looked down at the street. "Yeah, that's because they're all in the building with us. They probably managed to smash through the rear doors at some point. There were enough of them to do it."

"What do you reckon, Stu?" Jim asked, lighting a cigarette and blowing out plumes of grey blue smoke.

He coughed and spluttered, and soon regretted the decision. It only intensified his thirst. With disdain, he flicked the cigarette through the hatchway where it bounced off the face of a dumbstruck corpse as the showers of red sparks rained down over it.

"You mean about the radiation?" Stu asked as he turned to look at him. "Well, the birds are still singing and none of them are dropping from the sky, so it must be okay."

"That's good enough for me," Jim declared, and without any further debate, he was climbing through the hole and out on to the roof.

One by one, they carefully scrambled their way up to the top of the sloping roof, throwing a leg over each side and straddling the apex like a horse's saddle. They paused and surveyed the scene around them.

To their right, at the rear of the pub, the narrow and dark alley was empty. However, to their left, the street was packed with the shambling corpses of the town's previous residents. The two Range Rovers that they had arrived in were still in the middle of the road, swarming with the dead and with no hope of Stu and the other three being able to recover them.

"Well, looks like we're walking from here," Jim whispered over his shoulder as he began to shuffle along the rooftop.

Hussein looked down at the crowd and shuddered. It would only take a momentary loss of his balance and he would slip, unable to stop his descent, and fall into their clutching hands and snapping teeth. He concentrated on the tiles below his feet and the rounded terracotta of the apex that his sweating palms tightly gripped. He settled himself into a slow rhythm of lift and shuffle, taking extra care in where, and how, he placed his hands and feet.

Jim stopped and waited as the others caught up. He was right at the gable end of the building. In front of him was a sheer drop of twenty metres and the entrance to the empty alleyway below. He looked to the left and noticed a gate that blocked access to the passageway leading to the rear of the building from the main street. Beyond the barrier, thousands of bodies shuffled around, bashing into the gate and causing it to rattle in its frame.

None of the dead had noticed them on the rooftop.

'They always seem to be preoccupied with what was directly in front of them, or on the ground below their feet,' Jim noted to himself.

Stu caught up with him and stopped, panting from the effort of shuffling along the roof. Kieran was close behind but Hussein was lagging, taking his time and being particularly careful of his movements.

"Where do we go now then, Stu?" Jim asked over his shoulder.

Stu bit his lip and leaned forward to get a view of what Jim could see of the alleyway below.

"It's blocked off by a steel gate leading out onto the street," Jim pointed out when he noticed that Stu was trying to see past him. "It's clear at this end and they haven't seen us up here, yet. Thing is though, it must be open access in the other direction to have allowed them all to get around to the rear of the pub." He turned and looked Stu in the eye. "We could be trapped, buddy."

Without looking at him, Stu shrugged. "Nothing new there, then," he replied. "We can't stay here and our priority is to find water."

Hussein caught up with the others and took the opportunity to rest his hands and legs, and catch his breath. Despite the cold, he was saturated with sweat, but he feared risking removing his hands from the apex to wipe his brow. His rifle and ammunition were weighing him down. With his energy reserves depleted through lack of food and the onset of the effects of dehydration, he was terrified of losing his grip in his weakened state. Reclaiming the rifle, dealing with Stan and the fear and exertion, and having to fight off the dead, had sapped the last of his strength.

"Nothing for it," Stu declared. "It's down the drainpipe and standby to run."

He began slowly to slide down to the lip of the roof on his backside, using his feet out in front of him to act as a brake. He could feel the weight of his body magnified by the steep angle of the roof and threatening to throw him into an uncontrolled plunge, down to the lip of the guttering and beyond.

Without wanting to, he began to build up speed. He dug his heels in and spread his arms out wide, ensuring that as much of his body as possible was making contact with the slate tiles of the roof and acting as drag against his momentum.

"Shit," he hissed between gritted teeth as he saw the distance between him and the last of the tiles diminish far quicker than he would have liked. "Shit..."

He slapped the soles of his feet and the palms of his hands flat to the slate to bring him to a stop, risking his body being catapulted forward by the impetus of his descent.

With just centimetres to spare before he would have plummeted to the ground below, Stu stopped. He lay there for a moment, panting and sweating. His jaw was locked solid. He had been clenching his teeth so hard, they almost fused into one another.

Placing his toes on the lip of the guttering, he rolled over onto his stomach, turning to look up at the others. They watched him, concern slowly turning to relief but then back to concern as they realised that it was now their turn to try the same perilous stunt.

Stu nodded to Jim, signalling that it was his turn to descend. As Jim began, Stu made his way to his right and located the drainpipe he hoped would be there at the corner of the building. Huffing and grunting from the strain, he heaved himself over the edge and began to climb down towards the alleyway below.

Halfway down, a sudden clatter from above warned him to press himself in close against the walls of the building, as a number of heavy slate tiles sailed past, shattering loudly against the hard ground.

Stu looked up, furious that he had almost been hit by the falling masonry and because of the noise that they made when they hit the ground. In the otherwise still air, they sounded like a rock concert in Stu's head as their din echoed around in the narrow alley.

Jim peered down at him from over the lip and mouthed the word, *'sorry.'*

Stu shook his head and continued downwards. Soon, he was on the ground, his rifle firmly in his hands and checking the immediate area. Nothing moved. They seemed to have been spared from the possible repercussions of the falling tiles.

Jim was on the ground soon after and helping Stu to keep watch as Kieran clumsily began to climb down the pipe that was growing more rickety by the second.

Stu heard a scuffing noise to his right, from around the corner and towards the rear of the pub where they had been holed up for the prior three days. The hairs began to prickle on the back of his neck and a chill ran through his blood.

He looked across and clicked his fingers at Jim, who was looking in the opposite direction. The American turned to him and Stu pointed to his ear and then in the direction where he heard the noise.

Jim nodded and raised his rifle to cover the corner while Stu crept forward to investigate.

Slowly and carefully, he made his way towards the edge of the wall, his knees bent and his rifle in his shoulder. He placed himself flat against the bricks, making himself as hard to see as possible. He looked back at Jim and nodded. In his head, he began to count backwards from three.

He pushed his head past the corner and out into the open, getting a clear view of what was in the alley. He lingered there for no longer than a second or two, but long enough to get a lucid image of the rest of the passageway towards the rear of the pub. At the far end, roughly twenty corpses slowly shuffled and meandered about. They did not seem to be looking for anything in particular and were oblivious to the presence of Stu and his team, but nevertheless, they were there and blocking their only escape route.

Another body, the one whose feet Stu had heard dragging against the tarmac ground, was much closer and headed in their direction.

Stu pulled his head back in around the corner and remained pressed against the wall, waiting. He was unsure if the creature had seen him as he peered around the wall, but it did not matter; it was heading towards them and he would have to deal with it regardless of whether it was alerted to their presence or not.

Stu signalled across to Jim, indicating that there was one 'enemy' approaching. He drew his knife from its sheath, not wanting to use a firearm and attract every corpse in the city.

The knife blade created a dull metallic scrape as it came free. He raised it in his right hand and waited for the reanimated corpse to appear from around the corner.

It seemed to be taking forever and he almost began to suspect that the creature had turned around and headed in the other direction. Then he heard it. The scrape of its feet reached his ears as it drew near. He could hear its low groans and questioning sighs as it ambled along the narrow passageway of the alley.

Then, Stu heard something else. Something much more alarming and disturbing. A crunching sound to his left was quickly followed by an almost inaudible yelp. He turned just in time to see the drainpipe breaking free of the wall, and Hussein tumble through the air for the last three metres of his descent. He hit the ground with a heavy thump and his rifle clattered against the hard concrete of the pavement. He rolled to his right and groaned, clutching at his knee as Kieran raced over to help him.

In the distraction, Stu had taken his focus from the approaching danger. Now, he turned his attention back to the edge of the brick wall just as the festering corpse of a woman rounded the corner.

She saw him immediately, letting out a long howling moan, as she suddenly launched herself at him with speed that Stu did not believe possible from one of the dead. He brought the knife down in a powerful thrust, aiming it at the top of her cranium. The blade missed, slashing down the side of the dead woman's face and opening a wide gash that oozed pus and coagulated blood.

The creature collided with Stu and he felt her cold fingers begin to clutch at his flesh. Her lank blonde and blood stained hair clung to her scalp and face in strands. Her grey green mottled skin looked shrunken against her skull with numerous seeping sores, intensifying her demonic features. Her withered and drawn lips and receding black gums exaggerated the length of her teeth; her dead fishlike eyes, unblinking and without life or emotion, terrified Stu as he stared back into them, struggling to raise the knife for a second blow.

He brought up his knee and drove it into the midriff of the woman, knocking her backwards and forcing her to lose the grip she had on him. He threw himself forward, gripping her by her filth ridden and stinking jacket, and at the same time, brought the knife down. This time, the blow was accurate. It smashed into the top of her skull, piercing the brain and causing the corpse to drop immediately.

Stu stepped back, his chest heaving and his skin ashen. Jim nodded at him as Stu began to check himself for bites and cuts. He shook his head, blowing out a sigh of relief. He moved back over to Jim and Kieran, crouching over Hussein, who sat nursing his leg.

"What's the verdict?" he asked.

Jim looked at him. Stu looked shaken. His hands twitched and his voice quivered but he fully understood why. They had battled with the dead on countless occasions, but it was very rare that one would come so close to taking a bite out of either of them. To be caught out like that, having the putrid flesh and gnashing infected teeth so close to his skin, it was enough to shake even the toughest man to the core.

"Well," Kieran said, looking up at him, "his knee is fucked. I'm not a doctor so I can't give any better diagnoses than that."

Stu looked at the swelling that was even apparent under the cloth of Hussein's trousers. It looked like he had a grapefruit strapped to his leg.

"Can you walk?" he asked.

Hussein shook his head, his face grimacing with the pain. "I don't know, maybe."

Stu and Kieran helped him to his feet and supported him as he took a couple of hobbling steps. He soon collapsed to the floor again, gritting his teeth and growling with agony and frustration.

"How do we look at the far end of the alley?" Jim asked.

Stu shook his head. "Not good," he replied, staring down at Hussein and trying to come up with a solution. "There's a bunch of them down there, just mincing about. I don't think they know we're here though."

"We'll have to make a run for it," Jim replied, looking back at the turn in the alleyway, making sure that none of the dead had suddenly appeared as they came to investigate the noise.

Stu shook his head again. "How will we make a run for it? Hussein can hardly walk."

Jim was still watching the corner, deep in thought. "It was a figure of speech, Stu. What I meant was: we can't stay here."

"I'll carry him," Kieran volunteered.

Stu nodded acknowledgement. "Jim, grab Kieran's rifle and bring up the rear. I'll take the lead."

"Wait," Kieran hissed as he began to haul Hussein up from the floor and onto his back. "That little tramp, Johnny, he said they can be fooled and we can pretend to be like them if we just shuffle along, slowly."

Jim looked at Stu and raised an eyebrow. "I'm not sure I'm up for that, buddy. Rubber chickens, peanut butter, ball-gags...sure, I'm into all kinds of kinks, but walking about and pretending to be dead, amidst a bunch of pus-bags that want to eat me…?"

"Well, I'm not sure I can carry Hussein and fight them off at the same time, Jim."

"It's worth a try," Stu agreed. "Let's make like dead-fucks and if they make any move towards us, we go noisy, okay?"

Everyone nodded.

"Nice and slow, remember," Jim reminded them, "we don't want to look like athletes out there and get our asses bit off."

Stu stepped out in to the main passage of the alley. Before them, just thirty metres further on, a cluster of shadowy figures sauntered and roamed. They meandered from one side of the alley to the other, dragging their feet and colliding with one another as they stared blindly at the ground.

A few of them stopped and curiously studied discarded items that they picked up from the ground at their feet. One of the wandering bodies held a child's toy, a doll that was made to appear like a baby. It held the small lifelike figure up before it, studying it. The creature twisted and turned it in all directions as its cold eyes gazed at the plastic features and synthetic hair. Its shrivelled and brittle finger caught in the pull string attached to the doll's back. Its eyes opened; their bright blue irises sparkling in the cold air as a flurry of baby noises erupted from the voice box inside its chest.

Immediately, every reanimated corpse within hearing distance stopped and turned. They all heard the recorded noises of a young child that emerged from the toy, believing them to be the sounds of a real life human being. A chorus of moans and wails broke out in unison, as every decaying figure in the alleyway began to stagger towards the source of the alluring sounds.

The body holding the baby, a man in his early thirties and probably once having been a father of children, without any further hesitation, bit down on the face of the doll. His teeth sank deep into the artificial, rubbery flesh and tore a gaping hole in the area of the eyes and nose. The dark grey of the man's decaying flesh contrasted harshly with the bright and vibrant looking skin of the child's toy. As the dead man pulled his head back, a large chunk of the toy's face tore and came away, wedged between his teeth.

The baby noises continued as the creature began to chew. After a moment, the man's lifeless eyes looked down at the small figure in his hands, confusion apparent upon his face. He spat the false flesh from his mouth and shook the baby as it continued to gurgle and repeatedly pronounce the word, *'Mama, mama.'*

The other bodies in the alley converged on the man and doll, and began to crowd around, staring at what they believed was human flesh. A flurry of hands reached out and began to tear at the toy and the corpse that still gripped it, as he refused to let go.

Stu walked by slowly, watching in horror as the doll and its new owner was torn to shreds by the horde descending upon them. Limbs, plastic, and flesh and bone, were ripped from their sockets as the mob became more agitated by the continuous cries of, *'Mama, mama',* and newborn style gurgles and giggles.

The crowd of ravenous monsters growled and hissed as they continued in their frenzy, clawing and biting at anything that was placed in front of their mouth. Others became victims to the excitement of the moment, as teeth severed fingers, lacerated flesh, and bony hands clawed at the eyes and soft tissue of any that were unfortunate enough to be mistaken as prey.

In spite of the overpowering urge that he felt building up inside him, Stu kept his pace down to nothing more than a sluggish saunter, keeping his face to the ground and discreetly watching his peripherals.

Kieran, just a few paces back from Stu, kept a tight grip on Hussein, carrying him on his back, as the young Iraqi man watched in horror at the turmoil of the dead. Hussein kept a tight grip on his rifle, resting it on Kieran's shoulder and aiming it in the direction of the horde.

The four men slowly hobbled past at a distance of no more than three metres; close enough to hear the individual growls and moans, and smell the stench of their rotting flesh. Stu, Kieran, Hussein, and Jim, all fought against their instincts that screamed at them, telling them to run and put as much distance between them and the group of dead as possible.

Stu prayed to the Gods that no one became overcome by fear and bolted. That would attract every one of them and more from the surrounding area. Although his guts knotted and threatened to cramp, and every hair on his body stood on end, he was determined to continue in the same slow manner until they were away from the immediate danger. After that, his next concern was what was around the next corner, and which way they would go.

With Stan dead and Hussein injured, they had no choice but to head straight back to the safety of the park, but he had no idea of a plan of how to get them there. In his mind, he decided that the priority was to find a vehicle and be away from the main built up area, then formulate a plan and consider their next move.

Jim brought up the rear, protecting Kieran and Hussein from any attack from behind. He watched Kieran, as the weight of Hussein on his back seemed to take its toll. His hands were slowly losing their grip and his burden slid downwards. Any sudden jerking movements as Kieran attempted to adjust the weight distribution could attract the hungry eyes that lurked close by.

Jim increased his pace slightly, closing the distance between him and Kieran. He reached out and placed his hands underneath the seat of Hussein's trousers, taking his weight and allowing Kieran to adjust his grip.

"Slowly," Jim whispered, "pull him up, slowly."

Kieran did as he was told, and Hussein grimacing as he did so, climbed up the back of his human transport, his knee sending shooting pains through his nervous system.

"Cheers," Kieran whispered to Jim as he continued forward.

A loud resonating clatter from behind made Stu's blood freeze in his veins; he stopped and spun around, looking for the source of the noise and silently hoping that it was the group of dead, tearing into one another that had somehow created it.

Kieran and Hussein also stopped and turned to see Jim in a panic, as he reached for the ground to retrieve his weapon, which he had dropped.

"Fuck, God damn, fuck shit," Jim cursed through his gritted teeth, knowing he had endangered them all with his carelessness.

He scooped up his rifle and slammed it into his shoulder as he rose to his feet, spinning his body around and facing the decomposing swarm that were just a few metres from him.

They too had heard and seen him. They rose to their feet, forgetting about the crying doll and focussing their attention on the four men standing motionless and close by. They stood and stared back at Jim, their hungry dead eyes locked on him, as he remained rooted to the ground.

The group of corpses consisted of all types. Men, women, and children, in all manner of states of rot, watched Jim and the other three intently. Not all of them had full working senses, that much was obvious. Some were missing eyes, while others had heads damaged to the extent that there was no way of them being able to hear. However, as a group, they could hear and see together.

A tall, gangly figure dressed in the filth covered remains of what appeared to be a tracksuit, its face pitted with holes and its flesh a deep green, reached out and took a step forward. A moan of poignant accusation erupting from its throat as its bony claw-like fingers grasped at the air between it and the living human.

The rest of the crowd exploded with the same moans and immediately, they became more agitated and excited in their tone.

"Fuck," Jim cursed again.

He squeezed the trigger, the report echoing in the built up area as the crack of the round bounced from building to building. The bullet hit the tall figure squarely in the face, smashing a hole through its skull and killing it instantly. It dropped to the floor, causing the two other creatures immediately behind it to trip and tumble over it.

The other thirty or so ghoulish walking corpses advanced, wailing and quickening their step as they reached out towards Jim, who began to back up.

More shots pierced the air as Stu began to fire into the crowd, screaming for Jim to retreat. Five more bodies tumbled in quick succession, but in their panic and haste, Stu and Jim missed with their shots just as many times as they managed to hit home. Glass shattered and brick splintered as the stray rounds smashed into the buildings behind the advancing flesh-craving mob.

"Bug out," Stu called, encouraging Kieran to get himself and the crippled Hussein clear of the area. "Jim, move your arse, we're bugging out."

Jim turned and sprinted past Stu, following in the wake of Kieran who had taken flight at a speed that defied the heavy burden he carried.

Stu took off, close on Jim's heels, as they ran in the only direction that they could see was relatively clear. From behind every building and abandoned car, dozens of lurching shadowy figures sprang, all wailing and pursuing the living people as they tried to flee the area.

The entire town seemed to erupt with the wails of the dead.

Kieran was panting heavily. The initial adrenalin-fuelled influx of energy that was created by terror had burned itself out. Now, he was running on empty and his legs, back, and arms began to tire. His pace slowed as his feet slowly turned to lead and his lungs screamed at him for a reprieve in the tempo.

More and more moaning and screaming figures appeared from every doorway and from around every corner. All eyes locked on the fast moving, fleeing men, as they sprinted along the street.

Stu could see that Kieran was beginning to slow down and his grip on Hussein had slackened. Jim remained at the rear, running along and stopping only to dispatch any of the dead that he judged were too close or about to step into the path of Kieran or Stu.

"Kieran," Stu called as he ran up parallel, "pass him over, I'll carry him."

Kieran shook his head angrily and grunted as his thighs worked like pistons, powering him forward along the street.

"Just keep them off my arse," he gasped.

Hussein pleaded with Kieran to allow him to attempt to run for himself. Each time, his request was declined as the powerful young man adjusted his grip, tightening his hands around the legs of Hussein and drawing on all the energy reserves and determination he could muster.

"There," Stu called, pointing to a vehicle just fifty metres ahead of them.

The door of the driver's side hung open, giving them the opportunity of a quick inspection to see if it was still roadworthy and not waste time trying to gain entry.

As they drew closer, Stu realised that it was a police car. Its windscreen was cracked and smears of blood coated the entire exterior of the vehicle. It appeared that the occupants had been caught in the open, unable to get back to the safety of their vehicle, and now their ghastly remains littered the ground around the vehicle.

Stu raced forward to the car, dropping another four of the dead as they closed in on him. Jim appeared at his side, wrenching the rear doors open, covering Stu and ready for Kieran and Hussein to pile in.

Stu jumped behind the wheel and saw that the keys remained in the ignition. He reached down and gripped them in his trembling hands.

'Please, please start,' he silently prayed before turning the key.

The engine clicked and the starter motor groaned. He turned the ignition again, pumping the accelerator pedal and willing the engine to fire up, as the starter motor continued to turn and grind.

Kieran was twenty metres short of the police car, with hundreds of bodies closing in all around him. His mind was in a panic, but his eyes focussed on the vehicle before him.

"Nearly there," he grunted under his breath.

His hands, unable to bear the strain any longer, finally gave out and Hussein began to slip from his back. Kieran managed a few more steps, and then he could hold on no longer. It was no use; he could not carry the human burden on his back any further.

"I'm sorry," Kieran said, as he gasped for breath. Hussein dropped to the ground, groaning with the impact as his knee clashed with the hard surface.

"I'm sorry, Hussein," Kieran repeated, snatching Hussein's rifle and firing at a number of approaching corpses with only one round hitting its intended target.

Hussein nodded, understanding that Kieran had done his best and could not carry him any further.

"I understand," he said in resignation, knowing that he was incapable of walking, despite the gravity of the situation.

"Please, shoot me, don’t leave me for those things," he pleaded.

Kieran fired another volley and turned to look down at the man at his feet. Hussein looked back up at him, defiance burning in his eyes with bravery that Kieran had never seen before.

Kieran smiled for a second. "Dick head," he huffed, "you think that I'm fucking leaving you here?"

Without another word, Kieran reached down, grasping Hussein by the straps of his assault vest and hoisting him up on to his feet.

"No chance. You're coming with me and you owe me a beer for this," he groaned as he strained with the weight of Hussein.

With an almighty heave, Kieran threw Hussein over his shoulder, holding onto his legs while the Iraqi's head and body hung over his back in a fireman's carry. With the last of his strength, Kieran took off, sprinting towards the static police car.

13

The high-pitched scream of the engine subsided and the rotor blades settled to a slow spin as the pilot closed the machine down and stepped out from the cockpit.

Marcus, Steve, and Helen, stood watching as she removed her helmet to reveal an attractive woman with shoulder length brown hair. It was not what Marcus had been expecting. He felt slightly ashamed for assuming that it would be a man, even though he had known female pilots during his days in the army.

The co-pilot remained inside the helicopter for a while before being prompted by his pilot to join her outside. Reluctantly, he climbed out, his right hand instinctively reaching for and covering the handgrip of the pistol attached to his leg. His body language spoke volumes of unease. He was obviously suspicious, and maybe even afraid.

For a moment, the five people stood in silence, eyeing one another and making their own assessments of the situation.

Kelly felt uncomfortable and regretted shutting down the engine. They were vulnerable and in unfamiliar territory, and facing unknown numbers. They had no idea of their host's intentions, and it dawned on her that she might have left them both wide open to an attack. Seeing the flare in the sky and comparing the interior of the walls to the outside, she had been overwhelmed with the possibility of finding somewhere safe, with real living people and without the ever-present threat of death creeping up on her.

Their base was safe from the dead, but it was far from being a place of tranquillity, security and freedom. General Gibson ruled the island with an iron fist and the entire population was in a permanent state of unease and suspicion. That was exactly how the General wanted it, *'divide and conquer'*; he would always say when referring to the people under his command and so-called protection.

Before her stood two men and a woman, not exactly threatening in their appearance but one of the men definitely stood out from the others. Dressed in what she mistook to be a wetsuit at first, she now realised that he was actually wrapped in black plastic. To a degree, she feared asking why.

She looked past the three people and over towards the house. Dozens of faces peered back at her from behind the numerous large windows of the old mansion. Further up, and just visible over the lip of the roof, she could see two more figures watching them; at least one of them seemed to be holding a rifle.

They were outgunned and overlooked, but she did not feel under any immediate threat. She understood that people were scared and took nothing for granted when it came to their own safety and defending what they had built for themselves in the new world order.

They all remained silent, watching one another and waiting for someone to break the ice and begin the conversation.

The cold air caused goose bumps to form on Kelly's flesh and her breath formed in short rapid clouds that misted in front of her face. Apart from the sound of the gentle winter breeze and the distant hum of the multitude of dead beyond the walls, the silence was complete and eerie.

Kelly turned her head to her right and glanced at Joey for reassurance. It was hard to read his face or tell what he was thinking because he still had his helmet on with the sun visor pulled down, hiding his features and expressions. His body language was audible enough, though, as his hand remained hovering over the pistol at his side and his weight continually shifted from one foot to the other. He was nervous and ready to draw his weapon if needed.

She looked back at the three people in front of her and made a mental note of their weapons, still in the holsters attached to their hips. They did not seem to be in any rush to begin a gunfight and their body language came across more as cautious, not hostile, but all three of them stood ready.

The man in the centre, in spite of his dress sense, carried an air of leadership about him. His eyes bore down on her as he studied Kelly and Joey. She could see from the way he held himself that he was a tough man and knew what he was doing. He was cautious, but confident, and his posture was that of a man that could spring into action at the blink of an eye. If she did not know better, she would have guessed him to be a soldier with more than his share of experience in war.

The others, the man and woman, though clearly ready to fight if necessary, took their lead from the man in the centre, and continually looked to him for any sign of a change in his attitude.

Kelly decided that the silence had lasted for long enough.

"So," she began as she locked eyes with the man wearing the strange outfit, "what have you come as?"

Marcus was thrown off balance by the casualness of the question and looked down at his attire, feeling completely disarmed. He cursed himself for not having the forethought of stripping himself of the makeshift protective clothing, but in his defence, he had completely forgotten that he was wearing it.

He looked back at Steve in embarrassment and rolled his eyes.

"Uh, protection," Marcus stated, "what's your story? Why are you here?" he asked before the female pilot could quiz him further.

"You fired the flare," Joey spoke for the first time.

Marcus nodded. "Yeah, I did, but what I mean is, why are you in this area? Why is there a helicopter flying around so far inland? From what we know, there are no bases still in operation around here."

Kelly did not feel it was yet the time to give too much away of the reasons why they were there. Instead, she wanted to get a feel for their new hosts and their intentions.

"I'm Kelly," she said, changing the subject. She nodded to the nervous man at her side. "This is Joey, my co-pilot."

"I'm Marcus and this is Steve, and that is Helen."

"How many people you got here?" Kelly asked, nodding at the large house and, in particular, the two figures she saw watching them on the roof.

"Enough…"

"Enough for what?" Joey asked. "You do know you're surrounded, don’t you?"

Marcus nodded. "Yeah, we know, but I don’t think they can get inside the walls."

Kelly shook her head and glanced at Joey. They had flown over the whole area and had a clear picture to the extent of the size of the mass of dead flocking towards them from the surrounding area.

"No, you don’t understand. It's not just a case of a few thousand hanging around outside your walls. There are hundreds of thousands of them and more are on their way." Kelly sighed. "You're trapped here."

Marcus stepped forward, nodding as he approached her. He looked over his shoulder and up at the house, waving to Lee and Jake on the rooftop. Both of them stood up and waved in return.

"Look," Marcus said as he drew near, "we're well aware of our predicament, but you say there are more of them coming?"

Kelly nodded as Joey began to remove his helmet. Marcus looked at him, fixing him with a cold stare that seemed to unsettle the co-pilot even further. He looked back at Kelly and his eyes narrowed while he scrutinised the two newcomers.

"You both look tired and as though you could use some food," Marcus said softly, alleviating the tension of the standoff. "You can come inside and rest, but I must insist that you hand over your weapons, for now at least. We have families here and I would feel much more comfortable if you weren't carrying the means to do us harm."

Kelly understood; she knew that they did not have much of a choice. If they refused, the people before her could easily kill them. She reached down slowly and pulled her pistol from its holster, handing it to Marcus and nodding to Joey to do the same.

Marcus studied the weapons in his hand and grunted. "Do you have any more weapons in the whirly bird?"

"A couple of rifles and a GPMG," Kelly replied.

Marcus' eyes lit up as she mentioned the General Purpose Machinegun. She knew then that the man standing in front of her must be ex-military, probably infantry, judging by the delight in his eyes.

'How else would he appreciate the value of having a machinegun such as the GPMG?' she thought to herself.

"With about eighteen hundred rounds for the gun and plenty of loose for the rifles," Kelly added, wanting to seem compliant.

Marcus grinned at her. "You have a *'widow-maker'*?"

He looked back over his shoulder to Steve and Helen. "Grab the weapons and ammo from the chopper and bring it all inside."

A crash from far behind them, in the direction of the house, dragged Marcus' attention from the helicopter crew. He turned and saw Karen bounding down the steps. She marched across the gravel with her chest puffed out and a stern look on her face. Gary ran after her, trying to drag her back, but she rebuffed him each time, shrugging his hand from her shoulder and continuing towards Marcus.

Marcus felt uneasy. Her sole attention was concentrated on him and she scowled at him as she drew near. He was ready to fight with a helicopter, but he was not prepared for a confrontation with the 'battle-axe' that was Karen. Whatever it was that she was upset about, Marcus knew that he was about to receive the brunt of her wrath.

"Shame on you, Marcus," she reprimanded him, "how long are you going to keep them out here while you carry out your 'Spanish Inquisition' with all your guns pointed at them?"

She looked from Marcus to the two newcomers. Her expression was hard and stern when looking at Marcus, but softened as she turned to Kelly and Joey.

"I'm sorry about this one," she said to Kelly as she took her by the arm. "He's a little over protective of us all and sometimes forgets his manners."

Marcus felt like his grandmother had just rebuked him. "Karen, I was just about to bring…"

"You just leave them to me, Marcus," Karen said over her shoulder as she began to lead Kelly and Joey away, fixing him with a stare that took him right back to his childhood.

Karen reminded him of his grandmother in many ways and as a result, she would even get away with slapping his legs if she felt the need to. Marcus looked down at himself, half-expecting to see his bare legs protruding from a pair of school shorts. For a moment, he was filled with nostalgia for his 'Nan' and a half smile curled his lips, as he remembered things from a time long forgotten.

"You have their guns," Karen said as she headed towards the house, "so you just carry on doing your job while I do mine."

Marcus decided not to argue further. The pilot and co-pilot were disarmed and easy enough to deal with if they tried anything, so he allowed Karen to play the part of 'Mother Hen', a role that she enjoyed very much.

Gary looked at him and shrugged. "There's no stopping her once she has something in her head, Marcus."

He looked over his shoulder, making sure that Karen was out of earshot, and then took a step closer to Marcus while speaking in a hushed voice. "I learned a long time ago that she couldn't be stopped when she sets herself to something. I never told her to her face, but for years, I nicknamed her *'Attila'*."

Marcus grinned at the comparison.

Inside the house, as the helicopter's crew sat eating hot soup and being plied with all the boiling tea they could handle, Marcus and the others gathered around, watching them.

Kelly looked up from her bowl, the warm aroma of tomato drifting up to her face in wisps of steam. She breathed deeply, savouring the smell before dipping her spoon into the hot mix.

She glanced from her first taste and saw dozens of expectant eyes staring back at her. She could almost see the thousands of questions they wanted answers to. It was as if their minds were so crammed with them that the questions had taken physical form and had begun to seep out from their heads.

She braced herself for the bombardment.

"So," Jake began, "you're part of the counter offensive?"

Joey shook his head and let out a laugh that sounded more like a hiccup. "Not exactly; we were supposed to be gathering information and relaying it back to base."

"What sort of information, and where is your base?" Helen asked eagerly. She was desperate to learn of other places where people still survived.

"Jura," Kelly announced as she slurped soup from her spoon and avoided the first part of the question. "The Isle of Jura, off the west coast of Scotland. It was turned into a fortress early on as we evacuated the mainland."

"So, we still have an army?" Jake asked.

Kelly shook her head as she stirred her soup. "Not really, no. Most of what was left of our forces was destroyed during the counter offensive. There are still a few units on the island, but they're mainly for security."

"Destroyed?" Jake found it hard to believe that the entire army had vanished from the face of the earth, despite the billions of people that died since the dead began to rise.

"Yeah," Joey continued, "our head shed completely underestimated the enemy and entire regiments, brigades, and even divisions were swallowed up in the cities. There wasn't a thing we could do to help them; even the armoured units were lost. Their tanks and APC's were bogged down and turned into tombs, surrounded by thousands of those things."

Kelly looked across at Marcus sitting on the other side of the table. He stared back at her, still reserving his own judgement on them; still dressed in black plastic bags.

"So, how come you're dressed like that?" Kelly asked, unable to delay the question any longer.

"It's his turn to be the gimp for the day," Lee joked.

Jake let out an involuntary snort of laughter and immediately slapped his hand to his mouth to contain it. He looked across at Lee, his face turning purple as he fought hard to hold back the hysterics that threatened to burst through his efforts at self-control.

"I told you," Marcus replied, ignoring Lee's comment, "it's for protection."

Kelly's brow furrowed in confusion. "Protection," she asked, "from what? The dead can easily bite through that."

Marcus shook his head. "Not from the dead. Someone dropped a nuclear warhead and it's the best we could manage. We took shelter in the cellar and I came up to see if it was safe for the others."

Kelly almost laughed. She understood his concern and the reasons why he was dressed the way he was. She shook her head, feeling more relaxed that the outfit was not a part of the man's everyday attire.

"There's nothing to worry about where the bomb is concerned," Kelly confessed to them. "It was a low yield device, no bigger than five kilotons."

Steve leaned forward from the end of the table. He glanced at Marcus, then to Kelly. "What does that mean, *'five kilotons'*?"

"It means we're safe," Marcus said to him without taking his eyes from the helicopter pilot. "It was a tactical nuke."

"That's right," Kelly added in acknowledgement. "They're designed to take out military instillations and troop build-ups on the battlefield. The bomb dropped on Nagasaki at the end of the Second World War was twenty-one kilotons, so this was a baby in comparison."

"So you dropped it?" Jake asked accusingly.

Joey shook his head. "No, we didn't drop it. It was launched remotely from the silos that we still have access to on the mainland. We were supposed to record the after effects of it and report back to the General. We were on our way there to record our findings when we came across this place."

"The *'General'*? And which general is that?" Marcus asked, raising an eyebrow.

"Gibson," Kelly said with disdain. "The man is fucking mad." she glanced about her and noted the children that watched from the peripherals. "Sorry about the language, but it's true. He's completely insane."

"Never heard of him,"

"You were in the army?" Kelly asked, realising that Marcus must have been expecting to hear a familiar name.

"Used to be, a long time ago," he replied.

"Infantry?" Kelly asked, already knowing the answer.

Marcus nodded. His expression was stern and thoughtful. "The Parachute Regiment," he replied.

Kelly glanced at Joey knowingly, and then nodded at Marcus. Now that she knew, she could not picture him as anything but a paratrooper.

"Gibson wasn't always a general. He pretty much promoted himself. When he was given the command on Jura, he was a Colonel, but the power of being in charge of so many people must've gone to his head." Kelly reached for her glass and gulped down a large amount of water before she continued.

"After the failure of the counter offensive, he declared himself Chief of Staff and commander of all land forces."

Marcus' eyes widened and his forehead creased as his eyebrows were raised to their limit.

"Really? Sounds like we have a genuine old fashioned usurper up there."

Kelly nodded. "Yeah, well after we received reports that the Isle of Man was overrun, and the Channel Islands were at war with each other before losing comms altogether with them, Gibson decided that he would take command of the forces that were left and still loyal."

"Loyal to whom? I thought the government had been knocked out?" Helen asked.

"Loyal to him; he had an army of fifteen thousand troops at one point."

"So, what happened to them?" Marcus asked, anxious to know the fate of the armed forces.

Kelly looked down at the table, avoiding eye contact with Marcus as his question burned in her ears.

"Dead, mostly," Joey said casually and without looking up as he played with his spoon.

Kelly looked at him and then turned to Marcus, her eyes showing strong emotions as she held back powerful and horrific memories.

"That's right," she began, "Gibson took it upon himself to try to recapture Glasgow with ten thousand soldiers. He refused to listen to his staff about the disadvantages they faced."

She breathed deeply and splayed her hands on the table, still fighting with her feelings.

"Jesus, they didn't have a chance. They were too far from base and without any real support or resupply. When it began to turn against them, they had nowhere to retreat to and we didn't have enough aircraft to lift them all out."

"What about an evacuation or fall-back. Surely the operation was planned with 'actions-on' and contingencies?" Marcus asked, knowing that there was probably no such thing for the ill-fated forces in Glasgow.

Joey shook his head and looked at Kelly, unsure of what to say. He squirmed in his seat with discomfort and cleared his throat as he searched his mind for the right words to use.

"Uh, well that's where the General got the idea for nukes," Joey finally informed them. "He ordered a MOAB to be dropped on the city while the troops were still on the ground."

"Fuck me," Marcus gasped.

Steve looked at his brother, completely unaware of what they were saying. "What's a *'MOAB'*, is it an atom bomb?"

Marcus shook his head, his eyes locked on Kelly and Joey as they sat in silence before him.

"Massive Ordinance Air Blast, also known as the *'Mother of All Bombs'* or *'Daisy Cutter.'* It's the biggest non-nuclear weapon in the world and can take out an entire city, and that crazy bastard dropped it on his own troops."

Kelly nodded with fear in her eyes. She could see the expression on Marcus' face as he studied her with suspicion. She did not like the idea of them suddenly declaring her and Joey as a threat due to orders of an insane army officer.

"So he tried a nuke next?"

"No, he hit Newcastle and Leeds with another MOAB after that. Newcastle burned for three weeks before the fires finally died out."

She watched Marcus for any signs of change in his feelings, but he was hard to read. His face, although it was stern and his eyes piercing, showed no overt signs of aggression towards them, but at the same time, revealed no indication of understanding that Kelly and Joey were not responsible for the decisions of their commander.

"Look," Kelly began in an attempt at explaining herself and gesturing to Joey sat beside her. "You should understand as well as anyone, we have orders to follow. *We* didn’t decide to drop the bombs."

Marcus shook his head in disbelief. He imagined living people were probably still hiding within those cities.

"So, where was the nuke bomb dropped?" he asked in an unemotional voice.

"Which one?" Joey asked in reply, indicating to the people of the mansion that more than one nuclear bomb had been detonated.

Jake's head shot up with an expression of alarm. "Jesus, you mean they've dropped others?"

Kelly glanced nervously at the people staring back at her.

"A hydrogen bomb was dropped on London six days ago," she said with a sigh, feeling that they were digging themselves into a deeper hole. "It was so infested that it was decided the city was to be wiped from the map."

"As well as the surrounding towns…" Marcus added, knowing the size of the devastation that a hydrogen bomb could cause.

"I'm surprised you didn’t see or hear it," Kelly replied in a quiet voice, barely more than a whisper.

Marcus leaned forward, staring straight at her. "What about the bomb we saw a few days ago, the tactical nuke, where was it dropped?"

"Stoke-on-Trent."

"Shit," Steve exclaimed, "that’s only thirty miles or so from here. What about the radiation?"

Kelly shook her head, attempting to swallow another mouthful of soup. Since the conversation had turned so sour and she and her co-pilot were being looked upon as being responsible for the destruction of the cities, her appetite had begun to fade.

"I told you, it was a tactical nuke, low yield and the radiation is minimal, especially at this distance."

Marcus felt a sense of haste, as though he needed to get the information as quickly as possible.

"Right, where is the General planning on nuking next?"

Kelly shrugged her shoulders. "I don't know. We were supposed to report on the effects of the bomb at Stoke first, but obviously we haven't done that."

"Yet," Marcus interjected with a sneer.

Kelly looked at him and noted the change in his bearing. "Look, if you're wondering whether or not we plan to report your little gathering here, you needn't worry," she retorted in an aggressive and defensive tone.

"Our mission isn't to look for survivors or make contact with them if we come across any." She glanced at Joey before continuing. "If Gibson found out we had landed here, he would probably court martial us."

A shudder ran down Joey's back as he suddenly saw an image of them both hanging from a rope.

"I'm not going back, Kelly," he declared.

She shot him a look, the shock of the statement suddenly rattling her foundations. He looked up at her with an expression of complete calm etched across his face.

"I'm not going back to Jura. I can't."

He looked at Marcus pleadingly and then turned back to his pilot and friend. "If these people won't let me stay here, then I will take my chances on the outside, but I'm not going back to face the hangman."

"The *'hangman'*...?" Gary repeated questioningly.

Kelly sighed and looked down at the table. "Yeah, Gibson hangs people who speak out or disobey orders."

She realised that Joey was right. There was no life or real safety on Jura. Gibson's rule was totalitarian, and his most loyal troops and commanders enforced his law and will on the survivors there with a vigour that resembled the Gestapo, or KGB.

"And you two kids want to join our gang now?" Marcus asked sarcastically.

Kelly and Joey remained silent, as did the rest of the people that were assembled around the table. They all waited with anticipation to hear what Marcus would say next, but he continued to stare at the two newcomers without speaking.

Finally, he stood up and turned from the table.

"I will have to discuss it with the others," he announced, "but until we come to a decision, your weapons will remain with me and you will be placed under guard. For all we know, you could be part of a rogue unit looking for a place to stay and your story could be bullshit. You could be here to gather information on us and our defences."

Kelly nodded. She understood his suspicion and hesitation.

The next morning, as Kelly lay asleep on one of the large couches in the foyer, she was awoken by Marcus, as he nudged her in the back with the toe of his boot. She rolled over and turned to him, squinting in the semi darkness and rubbing her eyes. She looked at her watch and saw that it was almost six.

"You want a brew?" Marcus asked, holding out a cup of coffee.

She gladly accepted the steaming mug and slurped at the boiling dark fluid.

"Thanks," she croaked as the liquid ran down her dry throat.

"We've decided," Marcus began as he sat himself on the coffee table that was placed in front of the large leather sofa, "you and your buddy can stay, but you abide by our rules and you pull your weight."

Kelly looked up at him, feeling a sense of relief and optimism at the thought of not having to return to the island.

"Thanks."

"Don't thank *me*," Marcus replied, "I was all for kicking you both out, but one: you know we're here and could report it to your commander, and two: Karen and Jennifer have taken a shine to you and I don't want to get on their bad side," he said with a smile.

Marcus and the others had sat and debated late into the night. They had discussed the advantages and disadvantages of the helicopter crew becoming part of their group. Though Marcus was unsure of their real intentions, if they had any, he did reason that it would be better to have them close, rather than turn them loose.

Kelly attempted to return the smile, but it came across as more of a look of disgust as her tongue stuck to the roof of her mouth, and her teeth felt as though they had a layer of fur coating them.

"Who's Jennifer?" she asked.

"She's my wife and I'm trying to keep myself in her good books before I break the news to her," he said ambiguously.

"What news?"

"The news about what I and a few of the others will be doing with the aid of you and Joey."

His eyes glinted as he informed her that she was about to be put to the test.

Kelly's face tightened as she realised what he meant.

"Oh," she said with trepidation, "so you need us to fly you somewhere?"

Marcus nodded. "We have a few friends that have been outside the wall for the last four days and we need to look for them. I'm hoping that they're just taking cover somewhere, but if we can find them, then we need to bring them back."

Kelly shrugged. "Whatever it takes to prove that we're on your side," she replied. "Just one thing though." She looked up at him with a serious expression and then broke into a smile. "I desperately need a hot shower and a good meal first."

Marcus was about to reply when the front doors suddenly opened with a creek. Marcus spun to see what was happening and instinctively began to reach for his pistol.

A short stooping figure came scurrying in, taking small shuffling steps and mumbling, as it stared at the ground. It was Johnny. He looked even more bedraggled than usual and seemed to be completely in a world of his own as he made his way towards the stairs.

Marcus watched him with curiosity. No one had seen him since the nuke lit up the horizon, and many feared him dead.

"Johnny," Marcus called out.

The little vagrant stopped in his tracks, still mumbling to himself and staring at the floor. He did not look up or turn in the direction of Marcus' voice, and seemed to be counting something aloud.

"Johnny, you okay?" Marcus asked from across the room.

Johnny finally turned and looked up, his eyes searching the large open foyer for the source of the voice. His hair and beard were a tangle of matted strands, revealing just his eyes. They focussed on Marcus and he smiled broadly.

"Yes, I am Johnny. How are you, Marcus?" he asked matter-of-factly.

Marcus looked down at Kelly, a concerned look on his face.

"I'm fine, Johnny, what about you? We've been worried."

Johnny shook his head and smiled again, baring his stained teeth. He raised his finger and wagged it at Marcus.

"No, no, my dear sausage, you don’t need to worry about Johnny. Anyway, I have been quite busy lately and the answer is five," he nodded at Marcus who stared back at him in confusion.

"That’s right; five is the answer, on average," Johnny confirmed.

He turned and began to make his way up the stairs, continuing his count as he went, completely oblivious to the bewilderment of Marcus.

"Five what?" Marcus called after him.

Johnny stopped and leaned over the balcony. "Hmm…?"

The homeless man seemed to be in the dark as to what Marcus was asking; then he realised he had already given him the answer.

"Oh, yes, five. That's correct, on average, of course."

Marcus shook his head and put it down to the eccentricity of the strange man.

"By the way," Johnny called as he walked along the corridor that led to the bedrooms, "someone has parked their helicopter on your lawn."

"Who the hell is that?" Kelly asked as she struggled to come to terms with the strange sight she had just seen, and the completely incoherent conversation she had witnessed.

"Johnny," Marcus replied with a shrug of the shoulder. "He's our celebrity tramp. He was pretty well known around these parts, apparently, before the dead began to walk. The man even spent a long time wandering amongst them, pretending to be one."

"Jesus," Kelly rubbed her eyes, still unsure of the strange exchange she had just observed, and then drained the last of her coffee.

14

The sound of the helicopter was deafening, even from inside the house, as its engine howled and its rotors pounded at the air. The children, and even many of the adults, pressed themselves against the windows of the lobby. Their warm breath misting the cold windows as they crammed themselves shoulder to shoulder and peered out, speaking excitedly about the new addition to their band of survivors.

Naturally, the children all wanted to take a ride in the aircraft, but for now they had to contend with helping Gary and Sophie with their rounds through the park as they checked on the animals. They watched with envy at the awe-inspiring machine, as the power of the engines and downwash created a gale around it strong enough to flatten the grass in a wide area around the aircraft.

"Will we get to go up in the helicopter, Dad?" Sarah asked with glee.

Steve glanced at Claire, her mother, unsure of what to say and how to say it. He stooped and held her by the shoulders as he peered into her large brown eyes.

"I'm not sure if that would be a good idea, sweetheart."

He saw the deflation in her face and sighed, as he knew that his simple answer would not be enough. He led her away to one side and out of earshot from the others.

"Listen," he began in a reasoning voice, "I'm telling you this because I know you're strong enough to understand and handle it."

Steve paused and watched her. Her eyes focussed on him and immediately, she had become an adult.

She nodded.

"We're surrounded by those things, Sarah. A ride in the helicopter would not be very enjoyable right now. I'm not particularly looking forward to it myself."

The little girl with the ability to think in such a mature manner at times, nodded in understanding.

"Okay, Dad."

Steve kissed her on the forehead and ruffled her hair.

"I'll tell you what; when we get back, I will ask Kelly if she will take you for a ride to the north over the animal pens. That should be fun, don't you think?"

Sarah grinned, a smile that stretched the entire width of her face. "Yup, that would be brill, Dad."

She trotted back across to her mother and turned to grin at her father. She was excited and Steve knew there was no way she would let him off the hook when it came to his promise of a flight in the helicopter.

Claire looked at Steve with a disapproving expression. He could only shrug in return.

Steve, Helen, and Lee, were loaded down with all the ammunition that they could carry. Each had a rifle and their pouches were close to bursting point with the spare magazines. With the addition of the weapons and ammunition they took from the helicopter, they now had seven rifles amongst the group of survivors at the park, providing Stu and his men were still alive.

Kelly, dressed in her flight suit and carrying her helmet, walked in through the main door. She looked at Steve and nodded.

"We're ready to go, if you are," she announced as she gave him a thumbs up.

She glanced about her and realised that everyone's attention was focussed on her. They watched her admiringly as she stood in her green pilot's uniform, making her feel a little self-conscious as a result.

"Don't mind us," Jake said from the table where he sat holding a cup of coffee and grinning at Kelly. "It's not often that we see a pretty pilot walking about around here. In this day and age, you're a celebrity; bigger than the 'Beckhams'."

Kelly smiled at him and turned to Steve, gesturing that they should go.

Steve nodded and turned back to Sarah, still smiling at him as she stood holding Claire's hand.

"We won't be gone long, kiddo," he said, smiling and ruffling her hair once more as he walked by her.

A commotion behind him made him turn. Marcus was approaching, pushing the dishevelled and withered form of Stephanie before him. To the rest of the house members, she looked little different from the thousands of walking corpses that clambered at their walls.

Her long greasy hair was matted to her face in thick strands, obscuring her pale and gaunt features. The filth-encrusted and tattered clothes that were made for a much larger person hung from her shrunken frame. Her gait no longer bore the confidence that she once walked and strutted around the mansion with. Gone was the assertive and overbearing woman that Stephanie had once been, only to be replaced with a cowering wreck, shuffling gingerly with stooped shoulders and her face turned towards the ground.

She avoided eye contact with the people that stood around watching her. Her whole demeanour was one of fear and uncertainty. Her shoulders trembled and she whimpered continually as she was pushed along by Marcus.

Steve looked on in shock. He had seen Stephanie only in the shadows and gloom of her cell, her true appearance being obscured from him by darkness. He was well aware that she had been reduced to a glimmer of the woman she once was, but now, in the light of day and presented before him, he could see how delicate and unthreatening she had become.

For a fleeting instant, Steve almost felt a pang of guilt. He had never been a cruel man or the sort to stand idle while others suffered, but before his composure deteriorated into one of regret, the memories of what she had done and the resulting deaths sprang to the front of his mind, hanging before his eyes, a stark reminder of the reasons for the woman's suffering.

He clenched his teeth, staring down at the cowering Stephanie who seemed to have lost a foot in height during her incarceration. For a moment, he felt like snatching her away from his brother and dragging her back to the storeroom, and bolting the door shut until she finally died from malnutrition and infection.

He looked back up at Marcus, remembering the agreement that they had all come to the night before when they had sat discussing the fate of the helicopter crew. It had also been decided that Stephanie would be released far away from the park, in an area where she could cause them no further harm.

Lee had protested vehemently and stuck to his belief that they should feed her to the dead that surrounded their walls. It was only due to the influential objections of Gary and Jake that it was decided they would turn her loose.

Jennifer, the ever-present voice of reason in the ear of Marcus when his rage and testosterone threatened to boil over, had managed to convince her husband not to go to Stephanie's cell and put a bullet through her head to end the discussion, once and for all.

Kelly looked on in horror. She glanced from the bound woman being pressed forward by Marcus, to the people that stood around her, staring at the figure with hatred and the lust for revenge burning in their eyes.

At first glance, Kelly had believed the woman to be one of the dead, kept inside the house for whatever reason. It was only when she heard the whimpers that emitted from within the mass of filthy rags that she realised the being in front of her was alive.

In her mind, Kelly asked herself, *'What could this woman have done that was so terrible to make these people to hate her so much?'*

She looked to Marcus, questioningly.

Steve noticed her concern and stepped across to her.

"Her name is Stephanie," he whispered as he leaned in close. "She used to be a member of the group, and even worked here before all of this began. She tried to kill us all."

Kelly's head snapped around to face him, as she was finally able to tear her eyes away from the foul image making its way across the foyer floor.

"That's right," Steve continued, as he locked eyes with Kelly, "she and her husband opened the rear gate and let a bunch of those things in here. The thousands of dead that are now at our walls and surrounding the park…she led them here to us."

Steve paused to allow the information to sink in.

"She also sabotaged our fuel supply, which resulted in a couple of deaths when we went out to find more."

"What are you going to do to her?" Kelly asked, stealing another glance at the wretched appearance of the suffering woman.

Steve shrugged. "Turn her loose. We'll drop her far from here so she can't cause us any more drama. We've packed her a small bag of supplies that will give her a chance of survival, so it's all in her hands now."

Marcus continued towards the door, and Steve, Lee, and Helen followed. Kelly remained watching them, deep in thought, then snapped from her stupor and headed for the entrance. She felt unsettled by the events she had just witnessed. A group of people that seemed so intent on survival and based everything on harmony, strong in their unity and care for one another, yet they were capable of such cruel and draconian punishment of a living person.

She had no quarrel with having to deal with people that they viewed or had proved themselves as a threat in a harsh and unforgiving manner, but to keep them locked up and close to starvation seemed excessively brutal to her. Still, she was aware that she was new to the band of survivors at the Safari Park, and had not suffered the loss and pain that they had experienced at the hands of their prisoner.

She decided that it was not her place to judge their actions.

"And don't come back, you fat bitch," a voice called out from amongst the group.

Lisa jumped forward and placed herself between the doorway and Stephanie. Her face was red with anger and her lips curled back, revealing her snarling teeth.

"If it was up to me, I would feed you to those freaks out there," she spat. "If I ever see you again, you can bet your fat arse I will do exactly that."

As a final gesture, Lisa swung her arm, palm open, and whacked Stephanie across the face. The sound of the slap resounded in the hall of the house, sounding like the cracking of a whip.

Stephanie yelped and fell to the side from the force of the blow. Marcus caught her before she fell and pulled her upright, aiming her towards the door.

"That's enough, Lisa. She won't be able to hurt any of us now. I promise, you won't see her again," Marcus said in a calm and reassuring voice but with a tone that warned Lisa that he would tolerate no further attacks on his charge.

He placed his hand on Lisa's shoulder and gently steered her to the side, away from Stephanie. He felt no pity for the woman that had suffered at their hands for so long, but he did not see any reason to add to her misery by allowing the more aggressive and bloodthirsty of the group to exacerbate her condition.

Inside the helicopter, Marcus placed the headset over his ears so that he could remain in communication with the pilot over the din of the engine. Steve, Helen, and Lee sat buckled into their seats with Stephanie placed on the floor in front of them.

Marcus had decided that the doors of the aircraft should remain open to give them a better view and hope of finding Stu and the others as they followed their intended route. During the planning phase of Stu's task to find vehicles and supplies, he had given Marcus a detailed briefing of the locations they planned to travel to, including alternatives and the routes they would use.

Marcus hoped beyond hope that Stu and his team were holed up somewhere and still alive.

Over the past eight months, he had lost many friends to the rising of the dead, either directly or indirectly. Ian and Yan had been killed in battles with rogue military units and militia, as they had slogged their way from the other side of the planet. Sini had been lost because of his refusal to leave Sandra to die alone, and in the process, the tough Serb had saved the lives of Marcus, Stu, Jim, and Hussein.

In Baghdad, they had said goodbye to Nicky, Eddie and Paul. Insurgents that had left three other members of their team dead, and wounded Nicky in an attack. Eddie and Paul had parted company with them because they lived on the opposite side of the globe, and teamed up with other men from New

Zealand and Australia that were attempting to make a break out for themselves.

Marcus reflected for a moment, wondering if they were still alive and if they had made it home. He closed his eyes, picturing them safe and well with their families, but he knew that the odds had been stacked highly against them and the chances of them both making it were extremely unlikely.

The thought of losing more friends to the dead, and the circumstances that resulted from the new world, filled him with a dread that weighed heavy on his heart. They had been through so much together, and defeated every obstacle thrown against them, that Marcus saw it as a cruel twist if he was to be the only one remaining.

Steve felt the helicopter rise beneath him, carrying him with it into the air as the pitch of the engine rose and the beat of the rotor blades increased to a battering thump. He had never been in a helicopter before, and for a second; he grew with excitement before remembering the circumstances that had led to the moment, bringing him back to reality with an emotional bump.

He looked across at Marcus, who was speaking with the pilot through his headset and studying a map that he held in front of him. Steve watched his brother in awe for a few seconds, feeling blessed that they had such a man to lead them. Although he had never acknowledged it in the past, he now admitted to himself that he admired the man that Marcus had become; an immense feeling of respect grew within him.

Steve looked out to his left and saw the house shrinking beneath them as they gained altitude. He could see the people that had become a family to him, standing in the gravelled car park in front of the mansion, watching them take off in to the sky. Soon, they were so high that the figures on the ground had turned to little black specks, looking like ants in a model landscape with toy cars and a doll's house.

The wind howled around them and blew in through the open doors from the downwash of the spinning rotors, creating a gale within the aircraft. Conversation would have been impossible due to the noise, so Steve occupied himself with watching the landscape below and the actions of the pilot, as she manipulated the controls of the machine.

Kelly and Marcus were deep in conversation, obviously discussing the route and locations they needed to travel.

Lee seemed to be enjoying the ride and remained close to the door, one hand clutching the buckle of his seatbelt and the other holding onto his rifle, as he leaned forward and watched the ground below. His wispy, mousey-coloured hair flew in all directions and he squinted at the cold, stinging wind that blew against his face, but he remained enthralled with the sights below as he studied his surroundings.

Helen did not seem to be too eager to see the land below and the numerous dead that roamed the surface of the planet. Instead, she contented herself with keeping an eye on Stephanie, as she lay prone on the floor of the aircraft. She rested her head on Steve's shoulder and moved her body closer for comfort and warmth. She looked up at him and smiled, before kissing him on the cheek and mouthing the words that always made Steve grin like a child who had just been given the greatest present he could want.

"I love you, too," he screamed back, trying desperately to be heard over the noise of the aircraft.

It was only after he had said it that he realised how ridiculous the words sounded when they were screamed into the face of a person.

Helen smiled and shook her head. Steve felt her body convulsing gently at his side as she laughed at his attempt at airborne romance.

'Superman never had this problem with Lois,' he mused to himself, comparing the romantic flights of the fictitious superhero and his girlfriend to his own.

He looked down at the ground and saw the southern wall of the Safari Park pass by beneath them. The contrast between the interior and exterior of the park was breath-taking. Just moments before, he had seen lush green fields sweeping below. They seemed endless and completely untouched by the ravages of the dead.

As they flew over the stone barrier that held the hordes at bay, the blissful landscape gave way to the grotesque and horrifying image of thousands of decaying bodies clustering around the walls of the park.

A sea of black miniature shapes carpeted the ground like a bubbling oil slick, and stretched out far beyond the perimeter of the park. It was impossible to see anything on the ground below their feet, as every available space was crammed with the bodies of the dead.

As the helicopter passed over them, their ghostly faces turned upwards in unison as though being prompted to do so or controlled by an unseen force. That same driving force was the instinct that told them that the thundering machine passing over their heads contained living people, with warm blood flowing through their veins.

The dark seething mass surged with excitement as they stared at the aircraft above them. In all directions, the mottled sea below swelled and rippled towards the area directly below the helicopter, as the dead trampled and fought one another in their desire to get closer to the thing that they coveted more than anything; living flesh.

Lee shuddered and instinctively adjusted his position on his seat, moving himself back a little, away from the open door. He looked down and checked his harness, giving it a tug, confirming that he was still securely fastened in and unlikely to fall out. He decided that he no longer needed to be so bold. He could still see the uncountable figures below and that was enough.

He checked his belt again and gripped his rifle close to his body.

He looked across at Steve and realised he had been watching the whole time. Lee smiled and shrugged his shoulders.

"You never know," he bellowed across to his friend against the scream and thump of the aircraft.

He tried his best to appear casual, but he could see that Steve also held the same concerns and remained seated away from the door.

Steve nodded and smiled, unwilling to waste his effort in having a conversation that would be mostly drowned out by the noise of the engine.

A few hundred metres further out, the people in the helicopter could see that the crowds had thinned substantially. It was now possible to see the ground between the thousands of shambling figures heading in the direction of the park.

Although they were more spread out, their numbers were still immeasurable. It appeared that every member of the un-dead from the surrounding towns and villages, even cities, were converging on the Safari Park. They staggered and stubbornly made their way across the fields, along the roads and through the streets.

It was an exodus of decaying flesh.

Marcus felt a tinge of panic rising within him as he saw the scale of their predicament. Everywhere he looked, the ground was teeming with them as they slowly swayed and lumbered forward. He knew that it did not take much to attract the dead. Even the dead attracted the dead, and all it took was for one of them to become animated, and the others around them would take notice, following them blindly.

A few kilometres later, Marcus looked at his map and craned his neck to see over the pilot's seat and through the cockpit window. A large built-up area was approaching. A housing estate with sprawling streets and rooftops stretched off in the distance to the east and rural countryside, and farmland to the west, a wide dual lane carriageway separating the two contrasting landscapes.

"Okay, Kelly," he said into the mouthpiece as he leaned forward and tapped the pilot on the shoulder. "There's a major junction up ahead. Settle us there if you will, about fifty feet off the ground."

Kelly glanced back over her shoulder, unsure of why Marcus wanted her to hover in that area. She decided not to question it.

"Roger that," she replied.

At the given area, Kelly pulled back on the cyclic stick and reduced the lift on the collective lever, dropping the revolutions on the throttle. The angle of the rotors shifted slightly, allowing the aircraft to slow down and gently settle into a hover as they began to descend towards the ground.

Joey busied himself by checking the ground below them, calling out their altitude and making Kelly aware of any obstacles or hazards such as buildings and raised power cables.

Kelly concentrated on keeping the pitch of the aircraft level with the horizon, checking the instruments in front of her and using her own judgement as she looked out from the cockpit at the land around her. She continuously adjusted the cyclic and throttle lever to avoid stalling or descending too rapidly. At thirty metres, she pushed on the anti-torque pedals at her feet, manoeuvred the helicopter so that it was directly above the junction, and turned to face the housing estate to the east and into the wind.

"Twenty-five metres," Joey called through the intercom as he studied the ground below and kept Kelly informed of their altitude. "Pylons, one hundred metres to port, ground clearance good."

Kelly could see the streets of the housing estate beginning to fill with thousands of bodies as they became aware of the sound of the helicopter. They poured out from the buildings and houses, and soon they were staggering towards the junction, *en-masse*.

She began to feel nervous and remembered the mechanical issues they had suffered in the past with the old aircraft. Although she was confident in her ability to remain airborne and regain control of the machine from high altitude, she doubted that she would be able to recover them in time from just twenty metres above ground if they were to encounter a problem.

"Marcus," she called through her mouthpiece, "we don't want to be hovering like this for too long. This bucket is old and unreliable, at best."

"Understood," Marcus replied, "we won't be here long."

Joey looked back over his shoulder and saw Marcus climbing to his feet. He had no idea what the man was doing or what his intentions were, and he looked to Kelly with a raised eyebrow and motioned for her to check for herself.

Marcus was standing in the centre of the passenger compartment and lifting Stephanie to her feet. The woman's eyes were wide with terror as she was dragged over to the open door and forced to see the hordes of bodies approaching from the built-up area.

Steve looked across at Lee questioningly. He had no idea what it was that his brother was doing, and looked on as Marcus gripped Stephanie by the back of the neck and turned her face to his.

"You see that, Stephanie?" he screamed over the noise of the helicopter, her face just centimetres from his.

Steve, Helen, and Lee, could barely hear what he was saying, but Kelly could hear him clearly through the intercom.

"You tried to let them in, Stephanie. You tried to kill us all."

Stephanie trembled with terror and babbled away incoherently. She looked from Marcus, and then to Steve and Helen, pleadingly. Her eyes resembled a trapped animal's as she was completely at their mercy.

"You tried to kill us, Stephanie. My wife and kids are in that place and *you*, tried to fucking kill them all."

Marcus was red in the face and his words were accompanied with strings of spittle as his anger smashed its way through his composure. The veins and tendons in his neck protruded from his skin and his eyes flashed with wildness that Steve had never seen before in his brother.

"We're surrounded, Stephanie. There are a million of those cunts outside our walls and *you* fucking led them to us."

Stephanie had become limp in Marcus' grasp under the onslaught of his tirade, and he had to use all of his strength to keep her from collapsing to the floor. He grasped her by the hair, pulling her up, and began screaming in her face.

Steve looked on, seeing the rage in his brother's eyes and noting that his knuckles had turned white as he tightly clung to Stephanie's hair.

Kelly and Joey watched in concern. They saw a man close to madness and capable of anything as he unleashed his rage against his captive. Kelly shuddered and attempted to attract Marcus' attention through the intercom.

He turned and glared at her, making her shrink back in her seat.

The others looked on as Marcus continued his tirade.

"What did you think was going to happen, Stephanie?" he bellowed. "Did you think you would actually get away with what you did?"

He gripped her harder by her scalp and dragged her closer to the door so that her head and shoulders protruded outside the aircraft.

Below them, the first of the bodies had arrived. They hissed and snarled up at the helicopter, reaching and clutching into the air with their bony rotting hands. More of them were arriving by the second, and soon the ground was covered by the creatures, all clambering for the living flesh that they could see hovering above them.

Stephanie was screaming. Steve could hear her even over the engine. She struggled desperately, but in vain, against Marcus as he continued to bombard her with a torrent of verbal abuse.

Lee watched, a wry smile of amusement subtly creasing his face as he saw the hated Stephanie squirm the way he had so longed to see.

"I should fucking feed you to them," Marcus screamed as he wrenched Stephanie back into the helicopter, planting her just a short step away from the door.

She remained there, on her knees, her face turned to her lap as her shoulders convulsed with sobs.

Marcus sat back in his seat, glaring at the pathetic figure kneeling before him. Her misery was now complete. She had languished in the cell, suffering from depravation and praying for death, but now, after believing that her end was imminent, she desperately clung to life with terror filling her every sense.

"Okay, Kelly," Marcus nodded, his expression settling back to his normal 'poker face', "take us up."

Kelly complied and increased the throttle. The aircraft soared into the sky in a vertical lift as the ground dropped away below them.

Lee looked across at Marcus, glancing at Stephanie as he did so. He raised an eyebrow in wonder. Marcus just nodded and continued to watch dishevelled figure in front of him.

Helen also eyed Marcus, concerned that he was beginning to lose his mind and composure. She nudged Steve at her side without saying anything, but he knew what her question was.

Steve looked back at her with a frown and nodded as his face changed to a slight smile, telling her that everything was okay and Marcus was fine.

The helicopter continued to rise.

Steve saw a sudden flurry of movement to his right and looked up to see his brother springing from his seat. With lightning speed, Marcus pivoted and placed his boot into the area between Stephanie's shoulder blades, and with a heave, launched her forward and out through the door on the starboard side of the aircraft.

"I told you I would let you go," Marcus shouted after her.

Stephanie flew into the air, and with a barely audible scream, tumbled towards the ground.

Marcus did not bother to watch her land, but he knew her fate. The thousands of reaching arms that awaited her would cushion her fall, and then her true terror would begin as she was torn apart and eaten alive by the rapacious creatures below.

He turned around and saw five sets of eyes staring back at him.

The only face that did not have complete horror etched into it, was the one belonging to Lee. Instead, he looked on with an expression of compliance and understanding that Marcus' actions had been well founded and necessary.

"Okay, Kelly," Marcus said through the intercom in a casual tone and as though the incident had never occurred.

"Let's go get Stu and the others. Head north-east on a bearing of nine six zero mils for seven kilometres until we hit the main carriageway, then follow it east to the car dealership that Stu was headed for."

Marcus sat back down and turned to look at Steve and Helen. Both of them stared back at him with shock and concern.

"We couldn’t let her live," Marcus hollered as he leaned closer to them. "You knew her well enough. She would've done *anything* to carry out her vengeance against us."

Helen nodded and after a moment of reflection, Steve did too.

Marcus was right. Though his actions were savage and brutal, Stephanie needed to die and they could not risk leaving her alive and capable of returning to the park.

Marcus sat back and buckled his safety harness, catching a glimpse of Kelly's bulging and nervous eyes as she watched him through her mirror at the front of the cockpit.

Marcus smiled at her as the helicopter gained speed and headed northeast.

Steve sat thinking about what Marcus had said and done. He then remembered the punishment that they had dealt out to Tony all those months ago.

It was a brutal world and only the brutal could survive in it.

15

Something was happening in the road ahead of him. It was quite a way off, but there was definitely activity. At that distance, with his deteriorating eyesight, it was impossible to tell what was going on, but he could see movement and hear well enough.

There was a mass of moving shapes in the centre of the long and straight stretch of road. The bundle of silhouettes and colours remained low to the ground and in continual jerking and swaying motion. Shrieks and howls accompanied the shapes as they bobbed and weaved on the surface of the tarmac.

Blood-curding screams of agony from a creature that was trapped and dying echoed around the low-lying hills of the countryside, being carried for great distances in the otherwise still and peaceful air.

The noises struck terror into him and he could physically feel the fear as it crept over his skin. It was like an army of crawling insects, penetrating deep into his core, making him want to turn around and leave the area as quickly as possible before he was subjected to the same pain and horror.

He had never heard a sound like it; each howl seemed to be filled with more excruciating pain, and lasted longer than the previous gut-wrenching shriek.

Andy stopped, afraid to move any further along the road and approach the unknown. Fear tugged at every fibre in his emaciated body, warning him of imminent danger and tearing at his festering soul to turn him around.

He looked to his left and then his right, searching the area with his cold and frightening unblinking eyes that masked his true, pleasant and caring, nature. High hedgerows sprung up along the road on either side of him. Stripped of their leaves by winter and filled with pointed thorns and sharp branches that would tear at his flesh and strip his delicate body to the bone;

they created an impenetrable barrier that presented no possibility of him being able to negotiate.

He turned around and faced in the direction he had come. The memories of the destroyed city and the thousands of broken and burning bodies that now littered its streets tore at his mind. He could not go back. All that awaited him there was death and destruction with no hope of finding the beautiful things that he liked so much.

There were no trees left standing and no birds to flutter and sing in the skies above the ruined metropolis. They had been replaced by smoke and ash, clogging the air and turning the place into a twisted and grotesque reflection of the inhabitants that had roamed its streets before it was destroyed.

He had no choice but to continue. He could wait at the roadside for the howls to stop and the shapes to disperse, but he could be there for a long time, and there was always the chance of him becoming the next victim to disrupt the peaceful landscape with cries of anguish and torture.

It had been nearly a week since Andy had left the ruined city. He had headed deep into the countryside, hoping to find a place safe and far away from the others like him. His hopes of finding the people who had spared his life, and set him free, were dashed when he came across their convoy of trucks, burning in the road. They were surrounded by the shadowy monsters that tore and feasted on the bodies that were scattered in a wide area around their doomed vehicles.

Since then, he had meandered through the country lanes, avoiding any contact with the lifeless shapes roaming the land. He stopped from time to time when a building or an object that stirred a memory from deep within him, a murky and sometimes confusing reflection of his previous existence, roused his curiosity.

For two whole days, he had staggered along the road, completely transfixed with the football that he kicked before him, staggering after it with an excitement and pleasure that made him want to continue punting the bouncing sphere for all eternity.

In the garden of an abandoned house, he had discovered the ball amongst other discarded items. At first, he had been baffled by the object and unsure of what to do with it but, despite his bewilderment, something inside him had urged him to remain holding it. It was not until he dropped the ball that a cascade of emotions suddenly flooded his decaying mind. Thousands of images bombarded him all at once, almost knocking him flat with the sudden force and vividness of them.

The football bounced once, then again and again, all the time moving away from him with each impact with the ground.

Andy groaned with recognition as he watched it move and saw the distant memories of vibrant figures, running around with the grace of birds on lush green grass, chasing the football ahead of them.

The ball came to a stop in a clump of long grass. He moved towards it, his eyes fixed on the small black and white leather globe. As he staggered forward, he instinctively threw his leg out in front of him, the toe of his right shoe making contact with the object and launching it away from him.

It sailed through the air, no higher than a few centimetres from the ground, and collided with the tall fence of the garden with a resounding thump and rattle. It finally rolled to a stop in the long, unkempt weeds that sprung from the neglected flowerbed running around the perimeter of the garden.

Andy groaned with a delight that surged up from within him and released a renewed energy, making him want to kick it again. He remembered the joy he had gained from the same activity in the past as he and many others ran about, hollering to one another, kicking the ball for long distances and then sprinting after it.

Recollections of himself racing along a field, calling out to his fellow players chasing a football with vitality that he could no longer match, flooded his brain, and released an avalanche of powerful emotions.

He lumbered after the ball on rickety legs and, again, threw out his leg and kicked it once more. More grunts and groans erupted from his throat in triumph as he watched the round object glide through the air, higher and further with each kick, as he became more accurate with his aim.

For the entire day, Andy chased it around the large garden. The sounds of his groans of accomplishment and the crashes and bangs as the ball ricocheted from the fence, garden furniture and walls of the house, echoed long into the night.

He took the football with him and, for a long time, gently nudged it ahead of him with his foot as he continued his endless journey through the winding and twisting country lanes. Sometimes he would give it a powerful strike and send it bounding along the road, filling him with joy as he chased after it with clumsy strides.

The game came to an abrupt end when, on the second day, Andy launched the football with a powerful boot and sent it flying along the lane and into a ditch at the roadside. The trough was deep and filled with sludge, tangles of wire and broken branches and the ball sat snared in the centre, half-buried in the mire.

With a heavy heart, he had to leave the beloved sphere behind for fear of risking irreparable injury to his fragile body while trying to retrieve it. He continued along the country roads, alone and without the company of his football, feeling a sense of despair as he stared at the road below his shuffling feet.

His solitude was complete.

The few people that remained were afraid of him and would either run away or try to hurt him. The birds would never stay still long enough for him to get close to as they hopped along the tops of the hedgerows or pecked at the dirt on the roadside. The radiant and colourful flowers that he picked soon withered and died in his cold and twisted hands.

Andy was lonely.

His disgust and loathing for the others like him meant that he would always be caught between the two new worlds. The world of the living, and the world of the dead, and neither of them would ever accept him.

Cautiously, he continued forward. He was getting closer, and now, the howls of pain and terror had ceased, but the moving shapes that blocked his path remained. They were more visible now and Andy could see that they were figures with arms, legs and teeth. Biting, tearing teeth that ravaged everything before them, devouring flesh from bone. They were the figures of the repulsive monsters that he feared and despised.

He could hear their grunts and growls as they fought with one another over something that was on the ground in front of them. They snatched the shreds of meat from each other's hands and slurped hungrily as they stuffed the bloodied pulps into their gaping mouths.

When he was close and able to see clearly, Andy stopped and studied the scene just twenty metres ahead of him. A group of grey and grotesque beings knelt in the road over a torn open carcass. Its innards were spread in a wide area and the creatures feeding on them gorged and scoffed at the long strands of bloodied intestine, as they snatched clumps of flesh from one another and off the ground.

Two of the figures were tugging at the ribcage of the carcass, as they attempted to prise it open further to reach every morsel of flesh from within. Andy could hear the slap of blood-soaked meat against the hard tarmac of the road, and the sickening crack of bone as the ribcage was wrenched open and snapped from the spinal column.

He felt no desire to join them in their feast, or to snatch what meat he could and scurry away to feed. He wanted nothing to do with what the foul creatures did because he was not like them. He knew that he appeared much the same, but in his mind, though working less perfectly than it once had, he was completely different and held nothing in common with the monsters that now roamed the surface of the earth.

There was a gap to the left of the road. It was large enough to allow him to pass without coming into contact with the group. He decided that he would attempt to slip by the feeding misshapen monsters and continue on his way along the road.

Carefully, moving slowly so that he did not attract their attention with any sudden or clumsy movements, Andy moved towards the left hand edge of the road and began to negotiate his way through to the other side.

The ground beneath his feet was awash with blood and small pieces of blood-stained meat. Small shards of broken and gnawed bone lay discarded in a wide arc around the area of the carcass as the voracious creatures tore and stripped away the flesh from their victim.

Andy's foot scraped on a sliver of bone that then became lodged in the grip of his shoe and scratched at the surface of the road. The noise attracted the attention of the others and they turned to look at him, their concentration dragged from the bloodied remains on the ground. They snarled at him as they protectively crowded around their lifeless victim. Their pale and gaunt faces contrasted harshly with the smeared and glistening blood covering their features. Their sunken dark eyes watched Andy as he continued forward, shuffling through the narrow space between them and the edge of the road as he attempted to pass by them.

Without warning, the closest of the group, a creature that had once been a young and pretty woman, turned on him, groaning aggressively and reaching out towards him. She lashed at him with her clawed bony hands, catching Andy in the abdomen before he was able to step back or defend himself against the assault.

Her withered fingers, as sharp as talons, tore at the flesh of Andy's stomach, and ripped a long, gaping wound in his belly that threatened to tear further against the weight of his intestines and other internal organs pressing at the gash from within.

Andy clutched at his wound and shuffled backwards from his attacker as she approached for another assault. She wailed and snarled as she lunged again with her hands outstretched before her, reaching for his face and neck.

Suddenly, she dropped to the right and hit the ground with a loud crunch as her head bounced from the tarmac. A hole had appeared in the left hand side of her head, exposing the smashed skull and mangled brain.

Andy remained still, staring at the body at his feet and clutching the bloodied tyre iron in one hand and his torn abdomen in the other. He growled in anger at the fallen creature as he looked down and studied the damage she had inflicted on him. With a rage that seemed to fill his every thought, he brought the iron bar down again with all the force he could muster. It smashed into her head with a loud crunch, cracking the skull and separating the top half of the cranium from the rest of the head.

The exposed brain, pulped and coated in black, coagulated blood, oozed from the gaping hole in the dead woman's skull. Andy began to raise the weapon and pound away at the body repeatedly, smashing the head to an indistinguishable mush and almost severing it completely from the body, leaving it attached by just a few strands of sinew and vertebrae.

When it was no longer recognisable as a human face, Andy stopped. The remaining figures watched him, as they stayed crouched over the carcass in the road. None of them moved towards him, and after a moment of study, they turned their attention back to devouring the remains of the unfortunate creature that had wandered across their path.

Andy moved on, keeping his distance but his eyes remaining fixed on the despicable and misshapen monsters gorging themselves close by.

Only when he was almost clear of them did Andy realise that what they were feeding on was a dog. Its brown and black furry tail protruded out from beneath its bloodied and churned body. Its head lay discarded in a thick pool of blood just a short distance from the ravaging creatures.

He staggered onwards along the road, away from the revolting scene, holding onto the gaping wound in his stomach. He felt terrified of the damage that had been caused to him and he continually glanced down at his injuries, moaning softly to himself as he caught glimpses of his fetid innards protruding through the tear in his flesh.

He needed to find a way of repairing the damage. He was well aware that if left, the hole would tear further, compromising his flesh and threatening any chance of his continued existence.

Andy knew that the damage was not enough to finish him, but he also knew that if he left it untreated, the damage would spread and cause further harm to his already deteriorated body. In his mixed up and jumbled thought process, he was incapable of forming a solution to his predicament.

At a safe distance, he stopped and attempted to close his jacket over the wound, but no matter how hard he tried, the zipper would not fasten. His clumsy fingers and ill coordination added to his frustration and the state of his clothing was a further hindrance. The jacket that he wore was rotten and encrusted with filth. Grime and his own decaying flesh had penetrated every fibre, including the teeth on the zip. He let out a long groan in annoyance as he pictured his slow demise due to the damage caused in the attack from the foul and repulsive creature in the road.

A small sense of satisfaction grew within him as he remembered the death that he had dealt out to his assailant, but it was short lived.

No amount of vengeance would fix him.

He groaned again, louder and more poignant as he stared down at the tear in his flesh. He could see the swollen blue and grey internal organs pushing at the opening from inside, swarming with pale and bloated maggots that squirmed and riddled about in the soft tissue.

Panic and a feeling of complete defencelessness began to rise inside of him. He realised that, if he was attacked again there was little he could do to protect himself while in the condition he was in. He could easily find himself as nothing more than a limbless writhing mess, discarded in the middle of the road, like the countless bones strewn around the cities after being picked clean.

Something moved to his right within the thick bushes at the roadside. He spun in fear of another assault, raising the tyre iron above his head and ready to crush the skull of his foe.

The anticipated attack never came and Andy could see nothing.

He was about to continue walking when he heard a sound coming from the same bushes he had sensed movement from. He did not recognise the noise, but he somehow felt a sense of familiarity towards it.

It was not the moan of another of the beasts like him, nor was it the sound of a bird in the hedgerow, twittering and chirping as it hopped from branch to branch.

This sound was very different from what he was used to.

Andy stooped slightly, bending his creaking knees and craning his neck in an attempt to see into the thick undergrowth at the side of the country lane. It was hard to see anything in the shadow of the hedgerow and, at first; he hesitated in moving forward to inspect the source of the strange noise that he had heard.

The sound came again, clearer and louder than before now that his attention was focussed on listening for it. He stepped back slightly in apprehension, afraid of what could be creating the noise and concerned for his own safety.

The strange whimpering continued.

Andy's brow furrowed as he tried desperately to understand what the sound was and what was causing it. Suddenly, as though the comprehension had been thrust into his mind from the outside, he realised that there was no danger to him from the source of the sound. He crouched again and began to edge his way forward.

There, squatting amongst the bushes and barely visible, was a small form. It stared back at him, its bright eyes wild with fear and its body trembling as it watched the monstrous figure of Andy creeping towards it.

The figure whimpered and held its hands up to its face, covering its vision from the advancing terror that slowly approached with each step.

Andy stopped, suddenly alarmed that others may have seen him and become curious in his actions. He raised himself upright and looked along the length of the road to his left and right. Nothing moved in either direction and he was calmed in the realisation that he was still alone and unseen.

The bushes shook and branches snapped as the figure jumped to its feet and in a stoop, began to force its way through the tangled hedgerow, fighting its way through and out to the far side, away from the road and Andy.

He watched in alarm as he saw the little girl struggling against the thorns and branches that snagged at her clothing and skin, lacerating her flesh as she fled in fear. He stumbled forward, raising the hand that still grasped the tyre iron and moaned pleadingly after her as she crashed into the fields beyond, taking off at a sprint into the long grass.

Andy felt an overwhelming need to follow her, but he could not risk trying to force his way through the hedgerow and causing himself further damage. He bobbed and swayed, peering through the thick tangle of branches as he looked for the small girl on the other side. He could see the grass swaying as she ran through it. He looked beyond the area where she was and up along the rising grassy slope.

At the top of the hill, a row of trees ran from the road along the high ground, forming into a clump surrounding, and partially obscuring, a structure of some kind on the horizon. Andy, in his less than perfectly functioning brain, was able to deduce that she was heading for the building.

The little girl was gone from sight now and he felt pressed to find her as quickly as possible. He looked to his right along the road, searching for a gap in the hedge that he could climb through and then make his way into the field that the child had run through. He could not see any openings, and he did not want to search in that direction and have to come into contact with the group that were feeding on the dog again.

To his left, the road continued and twisted around to the right in a sharp bend. He turned and began to trundle along the lane at a pace that indicated a sense of urgency. As he moved, he kept an eye on the tall bushes to his right, glancing over his shoulder every now and then to check for any sign of the little girl.

He was also afraid of being followed by the creatures that he had encountered further down the road; he wanted to find an opening soon so that he could evade any wandering eyes.

Just beyond the bend, there was a wooden fence set into a wide gap in the hedgerow. Andy pushed and pulled against it but it would not budge. After a while of staring at the obstacle, bewildered, he concluded that he would need to scale the fence if he was to gain entry to the fields on the other side.

With one hand remaining pressed firmly against his abdomen, Andy began to climb.

At first, he was confused on how to begin his ascent. He could picture in his mind what he needed to do, but he could not get his feet and hands to do what was necessary. In frustration, he growled and hurled the tyre iron over the gate. It landed with a thud, protruding out from the packed mud on the other side.

Again, he attempted to climb, this time managing to coordinate his hands and feet a little better and gaining some height on the wooden slats of the fence. He became more confident, and soon a sense of joy at his conquest of the obstacle began to surge through him, as he scaled higher and higher and his limbs harmonized into a rhythm that allowed him to clamber up the wooden barrier.

At the top, he clumsily threw one leg over, catching the top of the fence and almost losing his balance. Straddling the obstacle, he paused and became confused again, unsure of how to make his way down on the other side.

For a long while, he remained seated astride the gate, unsure of what to do. He looked down to his left at the road and the ground he had come from. He knew that he did not want to go that way; to his right, the muddied and churned ground presented itself as an obstacle beyond an obstacle. He was aware that he needed to get himself onto the muddy side of the fence, but nothing came into his mind to guide him.

Eventually, Andy understood that he needed to do the same thing he had done climbing the fence, but in reverse. He clutched his left hand to his wound, holding it tightly, and with his right hand, he steadied himself as he began to lift his left leg in an attempt to bring it on the field side of the fence.

In his deteriorated condition, and with clumsy movements and lack of coordination, he misplaced his step. His foot skidded from the rung of the fence and his body lurched away from under him. He tried desperately to keep a grip on the gate with his right arm but it was no use; the weight of his body wrenched his fingers away from the top and he plummeted to the ground, landing on his side in the freezing wet mud.

Andy lay there for a while in the sucking filth that covered him from head to toe. He was afraid to move with the thought that he had caused himself further harm from the fall and hesitated in getting up.

He remained motionless, his head lying in the mire that surrounded him, staring at the miniature hillocks of muck and puddles just inches from his face.

He watched as a parade of beetles marched past his eyes, rolling clumps of dung with their hind legs and paying him no attention. For a while, he forgot about his predicament and the possibility of further injuries and lay, fascinated, studying the tiny creatures moving about in the slime around him.

Finally, he began to shift his weight in the wet dirt, testing the condition of his arms and legs, confirming that they were still attached to his body and functioning as normal.

Next, he began to drag himself upright into a sitting position, immediately checking the wound in his stomach and ensuring that his innards were still within his body.

He had seen many like him, walking with their intestines dragging along the floor in a long trail behind them. He recoiled at the thought of the same thing happening to him.

Slowly, and with great difficulty in the slippery mud, Andy climbed to his feet on unsteady legs. He paused and checked his surroundings to confirm that he was still alone, and had not attracted the attention of any of the wandering figures littering the landscape.

The air was silent and he detected no movement from close by. Even the birds and the tiny creatures that had been scurrying around in the dirt seemed to have dispersed and gone into hiding.

He turned, picked up his tyre iron and headed into the long unkempt grass of the fields, headed in the direction that the little girl had run. Although a part of his mind conveyed to him that he must move urgently, another part of his brain forced him to negotiate the ground cautiously.

Below his feet, the tangles of grass and weeds threatened to snare or trip him with every step, and the undulating troughs and mounds continually attempted to snap his bones and leave him stranded, to rot in the open field.

For what seemed an eternity, he carefully crossed the ground and steadily climbed the gentle slope of the hill. Finally, he was free of the long grass and staggered out onto a gravelled courtyard that surrounded a large farmhouse.

He stopped and studied the building. The house was old and strong looking with walls that appeared thick and impenetrable, covered in a carpet of creeping vines that ran up its brickwork and towards the roof. Its bright red door, thick and wide, looked as though it could withstand any number of creatures attacking it and never come close to breeching the solid wooden barrier. On either side of the main door, large bay windows were set high from the ground, out of reach of prying eyes and reaching hands.

Looking to the left and right of the house, Andy could see that a path ran around the outside, but it was difficult to see what lay beyond due to the tall and tightly spaced trees that surrounded the sides and rear of the building, casting it in shadow.

He turned to look in the direction he had travelled, down the slope and towards the road. Nothing moved in the long grass and there was no sign of anything moving by the fence or along the country lane in the distance.

To the right, a gravelled track that joined onto the courtyard ran away into the rows of trees leading down towards the narrow country lane. He had travelled along the road in that direction and had not noticed any turn off for a track that led up to the house.

He reasoned that he was under no threat from that direction and the little girl, if she were in the house, would be safe, for now.

He studied the windows, trying hard to view the interior of the house and see if there was any movement from within. He could see nothing. The windows afforded him no insight to the house or its occupants and reflected just a shiny blackness created by the light on the outside.

For some inexplicable reason, Andy felt obligated, duty bound, to ensure that the little creature that had run away from him at the roadside was okay and would remain so. He was aware that it was a child, and not a child that was in the same state as him. This child was one of the fast moving and beautiful sort, the kind with the vibrant flesh that made such wonderful sounds and moved with a grace that he envied so much.

He remembered what a child was and how delicate and vulnerable they were. For a moment, he reflected on his travels and the visions of the little girl, trapped in the car, that stared back at him with such beautiful but lifeless eyes. He felt a surge of sorrow flow through his body, as he recalled the memory of him putting an end to the misery that she so desperately wanted to be free from, causing a remorseful groan to rise in his throat.

He swayed for a moment, unsure of what to do as the dreadful memory faded in his mind. He took a step forward, his feet crunching the gravel on the ground and making him pause in fear of being detected.

Looking up, he eyed the windows but saw nothing, and then began to move forward again, placing each step as lightly as he could.

Soon, he was close to the front door of the house. He hesitated at the bottom of the steps and stared up at the large red wooden obstacle that blocked his path. He made a move as though to begin following the track that ran around the house, but then stopped. He stared back at the door, and then began to climb the steps. Grasping the large round handle in his hands, he attempted to turn the lock.

It moved slightly.

Andy placed his tyre iron on the ground at his feet and then gripped the handle with both hands, forcing it with all the strength he could muster. The lock clicked and the door opened a few centimetres, and then stopped.

At first, he felt afraid to push it any further, but then he remembered the reasons why he had come to the house. He needed to see the little girl, to be close to her, for a reason that he could not understand, but it was something that drove him forward in a way that no other force could.

With the tips of his bony fingers, he nudged the door open a little more. It creaked as it moved, making Andy glance back over his shoulder in fear that something had heard the sound and followed him. With nothing presenting itself to his rear, he stepped into the semi darkness of the hallway to the house.

The light pouring in from outside illuminated the interior only slightly, and Andy could see almost nothing beyond the first two steps of the entrance. He could see a set of stairs to his right, its white banister glowing in the gloom, and to his front, along a long dark corridor, he could see the frame of a doorway, lit up from the room beyond.

He moved further in, carefully closing the door behind him, not wanting to leave it open to any of the others that may be in the area, that may have followed him without his knowledge.

The house was silent. Nothing stirred in the eerie darkness. Andy began to feel deflated at the possibility that the child had gone elsewhere.

He let out a sigh and began to stagger forward, slowly making his way along the narrow corridor towards the light at the far end. Halfway along, a clunk resounded from the room ahead of him. Andy paused and attempted to focus his hearing on the sound, but the house remained deathly quiet and the noise did not repeat itself.

At the doorway, he stopped, fear of the unknown and what could be waiting for him beyond the frame of the door tugging at his instincts. He could see into the room and realised that it was a kitchen with a large table in the centre, piled high with cans of food.

Directly facing him, there was a long counter that ran along the far wall, stopping at another door that led out from the house and to the rear of the building. Andy glanced down and saw a small yellow bowl at the foot of the door. It was filled to the brim and overflowing with a brown substance that he did not recognise.

He grunted as he looked to the right and deeper into the kitchen. Pots and pans were stacked high along the counter; discarded tins and bottles littered the floor. In front of the cooker, situated on the far wall to the right, a lone chair stood close to the hob. A pan, steaming and with blue flames rising beneath it, sat on top of the cooker. The mixture inside the pot bubbled and spat itself onto the worktop.

Andy instinctively realised what the vision meant. Someone else was in the house.

He lurched into the room and turned in all directions, looking for any sign of the little girl, but she was nowhere to be seen.

Walking towards the cooker, his foot collided with a glass bottle in the middle of his path, sending it skidding and clattering along the brown tiles of the kitchen floor. The sound echoed around the room for a long time, sounding like a crescendo in Andy's ears, before it finally subsided.

Another noise could suddenly be heard, as though the sound of his clumsiness with the glass bottle had triggered it. The sound was the same that he had first heard at the roadside when he saw the child, cowering and whimpering in the hedgerow, but he could not see her anywhere in the room.

At the far end of the kitchen, to the right of the large old cooker, Andy saw a curtain that covered what appeared to be another doorway. He moved towards it, his feet scraping along the tiles.

The sound of weeping continued.

Andy's withered hand reached out in front of him and he gripped the cloth of the curtain, causing it to ripple and flutter.

The snivels and whimpers erupted into sobs of fear and helplessness as Andy tore back the curtain.

Shelves, stacked with boxes and cans, presented themselves to him as he peered into the small pantry, but there was no sign of the source of the noise. He looked down and, in the corner, saw a blanket that obscured a bulky form beneath it.

The blanket quivered and the crying continued from underneath.

He reached down and folded his fingers around the material. He pulled hard, wrenching the blanket away to reveal the little girl that he had seen earlier, coiled in the corner, sobbing and shaking uncontrollably.

In her hand, she clutched a large knife close to her chest, but she made no sign of any attempt to use it, as she remained curled into a ball with her eyes screwed tightly shut.

Andy peered down at her. Her tiny form and glowing skin, with the long strands of golden hair cascading over her shoulders, roused a hunger within him that overrode and blocked all other thoughts and emotions.

His mouth fell open and he bent slightly at the waist, moaning loudly with anticipation as he glared at the small child with envious and ravenous eyes.

An instinct tore at his every sense and filled his misfiring mind with visions of the warm soft skin of the child, and the euphoria that it would give him as he ripped the flesh from her bones.

He remembered the euphoria and excitement he had felt the last time he had tasted the living:

The warmth of the blood as it splashed over his face and into his mouth as he chewed and swallowed the flesh that he tore from the man in large chunks. It filled him with an overwhelming sense of exhilaration and revitalized him to the point where he felt restored to his former self.

He leaned in close, his clutching fingers reaching for the soft skin of the child's shoulders as he opened his mouth wide in anticipation of what he was about to experience again. His black fetid tongue slipped over his yellowed and broken teeth, appearing as a monstrous slug while toxic drool hung from his lips and a yearning groan rasped from his throat.

The little girl cringed and whimpered loudly.

Andy stopped, confusion clouding his mind, causing him to hesitate, blocking his desire for the flesh that crouched just before him. He suddenly remembered the revulsion and regret that he had felt in the aftermath of the last time he had torn into living flesh. Memories of the screams of terror and agony resonated in his ears and echoed through his mind, completely blocking out the sobs of the girl in front of him.

Visions of the consequences, of scattered body parts and large pools of blood, presented themselves before his eyes and the disdain he felt for the others that feasted and picked at the shreds of meat, still clinging to the bones, came racing back to him, causing him to take a step backwards in horror.

A grunt of disdain emitted from his throat, resolute in his realisation that his initial instincts were wrong and grotesque.

The child fell silent, as the terror and pain that she had expected never arrived. Gingerly, she turned her face upwards and peered at the figure in front of her, through squinted eyes filled with tears.

Andy watched her for a moment, a torrent of different emotions rising from within. They were sympathy and affection, and a yearning to protect and help the small and vulnerable creature that cowered in terror from him.

He reached out with his right hand, as though to offer her assistance in standing up, but the girl remained in the corner of the cupboard, confused and still clearly frightened, staring back at the discoloured and crooked fingers of the monstrous hand reaching out to her.

She recoiled from him, pushing herself further into the corner as she stared at his withered and rotted hand.

Andy sighed and his shoulders drooped, appearing almost like a shrug of resignation. He stepped back, his feet scraping on the tiles and his eyes remaining locked on the fragile figure in front of him.

He grunted again, and shuffled out from the kitchen.

16

"Just keep going, Stu," Jim snarled from the passenger seat, "just get us the fuck out of here, man."

Jim's head swivelled in all directions as Stu gunned the engine and raced along the street. The dead were closing in from every direction, pouring from buildings and side streets as they were attracted by the sounds of gunfire, and now the noise of the police car as the engine roared and the wheels screeched.

A mottled grey mass of lumbering shadowy figures appeared in all directions and the wails of the crowds erupted into a crescendo as they saw the living men attempting to escape from their trap. Some stumbled forward with clumsy steps, while others swayed from side to side, but they all advanced, united in their lust for the living flesh attempting to flee from them.

"Fuck me," Kieran exclaimed from the rear seat.

He was jostled from one side to the next and collided with Hussein as Stu threw the vehicle from left to right, trying hard to swerve around the dozens of corpses stepping into the path of the vehicle.

"Where the fuck are they all coming from? They're everywhere."

Heavy thuds and clunks resounded dully within the car, as bodies that Stu was unable to avoid impacted against it. They bounced across the front; crashing against the windshield and were tossed to the side as the heavy police vehicle smashed through them. Limbs were ripped from their sockets and bodies were crushed beneath the churning wheels, leaving trails and puddles of fetid sludge in the wake of the vehicle, as the entrails of the walking corpses exploded from their bodies.

The vehicle rocked and lurched as the suspension was buffeted from the numerous dead that fell beneath its wheels. The tyres spun and gripped alternately as they crushed the bodies underneath and lost grip on the tarmac. The road was fast becoming packed with the bodies of the walking dead, and it soon became impossible for Stu to see a way through and out to safety.

A dark repulsive figure, completely naked, its left arm missing from the elbow down, oblivious to the damage that would result in a head-on collision, threw itself into the path of the vehicle as Stu floored the accelerator pedal. The snarling creature stood its ground like a goalkeeper ready to save a penalty kick as the vehicle closed in on it. It waited with its one remaining arm outstretched and its mouth open wide, ready to receive the large steel and glass meal that raced towards it.

Its legs were smashed from underneath it, shattering at the knee as the bumper hit at full force and speed. The body was catapulted forward with such velocity that it exploded on impact with the hood of the car; its bloody entrails carpeting the front of the vehicle like a macabre hunting trophy.

The head; still attached to the spinal column, penetrated the windshield and became lodged in the glass with its face just centimetres away from Jim who recoiled in the passenger seat. For a moment, they stared at one another in complete surprise.

"Jesus fucking Christ," Jim howled as he raised his pistol.

He shoved the barrel into the gaunt face, smashing the muzzle through its teeth and into its festering mouth as it glared back at him, dumbstruck.

Jim winced and pulled the trigger.

The report of the weapon in the confined space of the police car sounded like the crack of thunder, almost blowing the eardrums of all inside, as the nine-millimetre round smashed a hole through the skull of the ghoul trapped in the glass.

Blood and bone splintered out from the exit wound and one of its eyes popped from its socket, as the vacuum travelling behind the bullet, faster than the speed of sound, ripped through the weakened flesh and shattered the bones of its face.

Stu lost control of the vehicle as the crack of the pistol exploded so close the side of his face. His ears threatened to implode. He felt as though someone had just slapped him on either side of his head, simultaneously.

His ears popped and whistled as his vision blurred and danced before him. The car swayed to the left as he lost his grip on the wheel and was unable to regain control in time. Travelling at speed, and out of control, the police vehicle ploughed through a dense throng of bodies and collided with an abandoned vehicle close to the edge of the road.

A loud crunch followed by an echoing bang reverberated around the city, bouncing from the concrete walls of the buildings as the two vehicles became infused with one another. The bumper of the police car caved in on itself and the steel hood crumpled like a sheet of foil being twisted into a ball. The doors to the passenger and driver's seats buckled and screamed in their frames, causing the glass to crack and splinter as the force of the impact rippled through the vehicle and the men inside.

They came to an abrupt stop, the four of them being thrown forward in their seats and crashing into whatever was in front of them.

For the two in the front it was the dashboard, and Stu felt his nose shatter as his face smashed against the steering wheel. Instantly, his eyes filled with water and blood gushed from his broken nose as he slumped back in his seat, the world around him spinning as his brain was jolted and kicked around inside his skull.

Jim heard the bones in his forearm crack as he raised his hands in front of his face to protect himself while he was hurled forward from his seat and into the windshield. His head crunched against the glass, just centimetres from the wrecked face of the corpse that had crashed through the front windshield.

The inertia dislodged the shattered head of the corpse and hurtled it through the air like a football, sending it bouncing across the roof of the car that Stu had crashed into when he lost control of the vehicle.

Jim rebounded and fell into the footwell of the passenger seat, crumpled in a heap and unconscious, with blood pouring from a gash in his scalp.

Hussein and Kieran were forced forward into the driver and passenger seats, their heads banging together and knocking them senseless as they were flung back against the rear seat in a tangle of arms and legs.

Kieran felt his shoulder pop from its joint as he smashed against the frame of the door. Instantly, a white hot flash of agony shot to his brain, making him yelp as he crashed back into Hussein beside him.

Stu groaned, holding his hands against his face in an attempt to stem the flow of blood. For a moment, he lost track of what was happening and where he was, but reality was soon brought back to him, as he heard the thumps against the windows and doors of the vehicle as dozens of the dead closed in and surrounded them.

Stu looked up and through his blurred and bloodied vision, saw the grey faces peering in at him longingly as they continued to pound against the glass. They pressed themselves so close that they blocked out the sun and cast the interior of the police car into semi darkness.

A black decomposing face, its skin full of gaping sores, smacked against the window beside Stu. Its thick bloated tongue flopped against the glass, leaving smears of putrid mucus across the cracked window. Maggots dropped from the gaping maw, becoming trapped in the sticky secretions of the corpse's mouth as it continued to drag its mottled blue tongue across the window of the driver's side.

Stu looked to his left and saw Jim struggling to climb up from the passenger foot-well.

"Shit," he groaned, "Jim, you okay?"

Jim did not reply but he grunted back in response, informing Stu that he was at least still alive.

Hussein began to pull himself up from his seat, grimacing at the pain that he felt in his head and his already damaged knee. He turned to look at Kieran, who sat growling with clenched teeth, holding his shoulder beside him.

Everyone reached for their weapons as the mob around them surged and assaulted the vehicle, sending it rocking from side to side as they tried desperately to get to the injured men inside.

Jim was up in his seat and staring back at the sea of grotesque faces that peered in at them. There were too many to begin to count.

"We're fucked, Stu," he said, calmly but loudly in order to be heard over the rising moans of the dead, and the bangs and thumps against the ruined vehicle.

Stu could not form a clear thought. Partially through the knock to the head he had received and partially through panic. Everywhere he looked, all he could see was a swarm of pale grey faces surrounding them. It was only a matter of moments before the windows gave way and left them as easy prey for the creatures outside.

The hood of the vehicle was the only area that was not covered with the pressing bodies. The front of the police car had become completely merged with the side of the other vehicle, smashing through the rear door and wedging the bumper and first half of the hood inside the rear passenger compartment.

Without any further consideration, Stu leaned back in his seat, raising his legs above the steering column. He began to kick at the smashed windshield with the heel of his boot.

Jim looked across at the new and sudden noise, realising what the new plan of action was, and joined Stu as they forced the glass from its frame, leaving the front of the vehicle open for their escape.

Stu leaned forward, pointing his rifle out through the gaping hole, and began to fire into the crowd of faces surrounding them. Heads exploded and bodies dropped, but each one was quickly replaced as another figure soon filled the gap.

Between the deafening blasts of each shot, Stu could hear a voice screaming, roaring close by. He realised that it was his own voice, bellowing in defiance of his imminent end as he became determined to die fighting.

"Fuck you," he hollered, "fuck you…you fucking cunts…"

Round after round erupted from his rifle, creating a bright flash of flame that shot out from the muzzle with an ear-splitting crack. Stu was in a rage, shrieking like a mad man and emptying his magazine into the rotting heads closest to him.

Despite the din, the crack of gunfire, the screams of his men, and the howls of the dead, he was acutely aware of the jingling sounds of the brass cases from his rounds, colliding with the vehicle interior as they were ejected from his rifle. Time seemed to slow down and all other sounds became distant and distorted except for the tinkle of the empty cases.

As his weapon ceased firing, he instinctively reached for the release catch, dropping the empty magazine into the foot-well. Without needing to look at the weapon, he reached for a fresh magazine from his vest and slammed it home, sending the working parts forward and chambering a live round.

Still roaring at the top of his lungs, he hurled himself forward and clambered through the hole created by the missing windshield. The vehicle swayed beneath him and he was tossed from side to side as he regained his feet and positioned himself on the hood, planting each boot firmly and continuing to fire.

More heads exploded and imploded as the hail of fire punched through them, sending sprays of blood and bone in all directions and bodies toppling to the ground.

"Move," Stu yelled into the vehicle, "move, Jim, get out of there."

As Jim, Hussein and Kieran began to scramble forward, Stu continued to pour his deadly fire over the sea of dead around him. The hood of the car was too high for the dozens of reaching hands and clambering bodies to reach him properly. Stu could feel their fingertips clutching at the heels of his boots as he danced like a boxer in an attempt to keep his balance and remain upright on the swaying vehicle.

"The roof," Stu ordered loudly as Jim climbed through the open windshield, "get onto the roof."

Jim did as he was told and quickly bounded up onto the top of the vehicle, wedging his feet beneath the red and blue lights to steady himself, as he gave supporting fire to Stu and the others.

Kieran screamed as his shoulder smashed down on the hood. The pain shot through his body like an electric shock, causing his head to spin and his hands to lose grip on his rifle. The weapon clattered across the hood, becoming wedged in the twisted and mangled grille attached to the front that protected the headlights that were partially buried inside the other car.

He rolled from the open window, almost crashing into the legs of Hussein, who now stood beside Stu, hobbling on his damaged knee and firing wildly into the ocean of walking corpses.

A rotted brown hand reached out and clamped around Kieran's forearm, its bony fingers closing tightly around the skin beneath his jacket. He wrenched his hand free and threw a kick into the face of his attacker, sending it reeling back into the crowd as he scrambled across to his rifle.

Moving quickly, and ignoring the pain that screamed at him through his shoulder, he scooped up his weapon and continued forward as his momentum carried him onto the roof of the abandoned car into which they had crashed. He could not risk trying to stop and losing his balance, so he allowed the impetus of his run to hurl him away from the grasping hands that were so close to his heels.

They were split, with Jim and Kieran on the roof of the two vehicles and Stu and Hussein standing their ground on the hood of the police car. All of them fired, hoping to thin the crowd closing in around them, but they could see thousands more approaching from the surrounding buildings and streets of the town.

More magazines were emptied and discarded as the brass casings piled up at their feet, accompanied by the deafening roar and crack of their rifles.

Stu and his men were beginning to run low on ammunition and they had failed to make even the slightest of dents to the mass of bodies pressing in around them.

"What do we do?" Kieran cried across at Stu as he continued to fire at the wailing and snarling faces below his feet. "What the fuck do we do now, Stu?"

Stu did not answer and maintained his rate of fire, his teeth clenched and his eyes burning wildly.

"Save your last round," Jim's voice screamed out over the noise of the gunfire. "Save it for yourself."

Kieran looked up to see Jim dropping an empty magazine and replacing it with his last full one. Looking down at his rifle, Kieran quickly took stock of his ammunition state. He was already down to his last magazine and he guessed that he only had ten rounds, maybe less, before he was empty and defenceless.

"Last mag, last mag," Stu hollered as he slapped the remainder of his ammunition into the magazine housing of his rifle.

Despite their weight of fire, they had been unable to clear any kind of path through the tightly packed bodies standing, shoulder to shoulder, all around them.

Hussein's rifle stopped firing. He looked down and saw that the cocking lever was fixed to the rear, giving him a view of the empty magazine inside. He drew his pistol and fired into the face belonging to the hand that had made a grab for his leg, catching him by the ankle and pulling with all its might, almost dragging him from the vehicle.

The pistol jerked in his hand and the round punched a hole through the eye of the partially decomposed face of a large fat woman. Her body slumped forward over the hood, but her hand remained firmly clutched around his leg.

Ignoring the pain he felt shooting up through his leg from his injured knee, Hussein kicked and stomped at the arm, breaking the bones and almost severing it from the rest of the corpse. He fell back and collided with Stu, almost knocking him from his position and into the waiting crowd of dead at his feet.

Stu was also out of ammunition for his rifle and firing with his pistol, counting each shot and ensuring that he would save the last round for himself.

"Five," he counted to himself as the weapon cracked and the round exploded from the chamber, *"four,"* another crack, *"three..."*

Jim had ceased firing. He was not out of ammunition, but something else had caught his attention.

A new sound, a rumbling, had joined the blast of their rifles and the crescendo of the dead. At first, it had been distant, but it was closing fast and growing louder by the second, and only he seemed to notice it.

He looked in all directions, trying desperately to identify the origin of the new sound, but all he could see was an ocean of rotting flesh surrounding their position.

He turned and caught a glimpse of movement in the sky.

"Stu!" he shouted as loudly as he could. He pointed into the air, waving his arms frantically. "Stu, look!"

No one could hear him through the sounds of their own weapons, and Jim watched in horror as Stu stopped firing and looked down at the pistol in his hand. Jim felt his heart miss a beat as he saw Stu close his eyes and begin to raise his pistol towards his face, opening his mouth wide and placing the barrel between his teeth.

"Stu..." Jim screamed again.

17

Marcus scanned the ground below. A multitude of grey rooftops and streets were laid out just a hundred metres beneath them, at a glance, appearing like a highly detailed model town.

Numerous bodies shambled through the streets, picking their way through the detritus left behind during the final days of chaos, before the dead seized control of the cities, and what was left of humanity, were forced in to hiding.

Cars; some burned to their frames, but most remaining neatly parked at the side of the roads or in their allocated spaces in the expansive car parks, lay abandoned and long since forgotten, as they slowly decayed along with the town and its inhabitants.

Whole buildings had collapsed in on themselves from the fires that had burned, unchecked, and spreading to the structures adjacent to them, destroying entire streets as the flames raged, engulfing the dead and the living alike. Now, the charred buildings lay as blackened ruins, bearing witness to the horror and chaos that had spread throughout the world as the dead began to rise.

The reanimated corpses of the dead infested the built-up areas, swarming like insects through the buildings and streets. Marcus could see hundreds of them swaying and shambling along the pathways and roads that criss-crossed the town. They all stopped and looked up with clouded eyes and gnashing teeth, staring at the helicopter as it passed overhead.

They had flown along Stu's intended route towards the car showroom. Although it was clear that something had happened there recently, they could not see any evidence of Stu and his team. The numerous bullet holes in the walls and vehicles around the main showroom building, and the smashed doors to the garage, were clear indicators that the five men had been and gone from the scene.

Marcus ordered Kelly to hover while he watched the ground below and studied his map. He dreaded the thought of suddenly catching sight of pools of blood and torn bodies on the ground, or worse, recognising one of the many lurching figures that he saw scattered around the area.

Although he was far from sure, he concluded that for some reason, Stu and his men had not been able to travel the same route back. The only other route that was clear and open, was the road that led into the built-up area and the town centre.

The carriageway leading off to the east was completely blocked, with static and overturned vehicles leaving Stu and the others no option but to turn south, and head towards the town itself.

They were only a few hundred metres from the outskirts of the town. If Stu's route west had been further blocked as he travelled through the suburbs, he could have ended up lost or even dead within chaos and confusion of the overrun centre.

Now, flying slowly and low over the rooftops, every set of eyes in the aircraft peered down into the dead streets, searching for any sign of the others.

Steve, Helen, and Lee, all took the extra precaution of keeping their harnesses fastened around their waists as they hung out as far as their nerves would allow in order for them to get a better view on the ground beneath the helicopter.

All of them were on edge and they instinctively, and regularly, looked back to ensure that their harnesses were still firmly secured to the frame of the aircraft.

The thing that Helen feared the most was not the danger of falling and being killed, but rising up as one of the walking dead afterwards. Even worse, she shuddered at the thought of falling and surviving, her bones smashed, leaving her unable to walk while she lay helpless as the rapacious monsters closed in around her.

"Something's happening up ahead," Joey called through his headset.

Marcus climbed forward in an attempt to see through the windshield of the cockpit. It was hard to make out, but he could clearly identify a mass of bodies filling an entire stretch of road to the south. Everywhere he looked, figures lurched towards the crowd, joining in on whatever it was that was going on there.

"Let's take a look, Kelly," Marcus ordered, and climbed back to his position by the side door. "Keep us low and reduce our speed."

Kelly was about to protest, remembering the mechanical issues that the old machine tended to suffer from, but she decided better of it and remained silent.

She pushed down on the anti-torque pedals and eased off on the throttle, bringing the helicopter's nose around so that it could move forward at a three hundred and fifty degree angle, giving Marcus a better view from the doors on the side of the aircraft.

Below them, a carpet of dead covered the ground for a depth of two hundred metres from the epicentre of the mass. Even over the thump of the blades swishing above them, the people in the helicopter could hear the excited cries of the crowd as they surged forward, pressing in towards whatever it was that had drawn their attention.

Over the scream of the engine, and without a headset to distort his hearing, Lee could hear other noises. At first, he could not place the faint cracks that sounded similar to branches snapping in a dense wood. He frowned as he angled his head and tried hard to focus his hearing to identify the source.

"Gunfire," he suddenly and triumphantly screamed up at Marcus, proud that he had identified the noise before anyone else did.

Marcus looked down at Lee's beaming face.

"Well fucking done," he hollered over the racket of the helicopter engine and the thump of the rotors. "I'll give you a cookie and a 'smiley face' badge when we get back."

Lee's face changed, his expression fading from delightful pride to embarrassment as he recognised the sarcasm from Marcus at his childish outburst.

"Fucking simpleton," Marcus grumbled as he removed his headset and began scanning the area at the centre of the crowd.

At roughly three hundred metres out, Marcus could see movement, fast and energetic movement and not the lumbering clumsy lumbering of the dead.

"There," Marcus shouted, pointing to an area where he could see people moving about on the rooftops of cars.

The sound of firing rifles could be heard more clearly as they drew nearer, and Marcus felt his heart leap at the prospect of finding what remained of his decimated team.

"Get us over to them and take us down, Kelly," he shouted into the cockpit at the top of his lungs.

Kelly and Joey manoeuvred the aircraft so that it shot forward with speed. The nose dipped slightly and the engine increased its revolutions as the helicopter raced towards the scene. Fifty metres out and Kelly eased off on the throttle, pulling back the cyclic stick and pushing down on the anti-torque pedals simultaneously, bringing the machine to a hover and spinning it around to the left so that the right hand side door faced the men trapped on top of the vehicles.

The sudden deceleration and turn of the aircraft made Steve and Helen need to hang on to their harnesses in fear of being thrown out through the left hand door. They gripped on, their legs suddenly becoming lighter than the remainder of their bodies as the centre of gravity inside the passenger compartment shifted with the sudden manoeuvre.

Marcus looked down and instantly recognised the stranded men. His men.

"It's them," he called over his shoulder as he placed his rifle into the aim.

Kelly was still bringing the aircraft into a hover position close to the men on the ground, and Marcus could not get a clear aim without the risk of shooting one of his friends. He growled under his breath as he watched his sight picture sway and oscillate, frustrated that he was unable to give accurate and safe fire support for his men below.

He watched as a figure that he recognised as Jim ran across the roof of a police car and threw himself at one of the others, Stu, standing on the hood of the vehicle with what appeared to be a pistol in his hand and pointing into his own mouth. Marcus looked on in horror as the two men collided. A flash erupted from the barrel of the pistol and they both tumbled forward, crashing into the hood of the car.

The dead reached for them, gaining a grip on Jim's arm, pulling him towards the edge of the vehicle's hood and into the waiting crowd.

Stu's body lay motionless, his head hanging down over the bumper and the dead scrambling around towards him as his body remained limp and helpless.

The helicopter closed the distance to twenty-five metres.

Marcus roared as he watched his friends fall. He began to fire, hoping that his shots would be accurate enough to give the men a fighting chance. Lee opened up beside him, firing into the crowd swarming around Jim as he fought desperately to climb back onto the hood of the police car.

"Closer, Kelly," Marcus shouted, "get us closer, for fuck's sake."

Kelly glanced out of the window and down to her right. She could see the illuminated red tracer rounds as they shot out from Marcus and Lee's barrels and ploughed into the mass of rotting faces swarming beneath them. She watched the tracer as they smashed through the bodies of the dead, illuminating them for a split second with a demonic red glow as they were lit up from inside by the pyrotechnic ammunition.

Some of the corpses, dried out and nothing more than parched husks, burst into flames as the heat of the tracer rounds caused them to spontaneously combust. The burning corpses did not seem to notice the searing flames engulfing them, and continued to pour forward, setting fire to others as they come into contact with them.

Soon, acrid black smoke began to rise from the crowd as more of them combusted.

Kelly pushed the cyclic to the right and increased the lift on the collective slightly, making the helicopter yaw towards starboard, bringing them closer and directly above the wildly waving arm of Kieran, as he stood his ground on the roof of a car, frantically screaming up at them for help.

She brought them lower, just metres above the heads of the dead that reached up for the underbelly of the green, roaring monster hovering above them. One of the wheels on the starboard side made contact with the tallest members of the swarm, as the helicopter swayed to the right, knocking them over and creating a domino effect as they all collided into one another from the force of the impact.

Marcus was just within reach of his men. Still firing, he screamed down to them to climb up as the helicopter closed the gap, centimetre by centimetre.

"Kieran," Lee screamed, hanging out from the side door and reaching down with his hand outstretched. "Come on, Kieran."

Kieran looked up at him, glanced at his hand and shook his head before leaping from the roof and onto the bonnet of the police car. The downwash from the whirling blades threatened to knock him off balance as he landed beside Hussein, screaming something into his ear before the young Iraqi made a leap for the grasping hands of Lee.

Steve and Helen had joined Marcus in the door and poured their fire into the bodies converging on Jim, as he fought desperately to keep them back and regain his position on the hood of the car.

"Magazine," Marcus screamed, dropping his empty magazine and reaching into one of his pouches for a replacement. He could see that Lee almost had Hussein in through the door to his left and turned his attention to the others.

Kieran leapt from the vehicle and landed in the crowd, close to where Jim was fighting for his life in an attempt to hold back the tide of dead.

Marcus' heart skipped a beat as he watched the powerful young Kieran disappear in a sea of rotting grey faces and swallowed up as they piled in around him.

The sudden distraction and disturbance in the bodies around him as Kieran jumped, allowed Jim to break free of the clutching hands refusing to let him go, and he began to scramble back up onto the hood of the vehicle.

Marcus, Helen and Steve increased their rate of fire as Lee hauled Hussein up the last few centimetres to safety.

Marcus scanned desperately in the area where Kieran had disappeared, hoping to catch a glimpse of him, and give him fire support and a chance of making it back to the safety of the police car, but he feared that Kieran was lost.

The crowd in the area where Kieran had been engulfed suddenly erupted like a volcano of rotting flesh. Kieran appeared, forcing himself upright from the ground and using his back to bear the weight of bodies that had heaped themselves on top of him. He threw himself upwards, pushing his body high on his powerful legs and clearing the space in his immediate area, allowing himself the fraction of a second that he needed to make his run.

He sprang forward, swinging his rifle in front of him like a medieval sword and smashing the skulls of the corpses attempting to close in on him. He threw his right leg forward, planting it firmly on the tyre of the police car, and with the momentum of his run, launched himself upwards and back onto the hood.

Together, Jim and Kieran scooped up the limp body of Stu and raised him up, as Kelly brought the helicopter in lower so that Marcus and the others could pull Stu in while Steve and Helen continued to fire into the mass of clambering bodies.

Marcus dragged Stu across the floor of the passenger compartment and crouched down beside him, checking his pulse as he stared down at his smashed and bloodied face. He could feel nothing from Stu's heartbeat. His stomach begin to churn and his throat seized as another friend lay dead in his arms.

Marcus looked down at his friend, his eyes already beginning to fill with tears as he expected to see a river of blood flowing from the exit wound of the bullet that had smashed through his head.

There was no sign of it. The back of Stu's head remained intact.

He checked Stu's pulse again and felt a powerful throb against his fingers as he held them hard against the carotid artery in Stu's neck. He began quickly checking the rest of his body in case the shot had hit him elsewhere, but apart from the damage to his face, Stu did not seem to have suffered any other injury, including a gunshot wound.

"Stu!" he screamed into his friend's face, shaking him in an attempt to bring him back to consciousness. "Stu, can you hear me? Wake up, Stu."

Jim and Kieran scrambled into the aircraft together with the aid of Steve and Lee as Helen loosed off another magazine into the dead below.

"Get us out of here, Kelly. We got them," Steve shouted, and with the swishing blades thundering above, Kelly began to lift the aircraft to a safer altitude.

Marcus remained by Stu's side but looked up at Jim questioningly.

Jim shrugged, and then winced with pain.

Marcus saw the blood running down his arm and pooling at his feet. Immediately, he feared the worst and assumed that Jim had been bitten during his fight. He moved to get up and examine the wound, but Jim waved him off, shaking his head dismissively.

"It's not what you think, Marcus," he shouted across to him, "it's a gunshot wound, not a bite. I'll be okay."

A look of concern crossed Marcus' face at the thought of one of them having accidentally shot Jim during the rescue.

Jim noticed his friend's anxiety and confusion. He grinned.

"It wasn't any of you guys," he roared over the engine, the veins in his neck protruding from the skin with the effort. "It was him."

Marcus glanced down to where Jim's finger was pointing and looked at Stu. He looked back up, frowning inquisitively.

Jim nodded with a smile.

"Yup, that's right. Stu, 'the bastard', shot me." He could see that more questions were on their way so he decided to put Marcus out of his misery. "Don't worry, buddy. He didn't do it deliberately. He was down to his last round, and was about to swallow it, then you turned up in a fucking helicopter."

Jim sat back, grinning at Marcus whose expression was already turning to one of relief. "I couldn't let him miss out on a helicopter ride, could I?"

As the helicopter rose into the air, Steve glanced about them, looking from one survivor to the next and doing a mental count. His brow furrowed and he glanced back down at the ground below where the dead continued to swarm around the vehicles where Stu and the others had made their stand.

The burning bodies had spread, and now a glowing ring of corpses surrounded the cars as more and the flames engulfed more bodies. A cloud of brown smoke hung low over the area, as the stench of burning, rotted flesh filled the air around them, but the dead were oblivious to the smell, as well as the danger of the spreading flames.

Steve looked back at the survivors from Stu's team, still frowning.

"Stan," he shouted to Kieran, struggling to be heard over the noise. "What about Stan? Where is he?"

Kieran did not reply. He remained sat with his back hunched against the rear of the pilot's seat, staring at the floor beneath his feet and clutching his painful shoulder.

Steve caught the eye of Jim who shook his head solemnly. He understood and leaned forward, placing a hand on Kieran's shoulder.

"Mate, I'm sorry," he shouted into Kieran's ear, unsure of what else to say.

Kieran nodded, his head slowly turning upward. His eyes were red with fatigue and sorrow and a tear escaped his lashes and ran down his cheek.

He blinked and wiped the tear away, nodding as he turned to look out through the side door.

18

Andy did not leave the house. He did not want to. He wanted to remain close to the vulnerable child, in one way or another. He was aware of his initial reaction and feelings when he laid eyes upon the girl as she hid from him. The urges that he had felt, and came so very close to carrying out, frightened him. He recalled the overpowering need to sink his teeth into her soft flesh and he snorted in disgust.

He paused in the hallway, unsure of what to do next. He made as if to turn back and head into the kitchen again, but the image of the child's terrified eyes upon seeing him forced him to hesitate. One thing he was sure of was that he was not going to leave, yet.

He turned right, halfway along the corridor, and walked through a door that led to a large sitting room. The curtains were drawn and very little light penetrated their thick material, casting the room in shadow and causing Andy to falter at the doorway, before entering the room proper.

In the centre, there was a wide-open space containing a small coffee table, flanked by two bulky couches. Beyond the table and set into the far wall stood a large iron and black marble fireplace, adorned with ornaments and photographs. Above it hung an enormous mirror, giving the impression that the room was much larger than it actually was.

Andy moved into the sitting room, catching a fleeting glimpse of his reflection in the mirror as he approached the fireplace. Immediately, he averted his eyes, afraid of seeing the hideous monster he knew he had become. He paused for a moment and considered his feelings towards himself. He understood that he looked very much like the other revolting, shambling figures roaming the streets, but he also knew that he was different.

He had come face to face with the living on a number of occasions, and after the initial urges that he felt to tear them limb from limb and feast upon their bodies, he resisted and caused them no harm.

He thought about the man that he had stood just a couple of paces from all those months ago in the abandoned supermarket, and the fear that had burned in the man's eyes as they stood staring back at each other.

Andy could have very easily attacked him. The small bearded man was cornered and had no way of defending himself, but Andy had pointed him to safety and remained where he was, watching as the man left and slowly walked through the street, away from him.

The little girl, hiding in the cupboard and defenceless against him, he could have easily torn into her, but he had fought against his instincts, knowing that it was wrong and that the child had caused him no harm. He would gain nothing from hurting her.

Even the men who had held him captive; he could have easily attacked them, but he had felt no urge to do so. His self-preservation had conjured up more powerful feelings inside of him, than the need to feed on them.

Pain; he distinguished that what he was capable of would cause great pain and suffering and he recognised that it was the main difference between him and the others outside. They did not think. They would not have hesitated to attack and devour the child, her screams of agony and terror falling on their uncaring ears and oblivious minds. They did not appreciate the beauty of the world around them or understand the things they did. They just did them and moved without any thought process, understanding or reason.

That is where Andy was different, and he recognised that characteristic in himself. He was not like them and he feared them in the same way that the child, hiding in the cupboard, feared him.

He looked back up and stared at his reflection in the mirror. Although the image staring back at him was that of a ghastly abomination, he could also recognise something different in his eyes. They did not carry the same glint or spark that the child's eyes did, but they saw the world around them and understood much of it, unlike the others that he despised so much.

He stepped closer in an attempt to view himself more clearly in the gloom.

His flesh was stretched taut over his features, making his cheekbones and eye sockets seem to jut out from his skull. The skin was a pale brown in colour with a green hue that appeared to radiate from beneath the outer layer.

His face had a waxy sheen about it, as though coated with a fine layer of grease, and the lips and tip of his nose were all but gone, leaving his teeth bared in a permanent sneer and his nasal cavity exposed to the open air.

The eyes staring back at him were dull and flat with a large, faded grey spot in the centre of each that was his misted and dilated pupils, but they were not vacant; he could see that. They did not just stare through the objects and reflections that they gazed upon; they studied and calculated. They understood and appreciated that the world in which he roamed had not always been that way.

Much of the hair that protruded from his scalp had fallen out over time, leaving strands and clumps of lank black tresses, flattened to his cranium and forehead with grime and filth.

He sighed, long and mournful, as he remembered how the man he had once been had appeared. He had been handsome once and looked upon with envious eyes by men and women alike.

Now, he was repellent to all that viewed him. He understood why the child had recoiled in fear, even after he had attempted to make it clear to the little girl that he meant her no harm.

He looked no different from the others and, despite his abilities and thoughts, the living's first reaction would always be one of fear whenever they laid eyes upon him. He would either die in the ensuing attack, or look on as they ran away; giving him no opportunity to prove to them that he did not want to hurt them.

He reached out and took hold of a picture frame that sat in the centre of the fireplace. He immediately recognised the smiling figure in the centre. It was the child that was still in the house, hiding from him in the kitchen. In the photograph, she looked happy, smiling from ear to ear, as she stood surrounded by a cluster of other people who appeared to be as content as she was when the picture was taken.

Andy ran a finger over the glass, stroking the faces of the joyful and beautiful people, frozen in time, and set in a decorative frame to be looked upon and remembered for years to come.

Stepping back, still holding the picture tightly in his hands as he continued to study it, he moved over to one of the couches. Slowly, he began to sit, his joints groaning and cracking as they bent and twisted in their parched sockets. He heard the noises that his body made in protest against his movements, but he was resolute and ignored them as he dropped into the soft cushions of the sofa.

There, he remained for a while, staring at the picture in his hands and admiring the simple beauty of the people that grinned back at him from beyond the thin pane of glass.

A shadow flickered its way across the room, causing Andy to turn with a start. In the doorway leading in to the room, and with the dim light from the hallway at its back, stood a motionless dark silhouette. It was too small to be anything but the girl, and Andy stared back at it, unsure of what he should do.

After a moment, the black figure stepped forward into the sitting room and paused at the end of the couch where Andy sat. The Girl watched him curiously, clearly fighting her fear as intrigue forced her to come and see what the strange creature was doing, as it was obvious that it had not harmed her, nor did it want to, and she knew it had not left the house.

They stared at one another, the child becoming less afraid and more confused. Andy was conscious of his actions and careful not to make any movements or sounds that would bring back her terror towards him.

Eventually, she walked past the coffee table and hesitantly sat down on the couch across from him. Andy remained sitting motionless, not wanting to move and scare her away. He eyed her from the couch and saw that she still held the large knife close to her chest. He could see that she was incapable of using it effectively, and that she clutched it more for comfort than defence.

The pair of them remained in silence, studying one another and taking in the atmosphere around them. There was nothing in either of their demeanour that activated any alarms in the other's minds, and soon, the little girl began to relax, placing the knife on the arm of the chair and sitting with her arms folded across her chest.

Andy, believing that a little imitation may be the right thing to do, gently lay the photograph on the cushion beside him, and attempted to fold his arms like the child had done. His first few attempts failed completely and left him with tangled arms and a confused mind. He was ready to growl in frustration, when he noticed the expression on the girl's face as she sat watching him, bemused and with a half-smile creasing the corners of her mouth.

Finally, he accomplished the intricate manoeuvre and sat staring down at his knotted arms with a sense of growing satisfaction in his achievement.

"Can you talk?"

Andy looked up, startled at the sudden noise in the otherwise silent room. The girl remained seated but watched him intently. He was not sure if the noise had come from her, and he glanced about him, expecting to see someone else entering through the door.

"I said…can you talk?" she repeated, looking directly at him.

He then grasped that she was speaking to him, something that no one had done in a long time. Her voice rattled around in his mind, ringing in his ears and sounding just as beautiful as the songs of the birds when he sat below the trees, watching in awe and listening to them intently.

He could hear her and see her lips moving, but he could not understand her words. He stared back at her, blankly.

She held her hand to her chest and pronounced her words slowly and deliberately. "I am, Molly."

He remained silent, staring back at her.

"My name, my name is Molly," she tried again.

She huffed and sat forward on the couch and continued to pat her chest as she stared at him, repeating her words.

"Molly," she said slowly, pronouncing each syllable, "Molly, my name is, Molly."

Andy gazed back at her, his arms still locked across his chest as he listened to the wonderful noises that emitted from her mouth. They were not like the sounds that he made, raspy and gurgling. Her words were animated and gentle on his hearing as the noises she made spiralled down through his ear canal and danced across his partially functioning brain.

"Can you hear me?" she asked, louder than before. "Molly. That is me, what is your name?"

Finally, something clicked into place. He suddenly understood that she was communicating with him and not just twittering with joyous sounds like the birds. He looked at her, concentrating his attention on the words that rolled from her tongue and the hand pressed against her chest.

'Molly,' she is, *'Molly.'*

His eyes grew wide and his brow creased as he recognised her words and actions, but frustration soon overtook him, as he could not communicate back to her. He unfolded his hands and reached forward, slowly and careful so as not to seem like he was lurching towards her. His fingers curled inwards, leaving his index digit extended towards the young girl.

Molly saw the realisation spread across his face and nodded, smiling at the thought of being able to communicate with him, to a degree.

"Yes," she said as she continued to nod encouragingly, "Molly. Can you say, *'Molly'*?"

Andy gurgled and followed it with a grunt but Molly was satisfied at the fact that she had made him understand. She beamed at him and clasped her hands together as she watched him begin to sit forward and reach for something behind him.

He struggled to coordinate his hands while they were out of sight from him, but eventually his fingers closed around the object for which he had been searching.

Groaning and leaning forward from the couch enthusiastically, Andy held out the worn and filthy leather wallet, motioning for Molly to take it from him.

At first, she hesitated, staring down at his withered, cold and bony hands, unsure of whether she should take the wallet for fear of him suddenly launching himself forward and attacking her. She reasoned to herself that the dead did not think and plan, or lure people into a false sense of security, and if he wished to hurt her, he would have already done it.

She took the small leather case, her eyes remaining fixed on his as she smiled nervously at him.

Andy remained sitting forward with the anticipation of the introduction and the possibility of hearing his name spoken.

Molly opened the wallet and peered over its contents. A few encrusted and tattered twenty-pound notes brought back memories of happier times to her as she stared down at the Queen's face. Then, she began to check through the multitude of cards before she finally found the one she was looking for.

She raised the small rectangular pink card and held it at an angle, pointing towards the doorway so that she could see the picture in the faint light filtering in from the hall. She studied the photograph of the Driver's License, seeing a young and handsome looking man smiling broadly with sparkling white teeth and glittering eyes.

She paused and looked up, comparing the picture to the figure that sat before her. There was no comparison between the withered and gruesome face of the creature sitting on the sofa and the vibrant head and shoulders of the man in the picture.

She looked to the right of the photograph.

"Andrew Moorcroft," she read aloud, slowly.

Andy's eyes grew wide again and his mouth fell open as he heard his name spoken in the angelic voice of Molly. A surge of elation raced through him and a soft muffled moan seeped from his raspy throat.

The girl looked up at him and saw the change in his expression.

"Andrew Moorcroft. That is you. Your name is Andrew, yes?"

He moaned again, gently, at her words.

Molly continued to read, then looked up at him after a while of thought and contemplation.

"I don't know what date it is," she said rhetorically, "but, I think you're twenty-eight years old."

She studied him again, subconsciously comparing him to the picture.

"I am nine, I think. I don’t think it's been my birthday, yet, but it must be soon."

Andy did not understand her words, but he revelled in the sound of her voice.

"Yes, I think I will be ten, soon. So, you're Andy and you're twenty-eight, and I am Molly and I am nine," she said, smiling at him.

"Sally," she suddenly shouted, "Sally, come here..." She stopped mid-sentence and grew silent, staring down into her lap.

Andy saw the change in her composure and noticed her shoulders sag. He grunted questioningly, concerned at her sudden change.

She raised her head and peered across at him, her eyes wet with tears.

"Sally was my dog," she informed him. "She was my best friend and those monsters out there killed her while she tried to protect me."

She pulled a faded and tattered photograph from her pocket and handed it to him. He gently took it from her hands and stared down at a picture of Molly, her arms wrapped around a brown and black fury animal, its tongue hanging from its mouth as it sat happily beside her.

Andy recognised the word '*dog*' and related it to the picture. The interaction with the child seemed to be re-opening the pathways and reigniting some of the neurons in his brain. He then realised that the carcass he had seen his attacker feeding on, was to what the little girl was referring.

He sighed heavily at the thought of Molly's pain and sadness.

Molly began to weep as the realisation sunk in that her dog was gone and would never come back.

Andy sat in bewilderment, unsure of what the noises emerging from the little girl meant, but he was able to conclude that they were not the sounds of joy and happiness. He sat watching her, listening to her crying softly.

He growled to himself, almost inaudible over the sound of Molly's lament. Her sorrow pulled at his own emotions, and he fought against the urge to join her with despondent moans and wails of his own, knowing it would only frighten her.

After a long time, she grew silent, and raised her head, wiping the floods of tears from her cheeks.

"Will Sally be like you, now?" she asked with a quivering voice.

The question was lost on Andy and he could do nothing but look back at her with his flat dead eyes. Although his eyes showed nothing, he felt her sorrow. It travelled through him like a wave, unsettling his thoughts and feelings and leaving him disorientated and unsure of what to do.

Molly looked over her shoulder and towards the curtained windows.

"It'll be dark soon," she announced, snorting back the rest of her tears. "I should go upstairs to my room."

She rose from the couch, wiped the tears from her eyes and looked across at Andy.

"Will you still be here in the morning, Andy?"

He looked back at her and attempted to rise to his feet. His knee joints creaked and groaned loudly and his hips seemed to rattle in the silence of the house.

Molly held out her hands, indicating for him to stop and remain seated as she listened to the deafening rasps of his bones.

"You should stay and rest, at least for tonight."

She walked towards the door and Andy followed her with his eyes, a sense of something that could only be described as compassion filling his senses, as he eyed the fragile and lonely little girl.

There was another emotion mixed in with the bombardment of feelings that assaulted his mind and silent heart: love. He knew the emotion, and he knew what it meant. There was no doubting it; he loved the little Molly and he wanted to care for her in her loneliness of the dangerous and terrifying new world.

"Good night, Andrew," Molly bid him as she left the sitting room.

Andy grunted softly and remained staring at the empty doorframe long after she had walked through. He sighed and picked up the framed picture from the cushion beside him.

Hours later, as the winter sun slowly rose above the horizon and cast its first glimmering rays over the dead land, Andy, had a sudden thought. He raised himself up from the couch and carefully placed the family photograph back on the fireplace, before making his way across to the window.

He pulled back the heavy thick curtains and peered out at the semi dark terrain surrounding the low ground around the house, stretching off into the distance towards the road that remained hidden by a freezing morning mist. The long grass of the fields to the west glinted with crystals of frosted dew as the sun began gently warming their stalks and releasing them from the cold night.

To the east, the sky was a bright vibrant blue, with pinkish clouds scattered high in the atmosphere. The sun began its climb and chased the shadow of the night towards the west, where the sky remained an inky black as it slowly turned from night to day.

Andy looked out across the gravelled courtyard and towards the row of trees that led down to the narrow country road. Nothing moved in the still and cold morning and he made a conscious decision to leave.

It was something he felt that he needed to do. Something he felt obligated to do for the little girl that had become his only friend.

As gently as he could, he removed the white dusty tablecloth from the dinner table beneath the window. He rolled it up in his arms and made his way out through the front door, picking up the tyre iron from the top of the steps as he left. He headed for the track.

A while later, and with great effort as he struggled his way along the long path beneath the tall overhanging trees, he returned to the house.

He remained outside in the gravel courtyard, staring up at the door, unsure of what he should do next. He alternated his gaze from the house to the large bundle he carried in his arms, wrapped in the sheet he had removed from the dinner table.

With a grunt, he decided that it would be best not to enter and began to make his way around to the side path that led towards the rear and garden of the house. His feet crunched across the gravel and, on a number of occasions, he almost lost his balance as he staggered around the narrow perimeter path of the building. He stopped, adjusting the bundle in his arms and using his body to brace himself against the brick walls of the house to regain his stability.

Finally, he gently placed his burden down at the foot of a tall and strong looking tree at the bottom of the garden. The thick, green branches hung low towards the ground, obscuring the area at the base of the trunk, protecting it from the elements.

Gently, he adjusted the position of the white sheet, and then proceeded to stumble about the area, picking up stones and rounded rocks, placing them around the tablecloth as neatly as his badly coordinated arms would allow.

He stopped and stepped back, staring down at the misshapen shrine that he had created, but something was missing. He turned in all directions, eyeing the bushes and shrubs that surrounded the expansive garden, but could not see what he was looking for. The closest he came was the dead and wilted weeds sprouting up from the cracks through the walls and paths of the garden. Their colours had faded, turning their yellows and blues to a dried and unattractive brown as they died in the winter air.

He looked back towards the house and, in the window of the kitchen; he saw a clutter of vibrant colours.

He turned and staggered back towards the house and the door that led into the kitchen. Inside, he reached for the windowsill and snatched up the plant pot containing the pretty flowers and radiant green leaves, and then headed back in to the garden.

"Andy?" Molly called from the door a short while later. "Andrew, where are you?"

She sounded anxious but Andy had no way of calling back to her as he remained below the tree, adjusting the position of the sheet and lie of the stones and flowers.

He raised himself to his feet and quickly glanced down at his creation. He grunted with satisfaction and turned towards the house, forcing his way through the overhanging branches that dripped with the melting dew.

As he stepped from the shade of the tree, he could see Molly standing on the step to the rear door of the house. She shivered in the cold morning air and rubbed the skin on her arms. As he stumbled into view, she looked at him, a smile spread across her face as he appeared in the open, raising his hand and attempting to attract her attention.

Andy saw the expression on her face and he felt something swell inside of him. Seeing Molly's appearance turn from one of concern to utter joy at the sight of him, ignited a fire within his chest and caused his head to throb with his own delight at her affection and acceptance of him.

She stepped out and walked towards him and, with a grunt and a huff, Andy beckoned her to follow him to the tree. She paused, watching the shadows beneath the heavy thick branches of the fir tree and looked back at Andy, unsure.

Andy stopped and looked directly into her eyes. He attempted to make himself appear less frightful by raising his brow. He could see her hesitation and he nodded to her encouragingly, hoping that she would see that he was no threat.

Molly fought with her feelings. Although she had been fearful at the thought that Andy may have left, and had felt happy when she laid eyes on him at the bottom of the garden, the sight of the dark shadows beneath the tree made her waver.

She still did not see him as a danger, but she had learned to stay away from the shadows and remain in the light, where she could see anything that was coming towards her.

She looked back at Andy and he gestured to her to follow him with a supportive grunt. His eyes held a spark of life that she had never seen before in one of the dead. As she paused and stared back at him and his expression, the look in Andy's eyes told her that he meant her no harm and that he only wanted to help her.

She nodded and followed him as he stumbled through the unkempt, dew sodden grass of the garden. He pushed the heavy branches aside and held them open so that she could enter the shadow beneath the thick foliage.

Below the tree, as her eyes adjusted to the semi-darkness, she struggled to understand what she was looking at.

Andy stood beside her, looking from her to the strange shape and collection of stones on the ground and grunting questioningly. Molly looked at him and realised that he was awaiting her approval, but approval to what, she did not know.

At her feet, she could see a white bundle surrounded by a crooked ring of stones, with a pot of flowers on the top. She failed to understand its significance or, the reason she needed to see it. She wondered if it was Andy's way of communicating to her, showing her that he was still capable of thought, with the ability to coordinate and build basic structures.

Andy realised that she did not understand and turned on his heel, staggering with urgency towards the house.

A minute later, he returned, carrying an object in his hands. Only when he had re-entered the shade of the tree did Molly recognise what it was that he was holding.

Andy had first seen the yellow bowl as he entered the kitchen the day before, looking for the little girl. He held it out to her, nodding his head towards her, encouraging her to take it from him. His eyes watched her, studying her reaction as he held out Sally's food bowl, still piled high with the now crusted-over dog food.

Molly took the bowl from him and looked down at the strange structure at the base of the tree, realising that what she saw was a grave.

She stared up at him, her eyes glistening brightly in the shade of the tree as she peered into the cold eyes of the dead man standing before her. Her heart pounded in her chest and her throat felt as though it was beginning to swell as a hard lump formed in her larynx. Her shoulders suddenly felt heavy and her lungs threatened to drop into her stomach. With each difficult breath, her body tensed and seemed to double in weight as she fought desperately to stop herself from collapsing with emotion.

Andy had travelled back to the road, wrapped her beloved Sally in the cloth and carried her back to the house, laying her to rest beneath the old tree and taking great care to ensure that she lay peacefully and surrounded in a rustic but strangely beautiful sculpture of stones.

Floods of tears began to cascade down Molly's cheeks. She could not hold them back any longer. She cried for the loss of her dog, Sally, and for the sentiment and care that Andy had shown to her. He had understood her sadness and cared enough to recognise that, Sally had meant a lot to her, and should not be left at the roadside, where she had died.

Molly looked down at the yellow food bowl clutched tightly in her hands. She snorted back her tears and nodded. She knelt down at the foot of the grave and gently placed the bowl on top of the white tablecloth.

Andy watched as the delicate little girl knelt, and he followed suit, slowly dropping to his knees beside her. The dried joints of his legs screamed out in protest and echoed around in the shaded and confined space beneath the tree, but they were of no concern to him as his concentration was fixed on the bereaved child at his side.

Her tears came in floods as sorrow wracked her body, causing her shoulders to convulse with each torrent of grief that washed over her like a tidal wave. For a long time she knelt at the stones as tears fell from her face, sprinkling over the grave of Sally.

"Thank you, Andy," Molly said as she turned to him, a half-smile creasing her puffed face and swollen red eyes while the tears continued to flow.

Andy understood the meaning of her words and grunted, nodding slightly and adjusting a rock that had fallen out of place from around Sally. He patted it back into position and rested his palm on the sheet covering the remains of Molly's beloved dog. He sighed softly and remorsefully, knowing that he could not change or take away the suffering of his new friend.

For a while, they sat in silence and thought.

Finally, Molly began to speak in a breaking voice that rose and fell in pitch as the emotion continued to force its way through her.

"She was my best friend and I will never stop missing her. I will love you always, Sally."

She kissed her fingertips and patted the white tablecloth before rising to her feet. She paused for a moment and stared down at the grave, and then she turned, and began to make her way out from the shade.

She stopped and waited on the other side of the low hanging branches, waiting for Andy to join her. She could hear him climbing to his feet and the echoing cracks and groans of his body as he clumsily fought his way through the foliage and out into the light of the garden.

Finally, he emerged, the branches lashing at his face and catching him on the side of the head, almost knocking him over. Molly smiled briefly at the sight and, rather than seeing, a walking horrifying dead man coming towards her, ready to attack, she saw an unfortunate and vulnerable soul. A man that had shown a great deal of care for her, more than anyone had done in a long time.

She realised that his appearance no longer frightened her, even though she was standing close and with his lifeless eyes peering down at her. Even his smell, though far from pleasant, was no longer as repulsive as she had first thought.

Andy was her friend. He had proven that to her, and already she began to feel safe around him.

As they walked slowly towards the house, she stopped and turned to Andy, looking up at him and smiling as he gazed down at her expectantly.

"We need to fix your knees or your legs will fall off," she announced, still wiping the remaining tears from her reddened eyes, but Andy just stared at her, dumbly.

Molly looked down at the large gaping hole in his abdomen and pointed. He followed her finger and instinctively reached his hand across his stomach to protect the wound, his expression turning to one of concern, as he suddenly remembered the damage that he had sustained the previous day.

"I think we can fix that too. Come on, Andy, I have an idea."

19

"How is he?" Marcus asked as he looked up from the table, watching Helen walking towards them after tending to Stu's wounds. He turned back to his stripped down rifle, the parts spread out on the table in front of him, and continued cleaning.

"A mild concussion, a few cuts and bruises, and he won't be pretty for a while. His nose is badly broken and his eyes are swollen, but he'll live," she sighed heavily and pulled a chair out from the table, sitting down next to Steve.

Steve looked at her and saw how worn out she looked. Her hair was a mess, standing out in all directions, looking like it had not seen a comb, or a bottle of shampoo, in a long time. Her hands, normally immaculate and manicured, were grimy with blood staining the nail beds and the pads of her fingers. Her face looked drawn and her complexion was pale and grubby from the events of the last few days.

No one had a real chance to wash and freshen themselves up since leaving the makeshift bomb shelter in the basement, and they had all taken on the appearance of a group of war veterans, fresh from the front, and in reality, that was exactly what they were.

Still, it did nothing to dull the feelings that Steve held for Helen. He saw through the grime and dust and never lost sight of the beauty that forced itself through the thickest layers of dirt and fatigue, but he knew that there was more to it than just physical attraction and lust. He loved Helen dearly. There was no doubt in his heart, and he truly believed that during all the chaos and horror, he had somehow found his soul mate.

He had discovered a woman who was able to accept him and all his faults. He was even comfortable just lying in bed beside her, watching the sun come up and pour its bright beams through their bedroom window, while talking about unimportant matters and giggling like children.

She never failed to make him laugh, and on so many occasions, he had reduced her to a quivering wreck with laughter at the silliest of jokes or comments.

Steve nudged her chair with the toe of his boot to catch her attention. She turned to look at him, blinking heavily with tired eyes and smiling lazily. Steve grinned back and leaned in to whisper in her ear.

"I'll run you a bath later, candles and all. Then, a good long back rub. How does that sound?"

Helen smiled sheepishly, embarrassed slightly, feeling like a teenager again. She turned to him with a smirk.

"You're on," she purred with a wink.

Marcus nodded, satisfied that Stu was in the best possible hands.

"What about the others? I think Jim lost quite a bit of blood."

Helen shook her head. "They're all patched up and Jim's shoulder wasn't as bad as it first appeared. He has a fractured radius too, and considering he is built like the gable end of a five pound note, without an ounce of fat on him, he was lucky that the round passed through his flesh without shattering his collar bone."

"Hussein's knee is bad," Jake added as he approached, drying his hands on a towel and dropping it onto the table as he sat down.

"How bad?"

"Well, he won't be running a Marathon in the near future," Helen said as she added her expertise. "It's badly twisted and I think there is cartilage and ligament damage. He needs to keep it rested. It may never be right without proper care."

"It's Kieran that I'm most worried about," Steve added to the conversation. "He's just lost his best mate and he's hardly spoken a word since he got back. He just locked himself away in his room."

Marcus shrugged. "I feel for the poor guy, I really do. We've all lost friends, but it's something that we just have to grin and bear, and get on with it."

"Yeah, but..." Gary began as he sat listening at the far end of the table. "You're looking at it from the perspective of a soldier, Marcus."

He paused before continuing in his usual mild, but wise, manner.

"You've experienced loss on a big scale, even before all of this began. The likes of us," he nodded at the others sitting around the table, "Jake, Helen, Steve and I, even crazy Lee, losing friends is new and something we never expected to face in such proportions, and especially so brutally."

"True," Marcus sighed.

"We need to keep an eye on the poor fellow and help him through his grief," Gary reasoned. "Karen is mothering him and trying to get him to eat, but we all need to do our bit and stand by him while he comes to terms with his loss."

"As always, Gary," Helen smiled, "you're the father to us all."

She reached across and scooped the cup from Steve's hand, emptying the contents in one gulp, feeling the lukewarm liquid slide down her dried throat.

"Cheers," she gasped, and immediately pulled a face. "Jesus, what kind of tea is that?"

Steve grinned at her, feeling a sense of satisfaction that she had swilled back his drink, hoping for a reaction from him, without knowing what it was.

"Special tea," he beamed, "half of the brew was whisky. My Nan was a huge fan of topping up her tea with a generous helping of the 'special stuff'. After today, I thought I could do with a little kick to my brew."

Helen wiped her mouth with the back of her sleeve, still grimacing at the aftertaste.

"It's disgusting, that's what it is," she groaned as a shudder ran from her shoulders to her feet.

"Each to their own, I guess. Here's to our Nan," Marcus grunted as he slugged back his own 'special tea'.

He smacked his lips and gasped with pleasure.

"So," Jake began, "what's the meeting all about? Have we missed anything? Where are 'Fly-Girl' and 'Fly-Boy'?"

"It's not a meeting, as such," Gary replied. "Kelly and Joey are outside, checking over the helicopter."

Jake looked at Marcus with concern. "I thought they were supposed to be under watch? Do we trust them now?"

Marcus shrugged and rubbed his face with his palm.

"If they want to leave, they can do. I'm not going to hold them prisoner and, after today, I think they've earned a little respect and understanding from us."

Helen looked at Marcus, studying his tired face as he stared down at the contents of his cup. It had been a long day for all of them, but Marcus looked far more exhausted than anyone else did.

"You sure that's wise?" she asked. "I mean, after watching you throw Stephanie out of the helicopter, they may think they could be next and take off."

"Eh?" Gary gasped, glancing from Helen to Marcus. "What do you mean, *'threw her out'*?"

Helen looked up, feeling uncomfortable for her slip of the tongue over the true fate of Stephanie.

"Sorry, I thought you knew," she said, sheepishly.

Steve leaned back in his chair and let out a long and loud sigh. He looked across at Gary and shrugged, raising his eyebrows indifferently.

"Like Marcus said, we couldn't let her live," Steve said, searching Gary's face for a hint of understanding.

"Come on, Gary, you knew Stephanie just as well, if not better, than the rest of us. That bitch would not have left it at that. Look at the mess we're in because of her."

He held his hand out, pointing through the large foyer windows and towards the area of the wall and gate.

Gary held up his hands and shook his head vigorously.

"Hey, I'm not judging you and I agree; it was the right thing to do. I was just surprised to hear it because I thought you were letting her go. I had already thought to myself that she could still be a threat to us if she was set loose, so believe me when I say it, it was justified and necessary."

He looked at each of the people around the table in turn, locking eyes with them to express his sincerity and support in their actions.

"I don't think we should make this public knowledge, though," he continued, "some people here may see it as a little excessive."

Gary paused for a moment, a frown creasing his brow as he thought about Steve's words.

"What do you mean; '*the mess we're in*'? I know we're surrounded, but how bad is it?"

"Pretty fucking bad," Marcus grumbled.

"They're coming in from all directions and there's more on the way," Helen began. "You know yourself, it only takes one of them to know we're here and in no time, there are thousands of them. The whole of the south, east and west walls are packed with them and their numbers stretch out far beyond the roads leading to this place."

"There's an exodus of them headed this way from the outlying villages, towns and cities. Jason and Stephanie must have put a lot of fucking effort in to screw us over. It must have taken weeks of hiding and sneaking about with all those things running around out there," Steve pointed out.

"And we've lost the CCTV, too," Jake added, matter-of-factly. "Not sure what the problem is, but it just seems to have finally given up the ghost."

"Could be the amount of weight against the gates," Helen offered. "Maybe the wiring has been damaged?"

"So," Steve concluded, "we're surrounded by those things, the gate is on its last legs and close to collapse and we can't see it happen because the cameras have packed up?"

Gary rubbed his face and nodded. "Yeah, that's about it."

"Great," Steve snorted. "I don't want to sound all doom and gloom here, but we're not exactly in the best of condition. We've just lost *another* one of our men and four others are injured, one of them with a gun-shot wound."

"Maybe we're running out of luck?" Jake suggested. "I mean, Stu and the others went out for vehicles and supplies, and came back with nothing but injuries and minus Stan. That's not mentioning the amount of ammunition that was used up during the rescue."

"And that is what we need to think about," Marcus added. "This place can't hold out forever. Eventually, one of the gates will collapse with the amount of weight those pus-bags can bring to bear," he nodded towards his brother.

"You said yourself that the hinges of the main gate are starting to give and that tanker we jammed up against it will only support it for as long as the gate remains intact."

Steve nodded as he leaned back and rocked on his chair.

"Wasn't that part of what Stu was supposed to be doing?" Jake asked. "Finding a possible place where we could run to?"

Marcus nodded. "Yeah, but in case you haven't been keeping up on current events, Stu got side-tracked."

Jake squirmed in his seat at Marcus' facetious reply.

"Tell him, Jake," Gary prompted him encouragingly, nodding towards Marcus. "Tell him what you were telling me this morning."

Marcus looked at Jake questioningly. "What? Tell me what?"

Jake was reluctant to speak in case he embarrassed himself again, but eventually, and after extra coaxing from Gary, he leaned forward and exhaled loudly.

"Right, okay," he began. "This will probably sound stupid to you, but it's just an idea and seeing as we're short on them, it's a start."

Marcus smiled wryly at Jake's discomfort. "Jake, stop flapping. I'm just teasing you," he grinned. "You're the only male 'sausage wallet' we have around here, so I have to take the piss from time to time."

Steve snorted and Helen shook her head, grinning down at the table from the expression Marcus had used to describe Jake and his sexual orientation.

Jake also smiled at Marcus' 'no punches pulled' and vulgar manner.

"Okay then," he continued, feeling more relaxed. "There's a holiday resort about a hundred miles or so north of here…"

"A *'holiday resort'*?" Steve interrupted.

Jake glanced across at him; already feeling like his suggestion would be mocked and discarded without a second thought. He looked back at Marcus, studying his face for a reaction, but, as usual, Marcus revealed nothing and would show no reaction until he had heard the full facts and considered it first.

Marcus held up his hand, silencing Steve. "Let's hear it, Jake."

"Yeah, a '*holiday resort*'," he continued, raising his voice slightly and asserting himself with more confidence. "It's up near the Lake District and in the middle of nowhere. You know the Lakes, they're secluded as it is, and this place is off the beaten track."

Marcus watched him intently, his elbow resting on the table and his hand supporting his chin. "How do you know this place? You been there?"

Jake nodded, encouraged by Marcus' question and the fact that his idea had not yet been dismissed.

"Yeah, I was there a few years ago, with my ex. It's one of those country retreat hideaway sort of places. The kind of place where couples go to relax and take in the scenery, or even families for the outdoor adventure thing. The place has everything."

"You got a brochure?" Steve joked from the opposite side of the table. "You sound like a holiday rep, Jake."

Marcus remained impassive and spoke in a monotone voice as he cross-examined Jake. "What about defences? Is the place secure?"

"That's the best part of it." Jake had become more animated and confident as he began to work on his sales pitch. "There's only one main road leading in to it and most of the...," he trailed off and looked up at the ceiling, placing his hand in front of his face and making something that resembled 'The Sign of The Cross' and mumbling to himself.

'Never, eat, shredded, wheat...,'

Marcus grinned as he recognised the phrase and realised that Jake was using the old teaching aid to help him remember the directions of the points on the compass.

"...the east side," Jake blurted enthusiastically. "Where the road is, it's walled, similar to what we have here, to stop people from just going in without paying. There's barriers and gates there too, the big heavy steel railing type."

"And what about the rest? Is that walled too?" Steve queried, leaning forward from his chair as he began to take an interest in what Jake was saying.

Jake shook his head.

"No, it's mesh fencing, surrounding the whole resort and beyond it, it has a thick pine forest and mountains. Seclusion and wilderness was the whole idea of the place, untouched and all that sort of stuff."

Marcus grunted and sat upright, placing both hands on the table. The others remained silent, watching Jake and Marcus alternately, waiting for the verdict.

Finally, Marcus nodded. "Sounds like it's worth considering, at least," he stated to the assembled. "How big is this place?"

"Big," Jake replied, opening his eyes wide to add weight to his statement. "I'm not sure of the square mileage, but there are hundreds of lodges and holiday homes there. It's a popular place." He paused before correcting himself. "It *was* a popular place."

"Gary," Marcus said across the table, "how many people do we have here?"

Gary looked up for a while, conducting a mental count. "Uh…twenty-four, including Kelly and Joey, I think."

"Have you counted Johnny?" Jake asked, concerned that the strange and humble man could be forgotten because of him rarely being around for long.

"Of course," Gary snapped back at him.

"That's a lot of people to move north in one group," Marcus surmised. "The heli will only carry a maximum of eighteen people, if I remember correctly."

"Yeah, that's right," a female voice said from behind, confirming Marcus' educated guess.

They all turned to see Kelly and Joey standing in the foyer, watching them as they wiped oil and lubricant from their hands.

"Eighteen, including the pilot and co-pilot, and that's pushing it on fuel," Joey added with a nod.

Marcus wondered how long they had been standing there, listening. He decided not to start at the beginning and hit them with the relevant questions that he needed answers to.

"What's the range on a Puma?" he asked as he turned in his seat to face them.

Kelly shrugged and approached the table.

"Depends," she said, pulling up a chair, helping herself to a cup of whisky from the bottle on the table.

She sipped it at first, closing her eyes and savouring its flavour, and then threw the cup's contents down her throat. She smacked her lips and gasped as the fluid burned in her throat and warmed her chest.

"Depends on what?"

"On whether you have a bucket of bolts Puma, or a good Puma," Kelly continued. "This one," she nodded over her shoulder, indicating in the direction of the main door, "is the bucket of bolts sort and its maximum range on our current fuel status is probably about two hundred kilometres, maybe less."

Marcus nodded. "Well, that gives us one lift, at least, but because of the distance, we won't be able to get an 'eyes on recce' of the place first. If we decided to go ahead with the move, we would be blind to anything that could be there waiting for us, and I'm not just thinking about those bags of shit roaming the planet these days."

"You mean other survivors?" Gary asked.

Marcus nodded. "Yeah, for all we know there could be thousands of people already there; even army units or, raiders."

"There is a similar place, a couple of hundred miles south-east of here, near Nottingham," Jake added as an afterthought.

Marcus shook his head.

"No good; it's too close to London and, according to Kelly here," he nodded to his left, "it's just been hit by a hydrogen bomb and the whole of the south will be covered with fall-out."

"I know the place *you're* on about," Kelly indicated with a tilt of her head towards Jake. "I've been there, too, about ten years ago with my parents and my ex-husband, and it's a safer place than here. We're surrounded by large towns and cities here."

"You think you could get us there?" Marcus asked, raising an eyebrow.

"Most of you, but like you said, we could only manage one trip and wouldn't have the fuel to come back."

"That's good enough for me, and at least it's an option we can consider," Marcus said, slapping his hands against the tabletop with enthusiasm.

He turned to Jake and winked. "You found it, buddy. Can you show me the place on a map?"

Jake nodded, staring back up at Marcus, surprised that his suggestion had even been considered in a serious manner.

"Well, come on then. I need you to give me as much detail as possible; routes in and out, the layout, even the surrounding towns and villages, anything you can remember about the place. Or did you spend all your time there biting a pillow?"

Jake began to laugh as Marcus beamed down at him. As brash and rough around the edges as the man was, Jake could not help but like and admire him.

Later, Marcus went to check on Stu. He entered the dark room and slowly walked towards the bed. Not wanting to wake his friend with a start, he opted for a more gentle approach.

"Hey, buddy," Marcus whispered, "how are you feeling?"

Stu rolled over and groaned, holding his head and wincing from the pain that throbbed behind his eyes, creating a tremendous amount of pressure there. He looked up and saw Marcus sitting at his bedside, grinning at him with a bunch of dead weeds in his hand.

"Here," Marcus began, "I've brought you some flowers. Isn't that what you're supposed to do when you visit a friend in hospital?"

Stu struggled to focus his vision and rubbed his eyes hard.

"Shove them up your arse, Marcus."

Marcus tossed the bouquet of weeds at his friend in mock offense. "Fuck you, then, you ungrateful bastard."

Stu forced himself to sit up, resting his head against the headboard of the bed. His throat was dry and a foul taste and texture coated the inside of his mouth. Before he could say anything, Marcus' hand suddenly appeared below his nose, holding a tall glass of water.

"Cheers," he whispered hoarsely as he took the glass and gulped greedily.

Marcus sat and watched him for a moment, his expression showing that he was eager to engage his friend in conversation, but he understood that Stu needed to come around slowly. He did not want to dwell on the incidents that had occurred earlier, but he felt strongly that he needed to at least, make fun of Stu over them.

"So," he began, "you felt you couldn't go on and wanted to end it all? Was it a 'Dear John' letter that pushed you over the edge?"

Stu smiled groggily. "You would've done the same, mate. We were down to our last rounds. How was I supposed to know that you would come to the rescue?"

Marcus sniggered and nodded.

"Where did the helicopter come from, anyway?"

"A new addition to our ORBAT," Marcus replied. "You saw the nuke?"

Stu nodded. "Yeah."

"Well, they were part of the group that dropped it and were on their way to record the results, when they found us and decided that they liked us."

"Group?" Stu queried. "Where they based?"

"The Isle of Jura, up on the west coast of Scotland, and according to Kelly and Joey," Marcus paused and realised that Stu had not yet been introduced to the new group members, "they're the pilot and co-pilot, and they won't be missed or looked for because of the distance."

Stu nodded his approval. "Kelly? Is she pretty?"

Marcus shrugged indifferently.

"I'm a married man so I wouldn't..." he began, but Stu cut him off without saying a word and lowered his head, staring at him in the same way that a school teacher would when catching a pupil chewing in class.

Marcus looked at him and shook his head, looking down at the floor with shame.

"Yeah, she'd get it," he beamed as he looked back up at the pulped face of Stu.

Both of the men laughed.

"A helicopter…a good piece of kit to have with us," Stu considered.

"Aye," Marcus nodded in agreement. "You're living proof of that.

"What about the others? Jim, Hussein, and Kieran, they okay?"

"They're fine. Bruised and battered, but they'll live," Marcus said reassuringly. "Listen, you get yourself back to fighting fit, and then I need to speak to you. We're planning a possible move north, to a holiday resort…"

The questioning expression on Stu's face made Marcus pause and smile.

"Yeah, a holiday resort; I'll tell you more about it when you're back on your feet, but we won't be moving until we're one hundred percent ready, and that includes all you sick, lame, and lazy people getting yourselves back to full strength."

Stu nodded as Marcus began to stand. As he moved towards the door, Marcus suddenly stopped and turned, glaring at his friend with an excited expression.

"Oh, I nearly forgot, I have a present for you."

"A present?" Stu retorted. "What *'present'*?"

Marcus grinned broadly and shook his head. "It's a surprise and you will have to wait till you're better before you see it."

"You fucking wanker," Stu growled at him. "You know I hate surprises and you're just saying that so that I get out of bed sooner than I should because *you're* fucking bored."

Marcus left the room, laughing loudly; Stu listened as his guffaws echoed along the corridor outside his room.

"Twat," he growled.

Marcus, Jim, Hussein and Jake stood around the table with a number of maps and road atlases unfolded and spread out over the table's surface, showing the area between their location and the holiday resort in the north. They had been studying the ground for a number of hours and asking around every survivor in the house to see if anyone else had been there, or to the area in the last twelve months.

Carl and his family had gone there the previous summer. Not to the resort, but the town that was closest, and he was able to help with his descriptions of the roads and built-up areas and give Marcus an up-to-date impression of the area in general.

From what Marcus could gather from Carl, Jake and Kelly's first-hand information, and bearing in mind that there had been a ten-year gap between Kelly and Carl going to the area, very little had changed in the road systems and size of the towns.

Many of the roads were still narrow; single-lane carriageways and urban areas, in true compliance with the National Park that the Lake District was, had hardly changed.

"It's purely hypothetical at this stage, Marcus," Jim spoke up as he stared at the large maps spread out on the table in front of him. "But, providing the road system hasn't changed too much since these maps were printed, and there aren't already people there, we could completely block off the entrance roads to the resort at the junctions a few kilometres to the north and south. I'm thinking we should do it with trucks; get them in place, remove the wheels and completely disable and reinforce them."

Marcus nodded as he bit down on his lip, deep in thought as he studied the lay of the ground, tilting his head and viewing it from different angles, as he turned the map into a three dimensional image of the whole area in his mind.

"I'm thinking we go a little further than that," he added to Jim's suggestion. "Yeah, we block off the access roads, but look." He pointed to the closest town on the map, situated roughly five kilometres to the northeast of the holiday resort.

It was placed close to the north shore of a large expanse of water. The Lake stretched for twenty kilometres to the south and the access road to the resort ran along the western edge, with a narrow stretch of land between the road and the lake, protecting the eastern flank and main entrance to the resort.

To the north of the town, high mountains and grasslands extended far into the distance, making it unlikely to be a possible approach route for large groups of wandering corpses, purely due to the lay of the land and the isolation. To the west of the resort, more mountains and high steep ridges stretched from north to south, cutting off any advance from the western flank.

"What we looking at?" Jake asked.

"You see the little red squiggly lines all over the map?" Jim replied, already recognising what Marcus had been considering.

Jake nodded as he leaned in close and studied the faint lines. "You mean the ones with numbers on them?"

"Yup," Jim nodded. "They're called 'contour lines' and they denote the rise and fall in the lay of the ground; hills in other words. The numbers that you see on some of them," he pointed with his pencil to one in particular. "That is the height above sea level."

Jake stared at the lines, forming a mental picture in his mind of what the ground must look like in reality. It was hard for him to do without ever having practiced it before, but he was beginning to grasp the general shape of the ground.

"So," he began, speaking deliberately and slowly, running it through his own head as much as anybody else's. "What you're saying is the place is protected by mountains to the north of the town, west of the resort and a fucking huge lake to the east, leaving just the south?"

"Exactly," Marcus grinned and slapped him on the shoulder. "We'll make a 'Rommel' of you yet, Jake. But, look closer at the road running through the town."

Jake squinted and, a moment later, leaned back from the map. "There's only one major road leading in and out?"

"Correct," said Jim, "and look what is covering the ground to the east of the road."

"A forest?"

Marcus nodded with an expression of encouragement, but Jake had become lost in the overall strategy of the plan.

"Okay," he began, his eyes locked on the map. "We have a lake and mountains covering our east and west, and the town is surrounded by hills and a forest with only one road. So, what does that mean?"

"We take the town," Kelly concluded as she stood watching from the side, all the time studying the map herself.

Marcus turned to her and smiled. "We take the town," he repeated, nodding slowly.

20

That evening, the temperature began to fall sharply. Carl could literally see the mercury inside the thermometer, rapidly dropping towards zero. By the time the sun had been extinguished for the day, it was just one degree above zero, and already he was shivering uncontrollably.

"Fucking hell," he gasped as a cloud of misted air blew from his mouth. "I feel like my blood is going to freeze in my veins."

Lee stood beside him, beating his hands and stomping his feet.

"Tell me about it," he replied as he pulled his woolly hat down over his ears and hunched his shoulders. "I can't feel my fingers or toes and I have three pairs of socks on. I'm scared of sitting down in case my arse freezes and ends up stuck to the chair. What time is it, anyway?"

Carl was reluctant to lift the sleeve of his jacket and expose his flesh to the cold air, but he wanted to check the time. He knew how long they had been left on guard duty before they could go back inside and warm up.

He looked down at his watch and squinted as he tried to see the dials in the darkness.

"Just gone eight. Less than an hour left then it's Sophie and Jake's turn to freeze their arses off for four hours."

Lee nodded, looking forward to the thought of getting into the warmth of the house. Then he realised the impact of Carl's words. Sophie would be on duty and he would have no one to cuddle up to when he climbed into bed. He had other intentions too. Activities that he would have liked them to share before the cuddle phase and, knowing that he would have to wait until the next night, he began to despair.

"Fuck's sake," he growled.

"What?" Carl asked as he turned to him, having to rotate his whole body for fear of exposing his neck to the icy air.

"Who wrote out this stupid guard list?"

"I don't know. I think it may have been Jake, or even Steve. Why, what's up?"

Lee shook his head and spat. "Nothing," he grumbled.

Carl laughed hoarsely. "Ah, I know why. Christ, Lee, you're like a dog with five dicks at times. It'll fall off with overuse, you know."

"Yeah, well, I intend to enjoy using it until it does," Lee retorted.

The night was completely still with not even a hint of a breeze. The moon had finally made an appearance, casting its ghostly light over the expansive grasslands of the park that stretched along the eastern side and down towards the wall. There was no noise at all, except for the occasional hoot from an owl in the woods to the west of the house, and the snap of a branch as the many nocturnal animals came to life in the darkness and scurried about in the underbrush.

"It's so quiet," Carl thought aloud.

"Always is," replied Lee, sniffing up the mucus that had begun to run from his nose due to the cold.

Carl turned to him.

"No, I mean more quiet than usual. Can you hear them?" He nodded to the south, indicating the thousands of corpses that he knew were on the other side of the large stone barrier of the perimeter.

Lee paused for a moment and focussed his hearing, raising his neck from his collar and tilting his head.

There was nothing there; not even the usual faint hum that could usually be heard as the dead sang their poignant chorus at the walls. No matter how dark the night became, or how far from the perimeter they were, the survivors of the mansion could always hear the distant hum of thousands of moaning and wailing voices, as they clambered at the perimeter of the Safari Park.

Lee looked at Carl in surprise. "You think they might have gone?"

Carl shook his head. "No, why would they? I don't understand why we can't hear them, though. I was up here this afternoon and there were a million of them."

"Can you see anything?"

Carl raised the binoculars and, for a long moment, scanned the wall. Finally, he brought his hands back down, a confused expression covering his face as he continued to look in the direction of the wall.

"I think I can still see them. It's hard to tell in this light but I'm sure they're still there. It's just that..." he trailed off in thought.

"Just what?" Lee asked as he reached for the binoculars.

"Well, they're not moving and we can't hear them either. It's fucking weird."

"Maybe they're just sick of their own tune?" Lee joked and laughed to himself. "Anyway, bollocks to it; we're finished here soon, and I need a brew and it looks like I will have to make do with just a 'mesome' tonight."

Carl looked at him in bewilderment, thinking that he had heard incorrectly, or Lee was stumbling with his words from the effects of the cold.

"A *'mesome'*? What's a mesome?" he asked with a screwed up face.

Lee turned to him with a mischievous grin.

"A mesome. It's a bit like a threesome, but with two less people."

Carl chuckled, his shoulders convulsing under the thick multiple layers that he wore.

"A *'mesome'*...I like that."

Carl and Lee returned to the roof eight hours later, to take the 'Dawn Shift' as it was known. They relieved Lisa and Claire, and neither of them had anything to report, except the eerie silence that had fallen over the land.

Both, Lee and Carl had brought extra quilted clothing and blankets, and stood completely immersed in thick layers of synthetic and natural fibres, shivering and complaining about the bitter cold, awaiting the dawn.

Carl had become infatuated with the thermometer that he had grown a habit of carrying with him whenever he was on the roof. Now, he stared at it in disbelief as it read five degrees below zero.

It was still dark and the sun would not bless them with its warming rays for another two hours. To prevent them from freezing on the spot, they both stomped and jogged around the rooftop in their cumbersome clothing and blankets in an effort to remain warm, stopping from time to time, staring to the east as the sky slowly changed colour. They both willed the sun to rise faster than usual, anticipating the radiant warmth of its rays that would free them from the icy night.

Finally, in the light of the new morning, the park came into view around them, stepping out from the shadows and joining them in the brightness of day. The sky was a clear blue, without a cloud to be seen, but it remained bitterly cold and the liquid metal mercury in the thermometer stubbornly refused to budge from minus five degrees.

As the light increased, Lee and Carl were able to see further.

The sun was still below the horizon, but it would soon make its glorious appearance as it rose above the trees, making its climb into the sky.

Carl could see the wall now with his naked eye; it was possible for him to make out the sea of dead that lurked just beyond it. Both of them had been waiting in anticipation to see if the mass of walking corpses were still there, both hoping to themselves, with an optimism that they knew was unfounded, that the voracious creatures had finally given up and moved elsewhere.

Now it was clear that their hopes had been dashed. There were just as many of the dark figures as there had been the previous day. Packed tightly together, they stood, staring at the walls and in to the park beyond.

"Fuck's sake," Lee mumbled, "there goes *that* idea."

Carl nodded and grumbled something under his breath as his eyes remained fixed on the mass of bodies. Something bothered him, though he was unable to place his finger on it. He watched them, squinting as the light brightened and the sun finally peeked above the trees, raising the binoculars and lowering them again as he studied the dead, intently.

"They're not moving, Lee," he finally realised.

"Eh...? What do you mean?"

Lee snatched the binoculars from Carl and began to look for himself.

"They're not moving; that's what I mean. They're just standing there, completely still. *None* of them are moving."

Lee saw it for himself. Carl was right, the thousands of dead, lining the roads, packed in tight against the walls, were standing motionless.

"I still can't hear them, either," Lee said from behind the binoculars. "They're not moving and they're not making a sound. What the fuck is going on?"

For a while, the pair of them stood at the edge of the roof, staring out at the sea of dark shapes, wondering and speculating on what could be wrong. Lee had come up with the suggestion that maybe they had all finally died for good and that is how the *'dead die'*, as he had put it.

Carl rejected Lee's proposal with a dismissive wave of the hand, almost resulting in the brake out of a fight between them as Lee took offense to his attitude.

After the pair had calmed, they went back to theorising and pondering, neither of them coming up with a sensible answer.

Finally, Carl gave up trying to understand what was happening and attempted to dismiss it from his thoughts.

"Bollocks to it," he groaned as he sat on the lip around the rooftop. "It's just another one of those strange things that happen in this new and mental world. Fuck me, they're dead; they shouldn't even be walking about in the first place, so how are we supposed to know what the hell they're doing now?"

He pulled out his thermometer to check if the temperature had changed since the sun made an appearance.

It had risen just one degree.

Carl grunted.

"Great stuff, winter is going to really kick the shit out of us now, Lee. It's eight o'clock in the morning and still minus four. Someone is going to end up freezing where they stand up here and..."

He trailed off and jumped to his feet, spinning around and looking at the legion of bodies outside the walls, and then staring back down at the thermometer in his hand.

"Fuck me," he gasped.

He turned, throwing the cumbersome blankets from his shoulders, and rushed for the door that led from the rooftop and in to the house.

"What? What's up?" Lee called after him, but Carl had disappeared down the narrow staircase, shouting for Marcus and Steve.

Steve and Marcus were in the kitchen, discussing their options for the move north over a pot of coffee when Carl barged in.

Steve looked up to see the big man as he stopped in the doorway, red in the face with an expression of excitement.

"Hey, Carl," he said, "cold up there this morning, is it? I've just made a fresh pot of coffee. Help yourself to a brew, mate."

Carl shook his head vigorously as he gasped for breath, his large chest heaving with the struggle.

"They're frozen, all of them," he gasped.

Marcus looked from Carl to his brother with alarm and uncertainty.

"Who? Who is frozen, Carl?" he asked as he began to rise from his chair, concerned that Carl was referring to the people on guard duty.

"Them," Carl replied, nodding his head to the right, "the dead, all of them are frozen solid. The temperature dropped to minus five last night, and they're now just blocks of ice, standing there."

Lee suddenly made an appearance in the doorframe of the kitchen, standing on his tiptoes and bobbing his head to see over the bulk of Carl.

"Steve," he said excitedly, "all the dead-heads are frozen solid."

"Cheers for that, Lee," Marcus replied with sarcasm as he turned to his brother. "Come on, we're going down to the gate."

"What time is the morning patrol due to leave?" Steve asked as he scooped up his coat from the back of his chair.

Carl looked at his watch.

"Any minute now, if they haven't already set out. It's Gary and Jennifer's turn this morning."

Marcus nodded and headed out into the foyer, making a beeline for the main doors, hoping to catch the Land Rover before they left.

Down at the gate, Gary brought the Land Rover to a stop in the shade of the trees without exposing them to the thousands of eyes and bodies at the main entrance.

The six people inside the vehicle stared out through the windshield, trying to see around the large white tanker blocking their view of the gateway.

"Can you see anything?" Jennifer asked Gary in a whisper, suddenly becoming unsure of why she was speaking in a hushed voice.

Gary's eyes remained fixed on the tanker, scrutinizing it and looking for any sign of movement. He shook his head.

"Not really, no," he said, distractedly, "the tanker is in the way, so I can't really tell if any of them are moving, or not."

"Right," Marcus announced from the back of the Land Rover as he began to push the rear door open. "Come on, let's have a look."

"What's the temperature, Carl?" Steve asked as he began to climb out.

Carl held his thermometer up to the cold air and paused for a moment, allowing the mercury to settle in the glass tube.

"Minus three," he said finally.

The six of them left the relative warmth of the Park Ranger's vehicle and began to make their way towards the main gate. Everything around them was frozen, leaving a white veneer of ice coating the grass and trees. Even the surface of the tarmac below their feet had a film of frost covering it.

The freezing air immediately assaulted any part of their exposed flesh, particularly their ears and fingertips. Faint grey mists surrounded them as their breath was instantly frozen the moment it was exhaled; their noses had already begun to run.

Marcus led the way and edged his way around to the rear of the tanker and towards the part of the gate that was not completely blocked by the truck.

"Jesus Christ," he exclaimed as he caught site of the dead on the other side.

Carl had not been wrong in what he had said; they were still there and, completely frozen. The bodies closest to the entrance were terrifying and, at the same time, curious to behold. Hundreds of them clung to the railings of the barrier, their hands frozen in a death-like grip and their faces solidified in their final expressions before they had succumbed to the sub-zero temperature.

Some had snarls fossilised into their faces, baring their teeth, their eyes fixed open. Others, their mouths agape with wide eyes as they froze in mid-wail and moan. All of them had a layer of white frost covering them, causing the browns and greys of their flesh to fade slightly, leaving them looking like grotesque and macabre rows of garden ornaments, placed and moulded against the gate.

Behind them, thousands upon thousands of heads could be seen, in all manner of positions and expressions. Arms were locked in place, reaching into the air, remaining motionless and giving the appearance of stone statues.

The vision was surreal, and all six of the living people stood staring, open-mouthed and unable to speak a word.

Marcus approached the gate, standing just an arm's length away from the closest of the solidified corpses.

"Careful, Marcus," Jennifer warned from behind him.

He turned and nodded. "It's okay, love."

He studied them up close, even being so bold as to lean in and hold his head close to theirs as he peered into their faces, looking for any signs of movement. Their frozen glass-like eyes did not move. They remained fixed on whatever they had been looking at during the time they had frozen over.

"You think they're dead?" Lee asked as he approached, standing at the side of Marcus. "I mean, *really* dead this time?"

Marcus shrugged his shoulders, unable to tear his eyes away from the mass of motionless corpses in front of him.

"I don't know," he said with a shake of his head.

He crouched and began to study the face of a child that was pressed up tightly against the bars of the gate. She could not have been more than four, maybe five. Her face was caught in a perpetual snarl, her teeth bared and her lips curled back. Her flesh, below the layer of frost, looked a pale blue in colour and her big unblinking eyes, locked in place, stared back at him with large black pupils.

Marcus looked down. One of her hands was firmly grasping the railings, her fingers curled tightly around them. He could see the frozen brittle skin and exposed bone of her worn knuckles. In her other hand, clutched tightly to her chest, Marcus could see the tattered and discoloured cuddly toy rabbit that she had obviously carried everywhere with her in life, and now clung to in death.

A wave of sympathy filled Marcus' heart and rushed through his body as he eyed the unfortunate and pitiful child standing before him. He stared at her for a long time, finding himself pondering on what she had been before she was turned into one of the millions of un-dead.

The sight of her, so close and unmoving, gave him the chance to reflect, considering how easily it could have been one of his own children in such a state. To Marcus, it was horrific and heart rending, and he wondered how any god could allow a child's innocence to be cursed and ravaged in such a way.

Finally, he raised himself to his feet again and forced himself to collect his thoughts and direct his attention to the matters at hand.

"How have they all frozen, then?" Lee asked as he stared at the mass of still bodies. "We were cold on the roof last night, but we didn't freeze, so how come they have?"

"You ask some bone questions at times, Lee," Gary remarked as he came closer.

Lee turned to him, his eyes narrowing.

"Okay, then, professor, you tell me why all these pus-bags have frozen all of a sudden."

"Because, they're dead and…"

"Yeah," Lee cut in impatiently, "I know they're frigging dead, Gary, but why are they frozen?"

"Well," Gary began with a sigh, a cloud of mist drifting from his mouth and nose as he struggled to keep his patience.

"If you would let me finish," he looked at Lee for his approval to continue. "Dead bodies don't have any circulation and that is how us *'living people'* keep warm and stop ourselves from freezing. They," he nodded at the rows of frozen corpses, "they don't breathe, their hearts don't beat and their blood doesn't flow in their veins. They have no body heat of their own and they are always the same temperature as the air around them. So, they froze because their body temperature dropped to minus zero."

Lee watched him for a moment, letting the words of the older and wiser man soak into his brain. He looked back at the gate, and then back at Gary, then at Marcus.

"Is that true?" he asked with an air of doubt.

"Yes, Lee," Jennifer confirmed, "it's true. When you're dead, everything is dead, and dead bodies don't have circulation."

She looked at her husband and rolled her eyes.

Marcus smiled back at her and made an almost invisible shrug of his shoulders as Lee stood looking at them in doubt and confusion.

"The gaps between the hinges are getting bigger," Steve remarked as he looked up at the edge of the gate. "They must've been really going for it down here before they froze."

Marcus looked up at the flaking concrete and hummed in agreement. He could see that the fissure had grown and that the barrier had more movement within the pillar that held it in place.

Jennifer, feeling bolder, stepped closer and peered out through the gate and over the heads of the sea of dead.

"There's so many of them," she remarked, rhetorically.

"Yup," a voice from behind agreed, "I would say that there are somewhere in the range of eight and nine hundred thousand of them surrounding us right now."

Everyone turned to see Johnny standing in the open area behind the tanker, staring past the living people and towards the gate, holding a sandwich in his hand. He reached up and took a large bite as Marcus and the others watched him curiously.

"How do you know that?" Jennifer asked as she stared at the strange man who looked back at her with an indifferent smile.

"Because I counted them," Johnny confessed, "not individually of course, oh no, my dear, that would take me forever."

"So how did you come to that number, then, Johnny?" Steve asked as he moved towards the vagrant.

Johnny stepped back, protectively holding his sandwich behind his back and shaking his head.

"You're not having a bite of my bacon butty."

"I don't want your sandwich, Johnny. I want to know how you counted them."

Quickly, the homeless man swept his hand from behind him and rammed the remainder of his breakfast into his mouth, chewing noisily and wiping his lips on the back of his sleeve with an expression of contentment spreading across his face.

"Easy," he said between chewing and swallowing, "I'm not stupid you know; my fellow sausage. While you were all hiding from the big bomb, I was walking about and enjoying the peace and quiet."

He grinned at Steve, his teeth filled with clumps of half chewed bacon and bread.

"I got bored and began to measure the walls. I counted how many of those ugly people were in each square metre; on average of course, multiplied that by the length of the walls, and then the depth of the crowd."

Marcus let out a low whistle as he calculated the figures in his own head then turned to Johnny who remained watching them impassively.

"Is that what you meant when you came into the house, telling me 'five on average'? Is that five per square metre?"

Johnny nodded.

"Jesus," Lee gasped, "that's more than I thought."

"What do we do?" Carl asked suddenly.

Steve turned to him and grinned. "Hope the cold lasts."

Back at the house, the remaining survivors were excited to hear the news. Some believed that it was the end of the dead; that they would finally die in their frozen state.

"We can't assume that right now," Gary announced, trying to stem the flow of over-optimism that seemed to spread through the building.

"Those things out there, they're already dead and there's no reason to believe that they are incapable of thawing out."

"Yeah, but maybe the cold will finally kill them all?" Sophie argued.

Gary nodded.

"I hope that is the case, but we don't know enough about them or what makes them tick, so we have to assume that when the weather changes, they will begin to move again."

The discussion continued until Marcus appeared, kitted up, wearing his ammunition strapped to his body and carrying his rifle in his hand. Behind him, Kelly and Joey also appeared, wearing their flight suits and making their way towards the doors.

Gary looked up and began to approach him.

"What's going on, Marcus? Are you going somewhere?"

"Yeah," Marcus replied, "a few of us are going to go out and collect what we need while we have the chance. We'll see if we can bring back some vehicles and equipment that will come in handy for the move north."

"Be careful out there, my friend. This *is* England, after all, and you know how easily and quickly the weather can change."

"Yeah, don't I know it?" Marcus replied with a smile. "The only place on the planet where you can get all four seasons in one bloody afternoon…in the middle of July."

Marcus heard the sound of footsteps coming down the stairs and looked around to see Stu, struggling with his equipment as he attempted to ready himself for the patrol.

"No, mate," Marcus ordered as he moved towards the bottom step, shaking his head at Stu. "You're staying here for this one."

Stu was about to protest but Marcus stood his ground, shaking his head resolutely.

"Stu," Gary interrupted, "you need to rest. You've took a serious knock and you would be more use to us here."

Stu looked from Marcus to Gary, realising that neither of them would stand in his corner over the matter. He knew they were right. His swollen nose throbbed and his blackened eyes burned. His body was weak and ached all over, and his head still ached from the concussion. He placed his rifle down and dropped his kit, looking deflated and rejected as he watched Lee and Steve join Marcus, ready to accompany him on the patrol.

"Stu," Marcus began encouragingly, "you, Hussein, Jim and Kieran, you were almost killed yesterday and you're lucky to be here. Don't worry, there'll be plenty more trips out that we will need you on in the future. In the meantime, get yourself back to fighting fit and chill the fuck out, mate. We can handle this one."

Stu nodded, but remained feeling dejected.

"Yeah, you're right," he agreed. He looked up at Marcus. "Before you go, what's this surprise you had for me?"

Marcus led Stu to one of the storerooms at the back of the foyer. He opened the door and grinned back at his friend.

"You're going to love this," he said with a glint in his eye.

Stu's eyes immediately fell on the black metal object in the centre of the room, the light glinting from the dull steel of its body and barrel.

"Where did you get this from, Marcus?" he asked with delight rising in his voice.

"The helicopter crew had it."

Stu stared down at the General Purpose Machinegun, his eyes lustfully running over the familiar shape.

"I want you and Jim to test fire it while we're gone," Marcus said as he watched his friend staring lustfully at the gun. "We have about eighteen hundred rounds for it, so don't get carried away testing it out. Just confirm that it's working okay and balanced right."

Stu nodded, unable to take his eyes from the weapon and the piles of linked ammunition stacked beside it.

"A, *'General'...,*" he whispered hoarsely, "we've got a *'General'.*"

21

"This will make you feel much better, Andy."

He stared back at her in confusion and watched as she reached for another bottle of the thick golden fluid. She unscrewed the cap and hefted the large container in her delicate and straining little hands. Holding it over the side of the bathtub, she tipped the contents into the bath, adding to the other liquid that was already beginning to rise to a reasonable depth in the tub.

Molly looked at him and saw the bewilderment in his eyes.

"It's okay," she smiled reassuringly as the bottle glugged and the last of the fluid drained. "It's just cooking oil. It won't hurt you."

Andy looked down at the wound to his abdomen. The row of staples and crude sutures that Molly had sewn to seal the tear in his flesh looked to be effectively holding him together. He ran his hand over the repair, feeling his fingertips brushing over the shining metal of the staples and across the thick knots in the rough cotton thread.

Molly had spent hours playing nurse to him as he sat silent and still, watching her work and revelling in the care and affection that she showed him.

He trusted her, and she trusted him.

Andy was allowing a member of the beautiful, fast moving kind to carry out surgery on him without wanting to end his existence. Molly, despite the fact that she had always run in fear from his sort with them wanting to tear her to pieces, seemed not to notice their differences anymore.

She accepted him completely and he was happy, truly happy, to sit and listen to the jumbled up noises that she made as she spoke to him, and completely oblivious to much of their meaning.

Now, they stood in the large bathroom of the farmhouse as Molly continued to fill the tub with the bubbling thick syrup. He could not understand what she intended it to be for, but he had concluded she was doing it for him; he was willing to follow her lead.

She tipped the final bottle of cooking oil into the bath and discarded the empty plastic container out onto the landing. Next, she reached down and lifted another object, but it looked different from the previous bottles. It was clunky and made of metal.

"This," Molly began, her voice straining as she hefted the weight, "is *'Castrol GTX',*" she said reading the label slowly.

"I've seen my dad putting it in generators and our tractor engine. He said it was to help machines from breaking when their joints were dry."

She looked up at him and then nodded to his knees and he followed her indication, looking down at himself.

"You have dry joints, so it won't do you any harm, I don't think," she reasoned.

The can of engine oil was tipped into the mixture along with anything else that she could lay her hands on. Shampoo, shower gel, toothpaste and even a bottle of mild disinfectant were thrown in, bringing the level of the bath even higher.

"Oh," Molly suddenly exclaimed excitedly, "wait here, I'll be back in a jiffy."

She ran out of the bathroom, leaving Andy standing, staring at the bath, completely bemused. A moment later, the child reappeared, barging through the door, her arms laden with more items.

"Look," she said, holding something out in front of her for him to view. He had no idea what it was.

"It's perfume," she said with a tone that sounded as though Andy should have rolled his eyes, accompanied with a 'tut' to himself for not realising.

Still, he had no idea what it was and just stared back at her, blankly.

Molly shook her head in disappointment.

She tipped the first, then the second, and continued until five bottles of her mother's expensive perfume had been added to the oily bath, absent-mindedly humming a song to herself as she worked.

Finally, she stepped back, wiping her hands on her trousers. She stopped and looked around for something, then saw what she needed in the corner, by the toilet.

"Ah-ha," she gasped with satisfaction.

She leaned over the bath and dipped the toilet brush into the mixture, and began to stir, still humming as she did so.

Andy watched and listened to her. Her movements were a delight to watch as her nimble feet danced around with such energy. Her voice and singing drifted to him, brushing delicately into his ears and wrapping his mind in a euphoria that almost sent him into a hypnotic state.

The little girl, Molly, meant everything to him now. She filled his every thought and he felt alive while he was with her. Her energy and life force seemed to radiate from her soul and infected Andy in the process through his proximity to her.

"There you go," Molly said, stepping back and clapping her hands together before wiping them on her trousers again.

"All ready for your bath?"

Andy remained standing still, staring at her and the bath alternately. He was able to deduce that the tub full of strange liquid was for him, but he did not know what she expected him to do with it.

Molly tried to encourage him to climb in, but all her hand gestures and words of instruction fell on ears that were incapable of understanding her.

She paused, placing her hands on her hips and huffing with resignation. She considered demonstrating what she wanted him to do, but she felt uncomfortable with the thought of getting undressed in front of Andy. Besides, the contents of the tub would not do her skin any good, she surmised.

Finally, a thought occurred to her and she instructed Andy to remain where he was while she went to find what she needed.

A while later, she returned with a brochure for a home furnishings store, turning to the pages containing the bathroom section and holding it up for Andy to see.

"You see," she said pointing at the pictures, "that's what I want you to do."

Andy's eyes narrowed as he scrutinised the images on the page and he focussed on the particular picture that Molly was pointing at for him.

He looked from the picture to Molly, who nodded approvingly at him.

"See? It's a bath, and that's *your* bath," she said, pointing at the tub to her right.

Andy could see that they were the same thing and in the picture, he saw the head and shoulders of a young woman protruding from the piles of bubbles that surrounded her, as she smiled for the camera.

Andy's eyes widened as he realised what he needed to do. Immediately, he began to position himself to begin climbing into the bath.

"Wait," Molly ordered.

Andy paused and turned to her, unsure of what it was that he was doing wrong.

"You need to get undressed, Andy. You can't have a bath with your clothes on."

He looked at her, his brain back to not understanding what she was saying or what she wanted from him. She pointed at his clothes and attempted to demonstrate that she wanted him to take them off, but it was impossible to get through to him.

"Undressed, Andy," she said slowly, "you need to get undressed."

Finally, with her patience wearing thin, she reached out to him and pulled on his jacket, attempting to remove it from his shoulders. Andy pulled against her and let out a groan of doubt, suddenly becoming feared and unsure.

"It's okay," Molly reassured him, holding up the brochure once more. "Look, the woman in the bath, she doesn't have any clothes on."

Andy scrutinised the picture again and looked down at himself, seeing the filth-ridden jacket and jeans clinging to his body. He looked back at Molly for her confirmation as he gripped the waistband of his trousers.

She nodded and then watched as Andy fumbled with his clothes. He was unable to undo the buttons of his jeans, so Molly reluctantly obliged him, turning her head and grimacing as she did so.

A new emotion crept into Andy, travelling through his limbs, making him unwilling to remove his clothing in front of the little girl. He trusted Molly, but something deep within told him that she should not be in the room when he began to undress.

Modesty was new to him and it made him feel vulnerable and exposed.

He looked at Molly and grunted, nodding slowly and indicating to his hands that tightly gripped the top of his jeans.

Molly smiled, partially with relief that she did not have to help him the whole way.

She pointed to the pile of towels and the bathrobe that she had placed on top of the toilet seat, and smiled at him as she headed for the door.

Andy watched her leave and then looked back down at himself. He had no idea how to go about undressing; a fear of literally falling to pieces once his clothes were removed skulked its way into the back of his mind.

He fought hard against his fears and, after a long struggle, he had removed all the filth encrusted and decaying clothing from his withered body.

He paused and looked down at himself.

His mottled, dark, wrinkly skin clung to his bones stubbornly. The muscle and flesh below had all but disappeared and his joints jutted out from his body.

Again, he ran his hand over the sealed wound in his abdomen as he stared at the bath with concern. He remembered the care that Molly had taken to repair him and his trepidation began to fade.

With a sudden influx of courage and determination, Andy climbed into the bath. He gripped onto the sides and slowly lowered himself in. He felt the liquid flow over his dried body and begin to penetrate his leathery flesh, surging into his brittle joints and bones.

He lay back and gasped.

It was a gasp of satisfaction, remembered more than physically felt, from the days when he had taken regular baths, and the sudden release of stress and tension that the hot steaming water had once given him.

He lay there for a long time, allowing his body to soak up much of the oils as they seeped into every fibre of his impaired frame.

After two hours of lying in the mixture, his skin had begun to soften. He touched the flesh on his forearm, feeling it move without breaking under his fingertips. Next, he raised his hands and rotated them, listening for creeks and groans as the joints rubbed against each other. They made no sound and moved smoothly as he watched their newfound suppleness with delight. He raised his legs and began working the knee and ankle joints, grunting with pleasure and excitement as they moved noiselessly.

Andy made his way down the stairs, wrapped in the bathrobe that Molly had laid out for him. It had taken him some time to climb from the bath and get the robe over his shoulders, but he was beginning to coordinate himself better than before, and was quicker at getting dressed than he had been at getting undressed.

He placed his steps carefully, taking his time for fear of losing his grip and slipping due to the oil that coated his skin. The fluid had soaked through the towel material of the white robe, leaving it a discoloured yellow, leaving a trail of oil in his wake on the carpet of the stairs.

While Andy was in his bath, Molly had lit a roaring fire in the sitting room. Even from the stairs, Andy could see its orange glow as it illuminated the sitting room. He staggered through the door, emitting a soft moan to inform Molly that he had arrived and was ready for her next instruction.

Molly looked up from one of the couches and placed the book that she had been reading to one side. She jumped from her seat, smiling broadly at him as she eyed him and began to walk towards him.

"How do you feel? Better?" she asked.

Knowing that her friend could not understand her words, she took him by the sleeve of the robe and led him over towards the couch, close to the fireplace. He sat down without a single groan or crack coming from his brittle body. He glanced up at Molly in surprise at the absence of noise from his joints.

"See, I told you it would make you better," she grinned, "you even smell better, too."

Andy stared back up at her, unsure of what she was saying but able to understand that she was pleased with him.

"You need to keep warm by the fire. It's very cold now," she instructed him as she checked the damage to his abdomen and confirmed that the stitches and staples were still holding his flesh together.

She sat on the coffee table in front of him, smiling at him affectionately.

"Would you like me to read you a story?" she asked eagerly, holding up a large colourful book for him to see. "It's one of my favourites, and there are pictures, too."

Andy settled into the soft cushions of the couch, slipping into a daze, listening to the gentle tones of Molly as she read to him.

He felt completely at peace and a wave of contentment coursed over his rejuvenated body.

22

On the orders of Marcus, the Puma helicopter conducted a low and slow sweep of the town centre. Nothing moved on the ground, and the deep freeze was complete. Everywhere they looked, grisly statues stood locked in place, frozen to the ground as the sub-zero temperature had crept over them while they lumbered through the streets.

Every surface of the built-up area looked opaque as the cold covered the land with a fine layer of frost, including the thousands of motionless bodies that filled the pavements and roads, and from the height, the numerous corpses took on the appearance of marble.

"Okay, Kelly," Marcus called through his headset, "find a clear place to touch down. Once we're clear, take off and stay on standby for a few minutes until I give the thumbs up, then return to base to save fuel."

"Roger that," Kelly replied as she began her descent towards an open piece of ground situated between a wide sprawling car park, and a large two-story building that looked like a college campus.

As the aircraft came in to land, the downwash from the rotors sent dozens of bodies scattering across the hard pavements and roads, their frozen limbs shattering as they were thrown and tossed against the concrete.

The wheels touched down with a jolt and Marcus felt the suspension bounce as the aircraft dealt with the hard surface below. He turned to the other three in the passenger compartment and, with a nod of his head, jumped from the starboard door and out onto the street.

His rifle was immediately brought up into the aim and he scanned the area around him, looking for any sign of movement from the dozens of figures that stood in all manner of stances around them.

Steve jumped from the door and joined his brother, while Lee and Carl exited the helicopter from the port side, covering their left flank.

"Okay," Marcus spoke through his personal radio to the other members of his team. "Push forward and cover the area. We'll remain static for a few minutes and allow a 'soak period'. Keep your eyes open, boys, we're in the lion's den here."

All four of them began to walk forward, away from the helicopter as the sound of its engine changed pitch and it began to rise back into the air.

Carl, kneeling down beside a wall, nervously looked over his shoulder and watched as the dark, bulky shape of the aircraft began to soar into the sky. Suddenly, he felt alone and completely detached from safety. He glanced across at Lee, who did not seem to notice the fact that the helicopter was leaving them on the ground in the middle of an infested city. As usual, Lee's attitude was one of complete indifference to danger and fear.

All around them, Carl could see hundreds of dark shapes, just standing there as if waiting for the order to begin moving again. He watched them, his brow sparkling with beads of sweat despite the freezing temperatures. At any moment, he expected the bodies of the dead to suddenly come to life and begin converging on the four exposed humans caught in the open. A shiver ran down his spine and he began questioning why he had volunteered, even insisted, on joining Marcus for the mission.

Carl's earpiece hissed and he heard Marcus' whispering voice speaking to him inside his own head.

"Okay, close in to me," Marcus commanded.

Lee turned and began to walk towards the wall of the college building where Marcus and Steve stood waiting for them. On the way, he stopped and began studying the closest of the frozen statues scattered along his path.

It was a woman, and despite the powerful downwash from the helicopter, she had remained standing when many of the others had toppled over like bowling skittles.

He eyed her up and down, and conducted a complete three hundred and sixty degree sweep around her as he inspected the unfortunate woman. Her clothes looked relatively well kempt and clean, and her flesh did not look as decomposed and ravaged as the other bodies that he was used to seeing.

She had been a recent newcomer to the army of the dead; a fresh kill, Lee surmised.

He could see no injury that immediately stood out to him, but he noticed a dark stain on the lower portion of the right leg of her jeans. The material was torn; he guessed that she had been bitten, and had succumbed to the ravaging virus and fever that would have raged through her body over the subsequent days.

Her eyes were flat and lifeless, as was expected from the dead. The large black spots in the centre that had once been her pupils covered nearly the entire iris, but Lee caught a hint of their natural colour around the outer edges of the blackness, and he was able to imagine her with a pair of piercing green eyes.

Her face was pale and tinged with a blue green hue, but it was still that of an extremely attractive woman in her early thirties, Lee guessed. Her dark, wavy shoulder-length hair retained the form and shine of a living person, as though she had deliberately made the effort to reanimate as a good-looking corpse.

Lee smiled to himself at the thought of her brushing her hair and applying a final touch of make-up as she lay in her final stages of life.

He looked down and saw the bulge of her pocket, and reached in to retrieve her purse. He held the green leather pocket book in his hand for a moment, before looking up at her face one final time then turning to join Carl and the others.

"You finished chatting up dead people, Lee?" Steve remarked as Lee joined them at the wall, glancing back at the frozen body that remained standing where he had left her.

Lee shook his head, a troubled look on his face; Steve recognised something in him that he had never seen before.

"What's up?" Steve asked.

"Not sure," Lee replied with a shrug, "just that woman over there," he said, hesitantly and nodding towards the body that he had been scrutinising. "She was fresh, and I mean *really* fresh."

"Nothing we haven't seen before, though," Steve replied.

"Yeah, but…she was a beauty; or at least, she used to be."

"Oh for fuck's sake," Carl sighed, mockingly, "Lee's got the horn for a corpse. I didn't realise you were in to necrophilia, Lee. First, it was running around naked with the monkeys at the park, and now it's *'mesoming'*, as you call it, over dead women."

"I don't even know what that word means, so I'll not knock your teeth out yet…"

"Necrophilia," Steve repeated as he grinned and winked at Carl, "it means that you like shagging dead bodies."

"You three, shut up," Marcus scowled as he approached after checking the next street from the corner. "I can hear you from fifty metres away."

Marcus stepped out into the open space and looked towards the helicopter, hovering just above the rooftops a couple of hundred metres away to the north. He waved his hands above his head to get their attention and then indicated to the east, telling Kelly that they should head back to base.

The helicopter crew obliged and turned the aircraft, pausing for a moment before powering forward and out of sight over the buildings of the town.

Marcus headed back to the others, and was about to tell them to move out when he saw that Lee was engrossed with something he was holding in his hand and was rummaging through, pulling out cards and pieces of paper.

"What's that?"

Lee did not take his eyes off the purse and simply nodded out into the open.

"That woman's purse," he said, and before Marcus could say anything, Lee continued. "Her name was Michelle; here's a picture of her with a little baby. I told you she had once been a good looking woman."

Carl took the picture that Lee handed around for all of them to look at. He nodded in agreement.

"Yeah, she was," he confirmed, "but that's just fucked up, Lee. Once they're dead, they're just walking bags of pus, you know that."

"Why are you so interested, Lee?" Marcus asked, beginning to get annoyed with their petty distractions.

"I don't know," he shrugged. "Just that she was a fresh kill by the looks and maybe if she had survived a few days longer, she would've been okay when the freeze came along and we might have found her."

"Aye," Marcus replied with a growl. "Would have, should have, could have… it's all bollocks and doesn't matter anymore. She's dead and there's fuck all any of us can do about it, so put your 'keep-sake' away and let's get moving. I want to be back before dark."

Lee stuffed the picture into his pocket and climbed to his feet. He turned and began to follow the others as they made their way along the wall and into the next street. Before he turned the corner, he paused and looked back at the woman one last time.

She remained motionless in the centre of the open area, her frozen eyes staring straight ahead of her. Lee turned away with a sigh, breaking into a jog to catch up with the others.

Two streets away, they stopped and stared at two large vehicles parked in the middle of the road, flanked by rows of buildings and shops. To the left of the vehicles, the sign above the door at the top of a set of steps read, *'The Nelson.'*

"Shit," Steve exclaimed as he eyed the name above the pub and looked at the two static vehicles. "They must be the Range Rovers that Stu and the others had to abandon."

Marcus nodded.

"Looks that way," he said, then turned to the others. "You think they will still be able to start?"

Carl shrugged. "I don't see why not. They've only been here for a couple of days."

They approached the first of the Range Rovers and began a slow circle of the vehicle, inspecting the damage they had sustained as the mass of bodies had closed in around them. The side windows were broken and numerous dents covered the bodywork, but Marcus could see no serious harm.

"Looks like most of the damage is mainly cosmetic," Carl announced as he finished his own inspection and stood at Marcus' side.

Marcus grunted and stepped closer. The driver's door was still open and a frozen corpse sat in the seat, its hands grasping the wheel with a confused look on its solidified face. Marcus reached up and gripped it by the sleeve of its jacket. He pulled at the body but it refused to budge. With a huff, he placed one leg against the frame of the door and yanked the lifeless man from the seat.

With a noise that sounded like a layer of sticky tape being removed from a smooth surface, the body tumbled from the vehicle, leaving its arms behind, still stubbornly gripping onto the steering wheel, fused from the frost. The remainder of the man crashed to the floor, breaking at the waist and cracking open like a frozen egg.

Marcus looked down at the shattered corpse and saw the congealed internal organs, all clumped together with ice, as they broke away from the ribcage and rolled onto the floor at his feet.

He screwed his face up at the strange and gruesome sight, spitting on the ground with disdain before climbing into the vehicle and prying the hands free of the wheel. He tossed them out into the road to join their owner.

In the seat, Marcus eyed the dashboard and the controls of the vehicle. He had once owned the same model, before Steve had wrecked and abandoned it months earlier while Marcus fought his way back from the Middle East.

He looked to his left and saw the key fob in the central panel where the gear stick was situated. He picked it up and pushed the button, and the dashboard lights came to life. He smiled ruefully and pressed down on the clutch, checked that it was in neutral and pushed the start button. Without any hesitation or sputter, the engine caught and came to life, grumbling menacingly beneath the hood.

Steve turned at the sudden sound as the roar of the engine filled the silent street all around them. He glanced about, nervously looking from one frozen statue to the next for any sign of movement. He checked the doorway to the pub behind him and eyed the mass of corpses that cluttered the entrance, standing shoulder to shoulder, as they had frozen while trying to fight their way out into the street.

"Carl," he hissed as he kept one eye on the nearest of the corpses, "what's the temperature right now?"

Carl fumbled in his pocket and pulled out the thermometer, holding it up in front of him as the mercury settled.

"Uh…," he began, as he squinted to see the small red numbers beside the glass tube, "minus one, I think."

Steve snatched the instrument from his hand and checked for himself to put his mind at ease. Satisfied, he handed it back to Carl with a nod.

"Keep an eye on it, mate."

"Will do," Carl replied, stuffing the thermometer back into his pocket.

Lee gingerly climbed the steps of the pub, holding his rifle tightly as he approached the cluster of motionless corpses filling the entrance. They were strange to look at, having frozen instantly in mid stride as they staggered, *en-masse* towards the door.

Each body supported the other, as they remained entangled with one another in their final strides and stumbles, their bodies fused together with ice. To Lee, the tangle of bodies and limbs reminded him of a strange sculpture that some modern artist may have come up with, depicting some struggling event in history, or even an interpretation of the workings of a depraved mind.

The dark and mottled flesh of the dead was mainly browns and deep greens, and looked almost bronze at a glance, especially with the fine shining layer of frost coating them from head to toe.

He leaned in close and inspected the nearest body, a gaunt and skeletal russet face, hardened in mid-snarl with one hand reaching out towards the open street. Its throat had been torn open and Lee could see the bone and dried ligaments of the neck within the ghastly wound, the shredded and wrinkled flesh looking like frozen and shredded beef jerky.

Lee placed his foot on the final step to get a closer look at the figure, his boot accidentally knocking against the leg of one of the frozen corpses that was joined to the first by a hardened layer of ice.

The body shuddered and rocked slightly.

The sudden movement sent the whole group oscillating, and within a couple of seconds, they all came crashing forward as Lee's clumsy footing had unsettled their delicate balance.

Lee screamed as the mountain of frozen corpses tumbled forward onto him, sending him reeling down the steps and falling flat onto his back. Before he could roll out of the way, dozens of stiff bodies piled on top of him, pinning him to the floor beneath their combined weight and sending him into a screaming panic, as he struggled to free himself of the repugnant trap.

Marcus and Carl raced to the scene, raising their weapons and, at first, believing that some of the bodies had managed to avoid the freezing process and had attacked Lee.

Lee's arms and legs had sprouted from the rotten mound while his muffled cries for help echoed hollowly from below.

Marcus and Carl realised that they were no immediate threat to Lee or themselves and stood by, watching their friend as he struggled and howled beneath the pile of rotting flesh.

Lee's head appeared from between two bodies, his eyes wide with terror and panic as he struggled to get free.

"Help me, for fuck's sake," he screamed up at Marcus and Carl as they stood watching with smirks creasing their faces.

"Fucking help me."

Marcus and Carl began to laugh as they watched Lee's face disappear into the midst of bodies again.

"He looks like that bloke from the movie, Titanic, doesn't he," Marcus laughed. *"Jack, don't leave me, Jack."*

"You been playing 'pus-bag Jenga' or something, Lee?" Carl added as he watched.

Steve appeared at the side of the pile of corpses and began pulling them off his friend. Finally, Lee was free of the pile and he scrambled to his feet, frantically brushing himself off as he spat continuously on the floor.

Steve turned away and headed back to the second vehicle, leaving Marcus, Carl and Lee standing by the mound of frozen dead.

"You wankers," Lee scowled as he stared at Carl and Marcus, his face red with anger and his body trembling from fear and rage.

"What's up, Lee?" Marcus asked with mock bewilderment. "I thought you had found a sudden liking for being up close and personal with the pus-bags?"

"Check to see if he's got a hard-on," Carl added, sending Marcus into fits of laughter at the expense of the enraged Lee.

"Fucking wankers," Lee grumbled as he stomped off to join Steve in the second Range Rover.

Steve got the other vehicle started as Marcus climbed back into the first, and soon the entire street echoed with the roaring engines. The two brothers pushed down on the accelerators and allowed the Range Rovers to move forwards a few metres, checking that their wheels were still serviceable.

After a few minutes, they switched off the engines. Marcus jumped from his vehicle with a broad smile spanning the width of his face. He could not believe their luck.

"Shame about the windows, bro," Steve remarked as they stood back and admired their new transportation.

Marcus waved his hand dismissively.

"Nah, we'll beef them up anyway when we get them back home. I was thinking that we should bar the windows and stuff like that."

"So we won't need the air conditioning, then?" Carl joked from behind.

"What now? Do we head back?" Lee grumbled, still sore from the ridicule that Marcus and Carl had dished out to him.

"We go shopping first," Marcus replied. "We may as well, while we have the chance. You never know how long this freeze will last."

He turned from the Range Rover and faced the others.

"We'll grab what we can from the closest of the stores. Don't head too deep into town and only take what we need. Once we've done that, we'll head for that big car park near where we landed and see if we can get a couple of 'people carriers.' What do you think?"

"Sounds good to me," Steve replied. "Lee, we'll check for food. Marcus, Carl, you grab equipment and clothing and we can all meet back here in say," he pulled up the sleeve of his jacket and inspected his watch, "thirty minutes?"

Marcus nodded. "Stay in comms," he said, tapping his earpiece. He crossed to the other side of the street with Carl in tow.

Steve and Lee headed in the opposite direction, towards the shopping arcade where they knew there would be an abundance of budget mini-supermarkets. Steve reasoned that during the chaos of the early days, the stores in the city centre might have been left unscathed, more or less, by the flood of panic-stricken looters for fear of becoming trapped by the increasing numbers of dead that had begun to fill the cities.

"Those two arseholes," Lee huffed as he walked along at the side of Steve.

Steve smiled.

"What? Come on, Lee, it *was* pretty funny and I'm sure that you would have laughed just as much if it had been someone else."

Lee shrugged and thought for a moment.

"Yeah, true," he admitted, "but they're still a pair of wankers."

They approached the arcade and paused at the large broken doors spanning the width of the entire entrance. The darkness from inside loomed out at them and the wind that flowed through the cavernous interior whistled and echoed as it howled through the length of the arcade, creating its own long and poignant moan.

Steve felt a shudder run over his goose-bumped flesh, as though an unseen force was warning him not to enter the darkness.

Lee stepped forward, his feet crunching on the countless beads of glass scattered across the ground. He hesitated at the threshold and looked at the doorframe to his right. It was twisted and buckled, having been forced inwards and broken from the hinges as thousands of the walking dead had descended on the shopping arcade.

He turned to Steve and raised an eyebrow.

Steve was unsure. Although the wind that rushed at him from beyond the doors and brushed his face was just as cold as the air outside, he still feared the unknown and imagined some of the dead managing to remain mobile inside the shopping centre.

Another haunting gust of wind moaned as it made its way through the darkness and out into the light.

Steve felt like turning away and running for the vehicles, but he fought against his fear, mainly to save face in front of his friend.

He shook his head to himself.

'Here I am, about to die because I don't want Lee to think I'm a pussy,' he thought.

Lee took a careful step through the doorway and paused again, allowing his eyes to adjust to the gloom. Steve followed suit and they stood, side by side, with their weapons at the ready in case a horde of unfrozen dead came hurtling towards them.

Nothing stirred inside.

There were no echoing footsteps or lingering moans from the dead, just the sound of the cold air gusting through the stores and wide corridors, and the heavy breathing of the two living men.

"It's a fucking tomb," Lee hissed through the darkness.

Steve nodded and grunted in agreement, but he still felt uneasy.

"Come on then, let's get on with it," Lee whispered, and he began slowly making his way deeper into the arcade.

Steve reached down and switched on the light that he had attached to the stock of his rifle. The narrow beam blazed out, illuminating anything that he pointed his barrel at, and he remembered Marcus' lesson when he was training them all on how to use the rifles they had brought with them;

'Wherever your eyes look, the barrel of your rifle should point.'

Steve kept his brother's wise words in mind. He dreaded the thought of being caught unaware with his weapon aiming in the wrong direction to where he was looking. He knew full well that a split second could be the difference between life and death.

The light cascaded over the broken and shattered windows and doors all around them as they crept through the eerie darkness.

Throughout the shopping centre, debris and bodies littered the floors. Some of the remains had clearly been killed and consumed by the dead, and others were the figures that had roamed the arcade and frozen in the sub-zero temperature, their bodies being knocked over by the gusts of wind flowing through the dark corridors.

Steve stepped closer to a figure that his light had illuminated as he scanned a doorway. It sat on the step to a clothing store, its hands resting on its lap and its eyes staring at the ground a few metres in front of it.

Steve moved nearer, the strange, frozen statue rousing his curiosity. It looked like the dead man had just decided to take a rest while the frost had set in. Steve almost expected the head to rise up and the eyes to lock with his.

He moved on, a shiver running down his spine as he imagined the corpse's head slowly turning to watch him as he walked further into the murky tomb of the arcade.

In the first store that they stopped at, they busied themselves clearing out what was left of the tinned food aisle, piling everything into a rickety trolley that Lee found on its side close to the entrance.

All of the large windows of the storefront were smashed inwards, with tables and stacking-shelves turned over and scattered around the threshold.

"Looks like someone tried to make a stand here," Steve suggested as he studied the debris and damage.

Dark stains of blood were smeared all along the floors and walls, with discarded bones of all shapes and sizes littering the narrow walkways between the shelving stacks. As he grabbed the last few remaining cans from the tinned section, Steve looked down and saw the tiny ribcage of a child at his feet. Its broken skull lay, discarded a few metres further along the aisle. There was no sign of the remainder of its body, and he involuntarily pictured the screaming child being torn apart and dragged away in different directions by the hordes of flesh-hungry creatures.

He shuddered and felt sick at the image that hung stubbornly in his mind; he shook his head vigorously to cast the sight from his thoughts.

He threw the tins into the shopping cart as Lee walked from another aisle, his arms bustling with packets of food.

"Noodles and rice," Lee said as he saw Steve looking at him and his burden. "These people weren't too keen on Chinese food by the looks of it."

They loaded up the last of the goods and added all the cases of bottled water that they could find, before moving on to the next shop.

Deep inside the arcade, they came to a large department store, and both of them stopped, staring into the pitch-black interior, unsure of whether they should go in.

Steve took a nervous glance over his shoulder, peering into the darkness behind him and searching for the creeping death that he was sure he could feel descending upon them. He looked across at Lee, his friend's face looking deathly pale and haunting in the glow of his torchlight.

Lee pointed his rifle into the store and cast its beam through the wide entrance. In the darkness, the layers of frost coating everything in sight twinkled as the light of Lee's torch reflected from it, appearing like a fine layer of sparkling dust. His shaft of light illuminated a number of frozen, grotesque statues in the aisles; their forms looked like strangely placed and disfigured mannequins to an unsuspecting eye.

Steve checked his watch, the face of it glowing green as he pushed in the button on the side. He was hoping that his watch would inform them it was time to head back to the vehicles, saving him the trouble of having to justify to Lee why he did not want to go into the store.

He saw the time, but his brain did not register it. Instead, his eyes saw something else.

"Jesus," he grumbled to himself.

"What?" Lee turned to his friend; shining his light in Steve's face and making him wince. "What's up?"

Steve waved his hand and Lee lowered the light. He looked back at his watch and shrugged.

"It's nearly Christmas, and none of us has even noticed."

Back at the vehicles, Marcus and Carl were already busy bundling their goods into the rear of the two Range Rovers. The rear compartments were already bulging and filled, almost to the point of bursting, with the winter clothing and camping equipment that they had liberated during their looting.

They looked up at the sound of the squeaking and rattling wheels of the shopping cart as Lee and Steve approached.

"What you got there?" Marcus asked, studying the piles of plastic bags that Steve carried in his arms and over his shoulders.

"Allsorts," Steve replied in a strained voice as he dumped the bags on the ground at the rear of the second vehicle.

"Looks like more than just cans of peaches and pears to me, bro."

Steve nodded as he watched his brother begin to rummage through the items that he had taken from within the shopping arcade.

Marcus looked up in confusion and annoyance as he began pulling out children's toys, board games, perfume gift-sets and piles of clothing and pyjamas of all sizes.

"What the fuck, Steve?" Marcus frowned, holding up a set of women's black lace lingerie. "You become a 'cross-dresser' now?"

Steve shrugged.

"It's not for me. It's for Helen. It's nearly Christmas and I thought…"

"You thought what, Steve, that you would do a little Christmas shopping? While we're off ram-raiding 'outdoor clothing' and 'camping' stores, grabbing sleeping bags, gas stoves, cold weather gear…you were busy browsing the knickers section in Matalan?"

"It was *'British Home Stores'…*"

"Shut the fuck up, Gorman," Marcus spat as he turned and glared at Lee, cutting him off in mid-sentence.

Marcus' face was red with anger, and his eyes bore a hole through Lee's face as he scowled at him. Lee looked away nervously, as if he was staring at an enraged animal about to attack.

Steve noted the fury and disappointment in Marcus' tone, and was about to reply with the argument that the survivors back at the Safari Park needed a break from the harsh realities of the new world.

"Shit," Carl suddenly gasped, indifferent to the ferocity of Marcus' appearance as he stood looking at the date on his own watch.

"I had no idea. My wife will kill me if I don't get her anything this year. I fucked up and forgot our anniversary in January, so here's my chance to make amends. Where did you get the sexy knickers, Steve?"

Marcus turned as Carl began to walk away in the direction of the arcade. He was about to say something when Steve and Lee suddenly tottered off to join him and collect more loot.

"Brandy, we need brandy too," he could hear Carl saying as they walked away from him.

"You can't have Christmas without brandy."

Marcus leant against the rear door of the Range Rover, shaking his head in disbelief as he sensed that his patrol had begun to fall apart around him, as every one of them decided to go on a shopping spree.

"Fucking civvies," he grumbled, brushing his hand over his hair and smiling to himself in resignation.

He glanced at the street around him, eyeing the shattered windows and broken doors. Nothing moved and the dead remained frozen in place. He checked his watch and nodded to himself. They still had four hours before nightfall.

"Fucking civvies," he said, shaking his head.

He turned and broke into a jog, following in the wake of the others as they disappeared into the arcade.

'Jenny would look good in some of that underwear', he thought to himself as he caught up with Steve, Lee and Carl.

23

"So," Jennifer began as she stepped closer to the helicopter, her shoulders hunched in her thick jacket as she protected her neck from the harsh cold. "Are you two going to be staying here, at the park?"

Kelly turned around and looked out from the passenger compartment of the aircraft. The large wrench that she carried in her hands glistened with oil and she dropped it onto the floor, where it landed with a heavy clunk. She wiped her hands on a cloth and smiled at Jennifer as she began to climb out from the door.

"I don't see why not," she said, studying the other woman's face for her reaction. "I mean, that's if you will have us and nobody objects."

Jennifer smiled and pulled a small hip flask from her pocket. She unscrewed the cap and took a generous gulp before offering it to Kelly.

"I've no objections," she said as Kelly took a swig of the spiced rum, "you've brought plenty to the table so far. This helicopter," Jennifer continued as she approached, and run the palm of her hand over the green painted metal of the aircraft's superstructure. "It's proven itself already. I mean, Stu and the others, they would be dead now if it wasn't for you and Joey in this helicopter."

Kelly nodded and looked up at the long rotor blades. "Yeah, she's old but there's still life in her."

"I'm glad you're staying," Jennifer turned to face her. "I know that Marcus can be a little scary at times, but he's a good man and will do *anything* to protect the people he cares about."

"You're referring to that Stephanie woman?"

"Yeah," Jennifer nodded. "Helen told me all about it. I know it must seem barbaric to you, but my husband was doing what he thought was best for the rest of us. He couldn't take any chances. You do understand that?"

Kelly nodded. "Yeah, I understand it now, but I will admit it freaked me out when I saw it and I wasn't expecting it."

"We're a family here, Kelly, and if you're part of our family, then Marcus will be just as savage in order to protect you and Joey."

"That's good to know," Kelly smiled.

"Anyway," Jennifer leaned in close with a glimmer in her eye and a hint of a whisper in her voice. "There's far too much testosterone around here and we need more of us girls to show them who's boss."

As the sun began to dip below the horizon, the survivors gathered in the foyer of the house, as they did every evening. Marcus and the others had still not arrived and people were beginning to get concerned.

"I'm sure there's nothing to worry about," Gary consoled Jennifer, "they're probably just busy getting as much stuff as they can, while they have the chance."

"The dead are still frozen," Claire added. "I was down at the gate with Jake just an hour ago and there's no sign of them thawing out, yet."

"You want us to go and look for them?" Kelly asked as she turned to Stu.

He shook his head.

"No, it's getting dark and we can't risk losing the heli as well."

He looked up at Jennifer who stared back at him in anger. Stu realised his mistake and began to backtrack as he stumbled over his own words.

"I mean," he said in an attempt to correct his slip of the tongue. "I mean…well, I don't mean that Marcus is lost, or that anything has happened to him. I just meant that…"

"It's okay, Stu," Jennifer sighed, "I know what you meant."

Stu glanced across at Kelly, sheepishly. She smiled back at him and she saw the discomfort he felt from his mistake.

Karen entered the foyer from the kitchen, with Sarah and the other children close on her heels. Her hands were wrapped in towels, tightly gripping a large steaming pan that she held out before her.

"Come on," she announced in her booming, but soothing, voice, "grab your spoons and dig in."

She placed the hot cauldron on the table and turned to Sarah.

"Go and get the bread, sweetheart. Be careful though, it's still hot."

"Bread?" Jake asked as he took a great interest in the hot steaming silver pan sitting in the centre of the table. "What we having?"

"Yes, bread," Replied Karen, impatiently. "The children and I have been baking bread all afternoon, and that is hot-pot," she pointed at the container. "Now make yourself useful, young man, and fetch the bowls from the kitchen."

Gary raised himself from the couch, rubbing his hands gleefully as he approached the large dining table.

"Oh, Karen's famous hot-pot."

He stopped suddenly and turned to look at Karen in confusion.

"Uh, where did you get the meat?"

Karen stared at him, her face turning red and her glare burned deep into her husband's eyes as she glowered at him.

"Uh..." she looked about, checking who was paying attention to her and making sure that none of the children had heard the question.

"You stupid old goat," she hissed at Gary as she leaned in close to him. "Where do you bloody well think I got the meat from?"

Gary suddenly understood and looked at his wife in horror.

"No, Karen," he said in disbelief and nodded at the steaming mixture of meat and vegetables in the large pan. "Please tell me that isn't from..."

Sophie noticed the drama that was about to unfold and jumped to the rescue, leaving Stu, Kelly, Jennifer, and the others distracted, talking about something completely different from the contents of Karen's hot-pot.

She pushed into the narrow space between Karen and Gary and began placing spoons in front of each of the closest chairs around the table, smiling absentmindedly and humming a tune to herself. She stepped to her left as Gary opened his mouth to say something, and she brought her heel down, deliberately stomping on his foot to silence him from asking any more questions.

He pulled away from her with an inaudible yelp and raised his foot, grasping it in his hand as he stared at her with uncertainty.

"Sophie, you just..."

"Gary," she leaned across to him, but kept her attention focussed on the place settings around the table. "Shut up and be quiet."

She fixed him with a look, leaving him in no doubt about how serious he should take her.

"In case you haven't noticed," she continued in a lecturing tone, "Tesco and Morrison's are shut and we have a lot of hungry mouths to feed around here."

She gestured over her shoulder at the people sat around, talking in the foyer. Gary looked at them and saw the children as they emerged from the kitchen, carrying the trays of bread that they had helped Karen to make.

"I love the animals here, just as much as you do," Sophie continued as the older man turned to face her again. "But when one of them dies, just like the old gazelle did this morning, it would be a shame, *and a waste*, not to eat them."

She paused and allowed Gary to let her words soak in.

He glanced at the pot, then to the people in the foyer, and then to the scolding face of his wife as she stood with her arms folded and her chest pushed out. Finally, he looked back at Sophie.

"You're right," he nodded as he turned to Karen. "Sorry, love, I just get so attached to these animals and forget what's going on at times."

Karen's face softened and she held out her hands, her fingers folding around the palms of her husband's as she smiled at him.

"It's okay, but you're still a silly old goat."

Marcus finally arrived as the remainder of the survivors finished their meal. The relief in many of the faces seated around the table was clear as they watched the four men begin, sweating profusely and dragging in all of the items that they had looted from the town.

Although they had originally intended to be back before darkness had fallen, Marcus and the others decided that they should take advantage of the sub-zero temperature, and the lull in the battle against the hordes of dead.

Marcus, Steve, Lee, and Carl, ransacked every store that they came across. They loaded their vehicles with their booty of essential and non-essential goods. Steve argued that *everything* they liberated from the abandoned town was essential, on account of the fact that receiving unexpected gifts and comforts would be a great boost to the morale of the people surviving within the walls of the Safari Park. A fact that Marcus finally came to understand and agree on, after a moment of reflection.

Once the two Range Rovers were filled to the point of bursting, they moved to the large car park close to the college buildings. It had taken them some time before they found exactly what they were looking for, but with the dead rendered immobile and posing no immediate threat, they had taken advantage of their newfound luxury of time as they checked each vehicle to see if it met their needs.

Finally, with all their loot in tow, they left the built-up area with the two Range Rovers and another two large people carriers. Altogether, in the four vehicles, Marcus estimated that they had enough space to move every member of the group, split between them and crammed into the vehicles, should the need arise.

"What's all this?" Stu asked as he looked down at the piles of clothing and equipment.

His eyes fell on the other items, things that were clearly not critical to their continued survival.

Marcus winked and smiled at him.

"Christmas presents."

Over the following days, Stu organized the work teams, and each day they travelled through the fields and out onto the country lane where the four vehicles waited. The two Range Rovers and people carriers were reinforced and strengthened to protect the living passengers from the dead. Grilles and wire mesh were attached to the windows for added protection and, once the work was completed, the vehicles were left to the north of the park, tucked away in a lay-by and stocked with food, fuel and equipment.

Every two days a patrol was sent out to them to check that they were still in working order and able to start. As part of the patrol's duties, they began clearing a path that ran through the centre of the overgrown fields.

At first, Stu and his work teams cleared all the long grass in a narrow channel, ripping up the tangles of weeds that grew close to the ground and threatened to ensnare anyone that ran into them. It took a lot of work and a lot of sweating and cursing as the work parties attacked the frozen ground with shovels and picks, flattening the miniature hillocks and filling in the deep ruts and holes.

Once the path was completed, stakes were placed in the ground at five metre intervals along the line of the track, with a length of rope attaching each to the next to help guide the survivors should they need to evacuate the house during dark hours.

A ladder, made of rope and wood, was constructed and placed against the cliff wall for people to scale, rather than having to try to descend the sheer rock face, which would inevitably lead to accidents and broken bones, even deaths.

Marcus wanted nothing left to chance and insisted on all eventualities being prepared for. Their equipment, weapons and ammunition were continually checked for serviceability and adjusted as new items were added to their loads. Map studies of roads and built-up areas along their intended route to their new location, far to the north, were carried out on a daily basis to the point where everyone knew the names, directions and distances of the roads and towns without having to check their maps.

Each member of the group was taken through the procedures of evacuation from the house and towards the vehicles to the north of the park. They practiced scaling the cliff and navigating through the fields, using the handrail made from ropes as Marcus observed and timed the drills.

Steve, Jake, Helen, Kieran, and Carl, were all nominated to be group leaders, having survivors allocated to them that they were responsible for during an evacuation. It was their job to ensure that the people under their care were guided from the house, through the fields and placed into the vehicles, while Marcus, Stu, Lee, Jim, and Hussein were the protection force, covering their retreat.

The drills were practiced and adjusted continuously, tweaked to perfection to ensure that no one was left behind and they could escape at short notice.

The primary plan, however, was to evacuate most of the group, including all of the children, by helicopter. The remainder would head north in the vehicles and meet up at a rally point that Marcus had specified from the map.

All was set and they were prepared for any eventuality.

Suggestions were made that they should take advantage of the weather and make the move as soon as possible, but Marcus argued that it would be too dangerous to go ahead without being fully prepared. If a thaw suddenly hit, the road team could find themselves in trouble without the correct equipment, personnel and preparation in place to deal with it.

The harsh cold continued as the people of the house celebrated the birth of Christ and exchanged presents, while the dead remained frozen at the gates, locked in a perpetual state of immobility.

On Christmas Eve, a banquet was organised with drink and games that lasted late into the night as the survivors forgot, for a short time, that the world they had once known had ended, and now millions of walking corpses roamed the earth, ravaging all who fell into their path.

It was never completely from their minds, though, and many, in between drinks and laughs, kept a watchful eye on the thermometer hanging in the hallway.

The next morning, as the children thundered down the stairs with excitement, and as many of the adults struggled to stem the pounding in their heads caused by the flowing alcohol from the night before, they were greeted by a blanket of brilliant white covering the entire land outside the windows of the foyer.

Marcus, with burning eyes and a dry throat, stared out at the thick layer of snow that carpeted everything in sight.

"Shit," he hissed as he realised what the snow would mean.

"What?" Jennifer asked as she stood beside him, admiring the view and revelling in the fact that they had a white Christmas; the first they had seen in many years.

"Snow," Marcus replied hoarsely as he moved towards the door.

"If it has snowed, then it means the temperature must have risen."

Jennifer realised his concern and followed him as he went to check on the thermometer. Marcus snatched it from the wall and stepped out through the large double doors. Howls of delight and excitement erupted from the children behind him as they began tearing into the presents sitting below the tree that Lee had erected in the foyer.

Outside, the cold air assaulted Marcus' flesh and made him cough and splutter as it seeped into his lungs. Instantly, his nose began to run as he stood staring down at the thermometer in his hand.

He prayed that his fears were unfounded.

Finally, after a moment, the mercury settled, reading zero degrees Celsius in the glass tube. He paused and looked out to the south, squinting in the harsh light of the winter morning. It was impossible to see anything from ground level.

He remained still and silent, Jennifer standing by his side and watching him intently. He angled his head and squinted, opening his mouth to cast out the sound of his own heartbeat in his ears as he focussed his hearing.

He could hear nothing.

The low murmur of thousands upon thousands of corpses was absent from the air and he began to relax as he turned to his wife and smiled.

"I think we're okay," he said with relief.

Jennifer smiled in return and was about to say something when her husband looked up towards the roof, and stepped back into the snow-covered gravel of the parking area in front of the house.

"Hey," he hollered into the cold air, "who's up there?"

Two heads suddenly appeared over the ledge of the roof, instantly recognisable as Jake and Kieran.

"What's up, Marcus?" Jake called down.

"You see anything moving out there? Are those pus-bags still frozen?"

The two heads paused and scanned to the south then looked back down to the ground at their leader as he stood watching them in anticipation of their reply.

"Yeah," Kieran shouted back down to him, "they're completely dead and frozen; just like a bunch of shitty ice-pops, Marcus."

"A little like my arse," Jake added, "it's fucking freezing up here."

"By the way," Kieran added, "Merry Christmas."

Marcus waved to them and headed back inside to the warmth. Jennifer linked her arm through his as she sidled up beside him, heading for the large wooden doors.

"You worry too much," she spoke to him softly.

"Someone has to."

"Yes," she replied, with a nod of acceptance, "but there are plenty of other capable people here, Marcus; people who have proven themselves many times over. So, just for today, let someone else do the worrying and play at being boss. The boys need their dad." She paused and smiled up at him. "I need you, too."

They remained standing at the top of the steps for a while, holding and kissing one another, completely oblivious to the cold air that wrapped around them as they embraced and revelled in each other's warmth.

24

The cold snap continued and the land remained frozen, locked in the grip of the sub-zero chill. The snow continued to fall and coated the ground, buildings and trees, burying them beneath a thick layer of brilliant white.

The dead remained motionless in the icy shells that their bodies had become, covered in the deep snow and hidden away from the eyes of the living, but they were never forgotten. The dead were never too far from the mind, as they stood frozen in place and awaiting the inevitable thaw.

For months, the reanimated bodies of the deceased had ravaged the earth, their ranks swelling each day as more people died and joined the legion of ravenous monsters that roamed the land, constantly in search of warm living flesh to devour and consume.

The cold brought a respite, a lull in the battle against the army of rotting corpses as their bodies, unable to generate heat, iced over and sent them into hibernation.

At first, Molly had not realised that Andy could also freeze over. She awoke one morning, thrilled about the thick blanket of snow that covered the ground outside her bedroom window and rushed down the stairs to tell her friend.

She burst into the sitting room, gibbering with excitement, to find an iced over and inert Andy, seated on the couch in front of the fading embers of the fire as it slowly died. Molly tried to get him to move with words of encouragement, thinking that her friend had just lapsed into a stupor, but the sight of his frost-covered eyes and hard, cold flesh made her realise that the dead were incapable of keeping themselves warm.

From then on, she kept the fire burning throughout the day and night as she fought hard against the elements to prevent Andy from freezing over again. On a number of occasions, she had seen his discoloured flesh begin to collect a coating of frost again, prompting her to add more fuel to the flames that warmed the room where her lifeless friend remained confined, as the temperature outside plummeted to the coldest winter she had ever experienced.

Andy sat quietly, watching as Molly continuously checked on him, encouraging him to stand as she observed and listened to his joints, ensuring that they had not seized up on him and that the oils were keeping him well lubricated.

As the weeks past, with little else to do other than sit and wait out the cold spell, Andy learned more and more from the little girl. She spoke to him, sometimes giving him instruction and other times telling him stories and making conversation to keep the boredom at bay that had begun to creep up on her.

He had remained inside and watched through the window as Molly ran around in the snow outside. She lay on the floor, flapping her arms and legs, making strange patterns in the dazzling white substance that seemed to bring her so much joy.

He looked on in confusion and curiosity as she collected a large mound of the snow and began rolling it into a ball, which grew larger as she guided it around the courtyard.

Something about Molly's activities seemed familiar to him as his dead eyes continued to stare out at her while she jumped about, laughing and waving to him through the window. Faint glimmers of memories came to him, from a time long ago when he used to do a similar thing when the ground turned cold and white.

Eventually, Molly stepped back, brushing the clumps of snow from her gloved hands and admiring her work.

"You see?" She called to Andy as he stood staring at the strange sculpture. "It's a snowman. A man made of snow, Andy."

He felt the urge to go out and help her, to join in with her delight as she ran around with a joy that he remembered once feeling himself when he played in the white brilliance, but her words echoed around in his decayed mind, ordering him to remain indoors. Words such as *'stay, no, danger'* and *'dead',* resonated through his ears as he remembered the possible consequences of him leaving the house, the danger and consequences that Molly had so vigorously explained to him.

He understood little of what she said, but he recognised certain words, and her body language was clear enough; *he was not to go outside while the whiteness covered the ground.*

With a sigh of disappointment, he turned from the window. He looked down at his lifeless hands and saw that his fingers had begun to turn white;

a layer of sparkling frost had crept over him while he stood close to the cold window.

Feeling the panic rise within him, he quickly moved back towards the fire. As he stood in front of the heat and flames, he saw the pale crystalline coating that had formed over his face and head in his reflection in the mirror. Slowly, the frost disappeared and the fear inside him subsided but he remained close to the heat, afraid of becoming locked in place while Molly remained outside.

Molly, one morning, in a moment of great wisdom, decided that his body was protected from drying out but not against the ravages of decay. She concluded that he needed extra protection from the rot that slowly ravaged his body. Molly reasoned that it would be in his best interest if she were to paint him with a layer of wood gloss from a tin that she found in the shed at the bottom of the garden.

Again, it was something that she remembered from watching her father when he painted the fence, and explained that the varnish would help to protect the wood from rot and prolong its existence.

She smiled at the idea of looking on Andy as a machine made from wood and engine parts.

Andy stood patiently in front of the fire, stripped naked apart from the old towel that was used to protect his newfound modesty and Molly's embarrassment. His young friend diligently applied the sticky brown substance to his flesh, giving him several coats as he stood with his arms outstretched and legs spread. As the varnish dried, his joints began to seize up, but Molly assured him that he would be fine and that eventually the stiffness would go away with continued exercise.

He looked down at the little girl, completely trusting in her knowledge as she gently brushed the varnish into his skin.

As an extra precaution, Molly wrapped his elbows, wrists, knees and ankles in bandages, soaked with oil to ensure they remained well lubricated.

She looked up at him and grinned and he replied in the only way that he knew how; a rasping gurgle which was the closest he could come to laughing. Molly found his attempts hilarious and broke into fits of laughter. Andy attempted to follow suit, grunting and spluttering, trying to mimic the sounds of the animated child as he flailed his arms and shook his head.

Once he was covered, she ordered him to remain standing in front of the fire with his arms and legs outstretched. As he dried, Molly re-entered the room with a bundle in her hands.

"Here you go, Andy. I thought you could do with some new clothes. I got these out of my dad's wardrobe, and he was *always* very smartly dressed."

He stared down at the pile of material on the couch. He looked back up at Molly in surprise while she stood before him, smiling as she began holding up each item of clothing.

"This is a lovely shirt, Andy. You will look very smart in your new clothes, don't you think? I think we should get you a hat, too."

Andy stood and stared at her as she folded the clothing. She really did care for him and he could feel the affection that she held towards him. It warmed him from within and if he had been capable of crying, tears would have flooded his dried and varnished cheeks. He had never imagined wearing new clothes, especially clothes that were given to him by a member of the beautiful people.

He adored the little child that gave him a feeling of life. She did not look at him as one of the vile creatures outside. She spoke to him and treated him as her equal, a friend that was lost in the same horrific and cruel world that he was.

Later, Andy stood before the mirror, staring at himself as he studied his new look. At first, he did not recognise his reflection and became confused by the man that stared back at him. It was only when Molly joined him at his side, he realised who he was actually looking at.

His skin no longer looked dry and brittle. It shone healthily with the layers of brown varnish that Molly had applied. He was far from looking like the attractive picture on the driver's license he carried in his wallet, but his flesh no longer looked like it was ready to fall from his bones.

His new clothes, free of the filth that had covered his old ones, fitted to his withered body in a much more flattering way than the rags he had discarded. As ugly as he believed himself to be, he was no longer terrifying to behold, even to himself as he stood staring back at his reflection in the mirror.

He felt a sense of pride rise up in him as he studied the figure staring back at him. The fresh and smart clothes with the dazzling white shirt and the jacket that covered the worn and bony shoulders that had jutted out from the old clothes, made him look far different from the despicable, shabby creatures that remained standing, frozen in the cold outside.

A dark green trilby hat and leather gloves were added as a final touch and at a glance; Andy appeared like a normal human being, an older man with weather-beaten skin and a touch of arthritis, standing beside his granddaughter in front of the mirror before leaving the house for a walk in the country.

For days, he strutted around in the sitting room, revelling in his new image and the joy it brought him each time he saw a fleeting glimpse of himself in the mirror.

It was early morning and, as the sounds of the singing birds drifted to him from outside, Andy raised himself from the couch. He could see the light beginning to shine through the curtains as the sun cast the night far towards the western horizon.

He staggered towards the window, glancing at the burning embers of the fire as he passed by, and then down at his own flesh to check that the frost had not begun to take its grip on his body again.

Reaching up, he pulled the curtains to one side, allowing the morning sun to penetrate the sitting room with its bright light, casting the shadows away into the far corners of the room. Around the window-frame, Andy noticed droplets of water, steadily dripping down from the melting icicles that had formed around the plinth at the top of the window.

He glanced down at the sill and realised that the snow was melting away steadily, turning to slush as the freezing cold released its grip on the land.

The snowman that Molly had made for him, no longer bore the appearance of fresh, sparkling white that it once had. Instead, its surface began to turn opaque as the frozen water slowly returned to its liquid form.

Andy let out a grunt as he eyed the strange sculpture. It had become misshapen and dull in its appearance, despite the radiance of the sunlight reflecting from its white body.

He considered going out into the courtyard to attempt to restore the snowman, to save Molly from disappointment when she awoke to see her hard work steadily turning into a slushy puddle. He did not want to see his young friend despair and as he considered his course of action, he noticed something else.

His eyes widened and his throat rattled as a grumbling moan forced its way up through his rasping larynx. Quickly, he turned and headed for the stairs. Climbing the steps as speedily as possible, he headed for Molly's room.

She lay in her bed, slumbering and completely unaware as Andy opened her door and slowly stepped over the threshold. He looked at her still form as she lay, wrapped in blankets and lightly snoring as she slept.

Andy grumbled and staggered forward into the room, his heavy feet scuffing against the carpet as he dragged himself to the side of Molly's bed.

She remained completely oblivious to his presence as he stared down at her. Her long, flowing hair covered much of her radiant face, leaving just a glimmer of the plump, soft flesh of her cheeks and her rose-tinted lips.

Andy paused, looking down at her, and feeling something spring to life inside of him. His hand reached out for her and he bent at the waist, bringing his face and mouth down towards her face.

His hand grasped her by the shoulder and a loud moan erupted from his mouth, his tongue flopped from the gap between his teeth as his jaw sprang open.

Molly's eyes shot open and she turned to see Andy's vacant eyes staring down at her, just centimetres from her face, his speckled black and blue tongue hanging from between his broken and discoloured teeth.

She stared back at him in horror, unable to move from fear as Andy's rotted face closed in on hers and his cold, clutching, bony hand remained tightly gripping her shoulder, pinning her to the bed as he moved in closer to her.

A whimper escaped from between her lips and she screwed her eyes tight, waiting defencelessly for the teeth of the dead man to close around her flesh and sink deep into her soft tissue.

The bite never came.

In its place, she heard the urgent grunts of Andy as he began shaking her by the shoulder. Gingerly, she peered at him through her squinting eyes, terrified of the figure that she no longer recognised as her friend.

Andy grunted again and pulled at her arm. She realised that he was not there to attack her, but he was trying to tell her something.

The terror that she had felt a moment before flooded from her body as she watched Andy's bulging eyes staring down at her with his own fear and concern.

"What is it?" she began as she stared back at him while he continued to grunt and groan urgently. "Andy, what's wrong?"

He pulled at her shoulder again then released his grip. He looked up at the window and raised his hand, his fingers closing inwards with his index digit pointing towards the world outside. He nodded, indicating that Molly should go and look, a long lingering moan surging from his mouth as he encouraged her to see for herself.

Molly jumped from the bed and headed for the window, sparing a backward concerned glance at Andy as he began to follow her across the room. She could see fear in him, but the fear was not for himself. She recognised that.

At the window, she realised immediately that the temperature had risen and the snow was already beginning to melt. The gravel of the courtyard was beginning to become visible in patches as the ice turned to liquid water.

The trees lining the track leading up to the house glistened as the snow and ice that clung to the branches liquefied, leaving them wet and dripping as the sun warmed their moss-covered bark.

Molly turned to Andy as he arrived at her side and looked out through the panes of misted glass. She saw that he was not looking at the courtyard, or the trees, and she followed his gaze out into the fields that surrounded the house.

Andy growled and bared his teeth as his brow furrowed into a frown, his cold and unblinking eyes fixed upon something that she had not yet seen.

There, in the long wet grass, Molly saw a number of stumbling figures, headed towards the house.

The dead had thawed.

She gasped at the sight of them, a cold tremble flowing over her skin as the icy hand of fear ran its creeping fingers across her flesh.

Andy growled again and Molly turned to face him, her eyes burning with terror as she glanced back down at the dark lurching shapes slowly making their way through the overgrown fields in front of the house.

He placed his hands on her shoulders and steered her away from the window. He looked down at her, his face softening as he clasped a hand on top of her head, ruffling her hair affectionately, before he turned for the stairs.

He gave a final grunt and pointed to the handle of the bedroom door, twisting the knob in his hands, and then closing it behind him as he stumbled along the landing.

Molly understood his command; she was to remain in the room.

Andy reached the bottom of the stairs and recovered his tyre iron from beside the main door. With a final glance up towards the first floor, he was satisfied that his young friend was safe from any immediate danger.

He pulled the door open and stepped out into the cold morning.

From ground level, he could not see the creatures as they converged on the house, but he knew they were there, creeping their way slowly through the grass.

Gripping his weapon in his hands, he waited at the edge of the gravelled courtyard, listening to the grunts and moans of the repugnant monsters, as they struggled through the weeds and up the slope of the hill.

Finally, the first of them appeared to his right, lurching from the swaying stalks of grass and out onto the crunching gravel.

It lumbered out into full view and looked up at the house, reaching out with its bony hands and wailing as its eyes fixed on the large red door.

Andy turned and snarled as he glared at the figure, feeling his anger soar and his protective instincts grip him like a vice.

It stopped and twisted its head to face him. Its skin sagged from its face, waterlogged and putrefying as the ice melted and turned its flesh to mush. Its clothing hung from its body with the weight of the water dripping from the fibres and stretching the material. It looked away from Andy, uninterested in him, and turned its attention back to the house.

It staggered forward again on uneasy legs and stumbling like a child learning to walk, groaning and grunting.

With a growl, Andy stalked after the walking abomination, quickly closing the gap between them as he raised his weapon high above his head.

Molly's care and devotion to the continued preservation of Andy gave him much more manoeuvrability than the others like him had. He was faster and suppler in his movements, stronger and more energetic.

The putrid creature turned and snarled; its mouth opening wide just as Andy brought down the weight of the iron in his hand, smashing it with all the force he could muster into the fetid face of the dead man.

The bones shattered immediately on impact, the tip of the tyre iron sinking deep, punching through the flesh, caving the face inwards and dropping the body to the ground where it landed in the gravel, scattering small stones in all directions.

Andy turned and saw two more emerge from the field and moved in on the closest. A rage had bubbled up inside of him, driving him forward with a determination that he had never felt before.

Growling and snarling, he lunged at the creature staring back at him with its blank eyes, its face turning to an expression of confusion when it saw the angered face of Andy glaring down at it, before the iron weapon was thrust through its skull.

The body let out a long gasp as it sank to its knees then fell forward into the slush on the ground, its face burrowing into the gravel of the courtyard, as its torn brains and coagulated blood seeped through the large hole in the top of its head.

Andy turned on his heel, letting out a loud moan in an attempt to attract the attention and stall the other figure as it lumbered towards the door of the house. The creature did not stop and Andy staggered after it, his legs powering him across the courtyard as panic gripped him.

He looked up and caught a glimpse of Molly at the window.

She stared down at him, her eyes full of tears and horror as she watched her friend battle with the dead attempting to reach the house.

The sight of her in such fear spurred him on and his eyes focussed on the back of the lumbering figure just a few metres ahead of him. Growling loudly, he rushed forward, his well-lubricated joints allowing a speed and strength that was unavailable to those like him, as he threw himself forward, smashing his tyre iron into the creature's shoulder.

They both tumbled to the ground, slipping in the wet stones.

The body of the dead woman continued to crawl forward, still headed for the door as Andy began to crawl up her struggling body, pulling at her legs and pinning her below him with his weight. Again, he raised his weapon and drove it down; embedding it deep in the head of the creature that wanted to hurt his friend.

Andy dispatched three more in quick succession as Molly looked on. She watched as the dead man that she had come to know and love as her friend, fought courageously to keep her from harm, completely oblivious to his own fears and safety.

Once the area was free of the threat from the dead, he paused and surveyed the scene around him. Six motionless bodies lay strewn across the courtyard, their skulls smashed, never to walk again.

Andy stared at them coldly and snarled with a strange feeling of satisfaction and relief. They would never again be able to hurt anyone.

Andy returned to the house and made his way to Molly, still safe in her bedroom.

He entered through the door and, immediately, the little girl ran to him, flinging her arms around his waist and hugging him tightly.

"I love you, Andy," she said, still firmly holding onto him with tears running down her cheeks.

Andy looked down at her, unsure of what to do but feeling an overwhelming sense of tenderness and fondness at the words she spoke. He understood what she had said to him and his soul inflated from the impact of their meaning.

His love for her was unquestionable. It was the one thing he was sure of in a world dominated by pain and death.

He folded his arms around her protectively, and pulled her close, grunting and murmuring as he began to stroke her hair, revelling in the feelings of life that she gave to him.

25

"What's the temperature, Carl?" Gary asked, keeping his eyes on the mass of bodies that remained pressed up against the gate.

"Fuck's sake," Carl huffed as he pulled the thermometer from his pocket. "I'm starting to feel like the weather man around here. Is this all I'm good for, telling you lot whether the day is going to be cold or not?"

Gary looked up into the air.

Apart from a few wisps of high clouds scattered in the stratosphere, the sky was a magnificent blue with the bright morning sun beaming down, now uninterrupted by the obscuring mass of grey snow-laden clouds that had filled the heavens for the previous few weeks.

"This country is a pain," Gary grumbled, "one minute, snow and freezing temperatures, then the next, the sun is cracking the flags."

"Not exactly flag cracking weather, Gary," Sophie added as she stood next to him, keeping a watchful eye on the grotesque, but still immobile, swarm surrounding their walls.

The ocean of corpses, frozen to the spot and partially covered by the heavy snow that had fallen, seemed endless, their numbers uncountable as they stretched as far as Sophie could see. She remembered the estimation that Johnny had come up with and the figure made her shudder.

She looked up at the gate, her eyes running the length of it and falling on the tanker that seemed flimsy when compared to the numbers of the dead pushing against it from beyond the walls.

"Plus two degrees," Carl finally informed them of the temperature. "It's only ten o'clock so it will probably go up to about five, by this afternoon."

Sophie turned to him.

"I don't know what you were complaining about, Carl. You seem to be enjoying predicting the weather for us."

Gary sighed then stepped forward to take a closer look at the hinges of the gate. They did not look as sturdy as they once had, but with the amount of bodies pressing against them, he was not surprised. The concrete that fixed them in place had become cracked, and in the area immediately around the fixture, a gap of a couple of centimetres had formed as the concrete had begun to break away. The fissure was big enough to allow the gate to move back and forth, slowly wearing more of the concrete away.

He looked from the frame of the gate and back at the endless sea of frozen faces in front of him.

They remained petrified, staring, snarling and locked in place in the positions they had been frozen in, slowly thawing out as the cold finally released its grip upon them.

"You think they'll be capable of moving again, once they're defrosted?" Sophie asked, looking from the gate, then to Gary.

Gary was too busy studying the tanker and its condition to notice the question had been directed at him. He estimated that the truck and its trailer probably weighed in at about seven or eight tons. Its body was placed so close to the gate that there was barely enough room to slide a sheet of paper between the tanker and the iron bars.

He looked back out at the swarm of corpses, then at the gate again. He knew that the barrier would eventually collapse and that the tanker, as heavy as it was, would do little to slow the tide of dead as they flooded into the park.

Finally, he turned to Sophie, a grave look etched onto his face as he considered the final collapse of the park entrance.

"Sorry, Sophie," he said as he realised that she was watching him expectantly, "did you say something?"

"Yeah, I did. I asked if you think they will thaw out and be back to trying to eat us?"

The older and wiser man looked back over his shoulder as he rejoined the others by the zebra striped Land Rover.

"I don't see why not. They're already dead and I doubt that a bit of ice will affect them much."

"What about the gate?" Sophie asked. "Will it hold?"

Gary shook his head.

"I don't know. There are so many of them and the concrete that's holding the hinge in place has begun to wear away, drastically. With enough force, they could collapse it and be in on us before we knew what was happening."

"Great," Carl grumbled, "maybe we should've done what Lee suggested and burned them all when we had the chance."

Sophie shook her head.

"There are too many of them. We couldn't burn the lot."

A resounding crack echoed in the still air around them, sounding like a branch being stepped on and snapping under the weight.

Gary looked at Sophie and then turned his attention back to the gate. The noise was followed by another snap, then another.

Carl moved forward gingerly, bowing at the waist and scrutinizing the mass of faces pushed up against the bars of the park's entrance. Although the bodies remained motionless, he could see that a number of lifeless eyes turned to look at him, glaring through their opaque film of thawing ice.

A cold shiver ran the length of his spine as he realised the dead were slowly returning to life, freed from their stasis and the freezing grip that had entombed them for the previous weeks.

"Shit," he hissed as he stepped back towards the others, unable to take his eyes away from the stares of the dead. "They're coming back."

More snaps echoed through the morning air as the bodies attempted to move again. Heads, free from their icy slumber, turned to face the living just beyond their reach. Arms and hands reached up with jerky motions, creaking loudly as the frost was broken from their joints. Throughout the entire swarm, the sound of fracturing ice and bone could be heard, assaulting the ears of the living as they looked on in horror as thousands of lifeless eyes turned to face them.

"Let's get back," Gary suggested in a trembling voice, his face ashen with fright. "We need to warn the others."

Lee finished tying the laces to his boots as he sat on the edge of his bed. He reached for his t-shirt and threw it over his head. He huffed and pulled a face at the taste in his mouth as he ran his hand through his dishevelled hair, which stood up on one side. Rubbing his eyes, and yawning loudly, he stretched the last of the slumber out of his body.

Sophie had been up early to do her rounds with the others, leaving him alone and able to take advantage of her absence with a well-deserved lie in. At least it was well deserved in his own opinion.

He stood and snatched his rifle up from the chair at the side of his bed and headed for the door. He was due to leave in an hour with Stu and Jim, to check on the vehicles that they had left on the far side of the fields, north of the park.

It was a daily routine that had begun to become monotonous, but he understood the need for the regular checks, and treated it more as an exercise in familiarity of the ground that they would need to cross to get there.

He had been part of the work teams that had cleared the track, and all too often, had pictured him as being the unfortunate soul that would trip and break his leg while evacuating the park. With daily repetition of the route to the vehicles, he surmised that he would know the track by heart and automatically place his feet in the correct places, even in the dark.

That was his reasoning and encouragement to himself.

He closed the door behind him and stepped out into the corridor, slinging his rifle over his shoulder and heading for the stairs.

As he walked through the dimly lit passageway, a noise stopped him in his tracks.

A groan, profound and lingering, drifted to him along the narrow hallway.

He paused, angling his head in an attempt to identify the direction from which the sound came. The house remained deathly silent around him and he felt the faint tendrils of fear creeping along his flesh, causing the hair on his forearms to stand on end.

He remained rooted to the spot, trying desperately to pinpoint the direction of the sound. After a while, without the lingering moan being repeated, he began to doubt himself.

He had been sure that it was the low rumbling moan of a man, or *dead* man, from somewhere inside the house. He had heard the same rasping lament a million times before and he knew what his gut feeling was telling him.

When the sound did not repeat itself, he turned to continue his walk towards the stairs, believing, convincing himself, that it was most likely the floorboards or walls of the old house, groaning from the cold and age.

Something in the back of his mind nagged at him, insisting that it was not the house or anything other than the mournful voice of the dead.

Before he reached the stairs, he stopped and looked back along the corridor and at each of the numerous doors that lined it. He squinted into the gloom and held his breath, trying hard to recognise any sounds from the rooms along the passageway.

He turned, about to begin his descent of the stairs to the empty foyer, when he heard a thud, followed by a muffled mutter, or whimper.

Lee turned, un-slinging his rifle from his shoulder and pulling back on the cocking lever. The working parts shot forward with a loud rasping clunk as the bolt scooped up a live round and fed it into the breach of the barrel.

His skin suddenly felt hot and flushed as his body surged and his nerves prickled his flesh. His eyes widened and his lungs began to take in large gulps of air. The muscles in his legs began to fill with oxygenated blood, and he could feel them beginning to tense as they prepared him for 'fight or flight.'

He was unsure of what to do next. He remained standing at the top of the stairs, staring at the door where he suspected the noise had come from with his rifle clutched in his sweaty palms.

The room was just five metres ahead of him on the right of the corridor, and his mind began to race as he pictured and feared the worst possible scenarios going on behind the thick wooden barrier.

Lee took a cautious step forward, holding his rifle tightly against his hip with the barrel pointing out in front of him. His body was coated with a cold film of sweat and his entire attention became focussed on the door where the noise had come from, as he slowly inched forward along the creaking floorboards.

Before he reached the end of the balcony overlooking the foyer, he hesitated and glanced down into the wide space below. No one was in sight and not a sound stirred within the house.

His heartbeat and heavy rapid breathing were the only noises he could hear as he continued his advance.

'Where is everyone?' he wondered to himself. *'Has something happened, have the pus-bags smashed their way through the gates and they've run away and left me here, alone?'*

Lee's mind raced and he pictured the other survivors driving away to the north, completely forgetting that he even existed as he lay asleep in his bed, and now he was left to fight and die in the house.

Another thud rang out from the room and Lee involuntarily ducked his head lower into his shoulders, as he expected a rotting figure to suddenly burst through the door and charge towards him.

He studied the entrance as he crept to within a couple of metres and realised that it was Jake's room, just two doors down from his own.

He stopped in the centre of the corridor and stole a glance to his left and then his right, checking that nothing had come up the stairs to join him in the narrow passageway and blocked his escape from the house.

He was still alone and the silence of the house remained oppressively still.

Stepping forward, he placed his feet as lightly as he could, trying to avoid any noise from the old floorboards beneath the thick carpet. He winced as he reached out with his left hand, intending to knock then thinking better of it. Instead, with his rifle held ready and his legs placed in a manner that he could spring backwards at a split second's notice, he leaned towards the door, placing his ear against the hard cold wood.

From inside, he could hear movement, but he was unsure of how to interpret the light rhythmic thuds and creeks. The different tones of the grunts and moans sounded like there was more than one of them in the room.

Lee stepped back, imagining Jake's body being torn into by a number of reanimated and rotting corpses, scattering his limbs and innards over a wide area and glistening with his blood, as it dripped from their gaping mouths.

He was terrified, but Jake had been his friend; the least he could do was ensure that the poor man would not come back as one of the dead to roam the earth, feeding on the living. Lee took a deep breath and nodded encouragingly as he steeled himself for what he was about to do.

"*Okay, okay,*" he whispered.

He reached out with his right index finger, feeling for the safety catch on his rifle and clicking it to 'fire.' He was ready. He would burst in, take care of Jake and then run for the main doors. After that, he had no idea what he was going to do, but he would keep on running until he was far from the park.

The weapon was brought up and pulled tightly into his shoulder. His left hand reached down and gripped the brass knob of the old door, twisting it slowly, careful not to make a noise and alert the dead to his presence.

The handle clicked, almost inaudibly, but in Lee's mind and with the house so deathly silent, it sounded like an explosion erupting in the still air.

With fear gripping him and his own voice screaming inside his head, Lee barged his shoulder against the solid wooden door, forcing it open with a crash, as it collided with the chest of drawers to the left of it, scattering bottles and other objects and sending them rolling across the floor.

The door shook and the echo of the impact reverberated around the room as Lee jumped over the threshold, his teeth gritted, a look of wild terror and aggression on his face.

He roared as he scanned his weapon to the left, bringing it into the aim and pointing it at the two figures struggling on the bed before him.

"*No,*" a voice screamed from amongst the tangle of limbs and sheets.

Lee had almost fired, but his finger soon dropped from the trigger as he looked on in horror at the scene that panned out before him.

His rifle lowered, his left hand losing its grip on the stock of the weapon. His right hand remained folded around the pistol grip, almost releasing his grasp on it and dropping it to the floor as his mouth fell open and his body became limp.

Lee remained staring at the bed in complete shock for a moment, unable to comprehend what he saw. His head swam and he could make no sense of the jumble of thoughts and feelings that suddenly converged on him all at once.

The two faces stared back at him, their eyes bulging with shock and fear as they watched Lee turn from a snarling, rifle-wielding maniac to a bumbling, gawking mannequin, frozen to the spot.

After a moment, the initial astonishment of the sight began to settle in Lee's system, allowing him to close his mouth and regain a degree of composure. He recovered his grip on the rifle.

The two figures in the bed remained motionless, looking at Lee with wide, bulging eyes, awaiting his response. After a while, when Lee did not say anything, they glanced at each other, embarrassed and terrified.

"Lee," Jake began, "it's not what you think."

Jake's words finally punched a hole through the opaque and disjointed reality that seemed to have shrouded and completely enveloped Lee.

He blinked and adjusted his stance, relaxing his knees, but regaining control of his shoulders as he brought them up from the slump into which they had drooped.

"Yeah, Lee, it isn't what you think," the other voice in the bed assured him desperately. "We uh...we uh..."

Lee looked at them both in turn, as they stumbled on their own words.

"What?" he asked finally. "You mean it was an accident and you both slipped?"

Jake looked at the person next to him, unable to think of an answer or excuse that could explain the situation that Lee had walked in on.

Without another word, Lee turned and walked from the room, heading for the stairs and shouting at the top of his lungs.

"Marcus, Steve," he hollered over the balcony. "Come and see. You won't believe what I've just found."

He bounded along the corridor and turned onto the stairs, leaping down them and taking three steps at a time as he continued to shout excitedly.

Steve arrived at the foot of the stairs as Lee was halfway down, still calling for the attention of anyone within earshot of his voice.

Steve looked up at him.

"What, Lee? What have you found?"

Lee was grinning from ear to ear, pointing over his shoulder with his thumb and shaking his head.

"I just walked in to Jake's room and found him and..."

Heavy footsteps thudded along the corridor above the stairs, warning Lee that someone was on the way to stop him from telling his tale. He turned to see the large figure arrive at the balcony, wrapped in a sheet.

Lee turned back to Steve and grinned ruefully.

Steve caught sight of the anger and embarrassment that burned in the eyes of Kieran and his brow furrowed as he looked back at Lee, wondering what his friend had now done to upset the big man.

"Oh, you won't believe this one, Steve. I've just caught..."

His report was cut short as the heavy double doors to the entrance of the house flew open with a resounding bang. Carl, Sophie, and Gary entered the foyer, out of breath and looking scared.

Steve turned to them, forgetting about the drama of what was happening above him, between Lee and Kieran.

Gary looked nervously at him and Steve raised an eyebrow as he glanced over his shoulder at Lee, then back at Gary. He was being flanked by dramatic events and he was unsure which to turn his attention to first; the grinning Lee and half-naked Kieran, or the fearful red face and panicked eyes of Gary.

"They're back," Gary finally gasped.

Steve stared back at them. "What do you mean, *'they're back'*?"

"Them," Gary nodded to the door, "the…, the…"

"The dead, they're thawing out," Sophie added with urgency as she saw that Gary was struggling with his words.

26

Throughout the day, as the temperature steadily climbed to six degrees above zero, the horde of corpses that surrounded the park slowly reanimated.

By the evening, their cries and wails could be heard even from inside the house as they resumed their assault against the walls and gates with vigour. The clangs and rattles of the iron railings resounded through the air. To the people standing on the roof of the house, it sounded like distant hammers being pounded against steel.

Marcus lowered his binoculars and scanned the length of the wall with his naked eye as the last rays of sunlight slowly faded below the tree line. His face bore the tell-tale signs of concern and he continuously bit down on his lower lip.

"They'll break through soon," Stu commented at his side, reading his friend's thoughts.

He stepped forward and rested a foot on the edge of the wall running around the outer rim of the roof, and balanced his rifle across his thigh.

"There's no chance of them getting through or over the walls, but by the sounds of it, that gate isn't going to hold out for much longer, Marcus."

Marcus nodded, squinting in the low sun as he continued to watch the black mass as it surged beyond the walls.

The weeks of freezing and the subsequent thaw seemed to have revitalised them in some way, re-energizing them, and now they threw themselves at the stone of the thick wall and the iron of the failing gate, oblivious to the damage they caused to themselves. Their only thought, goal, was to smash their way through the barricade, regardless of the cost.

Their screams and cries reached fever pitch, sounding like a football stadium holding a cup match in the days before the dead conquered the world and vanquished the human survivors into hiding.

The pulsing throng of reanimated corpses never ceased in their poignant song, which lingered and haunted the air for miles around.

"What are we going to do, bro?" Steve asked.

He had been standing there for a while, just a few paces behind Marcus and Stu, his presence unknown to them as he studied the sight for himself and made his own estimation of the situation.

Without turning to look at him, Marcus nodded with an unintelligible grumble and let out a long sigh of resignation.

"We need to leave, and as soon as possible, too," he eventually replied as he realised that Stu and Steve were waiting on his judgement.

"How's Hussein's knee and Jim's shoulder and broken arm? Will they be okay to begin the push north?"

Stu looked at him and shrugged.

"They don't really have much choice, do they? Jim's fine; it was just a flesh wound, really, and he told me to *'fuck off'* when I mentioned him going in the heli lift."

He paused as he shamefully remembered that it was he who had put the bullet in Jim in the first place.

"His broken arm is healing well and he won't take no for an answer, Marcus," Stu continued. "Hussein is still having trouble with his knee, but you know him; he's a tough little shit."

"When do we leave? Tonight?" Steve asked as he lit a cigarette and exhaled a long cloud of grey smoke into the cold air.

Marcus shook his head.

"No, we can't risk it in the dark unless we really have to. We'll leave at first light."

Steve looked up to the sky.

"You don't think the cold will come back, I mean the freeze and put them all back to sleep?"

Marcus also scanned the heavens.

"Not yet," he replied pessimistically. "Those dark clouds up there, they're full of rain, not snow. The sun is on its way down and there's no sign of the temperature dropping below zero again, not just yet anyway."

"Right then," Stu huffed, pulling his leg away from the wall and slinging his rifle over his shoulder. "We had better get everyone ready, hadn't we?"

Marcus nodded as he took one last long look at the hordes in the distance.

"Yeah, but don't cause a panic, and I want the guards doubled up tonight. Use the people earmarked to leave on the heli. The road team will need their rest."

Stu nodded. "Will do, boss."

That night, Marcus struggled to sleep. Many other people in the house suffered from the same; fear and uncertainty fuelled insomnia. Since the dead had revived and pressed their attack against the perimeter with more determination than ever, they all knew that it was only a matter of time before their position became unattainable.

Every member of the group of survivors had been informed of the intention to leave early the next day. Some had argued that it should only be done as a last resort, forcing Marcus to have to enlighten them about the imminent collapse of the gate.

Many faces had turned deathly pale with fright at the revelation from Marcus, and the thought of their sanctuary finally becoming compromised as the gates gave way. An uneasy silence had fallen over the house as people began preparing their belongings and family members for the move north.

Marcus held a final briefing with the group leaders, including Kelly and Joey, who would be transporting the bulk of the survivors in the helicopter. He went over the plan and the rendezvous points where they were to meet.

Fifty kilometres north of the park, on a stretch of highway that, because of its seclusion, Marcus believed would be free of the dead. The rally point was situated on a high point on the map, over thirty kilometres from the nearest city, offering the advantage of long-range visibility.

"You okay with that?" Marcus asked, indicating to Kelly and Joey as they sat drinking coffee and listening to the final briefing.

Kelly nodded as she blew at the steam rising from her cup.

"And if it's compromised or if you don't show?" she asked.

"Move to the second RV," Marcus shrugged with a nonchalant smile, "it's as simple as that. If we don't show within twenty-four hours, or if it's compromised and there are too many of the pus-bags to handle, move to RV number two."

He ran through the 'actions on', what they should do if the road team did not arrive at the meeting points, what they were to do if they had mechanical failure or had to ditch, and what they should do when they reached the new base.

Marcus and his men, who would be travelling by road, had numerous scenarios and 'actions on' that they had run through repeatedly during the weeks of preparation. None of them expected to make it through unscathed, but as long as they planned for every possibility, they believed they had a fighting chance.

The road team had conducted countless map studies, examining every section of road for their primary and secondary routes. The villages, towns, cities, even the service stations that they would pass close to on their move north, were etched into their minds.

The tension in the house could be cut with a knife and the fear and uncertainty carved into the faces of all was clear to see. Only the children seemed oblivious to what was happening. They seemed more thrilled about the helicopter ride and their excited questions and flitting eyes betrayed their innocence.

Jennifer was asleep, but Marcus remained transfixed by the ceiling, going through the plan in his mind, scrutinizing each phase for flaws or things he had missed.

He forced his body up from the springy mattress, swinging his legs out of the bed, and sat for a moment, massaging his burning eyes with his fingertips. He reached out for his boots, then realised they were already on his feet.

Marcus and Stu had advised everyone in the house to remain fully clothed, including keeping their shoes on, so that they could move at a moment's notice.

He glanced back at his wife as she lay slumbering peacefully, and then stood, picking up his rifle and assault vest from beside the bed and throwing them over his shoulder, as he crept towards the door.

Marcus left the room and made his way down the stairs to the kitchen, with the intention of making some coffee. The powerful aroma of the caffeine-rich drink was already lingering heavily in the air by the time he made it to the bottom step, and as he walked into the kitchen, he saw that there were a number of other people, also suffering from insomnia, already there and drinking from steaming mugs.

"You too?" Gary asked, looking up from the table as he noticed the tall bulky figure of Marcus move into the doorway.

Marcus smiled.

"Yeah, it must be the excitement," he replied jokingly.

The room remained quiet for a while, each in their own thoughts as the man who was about to lead them to their final realm of safety stood silently watching them from the door.

"Do you really think we need to do this, Marcus? I mean, maybe the gates will hold and they will never get in?" Gary asked optimistically.

"Gary," Marcus sighed heavily as he leaned against the doorframe and began massaging his tired eyes again.

"I know, I know," Gary began, waving his hand dismissively, "it's not a case of *if*, but *when* the gates collapse."

The room became hushed again as everyone's attention became focused upon the argument that threatened to break out between the two men.

Marcus just nodded and exhaled loudly, fixing Gary with a look that told him, he was not willing to get into a debate over it. The decision had been made to leave.

Gary submitted and remained quiet as he drank his coffee, staring down at the grain of the wooden table and running his finger along its surface. He had many fond memories linked to the old mansion and the park, and he did not relish the idea of abandoning the place. Over the weeks, since he had revealed his intentions of staying, no matter what, Sophie had kept on at him in secret, pleading with him and convincing him that he should go with them. Eventually, he had folded under her influence and agreed that he and his wife would move north with the rest of the group, but he had futilely hoped that the day would never come.

"Here," Stu said, holding out a cup as he walked towards Marcus. "We should go and see what's happening. It'll be first light in a couple of hours."

Marcus stepped through the door and out onto the roof. Immediately, he felt the cold drizzling rain pouring down from above, drenching him almost instantly as the fine spray coated his skin and saturated his bare head, sending rivulets of water running through his hair and down over his face.

It was cold, but the temperature of the rain and air refreshed him somewhat, and his eyes had stopped burning. He stood still in the centre of the roof and turned his face up towards the sky, holding out his tongue and relishing the cool rain.

"You should've been up here an hour ago," a voice said to him from the darkness.

"Fun was it?" Marcus replied, still facing the dark clouds and feeling the tiny sting of the rain on his tongue.

Carl shrugged as he approached.

"It came down in buckets and I'm drenched to the bone, mate. I don’t think I will ever dry out."

"Here, get some of this down your neck," Marcus said with a smile as he held out the cup of hot coffee that had already been half diluted with rainwater.

"How is everything?" Stu asked as he began to walk towards the lip of the roof.

"Hard to say," Lisa replied dejectedly.

She was sat on a stool, staring out over the park towards the wall with her shoulders hunched and her body trembling from the cold.

Stu looked down at her and smiled.

"I've spent many a night out in the rain, just like you are now, and wondering why the fuck I was there."

Memories of countless hours, days and weeks, spent in a hole in the ground, sodden with rain and mud as he stood guard over some piece of land that he did not know the name of, or even care about, flooded back to him with a nostalgia that only a soldier could understand.

Lisa looked up at him, pushing a thick strand of waterlogged fringe from in front of her eyes.

"Yeah, but, we know why we're here."

"True."

"It's a shame we lost the CCTV when we did. It would come in very handy right now, just to give us an idea instead of having to risk going down there."

She stood up and began patting and rubbing at the seat of her trousers.

"I hope I get the chance to change my knickers before we leave; they're soaking."

Stu tried hard, but he could not hold his laugh for much longer and it erupted from his throat like a spluttering howl.

Lisa looked on in bewilderment at his red grinning face.

"Simple things for simple minds, eh?"

Marcus continued to stand in the rain, staring out into the darkness, attempting to see through the black night and beyond the wall. He was tempted to go to the gate, to see what condition it was in, but he knew it was too much of a risk.

Throughout the whole day and evening, continuous reports had come down from the guards on the roof about the noises they heard and the movements they saw. On more than one occasion, as the hysteria and feeling of impending doom has spread, they had falsely believed that the gate had finally collapsed.

The dead were in a constant state of motion, their pulsing crowds surging back and forth, as they assaulted the walls repeatedly. No one had ever seen them so riled up and it was impossible to understand what had given them such vigour after their freezing hibernation. Many had hoped that the cold would have caused irreparable damage to them, leaving them permanently dead, or at the very least crippled and only capable of a much reduced speed and strength.

Instead, they threw themselves at the park as the 'fast movers' and 'infected' had done in the early days, at the start of the outbreak. Their cries and moans, louder and more vicious than ever before, echoed around for miles, terrifying the people as they stood guard on the rooftop of the house.

The rain continued to fall in fine sheets and, before long, Marcus and Stu were as drenched as the rest of the guard shift. The thought of dragging themselves through the fields to the north of the park after such a heavy rainfall was not an appealing one.

Marcus considered that, because of the sudden and heavy deluge and the low ground of the fields to the north, the track would be a quagmire of churned mud and swamp, resembling the battlefields of the Somme.

"Shhh…" Stu suddenly hissed, turning to Marcus with bulging eyes, a finger pressed against his lips. "Do you hear that?"

Marcus shook his head and the rest of the roof party took a step closer towards the edge of the wall, squinting into the murky night and trying to hear past the heavy drops of rain that splashed all around them from the outcrops of the roof, chimneys, and gutters.

"I don't hear any…" Claire began.

"Shut up, and listen," Stu growled with urgency.

Over the constant patter of the rain and the distant chorus of the dead song, another sound came drifting across the expanse of the park grounds and into their ears.

Carl frowned as he distinguished the new resonance from the other noises they had become accustomed to in the darkness. He looked at Stu questioningly. He was about to ask what he thought the new sound could be but Stu's contorted and frowning face discouraged him from speaking.

Marcus twisted his head and pointed his right ear towards the south. There was definitely something else adding to the ambient noise of the night. He could clearly hear the hum and wail of the thousands of reanimated corpses within the swish of the light wind, and echoing droplets of the rain, but something else, faint and distant, not a constant but still there, emitted from within the other noises.

"It," Stu began, and then paused, questioning his own thoughts before he continued. "It sounds like, a bit like…a *bell*."

Marcus, unable to hear anything, leaned back and glared at him, wondering if his friend had lost his mind.

"A bell?"

"My ears are better than yours, mate, and that's what it sounds like. I'm not saying it *is* a bell, but that's all I can describe it as."

"Oh fuck…" Carl exclaimed, suddenly realising what it was that he could hear.

He turned to the others, his face draining of all colour and his mouth beginning to tremble as he began to inch his way back from the edge of the roof.

"What?" Marcus asked as he stared at the pale-faced and rain-drenched, terrified man. "What can you hear?"

Carl glanced nervously from each of the people before him and then out, over their shoulders and towards the area of the main entrance that was obscured from their view by the numerous trees and darkness.

"The gate," he stammered as he turned to Stu, his voice quivering and on the verge of hysterics.

"It's not a bell, or anything else. It *is* the gate, collapsing. That's the sound of it bouncing against the steel tanker as hundreds of bodies climb over it."

Without another word, Carl turned on his heels and raced towards the door, disappearing down the steps into the house.

Marcus paused to listen, concentrating all of his efforts on his senses.

He heard it.

The sound was still there and the clangs of the two metal objects as they collided together, over and again, were unmistakable now.

"Shit, Carl's right," he gasped. "Get off the roof," he ordered the others, before turning turned to Stu.

"Get the general and get the road team up here. Keep everyone in the house and tell Kelly to get the heli started. She will have to pick the heli group up from the roof."

Stu turned to move, and then paused.

"Why the roof? Shouldn't we just load them in to the chopper?"

"We're out of time," Marcus replied with haste as he began searching the area to the south of the house with his binoculars.

"They're already in and Kelly may not be able to get it started before she's overwhelmed."

Stu took off through the house, screaming for everyone to get up and move. He burst into the kitchen where there was already a hive of activity going on as the word from Carl and the others had spread.

"Keep everyone inside," Stu ordered Sophie. "Marcus doesn't think that Kelly will be able to get the chopper started in time before the pus-bags get here."

He turned to Lee and Kieran, who were stood close by.

"Lock us down. Barricade the doors then get to the roof and bring every weapon and scrap of ammunition we have."

Before Lee and Kieran began dragging the tables and couches into place, Kelly raced out through the doors and into the rain, Joey following her as they headed for the helicopter. She drew the pistol from the holster on her hip, checked that a magazine was fitted, and pulled the top slide back towards her before released it again, ensuring that a round was chambered, as she readied herself for action.

Marcus watched as Kelly and Joey ran across the slippery wet grass and jumped into the cockpit of the aircraft. Immediately, they began flicking switches and preparing the engine to start.

To Marcus, it seemed to be taking forever as he stood keeping an eye on the open plains, the woods and the track leading up through the trees from the main gate.

In the house below, bangs and thuds resounded through the walls and roof as people began shoring up the doors and barricading the windows. Some had already begun to arrive on the roof. Children were crying and frightened voices from the adults attempted to comfort them as they asked incessant questions about what was happening.

Marcus heard an engine fire up from below, but it was not the sound of the Puma. It was a car engine; he looked down to see the zebra striped Land Rover racing across the gravel of the parking area with spinning wheels sending flying gravel and pebbles in all directions. It sped off towards the north of the park.

"Gary," Marcus yelled over the lip of the roof, "Gary, where the fuck…"

It was too late. The vehicle was too far away and, whether Gary could hear him or not, he clearly would not stop. Marcus watched as the rear lights disappeared over the rise to the north of the park, in the area of the animal pens.

Stu arrived at Marcus' side carrying the GPMG with coils of glistening linked ammunition draped over his shoulders.

"Here," he gasped as he slammed the machinegun down at the edge of the roof. "Lee and Kieran have the rest of the ammo between them."

Stu stood up straight and breathed deeply, his chest heaving and straining from the effort of organising the defence of the house then lugging the heavy weapon and ammunition up to the roof.

"How are we looking?"

"Come on, Kelly, come on," Marcus growled as he willed her to get the helicopter started and into the air.

A low whine heralded the electric motors cranking as they attempted to start the main engine of the aircraft. It continued to rise in pitch, and then a low rumble joined it as the powerful jet engines fired and began to grumble their way up through the revolutions.

"Come on, get it going, Kelly," Marcus encouraged as the main rotors made their first indication of turning and began to move, painfully slow, through the damp air as the motors began to howl.

To the south, specks of dark and distant moving shapes began to appear on the open fields that stretched out from the woods towards the east. Marcus did not need to raise his binoculars to see them, but instead turned his attention to the woods that were closer to the house and contained the track that led down, directly to the main gate.

'If they're already in the fields, then they'll be coming up the track too,' Marcus thought to himself as he eyed the dark woods.

"Steve," he yelled as he began to move towards the west side of the roof, "keep an eye on the heli and let me know when they're about to lift off."

Steve nodded and took up position with Jake and Helen on the eastern lip of the roof. They watched the helicopter intently as the blades picked up speed and the engine climbed in pitch. They could see that the mass of bodies approaching from the south were getting closer by the minute as they lumbered towards the house and the commotion from within and around it.

Marcus and Stu reached the western lip and stared down into the blackness of the park. They could hear the helicopter engine in the distance, and could hear the wind in the trees directly below them, but there was still no sign of the dead at their end.

"Set the gun up," Marcus ordered in an urgent voice as he began reaching into a pouch on his assault vest. "We'll need to buy Kelly as much time as possible."

A rifle opened fire at the eastern end of the roof, its muzzle flash lighting up the area and Steve, as he began pouring his rounds into the closest of the creatures approaching the helicopter from the south.

The howling engine continued to rise in volume and the rotor blades gathered speed as they thumped the air above the aircraft. Soon, they spun so fast that it was impossible to distinguish them individually. The engine screamed and the angle of the rotor blades changed slightly as the wheels began to gingerly bounce from the ground while Kelly increased the throttle and lift.

Screams, cries and panic could be heard from all around as more people poured out from the house and onto the roof. Unarmed and terrified, they huddled together in the rain, listening to the sounds of the aircraft as they desperately clung to their hope of rescue and watched the others around them defending the house from the dead assault.

Marcus quickly screwed the last of his mini-flares into the firing mechanism and cocked back the spring handle, which contained the firing pin. He held it up to the air, vaguely acknowledging the freezing rain running down the length of his arm.

Stu crouched beside him, the machine gun in his shoulder and a length of linked ammunition running from the feed-tray and through his left hand, held out to the side of the gun to support the weight of the rounds and prevent stoppages, or the link from snapping.

More shots rang out from behind them as Steve, Helen, and Jake continued to cover the helicopter crew while they attempted to bring the aircraft to the point where it had enough power flowing through the engine and was ready to take off.

The children whimpered and huddled close to the other members of the group that stood in the lashing rain, terrified that they would be stranded on the roof of the house as they watched, with wide eyes and growing terror, the dead making their way across the fields.

The flare shot out of Marcus' hand with a pop, blanketing the area in a blood red light as it soared into the air above the trees. In the ghostly crimson glow, hundreds of figures emerged from the darkness of the woods.

They staggered through the trees, their deathly pale and grotesque features illuminated by the flare as their eyes locked onto the source of the light and the two men who crouched close to the edge of the roof.

"Fuck, fuck," screamed Stu, as his eyes took in the magnitude of the crowd silently creeping towards them through the trees and along the path.

The advancing dead were everywhere, thousands of them, pressing towards the living as they staggered forward, shoulder to shoulder, through the underbrush of the woods and along the muddy track.

"Fuck..."

27

The barrel of the GPMG erupted with a roar and a jet of white flame as Stu squeezed the trigger, sending a burst of machinegun rounds into the nearest cluster that he had seen in the moment of the haunting red glow. The report of the gun was deafening, drowning out the sounds of the rifles that had seemed to open up all around him. Even the helicopter, as its engines screamed while it reached its maximum revolutions, was muffled by the blasting report of the powerful machinegun.

The butt of the gun juddered against his shoulder, sending vibrations through his whole body as he continued to squeeze the trigger for just two seconds at a time, sending out five round bursts.

The belt of ammunition flowed through the fingers of his left hand as he kept a tight grasp on the pistol grip with his right. All the time he swivelled the weapon from left to right, picking out fresh targets as they approached, mowing them down with a burst of searing hot metal.

One bullet out of every five was a tracer round and the woods became illuminated by streaks of glowing red, as the gun spat its venom at the mutilated bodies refusing to retreat from the ferocious defence.

Bodies fell in their droves and trees snapped in half as the large machinegun bullets punched through flesh and wood alike, devastating the ground immediately to the west of the house. Within a minute, the woods were nothing more than a smouldering and bloodied quagmire of mud and flesh as the dead were smashed by bullets and ricocheting tree splinters.

"Ammo," Stu screamed over his shoulder as he felt the belt of ammunition becoming lighter in his hand.

"More ammo, bring more fucking ammo."

Guns, pistols and rifles opened fire from all around the rooftop as everyone joined in on attempting to give Kelly the time that she needed. The noise was thunderous, sounding like a thousand hammers beating against a thousand steel drums. The bright red tracer bullets shot out in all directions, punching through flesh, splintering bone and wood, and ricocheting from rocks before rocketing vertically into the black sky.

The children screamed and covered their ears as they clung to their mothers. The people in the centre of the rooftop were helpless. They had no weapons to defend themselves and could only look on, as the rest fought with desperation to stem the tide of death that flooded towards the house.

The weight of fire did little to stop the advance of the dead. For every one that fell, it seemed a hundred more sprung up in their place. The death and destruction that obliterated everything around them did nothing to deter the mindless reanimated corpses.

They continued their onslaught, wailing with excitement and, even when battered with rounds that punched numerous holes through them, they pressed their assault.

Kieran appeared at the side of Stu and began to hand him bundles of the precious machinegun ammunition. The linked bullets slid from his shoulders in long, brass belts that sparkled in the bursts of light from the numerous weapons erupting all around them.

"Link them together," Stu screamed at him hoarsely as he let out another burst of fire into the darkness. "Make sure you get them the right way, for fuck's sake."

"Yeah, I know," Kieran screamed back at him over the roar of the gun, "you showed me this afternoon, remember?"

Kieran worked frantically, clipping the two ends of the ammunition belts together so that Stu could keep his rate of fire going without having to reload. He linked two more belts then stood up, raising his own rifle and taking aim at the advancing dead.

"Lee is still in the house," he hollered across to Marcus.

Marcus looked across at him, releasing his own trigger for a moment and trying to focus his hearing through the racket of the firing.

"What?" he yelled back.

Kieran, rainwater pouring down his face and into his mouth with his ears ringing from the deafening sound of the guns, pointed back towards the door that led to the stairs and into the house.

"Lee," he screamed to Marcus again, "he's still in the house, with Sophie."

"Shit," Marcus hissed and turned, ready to go after them.

Lisa had heard Kieran inform Marcus about Lee and moved towards the door. She had no weapon and served no purpose in the defence of the house from the rooftop.

"I'll get them," she screamed back at Marcus through the rain as she took off towards the door.

"Just don't forget and leave without me."

She raced through the house, screaming for Lee and Sophie, finding them in the foyer as they finished adding the last items of furniture to the barricaded main entrance.

They turned as the first thumps rocked the heavy wooden doors and echoed through the dark foyer. Lee and Sophie watched as the barricade of sofas and tables shuddered under the impact as more fists and bodies crashed against the door from the outside. The din of their assault on the house increased by the second, and soon, windows gave way, shattering loudly under the hammering of rotting hands.

The doors shuddered and reverberated under the impacts, shaking in their frames, and soon they began to splinter.

"Come on," Lisa screamed at them as the sound of gunfire, the helicopter engine, pounding fists and breaking glass threatened to carry her voice away into oblivion.

"You need to get out of here, now."

Sophie headed for the stairs, dragging Lee with her as he continued to stare at the rattling door that he knew would not hold out for long against such a ferocious onslaught.

"They're everywhere, Lee," Lisa yelled at him as they began to climb the stairs. "We can't hold them back."

Lee turned and raced up the final few steps with Sophie, dragging his attention from the failing barricade and heading for the rooftop.

Lisa lunged for the top step as Lee and Sophie took off along the corridor, the ball of her foot making contact with the thick carpet, but immediately losing its grip and forcing her ankle backwards, as the weight of her body pushed down on her foot.

Even over the deafening myriad of noise, she heard the bones snap.

She howled with agony and tumbled backwards, bouncing down the stairs as her arms and legs flailed through the air. She hit the tiled floor of the foyer with a sickening slap, her face smashing into the cold slate beneath her and sending her eyes rolling to the back of her head.

Blackness enveloped her.

Lee and Sophie burst through the door leading onto the roof and out into the midst of the chaos that seemed to reign supreme on top of the old house.

A large group of people stood huddled together in the centre. Mothers clutched their sodden children close to them as they shivered from the cold rain and trembled with fear. Marcus and Stu were to the right, pouring machinegun and rifle fire into the mass of corpses assaulting the house from the woods.

Jim, Steve, Hussein, Helen, and Jake, were firing over in to the open plains of the park, trying desperately to stem the tide of rotting flesh and give Kelly the time that she needed to get the aircraft off the ground.

"Lee," a voice yelled, and as he turned, a rifle was thrust into his hands from Kieran.

"We're out of time," Steve was screaming as he watched the helicopter struggling to take off. "We're out of time, they won't make it."

A number of corpses had already converged on the aircraft, surrounding it and pounding against its windows and sides, as the fuselage swayed and bounced under the thundering rotor blades, struggling to get airborne.

Hussein stared in horror as he saw more of the flesh-craving monsters arrive and surround the helicopter.

They would never be able to take off now.

"We're fucked, Marcus," Jim called across the roof as he began changing magazines. "The chopper won't make it. They're swamped with those things."

Marcus turned, quickly eyeing the ground around the house and seeing for himself that they had run out of time. The dead overwhelmed the helicopter; he knew that they would not be able to take off.

Reluctantly, he had to forget about Kelly and Joey, leaving them to their fate as they remained trapped inside the aircraft. Nothing could be done to help the aircrew; they were surrounded by too many of the dead for Marcus and his men to attempt a rescue. Kelly and Joey had their pistols, and Marcus knew that they would save the last rounds for themselves when the time came.

"Get off the roof," he hollered back at Jim. "Get everyone down, over the back and onto the ground from the kitchen roof."

Jim and Hussein began herding everyone to the far side of the rooftop. Children clung to their mothers for dear life as they shuffled to the edge, crying and whimpering helplessly as their bulging terror-filled eyes witnessed the pandemonium around them.

"I'll go first, Hussein," Jim shouted as he began climbing over the lip, ignoring the pain in his fractured arm. He was ready to drop down onto the lower roof of the kitchen just a couple of metres below.

"Once I'm down, start lowering the kids and..."

The deafening roar of the helicopter engine drowned out his words as it suddenly forced itself into the air above the house. The bulky fuselage of the Puma rose into view over the lip of the roof like a thundering titan, coming to the rescue of the survivors. Its engine howled with the strain and its rotors hammered at the air.

Marcus turned to see the aircraft as it soared into view and settled into a hover over the eastern edge of the house. Kelly began carefully manoeuvring it into a position where she could begin taking on passengers.

Its downwash was powerful enough to knock some of the people flat, and the heat from its exhausts and the spinning blades evaporated the torrential rain before the thick, heavy drops had a chance to land on the roof.

"Get them onto the heli," Marcus roared as he ran towards Jim and Hussein. "Get them in there, now. We can't hold for long."

Jim began dragging people towards the aircraft as Kelly brought the machine in lower, avoiding touching the roof with the heavy wheels for fear of causing a collapse. She fought hard with the controls as Joey called out the height and direction.

"Two metres," he said calmly over the intercom, staring down at the roof of the house and the windswept and frightened faces of the people rushing towards them.

"Come left, Kel, left. There, hold it there."

The port side door to the passenger compartment suddenly flew open and Kelly looked back over her shoulder to see Jim, hurling people inside and screaming encouragement to them, as he reached back for more.

Kelly checked her altitude and level as she toiled with the throttle and collective, trying to keep the cumbersome machine in the same place as the survivors were loaded. Through the muffled headset that she wore, she could hear the crack of the rifles and the growl of the machinegun, as the defenders continued to buy the remainder the precious time they needed to reach safety.

Marcus looked back, watching as Jennifer and his two sons were bundled into the aircraft, feeling a sense of hope that at least his family would make it. His eyes locked with his wife's and for a fleeting moment, they spoke a thousand words to one another without making a sound.

He smiled at her and nodded, before turning back to help Stu suppress the horde of putrefying flesh descending upon them.

Carl was the last to board the aircraft; unconscious after Jim had had to strike him hard across his jaw with the butt of his rifle. Carl had wanted to stay and help, but he had no weapons, and Marcus had already ordered that he should go with the helicopter group.

Sophie and Claire helped to drag him into the passenger compartment and tucked him into a corner.

Jim turned to Hussein.

"Okay, buddy, on you go," he hollered.

Hussein began to protest but Jim shook his head.

"Your knee is fucked, so you need to go with the others." Jim glared down at him and took the rifle from Hussein's hands.

"Give me your ammo, but keep hold of your pistol."

Hussein complied and handed over his magazines to Jim, an expression of dejection and guilt covering his face.

Jim slapped him on his shoulder and grinned.

"Don't worry, you'll get plenty more chances to kill bad-guys. Look after this lot." He indicated the people sitting in the passenger compartment of the helicopter. "They'll need you."

Hussein climbed in and Jim gave the thumbs up to Joey, who nodded back and shouted something unintelligible through the window on his side of the cockpit. Jim presumed that the co-pilot was wishing them luck and nodded in reply, before turning and heading towards Marcus.

The bulky Puma helicopter groaned and the engine squealed as Kelly adjusted the throttle and began to lift up into the air. Within seconds, they were high above the house where they hovered for a moment, then headed out into the dark sky, towards the north.

The noise on the rooftop seemed to settle slightly as the aircraft moved further away, despite the sound of gunshots and machinegun fire. The rain returned, without the rotors and exhausts to brush it aside, and the air stilled, leaving just the percussion of the weapons and the wails of the dead lingering around the house.

Marcus watched the aircraft fly away into the distance until it was gone from sight. He turned and looked around at the remainder of the survivors. There were eight of them still on the roof.

"Did we get everyone out?" he called as he leaned in close to Jim's ear.

"Yeah, I think so, apart from Gary, and I think Karen is with him."

"Cease fire, cease fire," Marcus shouted.

One by one, the weapons fell silent with smoke drifting up from their hot barrels, an eerie silence falling over them. Everybody turned to Marcus, waiting anxiously as the sound of the thousands of dead voices drifted up to the people on the roof without the sounds of exploding rifles to blot them out anymore.

Marcus felt a sudden calm.

Knowing that his wife and children were safe in the helicopter, out of harm's way, he could now think clearly despite the knowledge that they were about to be overwhelmed by the hordes of dead clambering at the failing doors and windows below them.

"Jim, give me an ammo count, and standby to bug-out." He eyed the others that stood close by. "Make sure you all have fresh magazines on your weapons and don't leave anything behind."

He turned and moved to the north side of the house, staring down onto the flat kitchen roof. He could see that there were a number of dark figures in the area, but there were much fewer there than at the front of the building. They would need to climb down and run for the north, fighting off any of the dead that had strayed into the area.

The thumps and bangs continued below, accompanied by the sound of the main entrance crashing inwards and the howls and screeches of the dead, as they began to pour into the old mansion.

As Marcus positioned himself to begin the descent from the roof, Jim came across to him with a grave look on his face.

"We have roughly twenty-two mags and about eleven hundred link' left for the gun, boss."

Marcus nodded in reply, estimating that they all had somewhere in the region of three magazines each for their rifles.

"Not fucking much is it?" he grumbled.

Marcus led the way, climbing down over the lip of the roof, holding on until his legs were still, then dropping down onto the kitchen, bending his knees and allowing his body to absorb the shock, creating as little noise as possible.

Stu was next.

As he threw his leg over the edge, the sound of a car horn blasting was carried to them on the night air over the crescendo that the dead made, as they continued to pile into the house.

Marcus looked to the east and saw the bouncing headlights of a car as it raced across the undulating ground of the plains, towards the house. The horn continued to blare while the lights repeatedly dipped to the ground then shot up into the sky, as the vehicle hit another rut, sending it bouncing through the long grass.

"Shit, it's Gary," Steve gasped.

Everyone headed to the east side of the roof, watching in horror as the zebra striped Land Rover came closer.

The multitude of dark and moaning figures below slowly turned and began to stagger towards the approaching vehicle, their voices rising with excitement as a new distraction entered their ravenous minds.

They knew that the roaring engine and howling horn meant living flesh, and they lurched with all the speed they could muster towards it.

Stu flicked down the bipod legs of the machinegun and rested them on the edge of the roof with the butt pulled firmly into his shoulder. Adjusting his aim, he released a string of glowing rounds into the path of the Land Rover, dropping numerous bodies in a single burst.

He continued to fire, aiming his shots so that he was clearing the way for Gary.

The rest of the survivors began to shout to him, waving to the vehicle, trying to gain his attention and direct him to the rear of the house. The vehicle did not slow and it seemed that Gary could not hear their cries from the rooftop. Instead, it ploughed through the mass of corpses, aiming for the main doors at the front of the house.

"What the fuck is he doing?" Jim cursed.

Stu desperately tried to thin out the numbers surging towards the vehicle, but it was impossible; there were thousands of them, in a sea of black that swelled and rushed towards Gary and Karen.

The Land Rover rocked and bounced as more and more bodies fell beneath its wheels and crashed against its bumper. Soon, the vehicle had slowed to a painful crawl because of the weight of the crowd pressing against it. Within seconds, Stu and the others could see nothing but the dull white roof and hood as it swayed from side to side, swallowed up by the swarming throng of rotting flesh.

The engine raced, but the wheels refused to propel the old Land Rover forward, leaving it sitting like a precarious life raft in a bubbling sea of death.

Even from the roof and over the moans and cries of excitement and lust from the dead, Stu and the others could hear the panic-filled screams of Karen, as the windows began to splinter and the doors buckled inwards against their frames.

Stu looked back over his shoulder at the silent and horrified faces of the others staring out at the stranded Land Rover containing Gary and Karen, as it bobbed in the frothing sea of dead. They were just fifty metres away, but between the vehicle and the safety of the roof, a thousand flesh-hungry corpses packed the area.

"There's nothing we can do for them," Steve whispered remorsefully.

He felt a hard lump form in his throat as he watched on, helpless to do anything for his friends.

"We can't help them."

Stu looked back at him and nodded solemnly, his eyes falling to the ground at his feet with the shame of their inability to do something to aid the two stranded and powerless people in the Land Rover, but there was one last thing *he* could do for them.

He brought the machinegun back up to his shoulder, clutching it tightly and adjusting his aim. The spike of the foresight rested on the area where he knew the driver's seat of the vehicle would be. Any sign of Karen or Gary was obscured by the mass of heads swamping the Land Rover, but Stu knew they would not be able to withstand the seven point six two millimetre rounds that he could spit from his powerful machinegun.

He closed his left eye, aiming carefully and taking a deep breath. He released it and then paused, settling the weapon and his sight picture.

'I'm sorry, Gary,' he whispered.

His finger squeezed the trigger, feeling it move under the pressure, and suddenly the heavy weapon juddered in his grip. A burst of bright red lines, like laser beams, flowed out from the end of the barrel and soared through the air towards the stranded vehicle and their friends. The rounds smashed through the heads and bodies of the dark figures that were in their path, shattering bone and splattering the side of the Land Rover with blood and gore. The heavy metal slugs continued through the organic material and punched through the thin metal and glass of the vehicle's front compartment.

He squeezed the trigger again, sending out more glowing death towards their own people, tearing large holes in the sides of the Land Rover. He continued to hammer away at the vehicle, sending flesh, glass and metal splintering into the night air, as he took careful aim at the area that he knew Gary and Karen would be.

Soon, the vehicle began to smoke as the tracer sounds burned through the flesh and material inside the driver's compartment. With one final burst that twisted the frame and caused the roof to cave inwards, Stu ceased fire, eyeing the scene with a heavy heart but telling himself that he had done the only thing that he could to end the suffering of Gary and Karen.

"Come on," he said with a subdued and heavy voice.

He stood up, turning away from the smouldering wreck and placed the cumbersome GPMG over his shoulder. He looked up at the horrified faces of Steve and Helen and felt his stomach churn. He had liked Gary and Karen very much, and although he knew that he had done the only thing left to them, he could not help but feel a deep hatred towards himself.

"Let's get out of here," he huffed as he walked towards the north side of the roof.

One by one, they climbed from the lip of the house and onto the flat space above the kitchen, where Marcus waited for them in the darkness.

"Is it done?" Marcus asked in a whisper as he stepped forward.

Steve nodded.

"Yeah, Stu took care of it, it's done."

Marcus knew instinctively what he meant and glanced at Stu, who avoided his gaze. Marcus also understood that Stu had had no choice, and he sympathised with the anguish and guilt that his friend would be battling against inside him.

Without wasting any more time, they began to scale down to the rear of the house. The small number of lurching figures that had arrived in the area were quickly dealt with as Lee, Jim and Kieran were the first to reach the ground. They set about clearing the area for the others and left a number of corpses, prostrate on the ground and with gaping wounds in their skulls from the blunt objects that had been used to smash them open.

Marcus was the last to descend, and once on the ground he conducted a quick head count. The house behind them echoed with the crashes and bangs of furniture being overturned and glass being smashed, as the dead rampaged through the rooms, searching for the living as more and more of them piled in through the gaping entrance to the foyer.

Marcus stood, glanced to his left and right, peering into the gloom of the night. He began to lead them off to the north, towards the cliffs, past the animal pens. Beyond that, they would cross the fields then reach the vehicles and head for the open road, and the rendezvous with the others.

The north of the interior of the park was free of the dead; they had all congregated around the house after making their way up from the main gate after its collapse. As they put distance between them and the house, an unsettling silence enveloped the survivors, making them nervous as they crossed the rain-soaked ground.

Marcus and his group were patrolling now, their pace steady and deliberate as they slowed to avoid running into trouble without being able to react. The blackness around them was complete, and the distance hum of the dead seemed a million miles away as they began to pass through the area of the enclosures.

Marcus suddenly stopped in his tracks, throwing his hand up to signal the others behind him to follow suit.

"What the fuck is that?" Jake hissed from the rear as he watched a large, lumbering shape pass by in front of them.

Everybody froze, staring into the darkness, ready to begin the fight all over again.

The shape continued to move, crossing their path from right to left as it lumbered towards the trees. A loud snort followed by a deep grumble came from the dark towering figure. It paused in the wet soaking grass, stamped its heavy foot and then let out a long, lingering grunt.

Marcus realised what he was seeing as the animal passed and he caught sight of its full silhouette.

"Elephant," he whispered over his shoulder, not wanting to draw the animal's attention and then have it charge down on them.

Soon, more dark shadows appeared in front of them as the herd headed into the trees towards the west of the park and away from the house.

"Gary must've set the animals loose," Steve hissed as he watched the parade pass them by, their huge lumbering hulks moving slowly through the night as they began making their own way to safety.

"Good luck," Jake whispered under his breath, hoping that the animals of the park could find a way to survive in the dead infested land.

Another figure suddenly emerged from the darkness, much smaller than the elephants; it was walking directly towards them.

Marcus raised his rifle and aimed at the man's head, ready to open fire.

The man did not move like one of the dead, nor did it lurch towards them, growling and moaning. As the silhouette closed in, Marcus recognised Johnny.

"Where have you been?" Jake asked in a hushed voice as he distinguished the familiar and dishevelled form of the eccentric vagrant.

"I went to help Gary with the animals, sausage," Johnny replied in a casual tone as he stopped in front of Marcus.

"Come on," Stu hissed, "we're getting out of here. We're overrun by those things and Gary and Karen are dead."

Johnny sighed heavily and glanced down at the sodden grass at his feet.

"That's a shame. They were good folks."

"Yeah," Marcus agreed impatiently. "Now come on, follow us."

"Sorry, sausage, but I'm going with the elephants. I don't really fit in with you crazy people and I'm not too fond of the Lake District either."

Johnny turned and began to head after the herd of elephants and into the darkness.

"Johnny," Jake hissed into the gloom, "Johnny, come back."

"Be careful of the lions; I think they might be a bit hungry," Johnny replied from the shadows as a parting farewell.

For a moment, the survivors of the park remained rooted to the spot, glancing at one another in disbelief.

"It's his choice," Jim finally whispered from the rear, anxious to get away from the park and the house.

"He'll be okay, now let's get going."

The rain had stopped, leaving a damp and cold mist clinging close to the ground, drifting between the long stalks of overgrown grass that glistened with moisture. The track leading through the fields beyond the cliff was as Marcus had expected; a quagmire filled with soft, sinking mud and scattered puddles.

The moon had made an appearance, peeking out from behind the blanket of dark clouds that threatened to open up with another downpour of heavy rain at any moment. Its ghostly light illuminated the field of mud and glistening high grass, giving Marcus the impression that he was staring at an old sepia or negative photograph.

As the remainder of his group scaled down the cliff, carefully placing their feet and hands along the rungs of wood and rope ladder, Marcus pushed forward, slowly placing each foot in the squelching mire and scanning the track for any sign of movement.

The moonlight reflected up from the numerous puddles along the narrow path, giving the impression that the passage was lit with floor lights, guiding them to safety.

He pushed on, honing his senses, listening and watching for any sign of the dead in front of them. Stu patrolled carefully behind him, his boots making a light sucking noise with each step that he took.

The grass to their left rustled and Marcus turned, his rifle clutched tightly in his hands and his finger gently stroking the trigger. His eyes narrowed as he pinpointed the position of the disturbance.

The grass seemed to move in the opposite direction to which the wind was blowing. Something was moving just metres away from them, watching their every step and stalking them.

He turned to Stu, about to give a signal when a howl erupted from behind them, to the right of the track. Marcus spun in time to see the pale wraithlike face as it closed on him, but he was too late to raise his weapon into the aim. His finger jerked on the trigger, a loud crack disturbing the silence and sending a round punching a hole through the chest of his attacker, but failing to slow its momentum.

The creature was already on top of Marcus and he tumbled backwards as its cold hands closed around his throat. He let out a yelp as his feet slipped from underneath him and both their bodies tumbled to the ground, landing in the thick, freezing mud with a sickening slap. Both of them struggled with one another as Marcus fought to break free from the cadavers grip.

Snarls, grunts and cries rang out in the still air.

Stu raced forward, his feet skidding in the wet mud. He could hear Marcus screaming and cursing as he flailed in the mud beneath the corpse that was sprawled on top of him, groaning loudly, its jaws continuously snapping at his flesh.

Stu made his final step, about to lunge forward to help his friend, when a blur shot from the long grass to the left of the track. A shape, large and pale in the moonlight, sprang from the undergrowth and leapt across the track. A deafening roar filled the air and, in a fraction of a second, it had snatched the corpse from on top of Marcus and back into the fields on the right of the track.

Stu stood in shock, staring at the magnificent beast as it stopped and turned to look at him. It growled and stared at him, its eyes glowing as they reflected the moonlight. In its mouth, hung the limp body of the corpse that had attacked Marcus, the lion's teeth sinking deep into its throat as it kept a tight grip on its prey. With a final growl, low and lingering for a long time, it turned and headed deep into the long grass, disappearing from sight.

Stu moved forward to help Marcus up from the mud.

"You okay, mate?"

Marcus climbed to his feet, brushing himself off but saying nothing as he recovered his mud spattered rifle from a puddle.

On the track in front of them, caught in the moonlight, Stu saw a number of silhouettes crossing their path and skulking into the underbrush. Each of them stopped and stared at the men for a moment before disappearing, their glowing eyes sparkling like diamonds in the darkness.

It was a pride of lions with a number of small cubs in tow, off to join in on the feast that the alpha male had just secured for them.

"Fucking hell," Stu exclaimed, "I don't think food is ever going to be a problem for that lot. Hey, you were just saved by a lion, mate."

Again, Marcus said nothing as he checked his weapon and cleared the mud from the muzzle and bolt area.

Stu watched his friend intently, his nervous movements jerky and rushed. His face was pale with shock as beads of sweat glistened on his forehead in the pale light.

"You sure you're okay, Marcus?" Stu asked with concern.

"Yeah, I'm fucking fine," replied Marcus, impatiently. He fixed Stu with a glowering stare. "Let's just get out of here."

28

The pounding and heavy thuds sounded distant, as though coming to her on the wind from miles away. Slowly, her ears began to focus and the noise of the hammering grew louder and more localised.

Lisa groaned and raised her head from the cold tiles, feeling her face throb and watching the room spin as she slowly opened her eyes. Then, as she attempted to sit up, the pain in her ankle shot red-hot searing lightning bolts through her body, attacking her nervous system like a thousand knives.

The agony of her shattered bones made her feel nauseous, making her head spin and her body grow weak. She looked down at her leg and saw the swelling immediately. Her ankle was twice its normal size, looking like a black and blue grapefruit protruding from her shoe.

She whimpered and convulsed as another wave of pain flowed up through her body from her smashed ankle, and into her spinning and floating brain. She very nearly lost consciousness again but the echoing thumps and juddering bangs quickly brought her back to reality.

She realised that she was inside the house.

She was on the cold floor of the foyer and confusion swept over her like a blanket as she tried to piece things together.

The loud noises continued to resonate around the room, but she could not understand where they were coming from or where everybody had gone.

"Gary?" she called out. "Jennifer, where are you all?"

No one replied from within the stillness of the house and she began to feel abandoned.

More noises drifted to her. Distant and muffled, but she could distinguish the sound of the helicopter's rotor blades, swishing and thumping through the air, and the screech of its engine. Accompanying the sounds of the aircraft, she could also hear the continuous rattle of gunfire, coming from above her, but from outside.

"Someone, help me," she cried out desperately, her voice bouncing from the walls and drifting around in the spacious but empty room.

"I can't walk, someone help."

Something moved behind her with a loud scraping noise. She suddenly became aware, through the fog of her confusion and spinning mind, that the other thumps and bangs were much closer than the gunfire and helicopter engines.

She turned, wincing at the pain as the movement jolted her leg, and looked towards the door. Piles of heavy furniture were stacked against the entrance to the hall and up against the windows.

All were juddering under the impacts of dozens of assaults. The furniture was slowly being pushed aside, grinding against the tiled floor.

She suddenly remembered; the gate had collapsed and the dead were in the park. Panic and terror assaulted her nerves and mind simultaneously, causing her blood to race through her veins, as she realised that the collapsing furniture and shattering windows was all that separated her from the hordes of flesh-hungry ghouls.

She began to drag herself towards the stairs, whimpering to herself and pleading for someone to come and help her.

A heavy crash behind her forced her to look back.

The large leather couch that had been placed on top of the barricade tumbled to the floor, exposing the windows set into the inner doors of the main entrance.

Lisa screamed involuntarily as she saw the rotting, gaunt faces of the dead pressed up against the glass, staring back at her.

The sight of the living human, just beyond their reach, sent the swarm of creatures into a state of frenzy as their hands and faces battered at the glass. The panes shattered, sending sharp splinters flying through the air and clattering across the tiles as they landed. Faces, cut to shreds from the shards that remained embedded in the frame, leered at her, their skin lacerated and falling from their heads, exposing the white bone beneath. Their ravenous, yet empty dead eyes, focused on the lone woman as she crawled away from them and towards the stairs.

Their howls of excitement erupted in unison, deafening in the space of the foyer as the chorus reverberated back and forth. They battered at the barricade with their bodies, and slowly it began to collapse.

The door steadily separated from its frame, creating a gap large enough for the dead to force their arms through. They used their limbs as levers against the heavy obstacle standing between them and the living flesh beyond, forcing the gap to grow wider with each passing moment.

Lisa reached the banister and dragged herself up, wincing with the pain from her broken ankle and holding onto the stairs for balance as she kept her damaged leg off the ground. With a yelp, she hopped up the first step, the impact of her landing vibrating along her body and jolting her shattered bones.

Sweat poured from her body, through fear, shock and exertion as she began to slowly, and painfully, climb the stairs one excruciating step at a time.

The dead continued to clamber at the barricade, shifting it further into the foyer with each thrust and expanding the gap between the door and the frame. The breach was now large enough to allow the heads and shoulders of the lead creatures to be thrust through, their bodies acting as wedges and forcing the breach to widen.

Lisa was halfway up the stairs, her legs shaking and threatening to give from underneath her when she heard the crash of the barricade finally collapsing, and the groaning of the wood as the door was barged open.

She glanced back, seeing the first of the snarling faces enter the foyer, their eyes locked on her as they lurched towards the stairway. Their moans filled the large empty room and their clutching hands reached towards her as they staggered to the stairs and began their ascent.

Panic filled her every sense as she continued to drag herself from step to step, crying uncontrollably as she heard and felt the dead closing in on her from below. Their moans and snarls echoed in her ears, growing in volume as more entered the house. She could almost feel their cold, bony fingertips clawing at her back as she reached the final few rungs of the staircase.

At the top, she pulled herself up, swinging her body around on the post supporting the thick, wooden banister. She looked down at the swarm of bodies that climbed up towards her along the stairs.

A thousand dead eyes remained fixed on her with snarling, drooling jaws that snapped continuously as rotting legs carried them forward, hypnotised by the soft and warm living flesh that lingered just before them.

Lisa's body shook uncontrollably as terror-filled whimpers fell from her throat. Her mind became overwhelmed with fear and her limbs almost froze, refusing to move any further as the dead closed in.

She glanced to her right and along the corridor towards the door leading to the steps and out onto the roof. It was a long way and she knew she would never make it. The mass of converging bodies were too close and gaining ground by the second. They would catch her before she managed to make it half way to the stairs.

Safety and protection from the others was so close, but in her condition, with a broken ankle and barely able to walk, they may as well have been a million miles away.

The sound of gunfire continued above her and she looked up at the ceiling, pleading for someone to come and help her, but she knew that no one would arrive. She had been left and abandoned to her fate.

The engine of the helicopter rose in volume, changing in pitch, and then began to fade into the distance amidst the roar of the battle that continued on the roof.

The helicopter was gone, leaving her to suffer at the cold hands of the dead.

Behind her, Lisa saw the door to Jake's room ajar and she turned, lunging towards the opening and crashing into the hard wooden frame. Her shoulder screamed at her from the impact, sending yet another flash of agony up to her brain and threatening to incapacitate her as her head began to spin.

She gripped the frame of the door and pulled herself inside. Slamming the door shut behind her, she immediately dragged the heavy chest of drawers across to block the entrance. She heaved with all the strength she could muster, bringing the heavy furniture into position, and then dropped to the floor as her legs gave way beneath her.

Within seconds, the door rocked and juddered as the mass of reanimated corpses arrived outside the room and began attacking the thick wooden barrier that they had seen their prey enter.

With each echoing bang, Lisa cried and whimpered. Each assault against the entrance brought her closer to death and the feeling of helplessness left her in a state of fright that seeped into her every sense, overwhelming her.

Her stomach churned with the feeling of dread and helplessness, and her body threatened to spill its contents upon the floor of the room.

She climbed to her feet again and hobbled back, tears flooding down her cheeks and her hands clutched together in front of her chest as she shook uncontrollably, pleading with unforeseen powers to spare her from the horror.

She no longer felt the pain in her ankle as she limped away from the door. The terror that filled her blood and soul was too overpowering and her pain receptors had become numbed from fear.

She felt her legs touch the mattress on top of Jake's bed and her knees bent, dropping her down to a sitting position, where she remained, staring at the door and howling in time to the beating fists as she watched the frame splinter.

There was nowhere left for her to run. She was trapped in the house with no weapons to defend herself, about to die at the hands of the dead in the same manner that she had lost her husband and children many months before, when the dead had first risen and begun attacking the living.

Finally, her body, under the pressure of such pain and horror, lost control of itself. Her shoulders shuddered, her legs shook and grew weak, and a dark patch of urine seeped out over the bed below her as her bowels and bladder released their contents; her failing mind became overwhelmed with panic and fear.

She remained sitting on the bed, dropping her head into her hands as she saw the lock of the door give way and the heavy chest of drawers begin to move. They were just seconds away now from crashing through her flimsy barricade, and she remained with her face buried in her hands, too afraid to look. She did not want to see their growling mutilated faces, the flesh hanging from their bones or their glazed dead and terrifying eyes as they descended upon her. She clasped her hands tightly to her face, not wanting to witness their gnashing teeth as they closed in around her soft flesh.

She cried; her shoulders shuddering with each sob and her body trembling as the door crashed open.

The dead piled into the room, moaning loudly as their ravenous eyes fell upon Lisa sitting on the edge of the bed.

They staggered forward, their cold clutching fingers reaching out for her and grasping her clothing, pulling at her and tearing the seams of her jacket.

More and more bodies poured through the open door as the first of Lisa's chilling screams rang out, echoing around the house from room to room as the teeth of the dead sank deep into her flesh. She felt the pressure of the sharp incisors burst through her tissue with a sudden pop, sending a searing, white-hot pain racing through her body. The jaws clamped shut, and then began to pull away from her, tearing a large portion of muscle and sinew from her upper arm.

Her blood-curdling screams rang out, muffled in her palms as she fought hard to keep her face covered while the sound of her agony seemed to excite the dead even further.

She remained curled into a ball as she felt the dead close in all around her, pulling at her, their cold flesh pressing against her own, their broken and jagged teeth tearing at her body while their rake-like fingers dug deep into her soft tissue.

She writhed and convulsed on the bed, a pool of blood growing larger around her as more of her body was torn from her.

Another bite punctured through the soft skin and muscle between her neck and shoulder, sending a searing hot pain surging through her, almost making her black out. The next was a large wad of flesh being ripped from her thigh, stopping her from falling unconscious from the previous bite and prolonging her agony, as more fleshy tissue and sinew was ripped from her quivering frame.

Her head was pulled back and she felt a sudden pressure around her windpipe as her throat was gripped between a set of powerful teeth that suddenly clenched shut, splitting the skin and then dragging away a large chunk of her throat. Her head jerked and snapped back and she felt her warm blood instantly gush from the wound, soaking her face and cascading down her chest.

She gurgled; bright red spittle spattered up from her mouth as her head slumped back and her glazed eyes stared blankly at the ceiling, at the gaunt and grotesque faces that surrounded her. Unable to muster the strength to scream anymore as the precious crimson fluid flowed from her body, spraying out in all directions while her carotid artery was severed, Lisa felt her life slowly fading from her.

She became distantly aware that she was being pulled in all directions, her failing brain registering that she was losing more flesh, blood and limbs, as the dead tore her to pieces. However, a strange calm seemed to envelop her, blocking out the pain as she slowly lost consciousness and died.

29

In the pitch-blackness of the night, and with no night vision goggles, Kelly had to rely solely on the instrument readouts in front of her, and the instructions from Joey relayed through her headset. He sat in his seat beside her in the cockpit, intently studying the map and continually checking their speed and bearing, gaining an accurate picture of where they were.

The interior of the aircraft was dark except for the faint green glow emitting from the panels in the front of the cockpit, casting the pilot and co-pilot's faces in an eerie green hue.

"Got a feature coming up on starboard, Kelly, altitude: one six eight metres," Joey said calmly as he stared down at the charts in his lap.

"Turn to three-five-zero degrees and hold that bearing for two point six kilometres."

Kelly complied and adjusted the direction of the helicopter, pushing down gently on the anti-torque pedals and lifting on the collective lever to gain altitude and clear the high ground to their right.

It had been almost forty minutes since they had left the Safari Park behind, the flash of the erupting gunfire fading into the distance as they flew away to the north, continuing with the plan, even though neither of them held out much hope of Marcus and the others making it out alive.

As they had lifted the survivors from the rooftop, Kelly and Joey had been able to see the scale of the situation more clearly. The swarm of putrid flesh stretched all the way down to the gate, and far beyond. Thousands of bodies spilled through the entrance every minute, all of them making their way towards the house and the stranded survivors on the roof.

Kelly's head swam.

The dead, despite their lack of mobility and speed, had overwhelmed them before they even had the chance to get their plan into motion. Their helicopter had very nearly been turned over, as the hundreds of rotting, walking corpses surged around the fuselage.

They were lucky to have gotten anybody out alive.

She looked back over her shoulder and into the passenger area. In the dim light, she was just able to make out the shapes of the people huddled together.

Sophie's face came forward, faintly lit in the dull green light of the cockpit.

"How long?" she hollered over the racket of the engine.

Kelly leaned across to her left, bringing her face close to the side of Sophie's head and shouting into her ear.

"About another forty minutes and we'll be at the first RV."

Sophie nodded and slumped back into the rear of the aircraft to pass on the message to the others, who remained sitting in the darkness, hungry for information.

Kelly looked out to her right. It was hard to see anything other than the different shades of dark as they flew over roads, fields and trees. It was impossible to distinguish depth and distance, leaving her completely reliant on the navigation skills of her co-pilot, Joey.

She checked her watch and saw that there was one more hour until dawn. At least then, they would have a better idea of how the ground looked, and the condition they were in. Until then, she would not even consider landing. In the darkness, they would be completely blind to any threat on the ground.

Her main concern was fuel. They were already getting low, and to remain airborne, circling for any length of time would bring them to the point where they would have absolutely no reserve left. That would leave them with no option but to land when they finally arrived at the new base location, regardless of the situation on the ground.

Their margin for error was growing narrower by the minute.

She turned to Joey, about to ask him how far they were from the nearest built area, when a flash of light erupted from the ground in front of them. A stream of red lights hung in the air, growing slightly larger, and then zipping past the fuselage at lightning speed.

"Incoming," Kelly barked, "we have incoming, Joey."

The red lights were tracer rounds, and soon more joined them as the firers on the ground adjusted their aim.

The air around the helicopter lit up with the red glow from the machinegun bullets as they soared through the area immediately in front of the aircraft, missing the nose of the machine by just a few metres.

Kelly slammed the cyclic to the left, sending the helicopter into a steep banking manoeuvre in an attempt to avoid the next burst of fire from below that would surely be more accurate after the first.

"Shit, Kelly," Joey cried as he felt himself being tossed and buffeted against his harness as Kelly pushed the aircraft into the drastic manoeuvre.

He slid in his seat, clutching at the leather straps hanging from the ceiling to stop him from crashing into the door on his left. He collided with the bulkhead frame, his head ricocheting around inside his helmet and sending his vision spinning, as he strained to keep himself upright in his seat to aid Kelly as much as he could.

More fire raced up towards them, this time striking the underbelly of the helicopter with heavy thuds, punching a number of holes through the fuselage, sending small splinters of metal flying through the air in all directions.

Over the noise of the straining engine, panicked voices and cries of fear and pain could be heard from the defenceless passengers in the rear as they were tossed into one another and into the superstructure of the interior. Some were knocked unconscious and others were caught by hot splinters of metal exploding through the inside at deadly speed.

Kelly increased the throttle to maximum revolutions, pushed down on the collective as she dipped the cyclic into a steep angle, pointing towards the floor and forcing the aircraft forward, losing altitude as they did so in the hope of getting below the rounds whipping through the sky all around them.

"Altitude, watch your altitude," Joey was yelling over the intercom as the helicopter was thrown from left to right and rapidly began dropping from the sky.

Kelly banked right and saw the muzzle flashes of the firing point just twenty metres below her as she forced the aircraft around in a tight loop, her hand twisting the throttle until it would turn no more to give them maximum power and speed.

With a roar, the aircraft passed over the ambush, low and fast with smoke pouring from the exhausts. With the manoeuvre of charging their attackers, Kelly hoped to gain some distance from them before they had the chance to turn and adjust their aim on her.

The feature that Joey had warned her about earlier rose up ahead of them like a dark giant monolith, and Kelly had to pull back sharply on the cyclic and increase the collective to gain altitude before crashing into the fast approaching rocky slope.

The engine screamed in protest and the rotors whined above as the sharp and sudden manoeuvre pushed the aircraft to its limit. They were almost vertical, soaring into the sky as more glowing red tracer rounds passed by;

snapping through the blackness like lightning bolts shot from an angry god. They whizzed by with resounding cracks, displacing the air around them just centimetres from the superstructure as they burned through the night, hitting rocks jutting out from the feature in front and ricocheting into the dark sky.

Kelly strained with the controls as Joey screamed at her, warning that more rounds were coming, as he desperately checked over his left shoulder, watching the blazing tracers zooming towards them.

"Bank right, Kelly. Bank right," he screamed frantically as he saw the enemy fire racing directly towards them, sure to hit their mark.

With gritted teeth, letting out a loud groan, Kelly squeezed the last of the power that she could from the aircraft and flung the cyclic to the right, turning them in a vertical one hundred and eighty degrees that sent them into another dive and plummeting towards the black earth below.

The engine whined and shrieked, threatening to explode as it struggled to keep them in flight.

At a low altitude, she again pulled hard on the collective, screaming to herself and trying desperately to gain some lift, as she kept the cyclic pushed slightly forward for speed and hoping that they had enough room between them and the ground to pull out of the dive in time.

The engines vibrated behind the passenger area, rattling in their foundations and threatening to tear them apart from the strain. Above them, the rotors, spinning so fast that they threatened to fly loose of their housing, hammered at the air with a whirling thump that sounded like one endless beat against a bass drum, echoing for an eternity and never losing its volume, while Kelly and Joey felt the cockpit juddering around them.

The helicopter began to pull up, its nose rising towards the horizon and climbing out of the steep dive. The ground raced by just fifteen metres below them while Kelly fought to gain some altitude.

Another series of flashes erupted close to their right and a stream of fiery red projectiles zoomed towards them. With no time to manoeuvre, Kelly braced herself, clenching her teeth and tensing her body, hoping that the heavy bullets would miss.

The helicopter shuddered and a series of holes exploded through the door of the passenger compartment. Loud thumps and thwacks rang out as the heavy metal slugs impacted all along the helicopter's fuselage, punching numerous holes and causing an untold amount of damage.

Even with the noise of the engine, Kelly heard the screams of the people behind her as the machine swayed and jerked below her while the cockpit shook violently, and the controls vibrated in her hands.

All around them, red lights began to flash and warning alarms began to blare, informing them that they had sustained serious damage.

More rounds punched through the outer shell of the helicopter, sending sparks erupting from the instrument panels in front of her and causing the glass of the windshield to shatter, as the bullets punched through the nose of the aircraft.

The engine coughed and spluttered and Kelly felt the sudden loss of power as the machine was mortally wounded.

"Shit, we're losing her," she screamed as she fought to keep control of the aircraft as they were thrown into a spin.

She pushed down hard on the anti-torque pedals, but they did not respond. She pulled up on the collective, but that too did nothing as she twisted and turned on the cyclic to regain some control.

She knew that a crash landing was inevitable, but to smash into the ground whilst in a spin and out of control would be catastrophic, and would result in the complete loss of life of everyone on board.

"Joey, we've lost the rear rotor, and hydraulics, too." She glanced across at him, fear blazing in her wide eyes and her face sparkling with beads of sweat.

"We're going down. I can't hold her, Joey."

Joey nodded, bracing his legs against the control panel and grasping the leather straps above him tightly with both hands. He pushed back against his seat and screwed up his face, ready to accept the hard landing racing towards them.

With great effort, Kelly managed to slow the spin with the throttle and the cyclic, but they were still falling and a crash was unavoidable. At fifteen metres, she saw the ground rushing up towards them and she raised her legs, throwing her head back against the seat.

"Brace, brace..." she screamed, hoping that the people in the back would hear her and do what they could to protect themselves.

With a roar and an ear-splitting crunch, the front of the helicopter disintegrated as it impacted with the hard ground.

Kelly felt the tremendous jolt of the collision travel through her body, and a split second later the darkness took her.

30

Claire heard the thuds against the helicopter; felt the sudden displacement of air as the gaping holes appeared in the walls of the fuselage around them, and then the hot fluid splashing against her face and neck.

The helicopter was spinning and she could feel her body being pushed towards the door from the centrifugal force of the whirling aircraft. She tried desperately to keep a tight grasp on Sarah with one hand and on the cargo nets attached to the seats with the other.

Over the roar and scream of the engine, she could hear numerous cries of fear and shrieks of pain from the other people being thrown about inside the passenger compartment. She could also hear her daughter, crying and shouting for her, as she felt her grip begin to loosen from her hand.

"Sarah, hold on," she cried over the deafening noise of the howling engines, thudding rotors and screaming people.

"Keep hold, Sarah, I've got you, honey."

Another row of holes exploded through the shell of the aircraft, faint shafts of light beaming through and red-hot glowing metal racing through the air. Another body squealed out in the darkness as fragments of bullet and helicopter pierced their flesh.

The engine coughed behind them and, with a series of whines, descending in volume and pitch, fell silent, leaving just the thumping rotors above them, still beating at the air, but clearly losing speed as the power to the motors was cut.

The spin of the helicopter had slowed and Claire was able to gain a better grip on the cargo net, looping her arm between the rungs and pulling Sarah in close to her, as she wrapped her legs around the steel legs of the seats bolted to the floor.

"Brace, brace..." she heard Kelly screaming from the pilot's seat. She closed her eyes tight, tensing every muscle in her body, waiting for the inevitable impact that was to follow.

Time seemed to slow down; it felt as though the helicopter was hanging in the air, moving in slow motion as she gripped her daughter tightly, whispering to her reassuringly as the ground approached them from below.

"Okay, Sarah, everything is going to be okay," she whispered in a breaking voice filled with fear and resignation.

"I love you, Sarah. I love you so..."

Claire's final words to her daughter were cut off as the aircraft made contact with the ground. The impact sent her flying forwards, despite her grip on the cargo net and seat, into the bulkhead behind to the co-pilot.

Her shoulder crashed against the hard metal and then tossed her towards the door. Her head snapped back, sending a shooting pain down through her spine and back up into her brain, as she hit the fuselage with a thud, barely clinging onto consciousness.

She was distantly aware of other bodies being thrown through the air, crashing into one another and into the frame of the aircraft. Some screamed, while others crashed about in silence, already knocked out, or dead.

The helicopter continued to move. She was jostled from the door and onto the ceiling as the aircraft began to roll over, causing glass to explode and bulkheads to collapse as the frames began to buckle in on themselves.

The rotors, still spinning at a rapid rate, smashed into the ground, splintering on impact and sending fragments flying in all directions. A large piece of one of the blades sliced its way through the body of the aircraft, cutting through metal and flesh as it swathed a path of destruction through the passenger compartment.

Howls of pain and fear echoed all around her as Claire precariously clung to consciousness.

She landed hard and felt a body tumble on top of her. She wrapped her arms around it, pulling it close and believing it to be her daughter, while gritting her teeth and accepting the beating that she received from the dying aircraft as it continued to tumble and slide across the rocky ground.

"Sarah," she screamed, her lungs feeling like they would burst as she clutched the limp body in her hand.

The destroyed helicopter rolled and disintegrated around Claire as the world closed in to envelop her.

Finally, she blacked out.

Moments later, Claire's eyes flickered open.

Everything was still and silent around her. At first, she felt confused to what had happened and where she was, and then it dawned on her as she remembered the screams and the crash.

She coughed, tasting the distinct flavour of blood in her mouth. The copper scent seemed to fill her nostrils and throat as streams of crimson sprayed from her mouth.

She wiped her face on the back of her hand, her fingertips brushing against the thick strands of hair of the head resting on her chest.

"Sarah," she whispered, "Sarah, honey. It's okay. We're safe. Sarah…?"

She began running her hands through the tangles of thick hair, feeling the shape of the face in the darkness, trying to identify her daughter.

"Sarah, speak to me," she said in a panic as her fingers ran over the mangled features.

Then, she felt the warm sticky mess that her palms sunk into as she brushed her hands along the body's neck and back. A feeling of dread rose up in her, making her head spin even more and her stomach churn as she realised that it was blood she could feel coating her fingers.

"Sarah, no, please, God, no," Claire whimpered as her hands felt further down along the torso.

Where the legs should have been there was nothing; Claire's fingers pressed deep into the warm, blood-soaked intestines and smashed pelvic bone that hung from the lower part of the body.

She gasped at the realisation and began to scream in both horror and anguish.

"Sarah," she screamed again. "Baby, no…"

Suddenly, a fragile and frightened voice spoke up from within the darkness of the deformed helicopter.

"Mum," the voice croaked desperately, "Mum, I'm here. Where are you?"

A flood of relief swept through Claire's body. She was almost overwhelmed by it and knocked unconscious again.

"Thank God," she whispered hoarsely. "Thank God."

Straining, she pushed the mutilated body away from her. It slumped to the side with a sickening thud as its exposed flesh and entrails smacked against the bare metal of the passenger compartment ceiling.

"Sarah, I'm here. Where are you?"

Claire reached out into the gloom and felt her hands touch the soft, warm face of her daughter. Immediately, she pulled Sarah close, squeezing her tightly as she cried uncontrollably with relief that she had been spared.

With a lot of effort and pain, Claire climbed from the downed aircraft and out onto the cold wet grass, dragging Sarah with her. Outside, she dropped to the ground, feeling the damp soak into her back. Her head throbbed and the pain in her neck and shoulder made her feel as though they were on fire.

Somewhere inside the twisted and mangled fuselage of the helicopter, someone groaned. She heard the thuds as a body moved and whimpers of pain and suffering drifted to her ears, forcing Claire to her feet and into action.

"Wait here, Sarah," she instructed her daughter.

She crawled back towards the carcass of the machine and forced her head and shoulders back in through the smashed and disfigured doorway.

Inside, her senses were overpowered by the smell of aviation fuel, oil, blood and human faeces. The reek almost made her vomit as she clasped her hand to her mouth, fighting hard to keep the bile at bay that was threatening to rise up from her stomach.

In the semi darkness, she could see a number of dark figures writhing in a tangle of arms and legs, mixed in with debris and equipment.

Somebody groaned close by, to her right. Claire turned to reach out to it and felt a hand clasp hers and begin to pull against her.

A sudden and horrific thought occurred to her:

'What if those who were killed have already turned?'

She began to panic, trying to break the hold that the dark figure below had on her hand. She pulled hard, trying desperately to get free. She reached out and began to pound her fist against the forearm of her attacker.

The body let out a yelp and immediately withdrew its hand, releasing its grip on Claire and sinking back into the darkness.

"Stop, stop... What are you hitting me for?" the faceless voice growled in anger and pain.

Claire paused, feeling ashamed as she recognised the voice below her.

"Sorry, Sophie," she began, "I thought you had turned into one of those *things*."

"Well, I'm not one of those *things*," Sophie hissed in reply. "Are you going to help me now, or just frigging stand there?"

Claire helped Sophie from the smashed helicopter and out onto the wet grass, placing her down beside Sarah.

Sophie groaned and rubbed her head as she looked around her, trying to find her bearings and make sense of what was happening.

"Are you hurt, Sophie? Are you okay?" Sarah asked in an innocent and genuinely concerned voice.

"Just my head, I think."

She looked up at Claire pleadingly. "What happened? How did we crash?"

Claire was about to return to help more of the survivors.

"I think we were shot down," she said, causing Sophie's eyes to bulge and a gasp escape from her throat.

"Who…," she began in astonishment, "who shot us down?"

Claire had already turned back to help the others.

More cries for help came from within the darkness of the passenger compartment. Claire's eyes had adjusted to the gloom; she was now able to distinguish a number of wriggling bodies in the tangle of flesh and helicopter.

She looked to the front, to where Kelly and Joey had been. There was virtually nothing left of the cockpit and Claire assumed the pilot and co-pilot were dead.

A noise to her right, outside of the wreckage, caught her attention.

It was a voice, carried to her on the wind from some distance. She stepped back and looked across the grassy hillside, and saw a number of torch beams bouncing in the darkness, coming towards them.

Instinctively, she knew that they could only be the people that shot at them. She suddenly felt exposed, caught in the open and vulnerable to another attack, as she heard the excited voices getting nearer.

Claire glanced at the helicopter, and then back at Sarah and Sophie, who had also spotted the lights in the distance. Both of them were climbing to their feet, their heads turned in the direction of the approaching menace, fear glinting in their eyes as they turned back towards Claire, searching for answers and instructions.

Leaning back into the passenger compartment, Claire hissed at the darkness.

"Someone's coming, you need to get out, now," she said urgently.

All she got in reply were more groans and whimpers from the injured survivors. It seemed that everyone that remained alive were either too hurt to help themselves, or in such a state of shock that their bodies refused to comply with what was needed of them.

"Come on," she tried again, hoping to force some of them into action.

"Come on, I'll help you out. We need to move, now."

Still, no one seemed coherent enough to understand the importance of the situation.

"Shit," Claire cursed as she pulled herself back from the door.

She turned to her daughter and Sophie.

"We can't do anything for them," she said in a quivering voice; her face was awash with shame.

She glanced down at the ground, then over towards the approaching lights and voices.

"We have to leave them." Sophie spoke the words for her, understanding the dilemma and regret that Claire fought with inside her.

Sophie grasped them both by the hands and turned away from the wreckage.

"Come on, we need to find somewhere to hide."

They ran away from the helicopter and towards a large, thick clump of trees that they could see in the distance against the slowly brightening sky as dawn approached. Their breaths came in gasps as their legs forced them forward, continually threatening to trip them as they waded through the long grass.

After a few hundred metres, Sophie's chest burned and she began to slow, but Claire dragged her on as she drew on her reserves, strength and fitness from all her years of running.

Claire continuously spoke to them in a hushed voice as they ran towards their new sanctuary, giving her daughter and Sophie words of encouragement, and reminding them that the tree line was just a couple of hundred metres away, and then they would be safe.

Claire glanced back and saw the shafts of light converge on the wreckage of the helicopter. She counted six torch beams dancing around in the darkness and guessed that there were probably more people with them.

As far as she could tell, the people around the helicopter had not noticed them as they ran for the woods; she hoped beyond hope that they could make the last one hundred metres without being detected.

With burning legs and pounding hearts, the three of them finally made it into the safety of the trees. They collapsed onto the soft pine leaves covering the ground, panting for breath and feeling the relief of having survived the crash, and then escaping the people who had shot them down.

Claire was more relieved over that fact that Sarah was safe and unhurt. She reached across, still on her knees, and pulled her daughter in close to her, stroking her hair and kissing her on the forehead.

"It's okay," she whispered gently as Sarah sobbed in her arms. "We're safe; no one's going to hurt you, now."

Sarah looked at Claire, her eyes filled with emotion. She snorted back tears.

"What about the others? Are they all dead?" her voice trembled.

"I don't know, sweetheart, but we *had* to leave them to get away from the bad men that were coming."

"What about Dad?" Sarah questioned her mother, as she became filled with concern and trepidation.

Before Claire could answer, a crack rang out from the darkness of the woods, echoing around between the tightly packed trees. It sounded like a branch being snapped under somebody's foot.

"Oh, I'm sure he'll be fine," a voice called out from the gloom. Its tone was of a mocking reassurance and Claire pictured a sneering smile behind the words.

A dark figure stepped out from between the tall trees and moved towards them. More dark shapes joined the first, appearing from all sides, surrounding the three crash survivors that had taken refuge in the woods, believing they were safe.

"Who are you?" Claire demanded, pulling her daughter even closer.

"That doesn't matter right now," the man replied in a calm but menacing voice as the men with him, pointing their weapons at Claire, Sarah and Sophie, closed in.

"What *does* matter; is that you're unhurt, which I am pleased about, of course, and now I must insist that you come with me. You can be my guests, if you like?"

Claire felt helpless; a tight knot began to form in her stomach. She knew that the offer of going with them was not really something she had the option of refusing.

31

The rain had started up again. Much lighter than it had been before, but it was heavy enough for Jim to judge it was time to flick on the windscreen wipers.

He concentrated intently on the road ahead of them, picking his way through stalled traffic and debris that littered their path on every stretch of the dual carriageway. The interior of the Range Rover was silent, except for the swish and thump of the wipers as they swept across the windscreen rhythmically, almost hypnotically and nearly sending Jim into a state of autopilot.

He knew he needed to stay focussed and alert, and tried to keep his mind occupied. It was not an easy thing to do. After barely making it out of the park, they had piled into the vehicles and headed through the country lanes and towards the north, pushing hard for the rendezvous with the group in the helicopter.

Now, with the adrenaline free from his system, and the fear and excitement of the events at the Safari Park left far behind them, fatigue had taken control and he faced a new battle to remain vigilant.

The bright beams of light that pierced the darkness before them, guiding them on their journey, illuminated the evidence of the mass chaos and confusion that had befallen humanity at the outbreak of the plague. Everywhere he looked, he could see the evidence of panic and fear strewn across the roadsides.

Jim was exhausted.

His eyes burned and his body ached, particularly the slowly healing bones in his fractured arm. His brain screamed at him for a rest, but he forced it to stay awake, fearful that a lapse in concentration could put them all at risk. If he allowed his mind to wander, he could plough into a static vehicle, or one of the many hasty blockades that they had passed through.

Even worse, he could fail to notice a crowd of dead, blocking the road ahead of them, until it was too late and driving them straight into an ambush of rotting flesh and gnashing teeth.

He looked to his left with the intention of engaging Marcus in conversation, but just one glance at the man told him that talking was not an option. Since leaving the park, Marcus had barely spoken a word.

Now he sat silent, staring at the road ahead, deep in thought with a look of exhaustion on his face that made him appear close to the point of collapse. His eyes were sunken and almost seemed to glow red in the dark interior of the vehicle. His cheeks were withdrawn and his skin looked pale with a glistening layer of sweat coating the surface.

"Hey, Marcus," Jim said with concern, "you okay, man? You really look beat."

Marcus did not reply. His eyes remained fixed on the road, illuminated by the powerful beams of the headlights, as he continued to grip his rifle between his legs, continually looking down at the dull black metal and nervously checking that the magazine was still securely fitted.

"Marcus…" Jim repeated as he watched the man with growing concern.

"What?" he snapped back, sounding annoyed and in no mood to talk.

Jim stared at him for a second, watching his features and glaring eyes as they remained fixed on the windscreen.

"Hey, look," sighed Jim, sounding just as agitated. "I just want to make sure you're okay, man. You've hardly spoken a word since we left the roof of the house. Are you worried about the others?"

"I'm fine, Jim," Marcus grumbled, "just keep your concentration on the road. The last thing we need now is a drama because you wanted to talk about the fucking weather."

Jim glowered at him and even considered swinging his arm back from the steering wheel and smacking him in the mouth. Marcus may be his commander and his friend, but Jim had never allowed anyone to speak to him in such a manner.

After a moment of thought and reflection, Jim swallowed his anger down. It slid along his throat stubbornly and he gritted his teeth with enough force to shatter them while his rage threatened to burst through his composure. His knuckles had turned white from gripping the wheel too tightly but finally, he shrugged.

"Fuck you then, Marcus," he huffed and turned his attention back to the road.

The convoy continued to weave its way through the detritus that filled the roads. Overturned and crashed vehicles were everywhere. Personal belongings lay strewn on the rain-drenched tarmac and stray bodies, roaming the land aimlessly, continuously stepped out ahead of them. They lunged for the vehicles, colliding with the heavy bumper with which Stu and his work parties had reinforced the lead vehicle. The dead were mown down, crushed beneath the heavy wheels or flung to the roadside, broken and smashed as they squirmed in their own entrails.

They were making good progress, sticking to their plan and filtering their way through the back roads, only venturing onto the main highways when it was necessary. Marcus' vehicle took the lead, with Jim behind the wheel while Stu and Steve brought up the rear in the second Range Rover. Helen was partnered with Jake in the first of the people carriers and Lee drove the second, with Kieran in the passenger seat.

"So," Lee began, keeping his eyes fixed on the road while he balanced a glowing cigarette between his lips.

He puffed on it, blowing out choking smoke that filled the interior of the people carrier.

"How long you been a bender, then?" he asked casually.

Kieran looked up from the cold tin of baked beans he held in his lap; the spoon was full and rising towards his mouth when Lee's question struck.

"A '*bender*'?" Kieran asked incredulously.

Lee nodded, glancing at him before pulling his eyes back to the road as he blew out another cloud of grey cigarette smoke.

"Yeah, you know, a bender, a chutney ferret, an uphill gardener."

Lee looked at Kieran again, noting the expression on the big man's face and mistaking his annoyance for confusion.

"Okay, a homosexual. How long have you been gay?"

"I knew what you fucking meant, Lee," Kieran growled at him. "I just don't want you referring to me as a fucking '*bender*'."

"Right then," Lee acknowledged, nodding to himself as he took note of Kieran's sensitivities. "Sausage bandit it is, then."

Lee began to howl with laughter as Kieran's face turned red while his blood boiled below the surface.

"One of these days, I'll lose it with you, big time. You're a fucking cock, Lee."

Lee continued to laugh, but after a while, he settled himself and turned to glance at the infuriated Kieran again.

"Okay, okay," he conceded, "I'm sorry, Kieran, and I don't mean any offence by it; well, not that much. I just love taking the piss and now that there are two of you, at least Jake could never say that I am picking on him or singling him out."

Kieran thought for a moment then shook his head, a smile creasing his face despite his determination to continue his angry appearance.

"You really are a dick, aren't you, Lee?"

Lee shrugged, pulling the cigarette from his mouth and folding his bottom lip up over the top and towards his nose as he considered Kieran's statement.

"I suppose I am, but you should be the first to recognise a dick when you see one, with you being dick daft and all that."

Both of them began to laugh as the convoy continued to head northwards, winding its way through the country and the remains of civilisation that now stood in ruins all around them.

Steve drove along at the rear of the convoy, carefully keeping his distance from the vehicle in front in case of them suddenly stopping and him needing to avoid colliding with the rear of them.

The first shimmering rays of dawn were beginning to brighten the sky to the east as the gaps in the dark rolling clouds to their right, changing from a deep purple, almost black, and slowly shifting to deep orange, becoming brighter by the minute as the sun began its slow climb into the winter sky. It would still be another hour before it was fully daylight, and Stu calculated that at their current rate, they should reach the first rendezvous within a couple of hours of first light.

Within forty minutes, the sky had brightened substantially, giving them a better view of their surroundings. The sun had still not risen above the horizon but the sky, cluttered with dark clouds, allowed enough light through for them to see the landscape beyond the beams of their headlights.

They had recently turned off from a junction and now found themselves on a stretch of carriageway, two lanes wide and running in a straight line, with hardly a kink in the road. To their right, a valley stretched off far into the distance with rolling countryside and small villages and towns dotted amongst the vast expanse of greenery.

To their left, and beyond the crash barrier at the side of the road, the ground rose up in a steady slope that was covered with long grass, swaying in the cold winter wind. Patches of snow still clung to the landscape, slowly melting away as the rains arrived. At the top of the rise, Stu could see it was crowned with a tree line that ran north along the crest of the hill, paralleling the road.

"This stretch should take us pretty much all the way there," Stu said from the passenger seat as he sat studying the map.

"How long?" Steve asked, anxious to meet up with the rest of their group.

"Depending on the road, an hour, maybe an hour and twenty minutes, shouldn't be much more than that, though."

Steve nodded, and began to speak again, but was cut off by Stu suddenly screaming over the radio that he held close to his mouth.

"Contact left, contact left…"

Steve's eyes shot to the left. From within the tree line above the road, he saw a number of flashes from the barrels of rifles and machineguns, sending red beams of tracer rounds down towards the convoy, particularly aimed at Marcus' vehicle in the lead.

The crackle of the firing weapons followed, and soon the air around them snapped and hissed with the sound of bullets flying overhead and smacking into the vehicles with loud, metallic thumps.

An explosion erupted somewhere ahead of the convoy, sending up a plume of black smoke and debris hurtling through the air, the deafening percussion making Stu's ears pop and ring, even though they were over two hundred metres away from it.

Marcus heard the panicked and hollering voice of Stu through the radio and immediately saw the rounds racing towards them. With sickening thwacks and clangs, the hot steel projectiles smashed through the front of their vehicle, mutilating the engine; instantly, clouds of smoke and steam erupted through the bullet holes in the hood.

The tyres hissed and exploded as they were hit with rounds and the vehicle began to lurch across the road.

A cluster of static vehicles, just fifty metres in front, disintegrated in a blinding flash that was accompanied by a deafening bang. The shockwave struck the Range Rover, knocking it from side to side and peppering it with shrapnel. The windows cracked and the chassis buckled under the force of the detonation, jolting the two men inside.

Marcus felt the pressure against the side of his head as the blast threatened to crush his skull and suck his eyes from their sockets. His ears rang and his eyes burned as Jim fought with the wheel and struggled to keep the vehicle on the road as it continued to roll forwards.

"We've lost power," Jim screamed over the crack of the rounds as more fire was poured at them, punching its way through the thin metal of the doors and shattering the glass.

The vehicle was still moving, rapidly losing speed as Jim tried to drive through the killing area and out of the line of fire, but it was no use; the Range Rover was too badly damaged and they would soon come to a halt, stranded at the mercy of their attackers as they rained down their fire at leisure.

"Out," Marcus cried as the widow beside him exploded from a round cracking past his face, just centimetres from the tip of his nose.

"Bail out, Jim, move."

Marcus had already begun to scramble across the centre console, dragging his rifle with him, intending to jump out from the opposite side of the contact and use the disabled vehicle as cover. He realised then that Jim had not moved as ordered, and was still in his seat as more rounds smashed into the body of their vehicle.

"Jim," Marcus screamed as he looked up and saw his friend clutching at his throat.

Blood pumped from between his fingers and spattered the windshield and dashboard. Jim's eyes bulged with panic, and he struggled to breathe as he gripped his torn flesh.

As the Range Rover rocked and shuddered under more impacts, Marcus reached across the gasping and writhing Jim, pulling the door handle and throwing it open before pushing Jim through and out onto the road.

Marcus followed him just as a burst of machinegun bullets ripped into the passenger seat where he had been sitting just moments before, sending up clods of shredded leather and padding.

He crashed from the stalled vehicle, landing on top of Jim, who lay on the tarmac, squirming as he grasped at his neck with both blood-soaked hands.

The crescendo of the shots cracking above them and striking the vehicle was ear splitting. Stray bullets smashed into the road, sending up fountains of loose tarmac that ricocheted in all directions and showered down on Marcus as he dragged Jim to safety.

Marcus placed his friend behind the front wheel, hoping that the axle and engine would be enough protection to stop Jim from taking any more hits.

He quickly peered over the hood of the Range Rover, hoping to gain an idea of the situation.

Another burst struck the vehicle, sending splinters of metal flying through the air at deadly speeds and forcing Marcus to duck back down into cover.

Smoke began to pour out from the car as the tracer rounds burned and ignited the material of the seats. Diesel began to seep onto the road, and the smell of burning oil filled Marcus' nostrils and stung his eyes.

More thumps and cracks rang out around them as hundreds of rounds hurtled down towards the road.

Marcus looked down at the frantic face of Jim as the blood continued to pour from his neck. He reached into his vest and began ripping open a field dressing, and placed it against the gaping wound in Jim's throat, pushing down hard in an attempt to stem the flow of blood. Jim's eyes stared back at him pleadingly as he gargled and coughed up thick strands of frothy blood that speckled his face and chin.

His arms flailed and his legs kicked as he struggled to breathe and cling to life. Already, Marcus could see his skin turning pale as the precious blood poured from his body.

To their right, a figure suddenly lurched out through the smoke and from behind the torn open vehicles that had exploded at the start of the ambush. It saw Marcus and reached out towards him, staggering forward on rickety legs.

More shadowy figures emerged from the smoke, lurching their way along the road and towards the smouldering vehicles and trapped men.

Marcus raised his rifle, but before he could shoot, the lead creature's head exploded as stray bullets ripped through its torso and skull, dropping it instantly.

"Shit," Marcus hissed as he saw the dead approaching.

The rate of fire that the ambushers released onto them was immense. Marcus was completely pinned down and unable to move, or return any kind of suppressing fire. The air around them cracked incessantly as the glowing projectiles flew overhead, striking the tarmac. Deafening clangs and thumps rang out as more bullets shredded the vehicle that Marcus and Jim took cover behind.

Marcus looked to his left, further along the road in the direction they had travelled from, and saw smoke and tracer as the rest of his team took incoming from the tree line.

Over the racket, he heard the distinct sound of the GPMG opening up. Its heavy rattle echoed in long bursts as Stu began firing along the crest of the high ground, hoping to force the enemy to take cover and slacken their rate of fire.

In the thick of the battle, Marcus found the sound of the machinegun strangely comforting, knowing that there was still someone alive from his group and they were fighting back.

He glanced back behind him, looking for any cover that they could retreat to, but he could see that they would be exposed for far too long before they were clear of enemy fire and probably would not make it more than a few metres.

"Fuck," he growled.

The enemy fire slackened for a moment and Marcus was able to raise his head, long enough to get an idea of the enemy's position. He watched as Stu's machinegun rounds strafed along the summit of the hill, their glowing red tracers smashing into the hillside and sending clods of dirt up into the air, and smashing large chunks of bark from the trees beyond.

More rifles joined in from the left, telling Marcus that at least some of his people had managed to survive the initial contact. He looked to his right, searching the ground for an area he could move to and assault from the right flank, then rolling up the enemy position.

There was nothing.

The area was too open and provided no cover for him to move to and launch an assault. Their ambushers had chosen their killing area with the tell-tale signs of experience, leading Marcus to believe that they were up against professional soldiers and not a gang of bandits.

"Stu," Marcus called through his radio. "Stu, Jim is down, Jim is down. Can you move to the left and assault from the flank?"

There was no reply and Marcus could hear the continued rapid rate of fire that Stu threw back at the enemy position.

"Marcus, it's Steve," a panicked voice replied through the radio, hollering over the noise of the roaring machinegun.

"We can't move left. Stu says it's too open."

"Roger that," Marcus replied dejectedly.

He shuddered to think that there was no other option but to launch a full frontal assault, taking the fight to the enemy and charging up the slope of the hill, with nothing to support them apart from their sheer aggression.

The vehicles around them were slowly disintegrating and beginning to collapse inwards. More rounds punched through the Range Rover, passing clean through and exploding out onto the far side. The smouldering wrecks would not provide adequate protection for much longer, leaving them with no choice to move.

"Steve," he shouted into his radio as another burst struck the vehicle. "Who is left at your end? Are Lee and the others still alive?"

There was a pause, and then his earpiece crackled.

"I don't know about Lee, but I can see Helen and Jake," Steve replied breathlessly.

"Right, send Jake and Helen to me. I need them to cover this side of the road," Marcus commanded.

He turned just in time to see the barrel of Jim's pistol rise up in front of him. It was pointed directly at Marcus.

Marcus' eyes narrowed as he stared back into the pale face and unfocussed eyes of his friend.

"Jim," he began, but his words were drowned out by the deafening blast that erupted from the barrel.

Marcus winced as the round cracked at the side of his head; he turned just in time to see the disfigured corpse of a woman crumple to the ground behind him.

Jim managed to force a smile at Marcus.

"Nearly had you there, buddy," he croaked hoarsely.

The sound of footsteps approaching from his left dragged his attention away from Jim. Jake and Helen suddenly appeared from the smoke that filled the road and crashed down beside Marcus, as a stream of bullets ripped up the patch of tarmac, across which they had just sprinted.

"All call-signs," Marcus hollered over the radio. "When I give the order, pour as much fire onto their positions as possible, and I mean, really fucking hammer them."

Marcus was preparing himself to assault the hill, alone and with the remainder of his team giving him fire support. He knew that the others, being mainly from a civilian background, would not be able to turn and face the enemy, charging through a hail of bullets and storming forward.

Stu was the only other person, apart from Jim, trained and experienced, and therefore reliable enough, but Marcus needed him to remain behind the gun, pinning the enemy down while he ran forward to a better position from where he could begin his one-man assault on the enemy.

"Helen," he said as he turned to face her, "keep an eye on Jim. Jake, you keep firing on the hill and don't let those bastards get too close."

Jake turned to look in the direction where Marcus nodded and saw the cluster of dead approaching along the road from the right.

"Oh fuck," he whimpered.

Marcus crouched behind the front wheel of the Range Rover, checking he had a fresh magazine on his rifle. He had one more in his vest and he knew that it would not be enough for his assault. He looked at Jim, who was still holding the dressing against the wound in his neck as more blood seeped from his mouth.

"Jim," he said as he reached into his friend's assault vest and began removing his ammunition, adding it to his own.

"I'll be back soon, buddy. Just hang on and we'll get you seen to."

Jim did not reply as Helen continued to fight the flow of blood. His eyes were rolling and his face was drained of colour. He seemed to be struggling to stay conscious as more blood soaked through the swollen dressing in his hands and down his chest.

Marcus took a deep breath and began to inch his way forward, towards the bumper. The fire aimed at him and his vehicle seemed to have tapered off a little, and was being concentrated upon the remainder of his team who continued to sporadically fire back.

It would not be much longer before they were all out of ammunition. They had been in the fight for well over a minute now, and he guessed that most of them would be down to their last magazines.

Soon, his fire support would diminish, leaving him exposed, but as long as the initial crescendo of fire was heavy enough to keep the enemy's heads down as he made his first bound, he could continue to rely solely on Stu's general purpose machinegun to cover him up the hill.

He breathed deeply, looking back over his shoulder at Jake and then in the direction of the other vehicles.

He could see the enemy rounds gliding through the air, across the road, ploughing into the static vehicles that littered the carriageway.

He checked his weapon one final time, feeling his knees tremble as he crouched, psyching himself up for the insane move that he was about to make.

'One good thing I have on my side is surprise. They must think I'm already dead,' Marcus thought to himself when he considered the reasons that the rate of fire towards his vehicle had dropped substantially.

More fire suddenly erupted from the hill in long rattling bursts, but it was now coming from somewhere to the right. Marcus looked up and saw the muzzle flashes, a hundred metres to the right of where he believed the main ambush to be situated.

"Shit," he hissed to himself, realising that it would now be impossible to move and believing their new attackers were one of the 'cut off' groups, closing in to help the 'killing group' finish the job.

He raised his rifle, aiming towards the new threat. As he looked through his sight, he noticed that the new arrivals in the battle were not aiming their shots towards him and his stranded team.

They were firing at the positions on the ridge.

Marcus watched for a moment as the tracer rounds zipped along the crest of the hill, smashing into the enemy ambush and adding to the weight of fire that Stu poured onto them with his machinegun.

Marcus had no idea who they were, or why they were suddenly coming to their aid, but he was happy to take full advantage of their added firepower.

"We got fire support from the right," Marcus called excitedly into the radio.

"Standby, standby…rapid…*fire*."

Stu's machinegun suddenly upped its rate of fire. Long, echoing bursts streamed forward, shattering the trees and sending up plumes of earth and rock all around the enemy position. Marcus paused for a moment, watching the scene and revelling in the weight of fire that he was suddenly able to bring to bear on an enemy that believed it had the upper hand in the battle.

Dozens of bright red tracer rounds shot into the area where the enemy took cover. They sailed across the ground at lightning speed, cracking and whizzing as they thumped into the mud and rock covering the crest of the hill.

Marcus almost smiled, a surge of triumph and pride rising from within.

He wanted revenge and his aggression and blood lust spurned him on as he launched himself forward across the road. His legs bounded in long strides and he vaulted over the crash barrier and into the long wet grass of the hill.

As the new and unexpected fire support continued to suppress the enemy from their right, Stu and the others hammered away at the enemy from the left. Marcus charged up the middle, his eyes fixed on the summit of the slope, his heart pounding and a silent voice screaming at him aggressively inside his head, forcing him forward and blocking all other thoughts from his mind.

A number of shots cracked over him as the enemy realised what was going on, but with the weight of fire that was brought to bear against them, their aim was far from accurate and their fire was sporadic at best.

The rattle of the weapons to his right continued and he was distantly aware of movement from that direction. As he forced himself forward, his chest heaving and his mind racing, he caught sight of two men moving forward along the ridge from the right, closing in on the position and supporting one another as they moved forward in bounds.

The ambushers were being overwhelmed. They had lost the advantage of surprise and their domination of firepower dwindled under the pressure that Marcus and the others had thrown at them.

Marcus' main concern now was that the enemy would retreat before he was able to make the final assault.

He was now just ten metres from the summit and was close enough to feel the air displacement as Stu's rounds cracked past him just a few metres to his left. As the red-hot projectiles shot by, they sounded like a thousand whips, snapping with an ear-splitting thunder by the side of his head.

"Move," Marcus hollered down the hill, waving his arm and indicating to the left as he continued forward.

"Left flank, attack from the left."

Stu saw the signal and understood what Marcus needed him to do. He pulled the machinegun from the hood of the car that he fired from and scooped up the long belts of ammunition, flinging them over his shoulder.

"Steve, you're with me," he shouted to his right as he began to move forward towards the left of the hill.

Drawing on the last of his strength and roaring at the top of his lungs, Marcus launched himself forwards onto the enemy position, his finger depressing the trigger as he fired on automatic, sending long rasping bursts into the bodies of the men occupying the summit.

The shock and awe of his deadly charge was complete. With the heavy fire coming in on them from their left and right, and then suddenly seeing Marcus charging towards them, the ambushers were too stunned to react.

Some of the men, their eyes bulging with terror as Marcus launched himself at them screaming like a wild man, his eyes ablaze with madness and the lust for revenge, tried to fling their arms up in surrender, but they were too late.

Marcus could see nothing. He was blinded by hatred and a violence that filled his every sense. His veins coursed with fire and venom and no force in the world could stop his rampage.

Rounds smashed through flesh and bone. Screams of fear and pain rang out as Marcus dropped down and began to race along the line of shallow trenches, firing into the bodies that were still concentrating their fire on the road below, not realising that their position was compromised until it was too late.

He continued to the left, growling and howling like an enraged wild animal, rolling up the enemy and cutting a swathe of blood along the hilltop.

More shots and screams rang out from behind him as the two newcomers that had come to their aid assaulted from the far end, picking off the remainder that Marcus had bypassed when he launched his final assault through the centre of the ambush.

Marcus' rifle stopped, the cocking lever remaining fixed to the rear and indicating that his magazine was empty. With no time to correct the stoppage, he drew his machete from the sheath attached to his waist and brought the blade down, burying it deep in the skull of one of the ambushers.

The steel of the blade stuck, embedded in the bone.

Marcus released his grip on the handle and instinctively hurled himself at the next man in line with his hands stretched out in front of him and his teeth bared.

The shocked face of the soldier turned towards him, his eyes widening with terror as he saw Marcus and realised that they were being overrun. He attempted to raise his rifle, twisting it in his hands and bringing it to bear at the insane snarling figure leaping towards him.

The soldier was too slow and Marcus dropped on top of him, using his weight to pin the much lighter and younger man below him. The man yelped and struggled to free himself as Marcus began to pound him with his fists, roaring down at him as he landed each blow.

Digging his fingers into the soft flesh of the soldier's neck, Marcus began to tear at him, hearing the young soldier's choked pleas but continuing with his blood fuelled vengeance.

Muffled screams sputtered from the man's throat while he struggled desperately, kicking out and clawing at Marcus' hands, which refused to slacken their grip from around his windpipe.

Howling furiously, Marcus brought his head down with all the power he could wield behind it. His forehead crashed into the young man's face, splintering bone and causing a torrent of blood to erupt from his nose and mouth. Repeatedly, Marcus smashed the face to a pulp beneath his heavy blows, all the time tearing lumps of flesh from the dying man's throat as he gurgled and choked beneath the assault.

Finally, when there was nothing left to recognise as a human face, Marcus released the body that continued to twitch, dropping it on the ground at his feet.

He spat and wiped the blood away from his forehead as it began to run in to his eyes.

The crest of the hill fell silent as the young soldier's screams faded, indicating that the attack was over. Marcus reached for his rifle and quickly changed out the magazine, ready to take on the next fight, but none came.

Looking around him, he could see the sprawled and bloodied bodies of eight men. Steaming pools of blood covered the ground beneath the mutilated corpses that had been chewed up by Stu's heavy bullets or by Marcus' rifle and hands, as he hacked and gouged his way through them on his rampage.

He turned and saw two men standing just a few metres away, staring at him.

Marcus did not raise his weapon or perceive them as a threat. Their weapons were not pointed at him and their body language indicated no malice. They were obviously the men who had come to their aid, attacking from the right and helping Marcus to storm the enemy position.

Stu appeared over the crest of the hill, panting hard with the gun thrown over his shoulder and long belts of brass ammunition hanging from the chamber. Steve arrived close behind him, his eyes like saucers and his face as pale as a sheet.

Steve surveyed the ground in shocked silence, staring at the carnage they, and in particular his brother, had created. He placed his hand over his mouth, trying hard to stem the gag reflex that threatened to overwhelm him as the aftershock and nerves from the battle took hold, making his head spin, his knees tremble and his stomach churn.

"How was your baptism of fire, bro?" Marcus asked with a grin that creased his blood- and filth-smeared face, making him look demonic.

"The cut-offs," gasped Stu, "they'll either be closing in to help, or they'll be making their escape."

Stu was referring to the two groups that would be placed far to the left and right of the 'killing group' to ensure that no one could escape from the killing area of the ambush.

"No need to worry about them," one of the men behind Marcus announced.

"We took care of them last night and they didn't bother with a 'rear protection group', either. There were only two men per cut-off, so it was easy enough."

Marcus climbed up from the shallow trench containing the dead body with the pulped face. He looked at the two men and walked towards them as he pulled out a bottle of water from one of the pouches on his vest. He poured half of the contents over his face and began gulping the rest. He wiped his mouth with the back of his hand and stood, quietly eyeing the two men for a moment with his finger resting against the trigger of his rifle.

Shots continued to ring out from the road below as Jake and the others took care of the numerous dead that had been attracted by the noise of the battle. Marcus glanced down at them and then turned to the two men behind him.

"Who are you and why did you come to help us?" Marcus spat, still feeling a surge of the aggression that was only slowly dissipating from his system.

The two men glanced at one another for a moment, and then one of them nodded to the other, indicating that he should do the talking.

"I take it that you were part of the helicopter bunch?" the closest of them asked.

Marcus' eyes widened and his grip on the rifle tightened.

"Yeah, that's right. What do you know of them?"

They glanced at one another again, nervously.

"They were shot down by this lot and a few of their friends," he said, nodding at the numerous bodies scattered around them.

Marcus swallowed hard and turned to look at Stu.

"How did we come out?"

"Kieran got hit," Stu replied, "he took one in the shoulder and one in the lower leg. All four vehicles are fucked and we're low on ammo, too."

Marcus nodded as he reached up and wiped his face, smearing the blood, sweat and dirt.

"Jim's hurt too. He took a round in the neck. I had to leave him down there with Helen and Jake."

Marcus paused for a moment, his eyes staring blankly at the ground.

"Take what you can from these fuckers," he grunted as he indicated the dead men around him. "Make sure they can't come back, either."

He turned back to the two men who stood watching him. The professional soldier in him had taken over and he had avoided asking too much about the helicopter until he knew the condition and situation of his team and their capability to continue fighting.

"The heli, are they all dead?" he asked in a tone that demanded a straight answer.

The closest of the men shook his head.

"No, they crashed and the survivors were taken towards the east, their camp. Then this lot broke away and came to ambush you."

"How do you know all this and why were you so keen to help us?" Steve asked suspiciously, as he stepped forward.

He was eager for information and battled to hold back the feeling of panic that was growing inside of him for Sarah.

"This same bunch of bastards ambushed *our* convoy, killing a lot of us, and then took the survivors to their camp. We've been watching them for weeks but we couldn't do anything because there were so many of them, and so few of us. We saw these guys coming out and we followed them and that's when we saw them shoot down the helicopter and realised that someone else must be coming for them to go through the trouble of laying an ambush."

"So few of you?" Stu asked as he pulled his knife out of a head that he had just ensured would not get back up.

"How many of you are there?"

Again, the men looked at one another then turned to Stu and shrugged.

"Uh…just two," the man standing furthest away replied.

Stu snickered and shook his head.

"Fucking hell, we're formidable."

"Who did they take?" Marcus asked in a calm but impatient voice.

"They took a bunch of women and kids with them, I think there may have been a few men, too, but it was dark, so we couldn't be sure."

Marcus nodded.

"Well then, it looks like we're going to be going after them. Can you lead us there?"

"Of course," the man replied, eagerly. "Like I said, they have our people, too."

"Okay, collect whatever weapons and ammo you can and prepare to move."

He turned to look down at the road, towards where Helen and the others remained and spoke into the radio.

"Jake, how's Jim and Kieran? Can they move?"

There was a moment's silence then Jake's voice crackled over the speaker.

"Jim's dead, Marcus."

The news hit him like a hammer blow. His legs grew weak and he had to sit down on the edge of the parapet of one of the shallow trenches that their ambushers had occupied.

"Fuck's sake," he hissed mournfully as he stared down at the dirt and blood soaked ground at his feet.

Stu remained standing, shaking his head and fighting to control his composure as the anger swelled inside of him.

"Cunts..." he grumbled, and then spat on one of the mutilated and churned bodies lying in a pool of its own blood and entrails.

"I'm sorry," one of the men said as he stepped forward and crouched by Marcus.

"I'm sorry about Jim, but we can hit the fuckers back and save the rest of our people. We'll wipe the bastards out."

Marcus nodded, his body wracked with grief as he remembered the last conversation he had had with Jim and the fact that it had not been a particularly pleasant one.

"My wife and kids are with them, I hope," he whispered hoarsely, turning to the man who crouched close by, staring back at him.

"My daughter, too," Steve added.

"Well," the second of the newcomers began as he finished stripping one of the bodies of all its weapons and ammunition and dumping it back on the floor before moving on to the next.

"We need to get moving. We'll help your injured guy and find a place that he can rest up while we push for the camp."

Marcus nodded in agreement, as he raised himself to his feet.

"We need to take care of Jim first," he said with the indication that it was not open to discussion. "We can't leave him to rot here and we *always* take care of our men."

The two men nodded, understanding Marcus' sentiment as they felt the same sense of duty towards their own fallen comrades.

"You two got names?" Marcus finally asked as he turned to head down towards the road.

"I'm Toby," the first man said, then pointed over his shoulder, "and this ugly bastard, his name is Robbie."

32

The icy shock of the freezing water made her gasp as the immense cold snatched the breath from her lungs. Her eyes flickered open, just as a blow hit her on the side of her face, causing her head to snap back, rocking the brain inside her skull and threatening to send her back into unconsciousness.

"Oh no, Captain MacReady, don't be going back to sleep," a calm but menacing voice spoke to her through the ringing in her ears and blurred vision.

She could make out the dark shape of a man sitting directly in front of her but the details of his face were obscured by her delirium.

"There are things I want to talk to you about before we allow you to rest, Captain MacReady."

Kelly's head swam and her eyes refused to focus. Her whole body was wracked with pain, especially her back and neck. Confusion reigned supreme in her clouded mind and she had no idea of where she was, or what had happened.

She tried to speak, but her words came out as nothing more than a slur.

Another open-handed slap to the side of her face sent her reeling backwards, almost falling from the chair that she sat on, but the restraints that were tied tightly around her kept her in place.

"You're not being very cooperative, Captain," the composed voice continued.

"Although, you never were the sort to tow the line, and that is why we find ourselves needing to have this little chat."

Finally, through the haze that shrouded her mind, she recognised the voice. No one referred to her as 'Captain MacReady'; no one except General Gibson.

His voice was now unmistakable. It was that same familiar, soothing and fatherly tone that always held a hint of threat, lurking just below the surface.

Her head rolled as she tried desperately to collect her thoughts and gain control of her mind and body. Everything threatened to close down on her and send her back into the blackness, but after hearing his voice, she became determined to face him coherently.

She knew that she would not live for much longer at the hands of Gibson, but if she could help it, she would meet her death standing on her feet and looking him in the eye.

Her sight began to clear as she angled her head, trying to focus her eyes like a drunk manipulating a mobile phone. She could see his smiling face more clearly now.

Gibson had never looked menacing in any way. His appearance was completely non-threatening. He was tall and extremely slim, bordering on malnourished, with a perpetual smile that exaggerated the deep lines and creases in his weathered face. Gibson looked no different than the average man, certainly not appearing as a monster, but his eyes; Kelly had always felt that they were as black and lifeless as the eyes of the dead and anyone that dared to look into them would be chilled to the bone by the evil that lurked just behind them.

"Ah, finally," Gibson smiled, "you're back in the land of the living."

He thought for a moment, contemplating the impact of his statement.

"Or, should I say, the living *and* the dead?"

He was clearly impressed with his little attempt at humour and he looked around the room for the approval of the other soldiers and officers that were assembled.

"Right then," he said excitedly, clapping his hands together then rubbing them against each other. "Let's get down to business."

Kelly watched him through one eye, still struggling to focus.

"What business?" she slurred. "You know you're going to kill me, just get on with it."

Gibson's face suddenly changed to one of mock offense.

"Oh, Captain MacReady, I don't want to hurt you. I just need some answers, like, where were you going in *my* helicopter before we shot you down?"

The memory of the crash suddenly flooded back to her. The flashing red lights, the warning alarms blaring in the cockpit and the crack and thump as the machinegun bullets that ripped into the aircraft while the passengers behind her screamed in fear and pain.

"We were looking for a new place to live. How did you find us?"

The effort of concentration was painful as Kelly fought hard to remain coherent and place her thoughts in to order.

Gibson shrugged.

"Very easily, Captain; all my aircraft have a transponder fitted."

He watched for her reaction and saw the confusion in her face that he had been waiting for.

"Ah, of course, you didn't know about the transponder, and that is because I didn't want you to know."

Kelly shook her head and adjusted her position on the chair.

A hand from behind gripped her by the hair, forcing her head back; a bottle of cold water was thrust before her face. She gulped the cold fluid greedily, much of it running down her chin and onto her chest.

"See, I'm not that much of a monster. You feel better now?" Gibson asked in a cheery voice.

Kelly gasped, feeling the benefits of the cold water as it drained down her parched throat, rejuvenating her to a degree.

"Anyway," he continued, "as soon as you and Lieutenant Palmer deviated from course, we knew that you were deserting. You know how I feel about deserters and disobeying orders, don't you, Captain?"

Kelly said nothing, but the visions of pilots and soldiers alike being hanged on his authority flashed before her eyes. She knew well how he felt about the subject.

"We've been watching you for quite some time. My men even infiltrated that zoo that you were living in. Who do you think it was that knocked out your cameras? We didn't want you to see that we were weakening your defences."

Kelly's eyes snapped up, both of them suddenly becoming completely focussed as she stared into the eyes of the insane General sitting in front of her.

"Yes," he said, smiling and nodding as he confirmed to Kelly that she had heard him correctly.

"I don't think that gate would *ever* have collapsed, if it wasn't for the hard work of my soldiers."

"You bastard," Kelly snarled at him, her eyes fixing him with a piercing stare.

Gibson's expression changed. The smile disappeared from his face and his eyes narrowed. From somewhere behind her, another blow struck her in the right side of her head, smashing against her temple and sending her crashing to the floor as the power of the punch launched Kelly and the chair to the side.

A number of hands grabbed her and forced her upright again. She sat slouched in the chair, slumped against her restraints and barely conscious.

Another torrent of freezing water was thrown into her face, making her scream from the shock as her flesh felt like it was being pierced by a thousand needles.

"Okay then, Captain," Gibson's tone had changed. He no longer attempted to conceal the malice in his voice.

"Now that the pleasantries are over, I need to know where you were headed before the crash."

Kelly remained silent.

"There's no need to be the martyr here," he continued, "I know about the convoy and they're being dealt with as we speak."

Kelly's head twitched at the mention of Marcus and his team as they pushed north in their convoy, headed for the rendezvous with her and the helicopter.

"Okay," he nodded, and then indicated to the man standing behind Kelly to escort her outside.

She was untied from the chair, but her hands remained bound behind her back. She was half carried and half dragged out through the door and into the open.

The cold air almost took her breath away as it assaulted her straining and burning lungs. It was still dark, with just a hint of morning light spreading across the sky from the east and the temperature was not many degrees above zero.

Kelly was forced across a muddied open area surrounded by a number of long rectangular buildings. She was thrown to the ground, the cold mud smearing her face and seeping into her clothing, clogging her hair into thick clumps.

She raised her head, coughing out the filth that had poured into her mouth, and saw a number of men, armed and wearing military uniforms, standing in a wide circle around the area of the courtyard.

From behind her, she heard doors being thrown open and more people approaching, their feet tramping in the soft mud. The distinct sound of whimpering children and crying mothers was unmistakable, and Kelly twisted herself to see what remained of the helicopter group.

Sophie and Claire were in front, holding Sarah, Liam and David close to them as they looked about in fear, clinging to one another for comfort in the early morning cold. More people, men, women and children were escorted from the outlying buildings. Kelly did not recognise any of them and believed them to be other prisoners of the insane General Gibson.

Next, another figure was dragged from a separate building. Two soldiers hauled the barely conscious body between them, and then dumped the unfortunate soul in to the mud beside her.

The figure let out a groan and slowly rolled onto its back. Through the blood and smeared filth, Kelly recognised Hussein's face.

"Well then, Captain MacReady, now that you're all together," Gibson said as he crouched down in the mud beside her.

She stared back at him then glanced at the others.

Gibson saw the expression on her face and smiled broadly.

"Yes, that is right, Captain," he gloated, "this is all that remains of your little band of survivors, except these two over here."

He turned and nodded towards two more figures that were tied to posts in the centre of the courtyard. Both of their heads drooped, covered in mud and hard to identify in the darkness. Their bodies slumped against the restraints while they groaned and their heads lolled, as they were clearly close to collapse.

Gibson turned back to Kelly and smiled warmly as he raised himself to his feet.

"Oh, but don't worry, we took care of the others in the helicopter for you. They won't be getting back up. See, we're not savages here, Captain MacReady."

He stepped back and viewed the soldiers and civilian captives around him.

"My aim this evening is to prove a point to you good people." the General spoke loudly in his usual warm manner, addressing all that were assembled, including the survivors from the Safari Park.

"Captain MacReady and Lieutenant Palmer decided to betray me, and in times of war, as we find ourselves now, we cannot afford to suffer mutineers. Therefore, examples must be set for us to maintain order and discipline. We cannot win this war without absolute obedience and *discipline*."

He stepped forward, his boots squelching in the freezing wet mud, and approached Claire as she stood, shivering from cold and fear. He looked down at Sarah who clung to her mother's waist and smiled at her. He squatted down and reached out, stroking her hair.

"You understand, don't you, little girl?" he asked, still smiling with unblinking cold eyes as he spoke to the terrified Sarah.

"Discipline is something that your teachers surely taught you about. The whole world depends on it. Whether it is in business, politics or war, success can *never* be accomplished if discipline is not enforced to its fullest."

Sarah stared back at him, her eyes wide and the whites glowing in the darkness. She was terrified. The man speaking to her was neither one of the living, or the dead. He was something else and much more frightening than anything that now roamed the earth. His voice was soft but his words turned to searing flames as they penetrated her ears and his eyes, they never blinked or showed a fraction of emotion.

The man was a monster and Sarah saw him as the Devil himself.

Gibson stood up and ruffled Sarah's hair, still smiling down at her as he stepped backwards to continue his address.

"Okay then, on with the show."

He turned to the two bodies trussed up against the posts and held a hand out towards them, indicating them to his audience.

"This is Lieutenant Palmer," he paused and thought, "or as you all may know him, Joey. He was one of my men. A man that I considered a good soldier and pilot, loyal and trustworthy, but he betrayed us."

Joey groaned and raised his head, exposing his battered and bloodied features, and for a fleeting moment, he and Kelly had eye contact. She could see the suffering he was going through and her heart pounded in her chest as she watched him, his swollen eyes pleading with her to help him.

"This," Gibson made a chopping motion with his hand towards Joey, leaving no one in doubt to whom he was referring.

"This man was one of mine and must now be disciplined."

He nodded to one of the soldiers standing close by. The man nodded back then strode towards Joey as he remained slumped and restrained against the post, unable to move as the soldier drew a long knife from a pouch on his hip.

Without a word, the soldier gripped Joey by the hair, forcing his head back against the post, and dragged the sharp blade across his throat, slicing deep and creating a wide chasm in Joey's flesh.

Instantly, Joey began to thrash and kick at his restraints as the soldier stepped back from him.

Bright red blood sprayed in a wide arc, soaking through Joey's clothing and splashing into the mud at his feet as he continued to convulse. A sickening, wet sucking noise and panicked gasps emitted from the gaping wound in his neck as he struggled for air, but with his trachea destroyed and his arteries severed, it was a matter of seconds before Joey became still and silent, falling back against his bonds, his head slumping forward.

Sarah screamed and buried her face in her mother's arms as Claire and Sophie stood watching in horror and crying uncontrollably, pulling the children close in an attempt to comfort and reassure them.

Kelly whimpered and buried her face in the cold mud below her as she watched the life slowly slip from her friend.

"You bastards," she cried softly to herself as her floods of tears mixed with the mud covering her face. "You, bastards..."

Two soldiers then came and untied Joey's body, allowing it to fall heavily into the filth, and leaving just a length of rope secured around one leg, attached to the post at the other end.

It was clear that General Gibson intended for Joey to reanimate.

Gibson then strode across to the second figure tied to the stake beside Joey. As he pushed the man's head back, Kelly recognised Carl.

He was just as badly beaten and disorientated as Joey had been and she feared that he would not survive for much longer.

"You, my friend," Gibson spoke soothingly in to Carl's face.

"You will remain here and wait for Lieutenant Palmer to wake up. Then you can have someone to keep you company. Wouldn't that be nice?"

Carl's head rolled in Gibson's hand and one eye prised itself open against the swelling, splitting the encrusted blood that covered his face.

"Fuck you," Carl grumbled.

Gibson smiled back at him then turned to his soldiers.

"Take the Captain back in to the interrogation room and bring the girl and her mother too," he ordered, "they can help us with our enquiries."

He then indicated to Sophie and the two boys, Liam and David, and then Hussein who remained in the mud beside Kelly.

"Throw the others back in the pig shed."

Kelly, Claire and Sarah were taken to the farmhouse and dumped in the kitchen. Claire and Kelly were bound and tied to the chairs but Sarah was left with her hands free as ordered by the General.

He sat watching them, his unblinking eyes studying the women, making them feel uneasy and unsure of what his intentions were.

"Would you like something to eat, little one? Maybe a drink?" Gibson asked as he turned to Sarah and smiled.

Sarah remained staring at the ground. She was terrified of looking into his cold, unfeeling eyes again, for fear of what she might see; even his voice, though calm and soft, was enough to send a shiver down her spine. She had seen the evil that dwelled behind his eyes and she had witnessed the merciless savagery that he was capable of just moments before in the courtyard.

The General nodded to the soldier standing by the door, and he left the room, returning a few minutes later with a bottle of orange juice, which he placed on the table in front of Sarah.

"Thank you," she mumbled, still staring at the floor and not wanting to upset the General or his men by showing a lack of gratitude.

Gibson smiled at her then turned to Kelly.

"You've seen what I am capable of," he spoke matter-of-factly, referring to the execution of Joey.

"Now, I need to know where you were going when we shot you from the sky, Captain MacReady."

"I told you," Kelly replied, her eyes fixed on her boots, "we were looking for a new place to live."

"Yes, I remember you saying that, but where? I don't believe for one minute that you did not have a plan. Don't forget, Captain, my men were watching you for quite some time. We saw your preparations and you clearly had a fixed destination. How else were the rest of your people that were moving by road going to find you?"

Kelly remained silent. It was only a matter of time before the beatings would start and she knew that she could not hold out forever.

"Well?" Gibson pressed.

"Listen, Captain, if you're worried about 'operational security', it doesn't matter anymore. You are not going anywhere, and the convoy, they have already been taken care of. You won't be seeing them again, I'm afraid."

Claire's eyes snapped up from the table.

"What do you mean? What have you done to them?"

"Only what *had* to be done, my dear," he replied casually.

He stood up and unfastened his belt buckle, slipping his pistol and holster from his waist and placing it on the table in front of him.

"They were a heavily armed group and needed to be neutralised. I couldn't have a gang of armed bandits roaming the country while I am trying to take it back from the enemy, especially while I am recruiting."

Kelly looked up, her gaze flicking towards the pistol on the table for a fleeting moment, then locking with Gibson's eyes.

"So that's what this is all about, you taking back the country and recruiting?"

He nodded.

"Of course, why else would I be on the mainland? In case you haven't noticed, Captain, I am running short on soldiers and need to replenish my ranks. That is why I want to know where you're going. Are there more there, waiting for you?"

Kelly shook her head and huffed, a wry smile spreading across her face.

"You lost all your men because you sent them into Glasgow, unsupported and then left them to die there."

She watched as the General's expression changed to one of concern as she continued to sneer and spit venom at him.

"You're fucking insane, Gibson. You're not fit for command. You're not even a *real* general and more people will die because of your ludicrous plan to conquer the world because you're on some fucking power trip. What's the matter, Gibson, were you bullied at school?"

Gibson's face turned red with rage and, in a flash, he was up from the table, striking Kelly across the face and sending her crashing to the floor as Claire and Sarah reeled in fear.

Kelly raised her head, looking up at the incensed Gibson standing above her. Her vision blurred and her ears began to ring as her senses lost control of themselves.

She was barely aware of the screams that suddenly rang out from the courtyard. The long howling shrieks of pain and suffering as the reanimated corpse of Joey ripped the flesh from Carl's body.

She lost consciousness.

33

His feet trod lightly on the multitude of dried leaves and twigs carpeting the ground below him. Each step was carefully placed as he stalked from tree to tree. He made no sound, his skill and experience illustrated through his movements and confidence in his own ability as he climbed the wooded hill.

In the darkness, further up ahead of him, he could see the distinct outline of the ridge as its dark shadow contrasted with the pale clouds above, sailing across the night sky.

He paused for a moment, crouching in the shadow of a large tree as he watched and listened, making sure that he had not been detected. His eyes scanned the ground ahead of him and peered into the darkness on either side. His ears, finely tuned and listening intently to the sounds of the night, detected nothing that he perceived to be a threat.

He was close, just a few more metres from the summit of the hill and the sentry position that he knew was there, somewhere in the darkness. He scanned the crest of the feature, looking for the guard, but saw no one and he began to fear that the soldiers might have broken camp and left the area.

Stepping out from behind the tree, he carefully moved forward and to the right, his sixth sense telling him that if there were a sentry position, it would be to his left. He began to skirt around in a wide arc, hoping to come up on the guard from behind and remain undetected until the last possible second.

He had left his equipment and weapons with Marcus and the others, choosing to travel light, leaving fewer chances of snagging himself against a branch and making noise. All he carried was his knife and radio. He held the knife in his right hand, the hilt wrapped in his palm with the blade running along the inside of his forearm, avoiding the risk of the steel glinting in the dull light.

He took a few more steps then stopped as something moved to his half left. He froze to the spot, not wanting to make any sudden movements, giving his position away. If someone looked in his direction, he could easily be mistaken for just another tree in the gloom of the thick wood.

The sound was not that of an animal in the undergrowth or anything else indigenous to the woods. It sounded like a foot scraping against the dirt, a shift in position.

Now, he had a point of reference to aim for and he hoped beyond hope that it was the sentry and not one of the dead, roaming through the trees in the dark.

He swallowed hard, glanced about and then continued in his arc, keeping his eye on the area from where he heard the noise. It was impossible to tell with a degree of accuracy where the sound had come from, and he would need to continue his silent stalk until he was virtually on top of the position, lunging at the final moment.

After a few metres, he stopped again, turning his body so that he faced down the hill and out beyond the trees. He remained crouched, surveying the scene and the lay of the land beyond the woods. The visibility was good and he could see all the approaches to the ridgeline from the north and west. If anyone were to come up the hill, he would be able to see their movements in advance before they got into position to launch an attack. He glanced back over his shoulder, seeing that he was well below the skyline and not silhouetting himself against the pale clouds.

'If I was going to put out a stag position to cover the north, this is where I would put it,' he thought to himself, coming to the conclusion that the sentry must be just ahead of him, a little further down the hill.

He knew that the soldiers would not place their defences right on the edge of the wood line; that they would be set back in the cover of the trees. He remained perfectly still, scanning the darkness and focussing his ears for any indication of the guard.

He was readying himself to move forward a couple of paces when a flash erupted out of the darkness ahead of him. The light brightened a wide area, flickering from the trees and, more importantly, illuminating the man holding the lighter.

Robbie watched as the sentry held the flame close to his face, bathing his pale features in a swathe of light. He then extinguished the lighter and puffed on his cigarette, the cherry shining brightly in the darkness, giving Robbie the aiming mark that he needed.

No other men had been revealed in the area as the light had exposed the position, and Robbie glanced up to the heavens, smiling and thanking the Gods for the gift that they had just dropped in his lap.

Crouched and moving forward slowly, Robbie closed in, both hands held out before him, ready to grab his victim and silence him before he could cry for help. He kept his eye on the glowing cigarette that danced about hypnotically in the almost pitch black of the shaded wood as the sentry enjoyed what would be his last ever smoke.

The adrenaline flowed through Robbie's veins and his senses heightened even more as the moment drew nearer. His legs felt light and nimble and his body was coiled like a spring; his strong, powerful arms flexed involuntarily as his body subconsciously limbered itself up, ready for the final leap.

He was just a couple of metres away now. Close enough to hear the faint crackle of the burning cigarette as the soldier drew on it and then exhaled the plumes of grey/blue smoke that drifted up in to the trees, seemingly creating a glow of its own.

Robbie could see the full shape of the man in front of him now, and a cursory glance to the left and right confirmed to Robbie that the sentry was alone.

He took a deep, silent breath, ensuring that his muscles had all the oxygenated blood that they needed for the imminent struggle, a struggle that he *must* win.

Without a sound, Robbie threw himself forward, towards the man's back. He landed on top of him, his weight knocking the surprised soldier forward in the sentry position and sending the bright glowing cigarette sailing through the air.

The startled man let out a gasp, but before he could turn it into a scream, Robbie's large meaty hands had closed over his mouth while his thickset body enveloped him. As they continued to tumble forward, the soldier tried to twist his position, but Robbie's weight and power was too great, and they crashed to the ground and into the dirt.

The steel of the blade in Robbie's hand flashed in the darkness as he brought it around and thrust it against the sentry's throat. He felt the flesh pop as he pushed the knife in deep, driving it into the area behind the windpipe, then pushing it forward, severing the trachea and cutting off any cry for help that the soldier could have mustered.

The body below him thrashed and kicked as the man felt his life being snatched from him. His survival instincts took over and he struggled with the strength of a bear as Robbie held on tightly, bringing the knife back towards the soldier's throat.

As the blood gushed and poured over his hands and down his arms, Robbie began hacking away at the flesh of the soldier's neck, sawing through sinew, muscle and arteries. The man continued to struggle, his severed throat emitting a gargling, rasping noise as his body fought desperately for air and survival.

Robbie continued to cut, feeling the warm, crimson fluid cascade over his hands and smelling the familiar iron-rich tang of blood as it flowed from the soldier's destroyed gullet.

Eventually, the man began to fall limp. His feet continued to scuff around in the dirt and his gaping windpipe sucked at the air, but he was close to death now.

Robbie was still hacking at his neck, ensuring that any message or warning from the dying man was rendered impossible. The blade struck bone as it sliced the top vertebrate of the spine, and Robbie stopped.

He sat back, his chest heaving heavily as he gasped for breath. His body was soaked in sweat and his hands glistened with blood, looking almost black in the dark shadow of the trees. His breathing came in rasps and his body shook uncontrollably, as it began to suffer from the after effects of the adrenaline and struggle.

The body lay still in front of him, the man's pale face staring back at him in the gloom that suddenly seemed brighter under the cover of the trees. The wide frozen eyes remained fixed and unblinking, fossilised in an expression of perpetual surprise and horror.

Robbie's breathing began to slow as he regained his composure. He knelt up in the dirt and rubbed his blood-soaked hands on the ground, then wiped the sweat from his face on the back of his sleeve, smearing more blood across his features.

"Fuck's sake," he snarled to himself as he realised his mistake, feeling the blood seeping into his eyes.

He reached down and keyed the radio.

"Position clear," he whispered.

Soon, the remainder of the team had joined him just below the crest of the hill as Robbie sat waiting patiently, cleaning the blood from his knife.

"Fucking hell," Tobias gasped with a grin when he saw the state of his friend and the smears of blood that coated his face.

"Did you eat the poor bastard?"

"Fuck off, Toby," Robbie sneered, and then grinned at his friend.

They spread themselves out along the ridge and peered down into the low ground at the farm complex below.

Tobias looked to his right and studied Marcus' face. In the faint light, he could see that the man was sweating profusely, despite the cold of the early morning. His skin was pale and shiny and he looked as though he had not slept in weeks.

Tobias hardly knew Marcus, but he could see that the man was close to collapse.

'You're one tough bastard, mate,' he thought to himself as he watched Marcus with a sense of admiration.

Since the ambush at the road, none of them had even considered resting. After learning about the helicopter being shot down and his people taken prisoner, Marcus had single-mindedly driven them forward while his blood coursed with a lust for vengeance.

Tobias and Robbie, after weeks of watching the farm, built a detailed model of the ground, buildings and outlying features and informed Marcus of the strengths and routines of the enemy.

The complex was set in a patch of low ground, with the ridgeline directly to the west of it and sprawling farmland to the east. A road led up to the farm from the south, following the contour of the small valley, which the farm sat at the head of.

According to Tobias and Robbie, the prisoners were being held in the long rectangular buildings on the west side of the complex, with the main farmhouse at the north end for the commander and his staff and the soldiers occupying the barn and stables to the east.

Two defensive positions were set on the southern approach, not far from the main gate, with another position further to the north, at the rear of the complex and covering mainly to the north and east.

"So much for the 'three up' rule," Marcus commented as Tobias informed them of the enemy numbers.

"What's the 'three up' rule?" Steve asked as he stared at the model.

"Military doctrine," Marcus replied as he coughed and spat to the side.

"If you're attacking a section strength position, you use a platoon, outnumbering the enemy by three to one. If it's a platoon held position, you would use a company to attack it, and so on," he paused and smiled at his brother. "We're attacking a platoon with less than a section, so it's arse backwards."

Marcus had formed his plan and issued his orders, covering every detail of the operation and ensuring that everyone knew what their job was.

A kilometre to the south, he had ordered that Kieran be left in a small wood, with Helen to watch over him. She had protested at first but Marcus had cut her off, insisting that his decision was final. The reason was not one of chivalry or chauvinistic values, but of logic. She was medically trained and Kieran needed her attention, and more importantly, he wanted Steve's head to be clear. They were about to go into battle and he did not want his brother being more concerned about the wellbeing and safety of his girlfriend, but he had kept the latter reason to himself during his justification to Helen.

From there, the remainder of them had pressed on towards the farm and their friends being held captive there.

Marcus and Tobias would be the main assault group, with Stu and Robbie controlling the two fire support groups with Steve, Jake and Lee, armed with the machineguns that they had stripped from the dead soldiers at the ambush site.

Now, they waited in their positions, watching the farm and checking their watches as H-hour approached.

Stu and Steve lay quietly, holding their weapons tight into their shoulders as they watched the minutes tick by. They were forward of the high ground where Marcus and the others would launch their attack from and at a right angle to their line of assault. They lay perched on a small rise in the ground to the south of the complex on the far side of the road, giving them an over watch on the front and east side of the farm. From there, they could deal with any reinforcement that would be sent to counter attack.

Robbie, Lee, and Jake were higher up to the west, on top of the ridge with a complete view of the farm, enabling them to pour fire into the positions ahead of Marcus and Tobias as they moved forward.

Without the gun group's weight of fire, Marcus and Tobias would be dead within seconds after launching their attack.

"Overwhelm the bastards," Marcus had said to them, repeatedly. "They need to be wiped out the moment we move. As we take one position, switch your fire to the next and don't give them a second to breathe or re-group."

The machinegun teams linked all their belted ammunition together, saving time on reloads and allowing them to keep a high rate of fire pouring down onto the unsuspecting enemy.

As they waited, each of them had time to reflect and consider what they were about to do. Their senses became aware of the smallest things, the cold breeze blowing the grass just below their faces, the sound of mice rustling in the underbrush and the birds twittering in the trees as they waited for the arrival of the new day.

Their minds drifted and thought of things that they had long since forgotten, the tiniest details becoming as vivid as though the events had happened only yesterday. More than anything, the waiting allowed their fear to grow.

Every one of them had a knot growing in their stomachs and icy shivers running along their spines. Regardless of whether they were veterans, like Marcus and Tobias, or whether they were ordinary men, unused to war, like Steve and Jake; all of them were afraid.

Their bodies trembled from the cold and the nervous tendrils that seemed to creep along, just below the surface of their flesh. The only difference between the veteran and the unseasoned was that the tried and tested warriors amongst them knew how to channel their fear, to use it as part of their will to live and fight for their survival. They could take the fear that threatened to overwhelm them and turn it against their enemy, adding it to their aggression as they stormed forward through the hail of gunfire.

Marcus looked down at his watch and then glanced at the slowly brightening sky. A cold breeze wafted against his face and he closed his eyes for a moment, taking pleasure from its cooling effect on his flushing skin.

"Five minutes," he said as he keyed the radio.

A number of double clicks, producing short moments of static, came through his earpiece in reply, informing him that the two gun groups understood and were ready.

He turned and looked at Tobias, their eyes locking for a moment. Tobias nodded, confirming that he was ready without Marcus having to ask.

The minutes ticked by and Marcus checked his watch continuously until the sweeping hand entered into the final minute on the countdown towards the initiation of the attack.

"Ten seconds," he whispered into the radio, gripping his weapon tightly and readying his body for the first leap forward.

"Three...two...one..."

Like the sound of a gigantic piece of tearing cloth, the guns opened up instantly, firing long bursts into their allocated targets. The air rang with the continuous echoing clatter of the machineguns as their rounds zipped and cracked through it, smashing into the positions and disintegrating anything that moved within their line of fire.

Marcus watched for a moment as the streaks of glowing red tracer rounds from Stu and Steve's guns glided along the shallow valley below him from the right, ploughing through the thick brick walls of the soldiers' living quarters to the east and causing the gable end to collapse within seconds.

More rounds whizzed in from higher up, along the ridgeline to his right, as Robbie, Lee and Jake hammered away at the sentry positions that were placed on the south side of the farm and directly in the line of assault for Marcus and Tobias.

Clods of dirt shot up around the makeshift bunkers, their mud and brick walls collapsing instantly as the heavy rounds thumped through them and into the men inside. Screams echoed from within the positions as flesh and bone was shredded and splintered by the devastating fire that rained in upon them.

Already, the forward positions were nothing more than smouldering holes in the ground, filled with shattered and broken bodies, their blood mixing into the mud below them as the thunder of the rapidly firing machineguns shook the valley.

"Move," Marcus cried as he leapt up and rushed forward, charging down the hill then dropping to one knee, firing into the men that began to spill out of the surrounding buildings behind the bunkers.

As Marcus fired, Tobias jumped from his position and bounded forward, the noise of battle ringing in his ears as the bass drumbeat of his heart was drowned out by the snapping rounds filling the air all around him.

Bright glowing bullets shot past him as the enemy tried to return fire, cracking loudly as they displaced the air. Clods of earth erupted all around him as the rounds thumped into the ground, barely missing him as he forced himself forward, and roaring as he did so.

The valley resounded with the racket of the pounding machineguns, their deadly fire never letting up for a moment as the gun groups covered the advance of Marcus and Tobias.

More men appeared from within the barn and began to fire at the two men charging towards them from the hill, their bullets exploding from their rifles and zooming towards their targets.

Robbie swung his gun around, the distant figures dancing before the point of his foresight. He squeezed the trigger, feeling the weapon jerk in his hands and buffet against his shoulder as he watched his searing rounds sail through the air and smash into the bodies of the men, sending them tumbling and spinning as they fell into the mud.

Steve and Stu watched as Marcus and Tobias closed in on their first objective, the sentry positions in front of the farm. Glowing tracer rounds whipped past them as they ran, but the two men refused to slow down or fall back as they continued to storm forward.

As their friends entered their arcs of fire, Stu ordered that they switch their aim to the right, concentrating it on the barn and the farmhouse.

The air above Stu and Steve suddenly exploded with the crack and thump of rounds passing close overhead. Instinctively they ducked, burying their faces in the dirt and pressing themselves to the ground. Clumps of earth and grass sprang up around them as the enemy concentrated their fire on their position, pinning them down.

"Crawl back," Stu screamed over the crescendo as more rounds smashed into the ground close by.

"Crawl back to cover."

Steve's ears rang with the deafening snaps of the speeding projectiles as they shattered the air. He was scared to move but seeing Stu begin to shuffle back prompted him to follow suit. As he crawled, he glanced behind him and saw a number of dark figures approaching along the road from the south. At first, he took them for soldiers, closing in on their rear, but a second glance revealed them as a cluster of roaming dead, attracted by the noise of battle.

"We've got pus-bags behind us," Steve hollered over the roar of fire raining down upon them.

Stu glanced back, judging the distance and time that it would take before they became any threat to them.

"Don't worry about them, for now. Follow me."

Stu dropped down from the small rise and into the dead ground, turning to his right, lugging the machinegun and his belts of ammunition with him while he looked for a new fire support position.

"Here," he shouted back to Steve as he dropped to the grass and began crawling up to a patch of high ground.

"Come on, Steve, move your arse."

Marcus crashed into the bunker of the first position and Tobias dropped in close behind him, landing on the mangled and bloodied remains of a soldier that had been torn apart by the machineguns.

Both of them quickly changed magazines and gingerly peered over the top of the parapet.

Their fire support had suddenly decreased and Marcus realised that only Robbie's group continued to spill their heavy rate of fire into the enemy, as they attempted to mount a counter assault.

"Shit," Marcus growled, "I think Steve and Stu have been taken out."

As if to confirm his fears, a burst of fire smashed into the ground at the lip of the hole where Marcus and Tobias were taking cover. Showers of dirt and debris rained down on top of them, forcing them deeper into the wrecked bunker.

Marcus quickly glanced over the lip and immediately ducked back into cover.

"Shit," he hissed at Tobias.

"They're trying to get round from the barn side. Without Stu's guns, they'll overrun us."

His earpiece suddenly crackled and he heard Robbie's voice.

"Marcus, they're flanking you. Stu and Steve are pinned down and we have no shot from here."

Marcus grunted as another volley disintegrated the top of the hole.

"Concentrate your fire on the barn, Robbie," he shouted through the radio, "pour it on 'em."

The fire from Robbie's group reached fever pitch, the echo of their guns rattling the cold morning. Their rounds snapped and whizzed through the air above Marcus and Tobias as they suppressed the enemy remaining in the barn.

Marcus raised himself into a crouch, staring up at the edge of their bunker.

"What are you doing, Marcus?" Tobias shouted over the din of gunfire as he watched Marcus readying himself.

Without a word, Marcus launched himself up and leapt from the hole. Tobias looked on in horror as the lip exploded in a hail of dirt and debris as the enemy soldiers concentrated their fire on Marcus.

Ignoring the danger, Tobias sprang from cover, charging in the wake of Marcus, screaming at the top of his lungs as they bore down towards the enemy, firing from the hip and throwing themselves forward in an uncontrollable rage.

Marcus stormed towards the soldiers, rounds zipping past close by, snapping at his ears and ploughing the ground in front of him. He was roaring like a wild animal, his rifle jerking in his hands and his rounds smashed into a number of men who stopped to take aim at him. Their bodies shook and convulsed as Marcus and Tobias' bullets ripped through their flesh, dropping them to the ground as they screamed in pain.

A powerful blow, like a punch from a heavyweight boxer, smashed into Marcus' stomach, causing him to lose his footing and trip; stumbling forward, he continued his assault. The weapon in his hands continued to shudder as he refused to slow his advance, sending more bullets tearing into the enemy and the walls of the barn.

Another heavy thump struck his shoulder, sending a burning flash up into his brain and turning him to his right as he staggered on uneasy legs.

Tobias was still moving forward, pressing the attack. He saw Marcus' body jerk and his stride begin to slow as the enemy rounds tore through him. He stumbled a few more paces, still howling with fury and firing his rifle from his weakening hands, when another round smashed into his side. His knees gave beneath him and he fell to the ground, his weapon dropping to the stone of the courtyard with a clatter.

Tobias continued to charge for the barn, waiting for the rounds to begin smashing into him, too, as the enemy changed their point of aim. He fired on the move repeatedly, bellowing at the soldiers and challenging them to face him as his adrenaline and aggression carried him forward.

Bullets continued to strike the ground all around him and crack in the air by his head, but he was still moving, and as far as he could tell, he had not been hit.

He raced past Marcus as he lay on the ground, struggling to climb to his feet as more clods of dirt and gravel erupted around him.

Tobias gritted his teeth, waiting for the shot that would take him down.

From the right, red streaks suddenly began to race across the area ahead of him, drilling into the soldiers that stood firing at him, smashing into the walls of the barn behind them. The fire from Stu's guns had opened up again, forcing the enemy to reel back in confusion and panic while many of them fell under the heavy bursts as Stu and Steve decimated them.

Tobias reached the barn and pressed himself against the wall. His chest hurt as he fought to catch his breath and sweat poured down his head and into his eyes. His legs shook and his hands trembled as he snatched the empty magazine from his rifle, replacing it with a fresh one.

He glanced back at Marcus.

He was still lying on the ground but he was no longer struggling to climb back to his feet.

"Stu," Tobias yelled in gasps through his radio.

"Close in to me. Robbie, move to the first position but leave one gun on the hill to cover the west side."

The enemy fire had petered off, leaving just sporadic single shots ringing out as the soldiers withdrew in chaos from the weight of the attack that had crashed down upon them.

Reaching for his radio, Tobias kept his eyes on the figure laying still on the ground just a few metres away from him.

"Marcus is down," he said painfully, between gulps of air.

"Marcus is down."

34

Kelly's head lolled and rolled as she slowly became aware of the clatter of gunfire somewhere close by.

The noise of battle was getting louder by the second; she could distinctly hear shouts and screams in between the long bursts of fire as her mind fought its way through the fog. Her eyes slowly opened just in time to see a soldier come bursting through the door.

He looked alarmed and frightened and he spoke to the General in an excited and panicked voice as the chaos raged behind him.

Gibson, still seated at the table, turned to look at Kelly and Claire, his eyes narrowing as he realised that they were under attack and it was not his soldiers shooting at the dead.

His face changed colour, turning pale as the scale of the situation dawned on him from the report that the soldier had passed on.

He jumped up from the table and raced to the door, standing for a moment and watching as his men ran about the courtyard in panic. He looked on as he saw the tracer rounds whizzing past the gate at the far side of the complex, smashing into the two sentry positions and thumping through the walls of the barn as his soldiers struggled to return fire.

He witnessed a number of his men fall, blood gushing from their wounds and spilling into the mud as they fell to the ground, dying in agony, their screams echoing around the enclosed area.

"Bastards," he growled in rage as he stared out from the farmhouse in anger, watching as his men were annihilated, his command ripped from his grasp.

"Bastards…"

As the sound of battle and men dying howled around them, Kelly remained tied to her seat, but her eyes and ears were now fully focussed and her attention was fixed solely on the pistol sitting on the table in front of her.

She twisted her hands, trying desperately to loosen the plastic zip-ties holding her wrists tightly together behind her back. She could feel them cutting into her flesh as she pulled, ignoring the pain and thinking only of the pistol that sat just beyond her reach.

She looked at Sarah, who sat staring at the door with fear blazing in her eyes as the deafening cracks and bangs of the clattering machineguns mixed with the blood-curdling screams of the dying men outside. She was frozen to the spot, unable to form a clear thought or run for cover.

Kelly glanced back at the door.

Gibson remained standing on the threshold, shouting to his men and watching them die in a hail of gunfire.

"Sarah," she hissed, "Sarah, listen to me."

Sarah's head and eyes snapped towards her, focussing on her as she was brought out of her state of shock and awe.

"Sarah, I need you to untie me. Do you understand? I need you to cut the ties from my hands, quickly."

Claire joined Kelly in trying to spur her daughter into action as she realised what was going on.

"Come on, baby. It's okay, come on."

Sarah remained sat in the chair, her gaze alternating from her mother and Kelly, and towards the man that she considered the Devil.

She was terrified of moving, of offending him and incurring his wrath. She had witnessed his wrath and she had heard the long agony-filled screams of Carl as Joey reanimated and tore in to him.

Sarah had been in a semi state of shock ever since.

"Sarah," Kelly tried again after checking that Gibson was still standing with his back to them.

"Quickly, Sarah, untie me so I can get the gun."

Sarah looked at Kelly blankly, then at the pistol on the table. Her eyes were wide, bulging with terror, and her legs were refusing to do what her mind screamed at her to do.

Gibson, finally recovering from the initial shock of the attack, turned to go back into the house, grab his weapons, and join his men, rallying them and leading the counter-attack.

He stepped through the door, feeling his blood boiling within his veins as he considered the audacity of someone trying to take away his command and kill his men.

He crossed over the threshold and stopped dead in his tracks.

His expression changed from one of anger, to complete surprise. He stood staring down the barrel of his own gun, feeling completely lost for words. His heart skipped a beat and a shiver coursed its way through his body.

Staring at the muzzle of the pistol, his shoulders slumped as he realised that he had no bargaining chip, nothing he could say to convince his executioner to spare his life.

Sarah could hear her Uncle Marcus' voice echoing through her mind as he instructed her on how to fire a pistol.

'Stand with your body square to the front, legs slightly bent at the knee, Sarah. Hold the weapon firmly and aim with both eyes open, looking over the sight. Squeeze the trigger, don't jerk it...'

Her hands trembled and her legs felt weak, but her determination was steadfast.

She glared at the man in front of her.

Gibson stared back at the little girl and the pistol trembling in her delicate hands. He saw the hatred and fear in her eyes, then the flash of vengeance that glinted for a fleeting moment as she tightened her grip.

"Fuck," he whispered.

The shot rang out, deafening in the small kitchen of the farmhouse, rattling the windows in their frames.

The bullet smashed into his throat, knocking him backwards, a geyser of blood spraying out from the exit wound as the nine-millimetre slug punched through his flesh. He let out a muffled scream as he staggered, reaching up to his torn throat, his eyes widening with shock.

A second explosion erupted from the barrel as Sarah squeezed off another shot, hitting him square in the chest and causing his body to double over.

He reached forward for the table, grabbing it to steady himself as he looked up at Sarah, his eyes pleading with her, but only finding a hateful fire in her expression.

Sarah took careful aim, seeing nothing in her sights other than the monster that the General was; he was worse than the dead that she had run in fear of for so long. She glared back at him, feeling no pity or remorse.

The gun jerked in her hands one final time as another round blasted from the barrel, ploughing into the monstrous face of General Gibson.

His shocked features caved inwards as the bullet drilled through his skull and burst through the back in a spray of grey matter and blood. His head dropped to the table, hitting it with a dull thud before his body slid to the floor, his mutilated brains seeping out through the exit wound and a dark red puddle spreading across the tiles of the kitchen floor.

Kelly and Claire stared at Sarah in silence as she placed the gun back on the table and reached for her bottle of orange juice.

The attack was over. The few surviving soldiers fled to the farmland to the east, realising that their commander was dead and their defence had crumbled and leaving their wounded behind, dying and screaming in the mud as their attackers closed in and began freeing the prisoners.

Shots continued to echo around the valley as Robbie and his team began ensuring that the fallen soldiers remained dead. Then, they turned their attention to the numerous corpses converging on the farm complex along the road and down the hills from all directions, attracted by the noise of the battle.

Screams erupted from the east as the walking corpses, moving towards the farm and filling the long grass, brought down the retreating soldiers.

Robbie's and Lee's guns continued to clatter as they kept the dead at bay while the freed prisoners began collecting equipment and vehicles, ready to abandon the farm on the orders of Stu who was organizing the round up.

Steve crouched down beside his brother, staring at the wounds that he had sustained and watching as he coughed and sputtered, clinging to life.

"Jennifer," Marcus said in a strained and faltering voice, "is Jen okay?"

Steve looked up at Kelly and Claire who kneeled on the other side of Marcus. Kelly looked back at him with saddened eyes; a slight shake of the head, barely detectable, but Steve saw and understood it.

He looked back down at his brother, the tears welling in his eyes as he struggled with his words.

"Yeah, bro," he lied, "Jen is fine, the boys too. You just stay with us, okay?"

Marcus smiled back at him, his eyes unfocussed as foaming blood began to seep from between his lips and his face drained of colour.

"Take them north, Steve. You have to take them north."

Steve fought against the emotion that bubbled up inside him and the invisible hand that gripped his throat, squeezing it shut. The floodgates that held back the tears welling in his eyes threatened to give way at any moment.

"We will, Marcus," he replied soothingly, holding his brother's bloodied hand in his own.

"Don't worry about that, though. We'll fix you up and get you back on your feet first."

Marcus slowly shook his head, a slight smile creasing his face.

"I'm going nowhere, mate. You're their leader now and you need to…"

Steve felt Marcus' grip tighten for a moment and his body tense as his final rasping breath exhaled from his throat, rattling from the torrent of blood that had seeped into his lungs from his wounds.

Marcus' grip slackened and eyes slowly closed as his body fell still and silent.

For a moment, Steve stared at his brother's face, his body wracked with grief and his stomach twisting into a knot as the tears began to cascade from his cheeks, splashing down onto the lifeless face of Marcus.

Stu stood close by, feeling the same sense of loss as he watched his friend and commander die and fade away in front of him.

"Why?" Stu asked in a hoarse whisper as his throat seized, still gazing down at his friend lying lifeless on the floor.

"Why did he charge them like that?"

Everyone remained silent; the shock of losing Marcus was like a hammer blow to all of them and something that they had never expected to face.

"Because he was already dead," Tobias said solemnly from beside Stu.

He stepped forward and knelt beside Steve, bowing his head in respect.

"Rest easy, brother," Tobias whispered.

He placed his hand on Marcus' forearm and pushed back his sleeve, revealing a gaping bloodied wound in his flesh.

The tear in Marcus' arm was dark and festering, the skin already blackened around the edges and deep red veins distended from just below the surface.

Steve stared at the bite wound, his mouth falling slack as he realised that his brother had sacrificed himself, already knowing that he was going to die.

"It must've happened at the park during the escape," Stu commented with shock as he stared down at the teeth marks in his friend's arm.

Tobias nodded.

"The tough bastard carried on, though, even when he knew he had no chance of living."

Steve, Stu and Hussein carried Marcus' body over to one of the vehicles that had been left behind by the soldiers.

They gently placed him in the back of one of the trucks, alongside the bodies of Carl and Joey, and Steve climbed in, pulling down the canvas and sealing himself inside while the rest waited in the courtyard.

A while later, the canvas covering the rear of the truck was thrown back and Steve appeared, wiping the tears from his eyes as he climbed down into the mud.

Stu stepped forward, his eyes locked on Steve's, sharing in his grief.

"It's done," Steve nodded as the bloodied knife slipped from his hand and splashed into the cold mud.

35

For a long time, Andy and Molly had remained close, looking after one another and growing together. She had taken care of him during the harsh winters and the blistering summers, doing what she could to keep him from falling apart or seizing up.

She spoke to him constantly, teaching him, and he learned from her, understanding much of what she said as her wonderful sounding words fell on his ears.

They had ventured out, scavenging, collecting food and water, repairing their fences and disguising their gates and tracks. They walked in the country; Andy enjoyed the sounds of the birds and the endless chattering of Molly as they picked flowers and kicked a football between them.

Andy's delight had soared and he found joy in every moment he spent with Molly.

He had protected her, acting as warning and deterrent against the dead whenever they approached. On numerous occasions, he had saved her from a grisly and painful end, beating the heads of the lurking monsters to a pulp and dragging her to safety.

Molly and Andy had grown to rely on one another for their continued survival. For a long time, he had felt at peace with himself and with what he was. He understood that he was different from Molly and, to a degree; he knew that he did not have the same life force flowing through him that she did. Nevertheless, she accepted him and loved him as a friend, and in return, he loved her.

The love and adoration for her was the one thing that he clearly understood and was absolutely sure.

Now, fear gripped him, squeezing his body in its icy grasp. He had taken care of whole groups of the revolting things in the past as they stumbled upon the house, but now their numbers had grown. There were too many of them, and more were coming, staggering through the smashed gates and fences, stumbling across the fields and along the track, headed for the house.

He turned in all directions, frantically swinging his tyre iron and crashing it into the heads of the advancing horde. They came from all directions, relentlessly stumbling through the fields and along the tracks, their attention completely focussed on the large house at the top of the hill.

Andy stood his ground, destroying the skulls of the creatures as they came near, their twisted bodies quickly piling up at his feet and their coagulated and black blood soaking into the gravel of the courtyard.

He anxiously looked around at the putrid faces of the figures, their vacant eyes staring straight ahead of them, paying no interest to him, despite his noises and movements as he desperately tried to fight them off.

Their moans and cries of excitement filled the air as they closed in on the house, forcing Andy to step backwards, yielding under their pressure and numbers and retreating towards the door.

He continued to beat scores of them to the ground but they refused to give up on their relentless advance. No matter how many of them he killed, more arrived to fill the gaps.

Andy moaned loudly, trying desperately to draw them away from the door and to turn their focus on him. He flailed his arms, wailing excitedly and staggering to the side, hoping to convince the swarm of repugnant figures to follow him, away from the house and into the long grass.

He had used the same ruse on many occasions, luring them away as they staggered after him in their herd mentality, believing that Andy was leading them to somewhere of interest. Then, once he knew that Molly was free from danger, he would turn on them, killing them one by one, as they stood staring at him in dumb confusion.

The mass of lumbering bodies did not notice Andy as he attempted his distraction. They single-mindedly kept their attention fixed on the large, red door in front of them, tripping and stumbling over the bodies of the dead at their feet, trampling them as they moaned and staggered towards the house, their skeletal arms reaching out and their bony fingers clutching at the air.

They failed to notice as Andy charged back towards them, thrashing at them and raining down blow after blow into the lead creatures, their skulls splitting open and their rotting brains spilling across the gravel of the courtyard as they crashed to the ground. He was incensed as he doggedly defended the house, snarling and growling at the dead as they drew near.

A scream from inside rang out, causing Andy to turn in panic. He stared up at the bedroom window, his eyes growing wide as he saw the frantic face of Molly staring back down at him. He heard the crash of glass and the cracks of splintering wood as from somewhere inside the house, a breach was created in their defences.

"They're inside, Andy," Molly called down to him, her voice filled with panic and terror.

He turned and scaled the few steps leading up to the front door, the crowd close on his heels as he pushed his way through the entrance. Before the dead advancing on the house from across the courtyard could reach the threshold, Andy slammed the door shut, quickly sliding the bolt into place and securing it.

He turned, and immediately, a decomposing and lifeless face loomed towards him from the semi darkness of the hallway.

Without hesitation, Andy brought his tyre iron up, thrusting the pointed end through the soft and decaying flesh below the creatures chin and driving it up into the brain, killing it instantly.

The body slid from the iron bar and dropped to the floor with a loud thud.

More of them advanced. They poured in through the smashed door at the rear and piled into the kitchen. The rooms of the house were already filled with the dead as they staggered about, knocking over tables and trampling ornaments and personal items into the threadbare carpets, as they ravenously searched for the living.

More of them were on the stairs, creeping up to the first floor as they chased after Molly, following her after the back door had collapsed and they had cast eyes upon her warm flesh. Now, they scrambled at the doors to the upper rooms, smashing their way through, searching for the vibrant human being that they had seen just moments before.

Molly's panicked screams, as she barricaded herself in her room, drew their attention and they soon converged and began to assault the door, smashing their decaying hands against the hard wood and gnawing at the frame, desperate to get at the living person beyond the barrier.

Andy looked up at the packed staircase in horror, feeling a crescendo of emotions fall upon him. Fear, panic, desperation and rage; they all assaulted him as one. With a roar, he raised his weapon above his head and ploughed, headlong, into the mass of stumbling corpses that dragged themselves up the stairs.

He began pulling at them, ripping their clothing and flesh, tearing limbs from their sockets as he fought his way through. Moaning figures tumbled down the steps and fell from the banister as Andy flung them aside, still howling and hearing the helpless screams of his friend as the barricaded door began to crumble.

He was halfway up the stairs, and still had a long way to go, when he heard the distinctive sound of splintering wood.

The moans of the dead grew in volume and tempo as they sensed that their goal was within reach; Molly's blood-curdling screams of alarm and fright rang out around the house.

"Andy," Molly cried, her pleading sobs reaching him as he continued to fight his way up the stairs.

"Andy, please help me."

He groaned helplessly as the compressed bodies in front of him halted his advance. He continued to drag them away, tossing them down the stairs behind him as he reached the top step, but more of them greeted him on the upper floor of the house.

They were shoulder to shoulder and packed in tightly as they surged towards the room where Molly had hidden, her horrified screams driving them into a state of frenzy, as they battered at the failing door.

A loud crack rang out, louder than the excited cries of the dead. Andy's head snapped towards Molly's room, recognising the sound as the lock finally gave way, the weight of the crowd continuing to push against the frame.

Above the mass of bobbing heads in front of him, he could see the top of the door. It moved, pushing away from the frame and then slamming shut again, as Molly threw her weight behind it.

"Andy, please, the door," she screamed beseechingly.

"They're coming in."

Renewing his efforts and attacking the backs of the figures in front of him, Andy continued his assault, pulling at the crowd and pushing his way through the slightest gap.

Another crunch rang out and he saw the door burst open. Molly's screams erupted from the room as the ravenous creatures poured in through the gap.

Andy cried out, his rasping wail drowning out the moans of the bodies around him as he heard the horrified voice of Molly calling out for him. He rushed forwards, but was shunted aside as the crowd surged, forcing him against the banister of the stairs. He was pushed further and he found himself unable to move as his back began to arch over the wooden rail.

The figures swelled and rushed forward towards the room, Molly's echoing cries exhilarating them and sending them into a state of energized rage, as their lust for warm flesh and blood filled their every sense.

In the sudden flood of putrid flesh, Andy was launched from his precarious position that he clung to on the banister, sending him hurtling down the stairs, landing on the heads of the dead that continued to climb the steps, following the cries of anguish from the rooms above.

He tumbled and tripped, landing face down on the hallway floor with a bone-rattling thud. The feeling of powerlessness was overpowering as he climbed back to his feet, moaning wretchedly as Molly's heart-rending screams changed from cries of fear, to shrieks of pain as the mass of gnashing teeth and tearing hands ripped into her soft flesh.

Her yells and screeches echoed through the house and far beyond, into the fields and through the trees outside.

Molly's howls of agony shook Andy to his core and his legs weakened at the realisation that he could not help her, that he had failed to keep her safe. He tried again to climb the stairs, but there were just too many of them blocking his path.

Molly's painful cries continued, mixed with the animated wails of the monsters tearing into her, and Andy was forced to listen. Her voice grew weaker as her life drained from her body in torrents of blood and flesh ripped from her bones.

His back crashed against the wall of the stairway and his body slid downwards as he listened to his friend die, sitting on the stairs, pounding his fists against the wooden steps in grief, anger and frustration through his powerlessness to help her.

He wailed loudly, howling above the din of the dead that filled the house as Molly's screams stopped and her voice ceased calling out to him.

He was overcome with sorrow and regret at not being able to save her and he hung his head in the realisation that it was all over.

Molly was dead.

For a while, Andy remained sitting on the stairs, groaning and whimpering as the bodies continued to stagger into the room to feast on the remains of his young friend. He heard the distinct sound of tearing cloth, the grunts of satisfaction and the slurping and smacking of lips as they sucked the flesh from Molly's bones.

Looking up, the rage flared inside of him, reaching heights that he had never before experienced. He growled and snarled at the backs of the figures that continued to climb the steps, his eyes glaring at them, seeing them for the monsters they really were.

He stumbled back down the stairs, grunting to himself and pushing against the bodies that continued to force their way in to the house. He fought his way through, knocking them to the side and pulling at their decrepit clothing and festering flesh.

He barged into the sitting room and stormed towards the fireplace. He reached up, grabbed the tin of fluid sitting on the mantle and began to pour it over the floor and furniture around him. He snatched the box of matches from the table, knocking more of the creatures out of his path as he continued to squirt the flammable liquid onto the floor and walls, even the numerous bodies in the house around him, before leaving a trail out towards the front door.

He wrenched the door open and, immediately, a mass of rotting skeletal faces rushed in towards him.

Andy pressed himself against the wall, allowing them to pass, resisting the temptation to begin fighting them and possibly disrupt his plan.

Slowly, he pushed his way through the doorway and out into the courtyard, still pouring a trail of fluid out from the can and dousing the clothing of the shambling creatures that passed by as they piled into the house through the open front door.

Finally, at the bottom of the steps, he stopped and turned, a scowl secreting from his rasping throat, his incensed eyes fixed on the mass of bodies crammed on the steps leading up to the house.

With an overpowering feeling of revenge bursting from his core, he pulled out a match and struck it against the rough material on the side of the box. The small thin piece of wood flared and hissed as the sulphur ignited and Andy stared at it for a moment, mesmerised by the brightness and dancing flame that seemed to have a life of its own, as it grew brighter.

Raising his head and glaring at the vile and repulsive figures that had killed his friend, he dropped the match.

The fluid ignited instantly and a glowing blue flame began to spread, racing up the steps and towards the house. Within seconds, dozens of the dead were ablaze as their clothing and parched flesh easily caught fire.

They staggered through the house, oblivious to the danger and searing heat that began to engulf them. They crashed into one another, spreading the fire, and soon the bright yellow and orange flames grew and filled the lower rooms, flickering brightly through the blackened glass in the windows and licking at the wooden frames.

Within minutes, the whole of the ground floor was burning, with black smoke pouring out through the doors and the windows, as the glass cracked and shattered from the heat.

Andy moved away, walking back across the courtyard as more of the wretched and unthinking figures stumbled by him, headed towards the house, ignorant of the flames and the searing heat that were now spreading to the upper floor.

As he reached the row of trees flanking the track, he stopped and turned, taking one last look at the place that he had grown to love, and remembering Molly, who had become the sole reason for his continued existence.

He turned away and grunted.

His body felt heavy and his legs barely had the strength to carry him forward. Sighing heavily, and wracked with grief, he stumbled away down the track and towards the open road.

Molly was gone.

Now, Andy was alone again, and lost.

EPILOGUE

Steve adjusted his position. He had been sat in the same spot for hours, staring out over the dead land, daydreaming and reminiscing, and his backside had begun to grow numb.

He glanced across to his left, across the sprawling suburbs that spread out from the city, slowly giving way to the expanse of countryside stretching out towards the west. The sun was beginning to sink towards the horizon, its rays turning the western sky from a bright blue to a radiant orange. Far to the east, the darkness was coming, creeping up on the earth as the sun began to set.

It would be time for him to leave soon.

Even after twelve years, he still did not like to be caught out in the open after dark. The dead still ruled the land and the living only borrowed it from them during the hours of daylight, when they could see clearly and had time to react.

In the darkness, the only light that the living had was the moon and stars, leaving much of the world in shadow.

The dead; they lurked in the shadows.

They never rested and the slightest sound or clumsy movement always attracted them. To be out after dark, miles from his home base, would be a death sentence for Steve.

He looked up again towards the skyline. The city was silhouetted on the horizon as its tall, black buildings reached towards the heavens.

It was hard for him to believe that the decaying metropolis had once been part of the life centre of civilisation. Its roads were slowly being overgrown with plant life, and the numerous buildings were now home to all manner of wildlife that scurried and scavenged through their rooms and hallways, claiming the old realm of man for their own.

Steve smiled to himself, thinking about how wrong humanity had been. The priorities of the old world had been backwards, and it had taken the rising of the dead to put things into perspective for the survivors.

In his mind, civilisation had already been on its head, and only when corpses began to reanimate and attack the living did their species correct its mistakes.

He guessed that by now, probably ninety-nine percent of the human race was dead, with a large majority of it roaming the earth as the walking dead.

Now, as an endangered species, humans had grown to understand what was important in life, and it was not their bank balance, their job or their car; it was survival and the safety of the people they cared about.

Steve had begun to realise that very early on, but it was not until the arrival at the holiday resort, nestled amongst the beautiful and protective mountains, peaks, and lakes that Mother Nature had created, that he truly understood the scale of the disaster that had hit the world, or enlightenment as he had come to see it.

After the death of Marcus and with half their number killed during the evacuation from the park, Steve had led the survivors on towards the north, continuing with the plan of reaching the safety of the Lake District.

It had taken them two days to get there, circumnavigating large built-up areas and continually having to fight off the swarms of rotting corpses littering the roads, sometimes completely blocking their path and forcing them to detour.

Once in the protective cover of the steep hills and valleys, the numbers of dead declined rapidly. Crossing mountains and fording rivers and lakes were not activities that came natural to the reanimated, and as the living had noted on so many occasions, the lifeless figures roaming the land always followed the path of least resistance, unless something attracted them to veer away from the flat tarmac that shuffled by beneath their feet.

As suspected, people had already taken refuge in the resort; close to one hundred survivors occupying the lodges and cabins, making a safe haven for themselves, tucked away in the middle of nowhere, far from the dangers of the urban areas.

Steve and his band had been welcomed with open arms, adding to the steadily growing community that began to thrive in the foothills of the mountains. The heavy weaponry that they carried with them had been a tipping point in the considerations of the people already there.

It was not long before Steve began a sudden rise to power, despite his reluctance. People naturally turned to him for guidance and looked on him as their leader. At first, he had fought against it, shunning the responsibilities of command, wanting to be left alone to get on with rebuilding his life and looking out for the people he cared for, but it was for this same reason that Steve found himself drifting into the seat of power. He was unable to control it and before he knew what was happening he was the mayor of their small colony, making the decisions and setting down the template for their continued survival.

They set about turning their original plan into a reality, and they took back the town, destroying the hordes of dead infesting the place, blocking off the entrances by sealing the roads that filtered into the area. They secured the perimeter, reinforcing the fences and walls, and setting up guard towers and early warning systems with alarms and cameras.

Within a year, people in the settlement had fallen into a routine of something that resembled an ordinary life.

Children went to school and every adult had a job; whether it was part of the protection force and long range scavenging teams, or growing crops, tending to cattle or part of the builders guild that had started up. It did not matter because every position was considered vital.

Every occupation that civilisation truly needed to survive, the colony had and the only payment that was required from anyone was the fact that they continued to live, in peace and safety, alongside the people that they cared for.

Steve let out a long sigh, his reminiscing coming to an end as he looked out across the land, a slight smile creasing the corners of his mouth. He glanced back down at the rifle in his lap, remembering Marcus, and feeling a strong link between him, the rifle and his brother.

"You would've been proud, bro," he whispered to himself, stroking the dull black metal of the weapon.

"We're a community now and we don't live in fear anymore."

A thin layer of tears formed in his eyes as he thought about Marcus and all he had been through and done for them, sacrificing his life for them before ever reaching their final destination.

The man had become a legend amongst the survivors, even to the people who had never met him. The teachers taught the young children about him, telling them about what he had been through, crossing half the world with his men, fighting every step of the way and then continuing to fight when he had finally made it home.

Each year, on the anniversary of their arrival at the resort, many parties and drunken toasts were held in his honour.

Liam and David, Marcus' two sons, had grown to be very much like the man that their father had been, strong and determined. Natural leaders, living up to the legend and becoming valued members of their little society.

Everybody spoke of Marcus with a great degree of respect and admiration, and they all paused occasionally to say thank you to the man who had led them from the darkness.

Steve laughed to himself.

"You're revered almost as a God, brother."

He sat for a few more minutes then began to climb to his feet, wiping the traces of tears from his eyes and snorting back the strong emotions he felt bubbling up inside him.

He missed his brother, even after all this time.

Down the hill, the lone corpse continued in its attempts to climb the slope, still struggling to negotiate the slippery grass that hindered its progress.

Steve watched it for a while, seeing its frustration as it fell once more, sliding down the hill after fighting so hard just to gain a few metres towards its goal. It grunted, climbing back to its feet and staring up at Steve, letting out a long, mournful and frustrated wail.

Steve turned to leave, heading to his car to begin the journey back to the colony, but another moan from the bottom of the slope made him stop and turn.

It was not the usual poignant groan of the dead; long, lonesome and thrown out to no one in particular. This grumbling cry seemed to call out to Steve, directed at him specifically, as if to say, *'hey you.'*

He stood still and watched the body below him. It did not try to climb the hill again and stood, staring back at him.

Steve watched for a moment, studying the figure, sensing that there was something different, something out of the ordinary from the usual dead that he came across.

Curiosity got the better of him and he began to carefully descend the hill, watching his footing and the corpse alternately, afraid of slipping and landing in the waiting arms of the creature below.

The reanimated man did not move, nor did it get excited or animated as Steve approached. It remained rooted to the spot, intently watching the living man walking towards it.

The hairs on the back of Steve's neck stood out from his flesh and a shiver ran down his spine as he closed the gap, still cautious of where he placed each step. When he was just five metres away, he stopped, gripping the rifle tightly in his hands, ready to put a bullet through the creature's head.

Gingerly, he took a few more steps as the dead man's eyes remained locked on his.

At the bottom of the hill, and on flat, even ground, they stood just metres apart, studying one another in the fading light and cool air.

The man's face was a mottled grey and brown and as thin as paper. The cheekbones were visible below the decayed skin with the remnants of deep festering sores revealing much of the skull's bone structure, leaving the rows of rear teeth visible through the gaps in the flesh.

Its eyes sat shrivelled and dried in their sockets, but somehow they seemed completely focussed and not the usual gazing, unseeing eyes of the millions of dead that Steve had seen over the years.

Its wispy, sun-bleached hair drifted upwards in a gust of wind, showing its bare cranium where a thin layer of skin had rotted away over the years.

Steve studied the man, unsure of how to feel as he gazed into its saddened eyes. The corpse before him did not seem interested in attacking him or feasting on his flesh. It was almost as if the thing just wanted company, to be close to a living human being.

For the first time in many years, Steve felt a pang of sorrow for one of the unfortunate creatures.

The figure before him was not a monster.

He had been a man once, with feelings and desires, ambitions of his own and opinions that he had felt strongly about. The man had experienced joy and unhappiness in life and, as Steve looked into his eyes, he saw that a deep sadness seemed to linger with him, even in death, shining through the lifeless eyes that stared back at him.

The two of them remained silent as they watched one another, their eyes locked and a torrent of unspoken words passing between them.

"What?" Steve finally asked; something inside him told him that the dead man would understand his words.

"What do you want from me?"

The eyes grew wide in the skeletal face and a grunt rasped from its ragged throat. It looked down at the rifle that Steve held in his hands.

Its long spindly fingers stroked the air, reaching upwards until it was pointing, gesturing towards the weapon.

The man grunted again and let out a huff as he raised his eyes to look back at Steve.

Steve glanced down at his rifle and back at the reanimated body in front of him, unsure of what he wanted him to do. Then, the dead man let out a low, relinquishing moan and suddenly dropped to his knees in the long grass.

Steve gasped as the man stared up at him, pleadingly. Again, the dead eyes fell on the weapon clutched in his hands and gave a clear and unmistakable nod.

'He wants to die,' Steve thought to himself in astonishment.

He realised that he had spoken the words aloud when the creatures eyes, recognising what he had said, locked with his and a confirmatory, sorrow-filled, grunt emitted from its mouth.

He stepped back, shaking his head, and for the first time in twelve years, fighting with his feelings about whether he should pull the trigger. He had never hesitated before, but he had also never come across a reanimated body that behaved like this one.

The man, still on his knees and staring back at him, nodded his head again and let out an encouraging wail, pleading with Steve to end his existence.

Steve was being bombarded with a torrent of emotions, unsure of what to do as he began to look on the figure as a living man.

He watched the grief-stricken eyes of the wretched figure as it stared back up at him, defiantly.

Finally, the rifle jerked in his shoulder, a loud crack shattering the silence around them and the echo of the discharge resounding across the land, causing the birds in the trees to suddenly take flight and scatter into the sky.

The round punched through the forehead of the man, shattering his skull and tearing through his brain. The neck snapped backwards with the force of the blast as the bone erupted from within.

The man's face seemed to hang for a moment, looking back at Steve with a peaceful expression spreading across his decaying features.

The body slumped and fell to the side into the long grass as the echo of the gunshot continued to ride out across the fields, towards the dead city in the distance.

The man lay still, his long existence as one of the un-dead finally over, and his body now at peace.

Steve looked down at him, a mixture of feelings rising up inside him, as he felt content to have carried out the man's wish for an end to his suffering, but on the other hand, ashamed that he had ended his existence when he was clearly not like the others that now roamed the earth.

"I'm sorry, mate," Steve spoke over the body.

He was about to turn away when he caught sight of something in the jacket pocket of the dead man.

He reached down, removed the wallet and began thumbing through it.

A picture of a little girl fell from one of the compartments, landing in the grass at his feet. He reached down and picked it up, then turned his attention to the pink driver's license that he pulled from the decaying leather wallet.

He studied the card and the face of the man that smiled back at him.

Steve laughed silently and grunted, noticing that the man had come from the same town as him and wondered whether they had ever met, maybe even said hello.

He looked back at the beaming face of the little girl in the photograph as she sat with her arm around a dog, clearly happy with life as she posed for the camera.

He turned it over and read the inscription on the back:

'To my best friend, Andy,

'You're the best,

'Love, Molly. X'

Steve nodded, understanding that the man had been grieving and wanted to end the wretched existence that he led.

With a tear in his eye, he crouched down beside the lifeless body and placed the picture of Molly between his cold, emaciated fingers.

"It's over now. You don't have to suffer anymore," he said as he raised himself up to his feet.

"Sleep well, Andy Moorcroft."

Steve bowed his head for a moment, then turned and walked back up the hill.

END

NIGHTMARE OF THE DEAD

VINCENZO BILOF

In a world of war and mayhem, a twisted nightmare of undead cannibals begins.

The outlaw Neasa Bannan uncovers a horrifying conspiracy engineered by the psychopathic mastermind behind the Confederacy's deadly flesh-hungry weapons. A homicidal gunslinger and a brotherhood of killers emerge out of Neasa's tragic, blood-soaked past while the living dead ravage the land.

With the fate of the country in the balance, Neasa must decide: save the Union from the undead menace, or surrender to Saul's vision of ultra-violence.

ICE STATION ZOMBIE
JE GURLEY

For most of the long, cold winter, Antarctica is a frozen wasteland. Now, the ice is melting and the zombies are thawing. Arctic explorers Val Marino and Elliot Anson race against time and death to reach Australia, but the Demise has preceded them and zombies stalk the streets of Adelaide and Coober Pedy.

The Coalition

When the dead rose to destroy the living, Ron Cutter learned to survive. While so many others died, he thrived. His life is a constant battle against the living dead. As he casts his own bullets and packs his shotgun shells, his humanity slowly melts away.

Then he encounters a lost boy and a woman searching for a place of refuge. Can they help him recover the emotions he set aside to live? And if he does recover them, will those feelings be an asset in his struggles, or a danger to him?

THE STATE OF EXTINCTION: the first installment in the **COALITON OF THE LIVING** trilogy of Mankind's battle against the plague of the Living Dead. As recounted by author **Robert Mathis Kurtz.**

MACHINES OF THE DEAD

The dead are rising. The island of Manhattan is quarantined. Helicopters guard the airways while gunships patrol the waters. Bridges and tunnels are closed off. Anyone trying to leave is shot on sight.

For Jack Warren, survival is out of his hands when a group of armed military men kidnap him and his infected wife from their apartment and bring them to a bunker five stories below the city.

There, Jack learns a terrible truth and the reason why the dead have risen. With the help of a few others, he must find a way to escape the bunker and make it out of the city alive.

TIMOTHY
MARK TUFO

Zombie Fallout
Mark Tufo
CURRENTLY IN DEVELOPMENT WITH
Illuminandi Media
ShaedStudios.com

5104891R00188

Printed in Great Britain
by Amazon.co.uk, Ltd.,
Marston Gate.